THE PEOPLE...

Scattered at random across the Earth when they first arrived, **The People** yearn always for The Home—the planet from which they came—and for each other. This second book of **The People** centers on an Assembly, where members tell stories of their adventures with The Others—those of us born here on Earth, who haven't The Gifts—and of their perils in getting to the happy Assembly itself.

THE PEOPLE: NO DIFFERENT FLESH confirms Zenna Henderson's special place among science fiction creators.

Other Avon books by
Zenna Henderson

THE ANYTHING BOX	34579	$1.50
HOLDING WONDER	24737	1.50
PILGRIMAGE	36681	1.50

The People:
No Different Flesh

ZENNA HENDERSON

◆ AVON
PUBLISHERS OF BARD, CAMELOT AND DISCUS BOOKS

T a whole alphabet of pleasant people,
pausing at G

and J

and M

and, of course,

V.

All of the characters in this book
are fictitious, and any resemblance
to actual persons, living or dead,
is purely coincidental.

AVON BOOKS
A division of
The Hearst Corporation
959 Eighth Avenue
New York, New York 10019

First Avon Printing, May, 1968
Ninth Printing

AVON TRADEMARK REG. U.S. PAT. OFF. AND
FOREIGN COUNTRIES, REGISTERED TRADEMARK—
MARCA REGISTRADA, HECHO EN CHICAGO, U.S.A.

Printed in the U.S.A.

CONTENTS

NO DIFFERENT FLESH

Meris watched the darkness rip open and mend itself again in the same blinding flash that closed her eyes. Behind her eyelids the dark reversals flicked and faded. Thunder jarred the cabin window where she leaned and troubled her bones. The storm had been gathering all afternoon, billowing up in blue and white thunderheads over the hills, spreading darkly, somberly to snuff the sunset. The wind was not the straight-blowing, tree-lashing, branch-breaker of the usual summer storm. Instead, it blew simultaneously from several directions. It mourned like a snow wind around the eaves of the cabin. It ripped the length of the canyon through the treetops while the brush below hardly stirred a twig. Lightning was so continuous now that glimpses of the outdoors came through the windows like vast shouts and sudden blows.

Lights in the cabin gasped, recovered, and died. Meris heard Mark's sigh and the ruffle of his pushed-back papers.

"I'll get the lantern," he said. "It's out in the storeroom, isn't it?"

"Yes." Lightning flushed the whole room, now that the light no longer defended it. "But it needs filling. Why don't we wait to see if the lights come back on. We could watch the storm—"

"I'm sorry." Mark's arm was gentle across her shoulders. "I'd like to, but I can't spare the time. Every minute—"

Meris pressed her face to the glass, peering out into the chaotic darkness of the canyon wall. She still wasn't quite used to being interested in anything outside her own grief and misery—all those long months of painful numbness that at the same time had been a protesting hammering at the Golden Gates and a wild shrieking at God. What a blessed

7

relief it was finally to be able to let go of the baby—to feel grief begin to drain away as though a boil had been lanced. Not that sorrow would be gone, but now there could be healing for the blow that had been too heavy to be mortal.

"Take good care of her," she whispered to the bright slash of the lightning. "Keep her safe and happy until I come."

She winced away from the window, startled at the sudden audible splat of rain against the glass. The splat became a rattle and the rattle a gushing roar and the fade-and-flare of the outdoors dissolved into streaming rain.

Mark came back into the cabin, the light in his hands flooding blue-white across the room. He hung the lantern on the beam above the table and joined Meris at the window.

"The storm is about over," said Meris, turning in the curve of his arm. "It's only rain now."

"It'll be back," he said. "It's just taking a deep breath before smacking us amidships again."

"Mark." The tone of Meris's voice caught his attention. "Mark, my baby—our baby—is dead." She held out the statement to him as if offering a gift—her first controlled reference to what had happened.

"Yes," said Mark, "our baby is dead." He accepted the gift.

"We waited for her so long," said Meris softly, "and had her for so short a time."

"But long enough that you are a mother and I am a father," said Mark. "We still have that."

"Now that I can finally talk about her," said Meris, "I won't have to talk about her any more. I can let her be gone now. Oh, Mark!" Meris held his hand to her cheek. "Having you to anchor me is all that's kept me from—"

"I'm set in my ways," smiled Mark. "But of late you've been lifting such a weight off me that I don't think I could anchor a butterfly now!"

"*Love* you, Mark!"

"*Love* you, Meris!" Mark hugged her tightly a moment and then let her go. "Back to work again. No flexibility left in the deadline any more. It has to be done on time this time or—"

Lightning splashed brightness against the wall. Meris moved back to the window again, the floorboards under her feet vibrating to the thunder. "Here it comes again!" But Mark was busy, his scurrying fingers trying to catch up with the hours and days and months lost to Meris's grief and wild mourning.

8

Meris cupped her hands around her temples and leaned her forehead to the windowpane. The storm was truly back again, whipping the brush and trees in a fury that ripped off leaves and small branches. A couple of raindrops cracked with the force of hail against the glass. Lightning and a huge explosion arrived at the same moment, jarring the whole cabin.

"Hit something close?" asked Mark with no pause in the staccato of his typing.

"Close," said Meris. "The big pine by the gate. I saw the bark fly."

"Hope it didn't kill it," said Mark. "We lost those two in back like that last summer, you know."

Meris tried to see the tree through the darkness, but the lightning had withdrawn for the moment.

"What was that?" she cried, puzzled.

"What?" asked Mark.

"I heard something fall," she said. "Through the trees."

"Probably the top of our pine," said Mark. "I guess the lightning made more than bark fly. Well, there goes another of our trees."

"That's the one the jays liked particularly, too," said Meris.

Rain drenched again in a vertical obscurity down the glass and the flashes of lightning flushed heavily through the watery waver.

Later the lights came on and Meris, blinking against the brightness, went to bed, drawing the curtain across the bunk corner, leaving Mark at work at his desk. She lay awake briefly, hearing the drum of the rain and the mutter of the thunder, hardly noticing the clatter of the typewriter. She touched cautiously with her thoughts the aching emptiness where the intolerable burden of her unresolved grief had been. Almost, she felt without purpose—aimless—since that painful focusing of her whole life was going. She sighed into her pillow. New purpose and new aim would come—would have to come—to fill the emptinesses.

Somewhere in the timeless darkness of the night she was suddenly awake, sitting bolt upright in bed. She pulled the bedclothes up to her chin, shivering a little in the raw, damp air of the cabin. What had wakened her? The sound came again. She gasped and Mark stirred uneasily, then was immediately wide awake and sitting up beside her.

"Meris?"

9

"I heard something," she said. "Oh, Mark! Honestly, I heard something."

"What was it?" Mark pulled the blanket up across her back.

"I heard a baby crying," said Meris.

She felt Mark's resigned recoil and the patience in his long indrawn breath.

"Honest, Mark!" In the semi-obscurity her eyes pleaded with him. "I really heard a baby crying. Not a tiny baby— like—like ours. A very young child, though. Out there in the cold and wet."

"Meris—" he began, and she knew the sorrow that must be marking his face.

"There!" she cried. "Hear it?"

The two were poised motionless for a moment, then Mark was out of bed and at the door. He flung it open to the night and they listened again, tensely.

They heard a night bird cry and, somewhere up-canyon, the brief barking of a dog, but nothing else.

Mark came back to bed, diving under the covers with a shiver.

"Come warm me, woman!" he cried, hugging Meris tightly to him.

"It did sound like a baby crying," she said with a half question in her voice.

"It sure did," said Mark. "I thought for a minute— Must have been some beast or bird or denizen of the wild—" His voice trailed away sleepily, his arms relaxing. Meris lay awake listening—to Mark's breathing, to the night, to the cry that didn't come again. Refusing to listen for the cry that would never come again, she slept.

Next morning was so green and gold and sunny and wet and fresh that Meris felt a-tiptoe before she even got out of bed. She dragged Mark, protesting, from the warm nest of the bedclothes and presented him with a huge breakfast. They laughed at each other across the table, their hands clasped over the dirty dishes. Meris felt a surge of gratitude. The return of laughter is a priceless gift.

While she did the dishes and put the cabin to rights, Mark, shrugging into his Levi jacket against the chill, went out to check the storm damage.

Meris heard a shout and the dozen echoes that returned diminishingly from the heavily wooded mountainsides. She pushed the window curtain aside and peered out as she finished drying a plate.

Mark was chasing a fluttering something, out across the creek. The boisterous waters were slapping against the bottom of the plank bridge and Mark was splashing more than ankle-deep on the flat beyond as he plunged about trying to catch whatever it was that evaded him.

"A bird," guessed Meris. "A huge bird waterlogged by the storm. Or knocked down by the wind—maybe hurt—" She hurried to put the plate away and dropped the dish towel on the table. She peered out again. Mark was half hidden behind the clumps of small willows along the bend of the creek. She heard his cry of triumph and then of astonishment. The fluttering thing shot up, out of reach above Mark, and seemed to be trying to disappear into the ceaseless shiver of the tender green and white aspens. Whatever it was, a whitish blob against the green foliage, dropped down again and Mark grabbed it firmly.

Meris ran to the door and flung it open, stepping out with a shiver into the cold air. Mark saw her as he rounded the curve in the path.

"Look what I found!" he cried. "Look what I caught for you!"

Meris put a hand on the wet, muddy bundle Mark was carrying and thought quickly, "Where are the feathers?"

"I caught a baby for you!" cried Mark. Then his smile died and he thrust the bundle at her. "Good Lord, Meris!" he choked, "I'm not fooling! It *is* a baby!"

Meris turned back a sodden fold and gasped. A face! A child face, mud-smudged, with huge dark eyes and tangled dark curls. A quiet, watchful face—not crying. Maybe too frightened to cry?

"Mark!" Meris clutched the bundle to her and hurried into the cabin. "Build up the fire in the stove," she said, laying her burden on the table. She peeled the outer layer off quickly and let it fall soggily to the floor. Another damp layer and then another. "Oh, poor messy child!" she crooned. "Poor wet, messy, little girl!"

"Where did she come from?" Mark wondered. "There must be some clue—" He changed quickly from his soaked sneakers into his hiking boots. "I'll go check. There must be something out there." His hands paused on the knotting of the last bootlace. "Or someone." He stood up, settling himself into his jeans and boots. "Take it easy, Meris." He kissed her cheek as she bent over the child and left.

11

Meris's fingers recalled more and more of their deftness as she washed the small girl-body, improvised a diaper of a dish towel, converted a tee shirt into a gown, all the time being watched silently by the big dark eyes that now seemed more wary than frightened, watched as though the child was trying to read her lips that were moving so readily in the old remembered endearments and croonings. Finally, swathing the small form in her chenille robe in lieu of a blanket, she sat on the edge of the bed, rocking and crooning to the child. She held a cup of warm milk to the small mouth. There was a firming of lips against it at first and then the small mouth opened and two small hands grasped the cup and the milk was gulped down greedily. Meris wiped the milky crescent from the child's upper lip and felt the tenseness going out of the small body as the warmth of the milk penetrated it. The huge dark eyes in the small face closed, jerked open, closed slowly and stayed closed.

Meris sat cradling the heavy warmth of the sleeping child. She felt healing flow through her own body and closed her eyes in silent thanksgiving before she put her down, well back from the edge of the bed. Then she gathered up the armful of wet muddy clothes and reached for the box of detergent.

When Mark returned some time later, Meris gestured quickly. "She's sleeping," she said. "Oh, Mark! Just think! A baby!" Tears came to her eyes and she bent her head.

"Meris," Mark's gentle voice lifted her face. "Meris, just don't forget that the baby is not ours to keep."

"I know—!" She began to protest and then she smoothed the hair back from her forehead, knowing what Mark wanted to save her from. "The baby is not ours—to keep," she relinquished. "Not ours to keep. Did you find anything, or anyone," she hesitated.

"Nothing," said Mark. "Except the top of our pine is still there, if you've bothered to check it. And," his face tightened and his voice was grim, "those vandals have been at it again. Since I was at the picnic area at Beaver Bend they've been there and sawed every table in two and smashed them all to the ground in the middle!"

"Oh, Mark!" Meris was distressed. "Are you sure it's the same bunch?"

"Who else around here would do anything so senseless?" asked Mark. "It's those kids. If I ever catch them—"

"You did once," said Meris with a half smile, "and they didn't like what you and the ranger said to them."

"Understatement of the week," said Mark. "They'll like even less what's going to happen to them the next time they get caught."

"They're mad enough at you already," suggested Meris.

"Well," said Mark, "I'm proud to count that type among my enemies!"

"The Winstel boy doesn't seem the type," said Meris.

"He was a good kid," acknowledged Mark, "until he started running with those three from the Valley. They've got him hypnotized with that car and all their wild stories and crazy pranks. I guess he thinks their big-town fooling around has a glamor that can't be duplicated here in the mountains. Thank heaven it can't, but I wish he'd wise up to what's happening to him."

"The child!" Meris started toward the bed, her heart throbbing suddenly to the realization that there was a baby to be considered again. They looked down at the flushed, sleeping face and then turned back to the table. "She must be about three or four," said Meris over the coffee cups. "And healthy and well cared for. Her clothes—" she glanced out at the clothes line where the laundry billowed and swung "—they're well-made, but—"

"But what?" Mark stirred his coffee absently, then gulped a huge swallow.

"Well, look," said Meris, reaching to the chair. "This outer thing she had on. It's like a trundle bundle—arms but no legs—just a sleeping bag thing. That's not too surprising, but look. I was going to rinse off the mud before I washed it, but just one slosh in the water and it came out clean—and dry! I didn't even have to hang it out. And Mark, it isn't material. I mean fabric. At least it isn't like any that I've ever seen."

Mark lifted the garment, flexing a fold in his fingers. "Odd," he said.

"And look at the fasteners," said Meris.

"There aren't any," he said, surprised.

"And yet it fastens," said Meris, smoothing the two sections of the front together, edge to edge. She tugged mightily at it. It stayed shut. "You can't rip it apart. But look here." And she laid the two sides back gently with no effort at all. "It seems to be which direction you pull. There's a rip here in the back," she went on. "Or I'll bet she'd never have got wet at all—at least not from the outside," she smiled. "Look, the rip *was* from here to here." Her fingers traced six inches across the garment. "But look—" She carefully lapped the edges of the remaining rip and drew her thumb nail along it.

13

The material seemed to melt into itself and the rip was gone.

"How did you find out all this so soon?" asked Mark. "Your own research lab?"

"Maybe so," smiled Meris. "I was just looking at it—women look at fabrics and clothing with their fingers, you know. I could never choose a piece of material for a dress without touching it. And I was wondering how much the seam would show if I mended it." She shook the garment. "But how she ever managed to run in it."

"She didn't," said Mark. "She sort of fluttered around like a chicken. I thought she was a feathered thing at first. Every time I thought I had her, she got away, flopping and fluttering, above my head half the time. I don't see how she ever— Oh! I found a place that might be where she spent the night. Looks like she crawled back among the roots of the deadfall at the bend of the creek. There's a pressed down, grassy hollow, soggy wet, of course, just inches above the water."

"I don't understand this fluttering bit," said Meris. "You mean she jumped so high you—"

"Not exactly jumped—" began Mark.

A sudden movement caught them both. The child had wakened, starting up with a terrified cry, "Muhlala! Muhlala!"

Before Meris could reach her, she was fluttering up from the bed, trailing the chenille robe beneath her. She hovered against the upper windowpane, like a moth, pushing her small hands against it, sobbing, "Muhlala! Muhlala!"

Meris gaped up at her. "Mark! Mark!"

"Not exactly—jump!" grunted Mark, reaching up for the child. He caught one of the flailing bare feet and pulled the child down into his arms, hushing her against him.

"There, there, muhlala, muhlala," he comforted awkwardly.

"Muhlala?" asked Meris, taking the struggling child from him.

"Well, she said it first," he said. "Maybe the familiarity will help."

"Well, maybe," said Meris. "There, there, muhlala, muhlala."

The child quieted and looked up at Meris.

"Muhlala?" she asked hopefully.

"Muhlala," said Meris as positively as she could.

The big wet eyes looked at her accusingly and the little

14

head said no, unmistakably, but she leaned against Meris, her weight suddenly doubling as she relaxed.

"Well now," said Mark. "Back to work."

"Work? Oh, Mark!" Meris was contrite. "I've broken into your workday again!"

"Well, it's not every day I catch a child flying in the forest. I'll make it up—somehow."

Meris helped Mark get settled to his work and, dressing the child—"What's your name, honey? What's your name?"—in her own freshly dried clothes, she took her outside to leave Mark in peace.

"Muhlala," said Meris, smiling down at the upturned wondering face. The child smiled and swung their linked hands.

"Muhlala!" she laughed.

"Okay," said Meris, "we'll call you Lala." She skoonched down to child height. "Lala," she said, prodding the small chest with her finger. "Lala!"

Lala looked solemnly down at her own chest, tucking her chin in tightly in order to see. "Lala," she said, and giggled. "Lala!"

The two walked toward the creek, Lala in the lead, firmly leashed by Meris's hand. "No flying," she warned. "I can't interrupt Mark to have him fish you out of the treetops."

Lala walked along the creek bank, peering down into the romping water and keeping up a running commentary of unintelligible words. Meris kept up a conversation of her own, fitting it into the brief pauses of Lala's. Suddenly Lala cried out triumphantly and pointed. Meris peered down into the water.

"Well!" she cried indignantly. "Those darn boys! Dropping trash in our creek just because they're mad at Mark. Tin cans—"

Lala was tugging at her hand, pulling her toward the creek.

"Wait a bit, Lala," laughed Meris. "You'll fall us both into the water."

Then she gasped and clutched Lala's hand more firmly. Lala was standing on the water, the speed of the current ruffling it whitely against the sides of her tiny shoes. She was trying to tug Meris after her, across the water toward the metallic gleam by the other bank of the creek.

"No, baby," said Meris firmly, pulling Lala back to the bank. "We'll use the bridge." So they did and Lala, impatient of delay, tried to free her hand so she could run along the

15

creek bed, but Meris clung firmly. "Not without me!" she said.

When they arrived at the place where the metallic whatever lay under the water, Meris put Lala down firmly on a big gray granite boulder, back from the creek. "Stay there," she said, pushing firmly down on the small shoulders. "*Stay* there." Then she turned to the creek. Starting to wade, sneakers and all into the stream, she looked back at Lala. The child was standing on the boulder visibly wanting to come. Meris shook her head. "Stay *there*," she repeated.

Lala's face puckered but she sat down again. "Stay *there*," she repeated unhappily.

Meris tugged and pulled at the metal, the icy bite of the creek water numbing her feet. "Must be an old hot water tank," she grunted as she worked to drag it ashore. "When could they have dumped it here? We've been home——"

The current caught the thing as it let go of the mud at the bottom of the creek. It rolled and almost tore loose from Meris's hands, but she clung, feeling a fingernail break, and, putting her back to the task, towed the thing out of the current into the shallows. She turned its gleaming length over to drain the water out through the rip down its side.

"Water tank?" she puzzled. "Not like any I ever——"

"Stay there?" cried Lala excitedly. "Stay there?" She was jumping up and down on the boulder.

Meris laughed. "Come here," she said, holding out her muddy hands. "Come here!" Lala came. Meris nearly dropped her as she staggered under the weight of the child. Lala hadn't bothered to slide down the boulder and run to her. She had launched herself like a little rocket, airborne the whole distance.

She wiggled out of Meris's astonished arms and rummaging, head hidden in the metal capsule, came out with a triumphant cry, "Deeko! Deeko!" And she showed Meris her sodden treasure. It was a doll, a wet, muddy, battered doll, but a doll nevertheless, dressed in miniature duplication of Lala's outer garment which they had left in the cabin.

Lala plucked at the wet folds of the doll's clothes and made unhappy noises as she wiped the mud from the tiny face. She held the doll up to Meris, her voice asking and coaxing. So Meris squatted down by the child and together they undressed Deeko and washed her and her tiny clothes in the creek, then spread the clothes on the boulder in the sun. Lala gave Deeko a couple of soggy hugs, then put her on the rock also.

16

Just before supper, Mark came out to the creek-side to see the metallic object. He was still shaking his head in wonderment over the things Meris had told him of Lala. He would have discounted them about ninety per cent except that Lala did them all over again for him. When he saw the ripped cylinder, he stopped shaking his head and just stared for a moment. Then he was turning it, and exploring in it, head hidden, hefting the weight of it, flexing a piece of its ripped metal. Then he lounged against the gray boulder and lipped thoughtfully at a dry cluster of pine needles.

"Let's live dangerously," he said, "and assert that this is the How that Lala arrived in our vicinity last night. Let us further assert that it has no earthly origin. Therefore, let us, madly but positively, assert that this is a Space capsule of some sort and Lala is an extra-terrestrial."

"You mean," gasped Meris, "that Lala is a little green man! And that this is a flying saucer?"

"Well, yes," said Mark. "Inexact, but it conveys the general idea."

"But, Mark! She's just a baby. She couldn't possibly have traveled all that distance alone—"

"I'd say also that she couldn't have traveled all that distance in this vehicle, either," said Mark. "Point one, I don't see anything resembling a motor or a fuel container or even a steering device. Point two, there are no provisions of any kind—water or food—or even any evidence of an air supply."

"Then?" said Meris, deftly fielding Lala from the edge of the creek.

"I'd say—only as a guess—that this is a sort of lifeboat in case of a wreck. I'd say something happened in the storm last night and here's Lala, Castaway."

"Where did you come from, baby dear?" chanted Meris to the wiggly Lala. "The heavens opened and you were here?"

"They'll be looking for her," said Mark, "whoever her people are. Which means they'll be looking for us." He looked at Meris and smiled. "How does it feel, Mrs. Edwards, to be Looked For by denizens of Outer Space?"

"Should we try to find them?" asked Meris. "Should we call the sheriff?"

"I don't think so," said Mark. "Let's wait a day or so. They'll find her. I'm sure of it. Anyone who had a Lala would comb the whole state, inch by inch, until they found her."

17

He caught up Lala and tossed her, squealing, into the air. For the next ten minutes Mark and Meris were led a merry chase trying to get Lala down out of the trees! Out of the sky! She finally fluttered down into Meris's arms and patted her cheek with a puzzled remark of some kind.

"I suppose," said Mark, taking a relieved breath, "that she's wondering how come we didn't chase her up there. Well, small one, you're our duckling. Don't laugh at our unwebbed feet."

That evening Meris sat rocking a drowsy-eyed Lala to sleep. She reached to tuck the blanket closer about the small bare feet, but instead cradled one foot in her hand. "You know what, Mark?" she said softly. "It's just dawned on me what you were saying about Lala. You were saying that this foot might have walked on another world! It just doesn't seem possible!"

"Well, try this thought, then." Mark pushed back from his desk, stretching widely and yawning. "If that world was very far away or their speed not too fast, that foot may never have touched a world anywhere. She may have been born en route."

"Oh, I don't think so," said Meris, "she knows too much about—about—*things* for that to be so. She knew to look *in* water for that—that vehicle of hers and she knew to wash her doll in running water and to spread clothes in the sun to dry. If she'd lived her life in Space—"

"Hmm!" Mark tapped his mouth with his pencil. "You could be right, but there might be other explanations for her knowledge. But then, maybe the real explanation of Lala is a very pedestrian one." He smiled at her unbelieving smile and went back to work.

Meris was awake again in the dark. She stretched comfortably and smiled. How wonderful to be able to awaken in the dark and smile—instead of slipping inevitably into the aching endless grief and despair. How pleasant to be able to listen to Mark's deep breathing and Lala's little murmur as she turned on the camp cot beside the bed. How warm and relaxing the flicker of firelight from the cast-iron stove patterning ceiling and walls dimly. She yawned and stopped in mid-stretch. What was that? Was that what had wakened her?

There was a guarded thump on the porch, a fumbling at the door, an audible breath and then, "Mr. Edwards! Are you there?" The voice was a forced whisper.

18

Meris's hand closed on Mark's shoulder. He shrugged away in his sleep, but as her fingers tightened, he came wide awake, listening.

"Mr. Edwards!"

"Someone for Lala!" Meris gasped and reached toward the sleeping child.

"No," said Mark. "It's Tad Winstel." He lifted his voice. "Just a minute, Tad!" There was a muffled cry at the door and then silence. Mark padded barefoot to the door, blinking as he snapped the lights on, and, unlatching the door, swung it open. "Come on in, fellow, and close the door. It's cold." He shivered back for his jacket and sneakers.

Tad slipped in and stood awkwardly thin and lanky by the door, hugging his arms to himself convulsively. Mark opened the stove and added a solid chunk of oak.

"What brings you here at this hour?" he asked calmly.

Tad shivered. "It isn't you, then," he said, "but it's bad trouble. You told me that gang was no good to mess around with. Now I know it. Can they hang me for just being there?" His voice was very young and shaken.

"Come over here and get warm," said Mark. "For being where?"

"In the car when it killed the guy."

"Killed!" Mark fumbled the black lid-lifter. "What happened?"

"We were out in that Porsche of Rick's, just tearing around seeing how fast it could take that winding road on the other side of Sheep's Bluff." Tad gulped. "They called me chicken because I got scared. And I am! I saw Mr. Stegemeir after his pickup went off the road by the fish hatchery last year and I—I can't help remembering it. Well, anyway—" His voice broke off and he gulped. "Well, they made such good time that they got to feeling pretty wild and decided to come over on this road and—" His eyes dropped away from Mark's and his feet moved apologetically. "They wanted to find some way to get back at you again."

Then his words tumbled out in a wild spurt of terror. "All at once there was this man. Out of nowhere! Right in the road! And we hit him! And knocked him clear off the road. And they weren't even going to stop, but I grabbed the key and made them! I made them back up and I got out to look for the man. I found him. All bloody. Lying in the bushes. I tried to find out where he was bleeding—they—they went off and left me there with him!" His voice was outraged. "They

19

didn't give a dern about that poor guy! They went off and left him lying there and me with not even a flashlight!"

Mark had been dressing rapidly. "He may not be dead," he said, reaching for his cap. "How far is he?"

"The other side of the creek bridge," said Tad. "We came the Rim way. Do you think he might—"

"We'll see," said Mark. "Meris, give me one of those army blankets and get Lala off the cot. We'll use that for a stretcher. Build the fire up and check the first aid kit." He got the Coleman lantern from the storeroom, then he and Tad gathered up the canvas cot and went out into the chilly darkness.

Lala fretted a little, then, curled in the warmth Mark had left, she slept again through all the bustling about as Meris prepared for Mark's return.

Meris ran to the door when she heard their feet in the yard. She flung the outer door wide and held the screen as they edged the laden cot through the door. "Is he—?"

"Don't think so." Mark grunted as they lowered the cot to the floor. "Still bleeding from the cut on his head and I don't think dead men bleed. Not this long, anyway. Get a gauze pad, Meris, and put pressure on the cut. Tad, get his boots off while I get his shirt—"

Meris glanced up from her bandage as Mark's voice broke off abruptly. He was staring at the shirt. His eyes caught Meris's and he ran a finger down the front of the shirt. No buttons. Meris's mouth opened, but Mark shook his head warningly. Then, taking hold of the muddied shirt, he gently turned both sides back away from the chest that was visibly laboring now.

Meris's hands followed the roll of the man's head, keeping the bandage in place, but her eyes were on the bed where Lala had turned away from the light and was burrowed nearly out of sight under the edge of Mark's pillow.

Tad spoke from where he was struggling with the man's boots. "I thought it was you, Mr. Edwards," he said. "I nearly passed out when you answered the door. Who else could it have been? No one else lives way out here and I couldn't see his face. I knew he was bleeding because my hands—" He broke off as one boot thumped to the floor. "And we knocked him so far! So high! And I thought it was you!" He shuddered and huddled over the other boot. "I'm cured, honest, Mr. Edwards. I'm cured. Only don't let him die. Don't let him die!" He was crying now, unashamed.

"I'm no doctor," said Mark, "but I don't think he's badly

hurt. Lots of scratches, but that cut on his head seems to be the worst."

"The bleeding's nearly stopped," said Meris. "And his eyes are fluttering."

Even as she spoke, the eyes opened, dark and dazed, the head turning restlessly. Mark leaned over the man. "Hello," he said, trying to get the eyes to focus on him. "You're okay. You're okay. Only a cut—"

The man's head stilled. He blinked and spoke, his eyes closing before his words were finished.

"What did he say?" asked Tad. "What did he say?"

"I don't know," said Mark. "And he's gone again. To sleep, this time, I hope. I'm quite sure he isn't dying."

Later when Mark was satisfied that the man was sleeping, in the warm pajamas he and Tad had managed to wrestle him into, he got dressed in clean clothes and had Tad wash up, and put on a clean flannel shirt in place of his blood-stained one.

"We're going to the sheriff, after we find the doctor," he told Tad. "We're going to have to take care of those kids before they do kill someone or themselves. And you, Tad, are going to have to put the finger on them whether you like it or not. You're the only witness—"

"But if I do, then I'll get in trouble, too—" began Tad.

"Look, Tad," said Mark patiently, "if you walk in mud, you get your feet muddy. You knew when you got involved with these fellows that you were wading in mud. Maybe you thought it didn't matter much. Mud is easy to wash off. That might be true of mud, but what about blood?"

"But Rick's not a juvenile any more—" Tad broke off before the grim tightening of Mark's face.

"So that's what they've been trading on. So he's legally accountable now? Nasty break!"

After they were gone, Meris checked the sleeping man again. Then, crawling into bed, shoving Lala gently toward the back of the bunk, she cuddled, shivering, under the bedclothes. She became conscious of the steady outflow of warmth from Lala and smiled as she fanned her cold hands out under the cover toward the small body. "Bless the little heater!" she said. Her eyes were sleepy and closed in spite of her, but her mind still raced with excitement and wonder. What if Mark was right? What if Lala had come from a spaceship! What if this man, sleeping under their own blankets on their own cot, patched by their own gauze and adhesive, was really a Man from Outer Space! Wouldn't that

21

be something? "But," she sighed, "no bug-eyed monsters? No set, staring eyes and slavering teeth?" She smiled at herself. She had been pretty bug-eyed herself, when she had seen his un-unbottonable shirt.

Dr. Hilf arrived, large, loud, and lively, before Meris got back to sleep—in fact, while she was in the middle of her *Bless Mark, bless Tad, bless Lala, bless the bandaged man, bless—* He examined the silently cooperative man thoroughly, rebandaged his head and a few of the deeper scratches, grabbed a cup of coffee, and boomed, "Doesn't look to me as if he's been hit by a car! Aspirin if his head aches. No use wasting stitches where they aren't needed!" His voice woke Lala and she sat up, blinking silently at him. "He's not much worried himself! Asleep already! That's an art" The doctor gave Meris a practiced glance. "Looking half alive again yourself, young lady. Good idea having a child around. Your niece?" He didn't wait for an answer. "Good to help hold the place until you get another of your own!" Meris winced away from the idea. The doctor's eyes softened, but not his voice. "There'll be others," he boomed. "We need offspring from good stock like yours and Mark's. Leaven for a lot of the makeweights popping up all over." He gathered up his things and flung the door open. "Mark says the fellow's a foreigner. No English. Understood though. Let me know his name when you get it. Just curious. Mark'll be along pretty quick. Waiting for the sheriff to get the juvenile officers from county seat." The house door slammed. A car door slammed. A car roared away. Meris automatically smoothed her hair, as she always did after a conversation with Dr. Hilf.

She turned wearily back toward the bunk. And gasping, stumbled forward. Lala was hovering in the air over the strange man like a flanneled angel over a tombstoned crusader. She was peering down, her bare feet flipping up as she lowered her head toward him. Meris clenched her hands and made herself keep back out of the way.

"Muhlala!" whispered Lala, softly. Then louder, "Muhlala!" Then she wailed, "Muhlala!" and thumped herself down on the quiet, sleeping chest.

"Well," said Meris aloud to herself as she collapsed on the edge of the bunk. "There seems to be no doubt about it!" She watched—a little enviously—the rapturous reunion, and listened—more than a little curiously—to the flood of strange-sounding double conversation going on without perceptible pauses. Smiling, she brought tissues for the man to mop his face after Lala's multitude of very moist kisses. The man was

22

sitting up now, holding Lala closely to him. He smiled at Meris and then down at Lala. Lala looked at Meris and then patted the man's chest.

"Muhlala," she said happily, "muhlala!" and burrowed her head against him.

Meris laughed. "No wonder you thought it funny when I called you muhlala," she said. "I wonder what Lala means."

"It means 'daddy,' " said the man. "She is quite excited about being called daddy."

Meris swallowed her surprise. "Then you do have English," she said.

"A little," said the man. "As you give it to me. Oh, I am Johannan." He sagged then, and said something un-English to Lala. She protested, but even protesting, lifted herself out of his arms and back to the bunk, after planting a last smacking kiss on his right ear. The man wiped the kiss away and held his drooping head between his hands.

"I don't wonder," said Meris, going to the medicine shelf. "Aspirin for your headache." She shook two tablets into his hand and gave him a glass of water. He looked bewilderedly from one hand to the other.

"Oh dear," said Meris. "Oh well, I can use one myself," and she took an aspirin and a glass of water and showed him how to dispose of them. The man smiled and gulped the tablets down. He let Meris take the glass, slid flat on the cot, and was breathing asleep before Meris could put the glass in the sink.

"Well!" she said to Lala and stood her, curly-toed, on the cold floor and straightened the bedclothes. "Imagine a grown-up not knowing what to do with an aspirin! And now," she plumped Lala into the freshly made bed, "now, my Daddy-girl, shall we try that instant sleep bit?"

The next afternoon, Meris and Lala lounged in the thin warm sunshine near the creek with Johannan. In the piny, water-loud clearing, empty of unnecessary conversation, Johannan drowsed and Lala alternately bandaged her doll and unbandaged it until all the stickum was off the tape. Meris watched her with that sharp awareness that comes so often before an unwished-for parting from one you love. Then, with an almost audible click, afternoon became evening and the shadows were suddenly long. Mark came out of the cabin, stretching his desk-kinked self widely, then walking his own long shadow down to the creek bank.

"Almost through," he said to Meris as he folded himself to

the ground beside her. "By the end of the week, barring fire, flood, and the cussedness of man, I'll be able to send it off."

"I'm so glad," said Meris, her happiness welling strongly up inside her. "I was afraid my foolishness—"

"The foolishness is all past now," said Mark. "It is remembered against us no more."

Johannan had sat up at Mark's approach. He smiled now and said carefully, "I'm glad my child and I haven't interrupted your work too much. It would be a shame if our coming messed up things for you."

"You have a surprising command of the vernacular if English is not your native tongue," said Mark, his interest in Johannan suddenly sharpening.

"We have a knack for languages," smiled Johannan, not really answering anything.

"How on earth did you come to lose Lala?" Meris asked, amazed at herself for asking such a direct question.

Johannan's face sobered. "That was quite a deal—losing a child in a thunderstorm over a quarter of a continent." He touched Lala's cheek softly with his finger as she patiently tried to make the worn-out tape stick again on Deeko. "It was partly her fault," said Johannan, smiling ruefully. "If she weren't precocious— You see, we do not come into the atmosphere with the large ship—too many complications about explanations and misinterpretations and a very real danger from trigger-happy—or unhappy—military, so we use our life-slips for landings."

"We?" murmured Meris.

"Our People," said Johannan simply. "Of course there's no Grand Central Station of the Sky. We are very sparing of our comings and goings. Lala and I were returning because Lala's mother has been Called and it is best to bring Lala to Earth to her grandparents."

"Her mother was called?" asked Mark.

"Back to the Presence," said Johannan. "Our years together were very brief." His face closed smoothly over his sorrow. "We move our life-slips," he went on after a brief pause, "without engines. It is an adult ability, to bring the life-slips through the atmosphere to land at the Canyon. But Lala is precocious in many Gifts and Persuasions and she managed to jerk her life-slip out of my control on the way down. I followed her into the storm—" He gestured and smiled. He had finished.

"But where were you headed?" asked Mark. "Where on earth—?"

"On Earth," Johannan smiled. "There is a Group of the People. More than one Group, they say. They have been here, we know, since the end of the last century. My wife was of Earth. She returned to the New Home on the ship we sent to Earth for the refugees. She and I met on the New Home. I am not familiar with Earth—that's why, though I was oriented to locate the Canyon from the air, I am fairly thoroughly lost to it from the ground."

"Mark," Meris leaned over and tapped Mark's knee. "He thinks he has explained everything."

Mark laughed. "Maybe he has. Maybe we just need a few years for absorption and amplification. Questions, Mrs. Edwards?"

"Yes," said Meris, her hand softly on Lala's shoulder. "When are you leaving, Johannan?"

"I must first find the Group," said Johannan. "So, if Lala could stay——" Meris's hands betrayed her. "For a *little* while longer," he emphasized. "It would help."

"Of course," said Meris. "Not ours to keep."

"The boys," said Johannan suddenly. "Those in the car. There was a most unhealthy atmosphere. It was an accident, of course. I tried to lift out of the way, but I was taken unawares. But there was little concern——"

"There will be," said Mark grimly. "Their hearing is Friday."

"There was one," said Johannan slowly, "who felt pain and compassion——"

"Tad," said Meris. "He doesn't really belong——"

"But he associated——"

"Yes," said Mark, "consent by silence."

The narrow, pine-lined road swept behind the car, the sunlight flicking across the hood like pale, liquid pickets. Lala bounced on Meris's lap, making excited, unintelligible remarks about the method of transportation and the scenery going by the windows. Johannan sat in the back seat being silently absorbed in his new world. The trip to town was a three-fold expedition—to attend the hearing for the boys involved in the accident—to start Johannan on his search for the Group, and to celebrate the completion of Mark's manuscript.

They had left it blockily beautiful on the desk, awaiting the triumphant moment when it would be wrapped and sent on its way and when Mark would suddenly have large quantities of uncommitted time on his hands for the first time in years.

"What is it?" Johannan had asked.

"His book," said Meris. "A reference textbook for one of those frightening new fields that are in the process of developing. I can't even remember its name, let alone understand what it's about."

Mark laughed. "I've explained a dozen times. I don't think she wants to remember. The book's to be used by a number of universities for their textbook in the field *if*, if it can be ready for next year's classes. If it can't be available in time, another one will be used and all the concentration of years—" He was picking up Johannan's gesture.

"So complicated—" said Meris.

"Oh yes," said Johannan. "Earth's in the complication stage."

"Complication stage?" asked Meris.

"Yes," said Johannan. "See that tree out there? Simplicity says—a tree. Then wonder sets in and you begin to analyze it—cells, growth, structure, leaves, photosynthesis, roots, bark, rings—on and on until the tree is a mass of complications. Then, finally, with reservations not quite to be removed, you can put it back together again and sigh in simplicity once more—a tree. You're in the complication period in the world now."

"Is true!" laughed Mark. "Is true!"

"Just put the world back together again, someday," said Meris, soberly.

"Amen," said the two men.

But now the book was at the cabin and they were in town for a day that was remarkable for its widely scattered, completely unorganized, confusion. It started off with Lala, in spite of her father's warning words, leaving the car through the open window, headlong, without waiting for the door to be opened. A half a block of pedestrians—five to be exact—rushed to congregate in expectation of blood and death, to be angered in their relief by Lala's laughter, which lit her eyes and bounced her dark curls. Johannan snatched her back into the car—forgetting to take hold of her in the process—and un-Englished at her severely, his brief gestures making clear what would happen to her if she disobeyed again.

The hearing for the boys crinkled Meris's shoulders unpleasantly. Rick appeared with the minors in the course of the questioning and glanced at Mark the whole time, his eyes flicking hatefully back and forth across Mark's face. The gathered parents were an unhappy, uncomfortable bunch, each overreacting according to his own personal pattern and the boys either echoing or contradicting the reactions of their own parents. Meris wished herself out of the whole unhappy mess.

Midway in the proceedings, the door was flung open and Johannan, who had left with a wiggly Lala as soon as his small part was over, gestured at Mark and Meris and un-Englished at them across the whole room. The two left, practically running, under the astonished eyes of the judge and, leaning against the securely closed outside door, looked at Johannan. After he understood their agitation and had apologized in the best way he could pluck from their thoughts, he said, "I had a thought." He shifted Lala, squirming, to his other arm. "The—the doctor who came to look at my head—he—he—" He gulped and started again. "All the doctors have ties to each other, don't they?"

"Why I guess so," said Meris, rescuing Lala and untangling her brief skirts from under her armpits. "There's a medical society—"

"That is too big," said Johannan after a hesitation. "I mean, Dr.—Dr.—Hilf would know other doctors in this part of the country?" His voice was a question.

"Sure he would," said Mark. "He's been around here since Territorial days. He knows everyone and his dog—including a lot of the summer people."

"Well," said Johannan, "there is a doctor who knows my People. At least there was. Surely he must still be alive. He knows the Canyon. He could tell me."

"Was he from around here?" asked Mark.

"I'm not sure where here is," Johannan reminded, "but a hundred miles or so one way or the other."

"A hundred miles isn't much out here," confirmed Meris. "Lots of times you have to drive that far to get anywhere."

"What was the doctor's name?" asked Mark, snatching for Lala as she shot up out of Meris's arms in pursuit of a helicopter that clacked overhead. He grasped one ankle and pulled her down. Grim-faced, Johannan took Lala from him.

"Excuse me," he said, and, facing Lala squarely to him on one arm, he held her face still and looked at her firmly. In the brief silence that followed, Lala's mischievous smile faded and her face crumpled into sadness and then to tears. She flung herself upon her father, clasping him around his neck and wailing heartbrokenly, her face pushed hard against his

27

shoulder. He un-Englished at her tenderly for a moment, then said, "You see why it is necessary for Lala to come to her grandparents? They are Old Ones and know how to handle such precocity. For her own protection she should be among the People."

"Well, cherub," said Mark, retrieving her from Johannan, "let's go salve your wounded feelings with an ice cream cone."

They sat at one of the tables in the back of one of the general stores and laughed at Lala's reaction to ice cream; then, with her securely involved with two straws and a glass full of crushed ice, they returned to the topic under discussion.

"The only way they ever referred to the doctor was just Doctor—"

He was interrupted by the front door slapping open. Shelves rattled. A can of corn dropped from a pyramid and rolled across the floor. "Dern fool summer people!" trumpeted Dr. Hilf. "Sit around all year long at sea-level getting exercise with a knife and fork then come roaring up here and try to climb Devil's Slide eleven thousand feet up in one morning!"

Then he saw the group at the table. "Well! How'd the hearing go?" he roared, making his way rapidly and massively toward them as he spoke. The three exchanged looks of surprise, then Mark said, "We weren't in at the verdict." He started to get up. "I'll phone—"

"Never mind," boomed Dr. Hilf. "Here comes Tad." They made room at the table for Tad and Dr. Hilf.

"We're on probation," confessed Tad. "I felt about an inch high when the judge got through with us. I've had it with that outfit!" He brooded briefly. "Back to my bike, I guess, until I can afford my own car. Chee!" He gazed miserably at the interminable years ahead of him. Maybe even five!

"What about Rick?" asked Mark.

"Lost his license," said Tad uncomfortably. "For six months, anyway. Gee, Mr. Edwards, he's sure mad at you now. I guess he's decided to blame you for everything."

"He should have learned long ago to blame himself for his own misdoings," said Meris. "Rick was a spoiled-rotten kid long before he ever came up here."

"Mark's probably the first one ever to make him realize that he was a brat," said Dr. Hilf. "That's plenty to build a hate on."

"Walking again!" muttered Tad. "So okay! So t'heck with wheels!"

"Well, since you've renounced the world, the flesh, and Porsches," smiled Mark, "maybe you could beguile the moments with learning about vintage cars. There's plenty of them still functioning around here."

"Vintage cars?" said Tad. "Never heard of them. Imports?"

Mark laughed, "Wait. I'll get you a magazine." He made a selection from the magazine rack in back of them and plopped it down in front of Tad. "There. Read up. There might be a glimmer of light to brighten your dreary midnight."

"Dr. Hilf," said Johannan, "I wonder if you would help me."

"English!" bellowed Dr. Hilf. "Thought you were a foreigner! You don't look as if you need help! Where's your head wound? No right to be healed already!"

"It's not medical," said Johannan. "I'm trying to find a doctor friend of mine. Only I don't know his name or where he lives."

"Know what *state* he lives in?" Laughter rumbled from Dr. Hilf.

"No," confessed Johannan, "but I do know he is from this general area and I thought you might know of him. He has helped my People in the past."

"And your people are—" asked Dr. Hilf.

"Excuse me, folks," said Tad, unwinding his long legs and folding the magazine back on itself. "There's my dad, ready to go. I'm grounded. Gotta tag along like a kid. Thanks for everything—and the magazine." And he dejectedly trudged away.

Dr. Hilf was waiting on Johannan, who was examining his own hands intently. "I know so little," said Johannan. "The doctor cared for a small boy with a depressed fracture of the skull. He operated in the wilderness with only the instruments he had with him." Dr. Hilf's eyes flicked to Johannan's face and then away again. "But that was a long way from where he found one of Ours who could make music and was going wrong because he didn't know who he was."

Dr. Hilf waited for Johannan to continue. When he didn't, the doctor pursed his lips and hummed massively.

"I can't help much," said Johannan, finally, "but are there so many doctors who live in the wilds of this area?"

"None," boomed Dr. Hilf. "I'm the farthest out—if I may

use that loaded expression. Out in these parts, a sick person has three choices—die, get well on his own, or call me. Your doctor must have come from some town."

It was a disconsolate group that headed back up-canyon. Their mood even impressed itself on Lala and she lay silent and sleepy-eyed in Meris's arms, drowsing to the hum of the car.

Suddenly Johannan leaned forward and put his hand on Mark's shoulder. "Would you stop, please?" he asked. Mark pulled off the road onto the nearest available flat place, threading expertly between scrub oak and small pines. "Let me take Lala." And Lala lifted over the back of the seat without benefit of hands upon her. Johannan sat her up on his lap. "Our People have a highly developed racial memory," he said. "For instance, I have access to the knowledge any of our People have known since the Bright Beginning, and, in lesser measure, to the events that have happened to any of them. Of course, unless you have studied the technique of recall—it is difficult to take knowledge from the past, but it's there, available. I am going to see if I can get Lala to recall for me. Maybe her precocity will include recollection also." He looked down at his nestling child and smiled. "It won't be spectacular," he said, "no eyeballs will light up. I'm afraid it'll be tedious for you, especially since it will be subvocal. Lala's spoken vocabulary lags behind her other Gifts. You can drive on, if you like." And he leaned back with Lala in his arms. The two to all appearances were asleep.

Meris looked at Mark and Mark looked at Meris, and Meris felt an irrepressible bubble of laughter start up her throat. She spoke hastily to circumvent it.

"Your manuscript," she said.

"I got a box for it," said Mark easing out onto the road again. "Chip found one for me when you took Lala to the rest room. Couldn't have done better if I'd had it made to measure. What a weight—" he yawned in sudden release— "What a weight off my mind. I'll be glad when it's off my hands, too. Thank God! Thank God it's finished!"

The car was topping the Rim when Johannan stirred, and a faint twitter of release came from Lala. Meris turned sideways to look at them inquiringly.

"May I get out?" asked Johannan. "Lala has recalled enough that I think my search won't be too long."

"I'll drive you back," said Mark, pulling up by the road.

"Thanks, but it won't be necessary." Johannan opened the

door and, after a tight embrace for Lala and an un-English word or two, stepped out. "I have ways of going. If you will care for Lala until I return."

"Of course!" said Meris, reaching for the child who flowed over the back of the seat into her arms in one complete motion. "God bless, and return soon."

"Thank you," said Johannan and walked into the roadside bushes. They saw a ripple in the branches, the turn of a shoulder, the flick of a foot, one sharp startling glimpse of Johannan rising against the blue and white of the afternoon sky and then he was hidden in the top branches of the trees.

"Shoosh!" Meris slumped under Lala's entire weight. "Mark, is this a case of *folie à deux,* or is it really happening?"

"Well," said Mark, starting the car again. "I doubt if we two could achieve the same hallucinations simultaneously, so let's assume it's really happening."

When they finally reached the cabin and stopped the motor, they sat for a moment in the restful, active silence of the hills. Meris, feeling the soft warmth of Lala against her and the precious return of things outside herself, shivered a little remembering her dead self who had stared so blankly so many hours out of the small windows, tearlessly crying, soundlessly wailing, wrapped in misery. She laughed and hugged Lala. "Maybe we should get a leash for this small person," she said to Mark. "I don't think I could follow in Johannan's footsteps."

"Supper first," said Mark as he fumbled with the padlock on the cabin door. He glanced, startled, back over his shoulder at Meris. "It's broken," he said. "Wrenched open—" He flung the door open hastily, and froze on the doorstep. Meris pushed forward to look beyond him.

Snow had fallen in the room—snow covered everything—a smudged, crumpled snow of paper, flour, sugar, and detergent. Every inch of the cabin was covered by the tattered, soaked, torn, crumpled snow of Mark's manuscript! Mark stooped slowly, like an old man, and took up one page. Mingled detergent and maple syrup clung, clotted, and slithered off the edge of one of the diagrams that had taken two days to complete. He let the page fall and shuffled forward, ankle-deep in the obscene, incredible chaos. Meris hardly recognized the face he turned to her.

"I've lost our child again," he said tightly. "This—" he gestured at the mess about them, "—this was my weeping and my substitute for despair. My creation to answer death."

31

He backhanded a clutter of papers off the bunk and slumped down until he lay, face to the wall, motionless.

Mark said not a word nor turned around in the hours that followed. Meris thought perhaps he slept at times, but she said nothing to him as she cautiously scrabbled through the mess in the cabin. She found, miraculously undamaged, a chapter and a half of pages under the cupboard. With careful hands she salvaged another sheaf of papers from where they had sprayed across the top of the cupboard. All the time she searched and sorted through the mess in the cabin, Lala sat, unnaturally well behaved and solemn, and watched her, getting down only once to salvage Deeko from a mound of sugar and detergent, clucking unhappily as she dusted the doll off.

It was late and cold when Meris put the last ruined sheet in the big cardboard box they had carried groceries home in, and the last salvageable sheet on the desk. She looked silently at the clutter in the box and the slender sheaf on the desk, shivered and turned to build up the dying fire in the stove. Her mouth tightened and the sullen flicker of charring, wadded paper in the stove painted age and pain upon her face. She stirred the embers with the lid-lifter and rebuilt the fire. She prepared supper, fed Lala, and put her to bed. Then she sat on the edge of the lower bunk by Mark's rigid back and touched him gently.

"Supper's ready," she said. "Then I'll need some help in scrubbing up—the floor, the walls, the furniture." She choked on a sound that was half laughter and half sob. "There's plenty of detergent around already. We may bubble ourselves out of house and home."

For a sick moment she was afraid he wouldn't respond. *Just like I was,* she thought achingly. *Just like I was!* Then he sat up slowly, brushed his arm back across his expressionless face and his rumpled hair, and stood up.

When they finally threw out the last bucket of scrub water and hung out the last scrub rag, Meris rubbed her water-wrinkled hands down her weary sides and said, "Tomorrow we'll start on the manuscript again."

"No," said Mark. "That's all finished. The boys got carbon-copy and all. It would take weeks for me to do a rewrite if I could ever do it. We don't have weeks. My leave of absence is over, and the deadline for the manuscript is this next week. We'll just have to chalk this up as lost. Let the dead past bury the dead."

He went to bed, his face turned again from the light.

Meris, through the blur of her slow tears, gathered up the crumpled pages that had pulled out with the blankets from the back of the bunk, smoothed them onto the salvage pile, and went to bed, too.

For the next couple of days Mark was like an old man. He sat against the cabin wall in the sun, his arms resting on his thighs, his hands dangling from limp wrists, looking at the nothing that the senile and finished find on the ground. He moved slowly and reluctantly to the table to push his food around, to bed to lie, hardly breathing, but wide-eyed in the dark, to whatever task Meris set him, forgetting in the middle of it what he was doing.

Lala followed him at first, chattering un-English at her usual great rate, leaning against him when he sat, peering into his indifferent face. Then she stopped talking to him and followed him only with her eyes. Then the third day she came crying into Meris's arms and wept heartbrokenly against her shoulder.

Then her tears stopped, glistened on her cheeks a moment, and were gone. She squirmed out of Meris's embrace and trotted to the window. She pushed a chair up close to the wall, climbed up on it, pressed her forehead to the chilly glass and stared out into the late afternoon.

Tad came over on his bike, bubbling over with the new idea of old cars.

"Why, there's parts of a whole bunch of these cars all over around here—" he cried, fluttering the tattered magazine at Mark. "And have you seen how much they're asking for some of them! Why I could put myself through college on used parts out of our old dumps! And some of these vintage jobs are still running around here! Kiltie has a model A— you've seen it! He shines it like a new shoe every week! And there's an old Overland touring car out in back of our barn, just sitting there, falling apart—"

Mark's silence got through to him then, and he asked, troubled, "What's wrong? Are you mad at me for something?"

Meris spoke into Mark's silence. "No, Tad, it's nothing you've done—" She took him outside, ostensibly to help bring in wood to fill the woodbox and filled him in on the events. When they returned, loaded down with firewood, he dumped his armload into the box and looked at Mark.

"Gee, whiz, Mr. Edwards. Uh—uh—gee whiz!" He gathered up his magazine and his hat and, shuffling his feet for a moment said, "Well, 'bye now," and left, grimacing back at Meris, wordless.

Lala was still staring out the window. She hadn't moved or made a sound while Tad was there. Meris was frightened.

"Mark!" She shook his arm gently. "Look at Lala. She's been like that for almost an hour. She pays no attention to me at all. Mark!"

Mark's attention came slowly back to the cabin and to Meris.

"Thank goodness!" she cried. "I was beginning to feel that I was the one that was missing!"

At that moment, Lala plopped down from the chair and trotted off to the bathroom, a round red spot marking her forehead where she had leaned so long.

"Well!" Meris was pleased. "It must be suppertime. Everyone's gathering around again." And she began the bustle of supper-getting. Lala trotted around with her, getting in the way, hindering with her help.

"No, Lala!" said Meris, "I told you once already. Only three plates. Here, put the other one over there." Lala took the plate, waited patiently until Meris turned to the stove, then, lifting both feet from the floor, put the plate back on the table. The soft click of the flatware as she patterned it around the plate, caught Meris's attention. "Oh, Lala!" she cried, half-laughing, half-exasperated. "Well, all right. If you can't count, okay. Four it will be." She started convulsively and dropped a fork as a knock at the door roused even Mark. "Hungry guest coming," she laughed nervously as she picked up the fork. "Well, stew stretches."

She started for the door, fear, bred of senseless violence, crisping along her spine, but Lala was ahead of her, fluttering like a bird, with excited bird cries against the door panels, her hands fumbling at the knob and the night chain Meris had insisted on installing. Meris unfastened and unlocked and opened the door.

It was Johannan, anxious-eyed and worried, who slipped in and gathered up a shrieking Lala. When he had finally un-Englished her to a quiet, contented clinging, he turned to Meris. "Lala called me back," he said. "I've found my Group. She told me Mark was sick—that bad things had happened."

"Yes," said Meris, stirring the stew and moving it to the back of the stove. "The boys came while we were gone and ruined Mark's manuscript beyond salvage. And Mark—Mark is crushed. He lost all those months of labor through senseless, vindictive—" She turned away from Johannan's questioning face and stirred the stew again, blindly.

34

"But," protested Johannan, "if once it was written, he has it still. He can do it again."

"Time is the factor." Mark's voice, rusty and harsh, broke in on Johannan. "And to rewrite from my notes—" He shook his head and sagged again.

"But—but—!" cried Johannan still puzzled, putting Lala to one side, where she hovered, sitting on air, crooning to Deeko, until she drifted slowly down to the floor. "It's all there! It's been written! It's a whole thing! All you have to do is put it again on paper. Your word scriber—"

"I don't have total recall," said Mark. "Even if I did, just to put it on paper again—come see our 'word scriber.'" He smiled a small bent smile as Johannan poked fingers into the mechanism of the typewriter and clucked unhappily, sounding so like Lala that Meris almost laughed. "Such slowness! Such complications!"

Johannan looked at Mark. "If you want, my People can help you get your manuscript back again."

"It's finished," said Mark. "Why agonize over it any more?" He turned to the blank darkness of the window.

"Was it worth the effort of writing?" asked Johannan.

"I thought so," said Mark. "And others did, too."

"Would it have served a useful purpose?" asked Johannan.

"Of course it would have!" Mark swung angrily from the window. "It covered an area that needs to be covered. It was new—the first book in the field!" He turned again to the window.

"Then," said Johannan simply, "we will make it again. Have you paper enough?"

Mark swung back, his eyes glittering. Meris stepped between his glare and Johannan. "This summer I have come back from the dead," she reminded. "And you caught a baby for me, pulling her down from the sky by one ankle. Johannan went looking for his people through the treetops. And a three-year-old called him back by leaning against the window. If all these things could happen, why can't Johannan bring your manuscript back?"

"But if he tries and can't—" Mark began.

"*Then* we can let the dead past bury the dead," said Meris sharply, "which little item you have not been letting happen so far!"

Mark stared at her, then flushed a deep, painful flush. "Okay, then," he said. "Stir the bones again! Let him put meat back on them if he can!"

The next few hours were busy with patterned confusion. Mark roared off through the gathering darkness to persuade Chip to open the store for typing paper. And people arrived. Just arrived, smiling, at the door, familiar friends before they spoke, and Meris, glancing out to see if the heavens themselves had split open from astonishment saw, hovering treetop high, a truly vintage car, an old pickup that clanked softly to itself, spinning a wheel against a branch as it waited. "If Tad could see that!" she thought, with a bubble of laughter nudging her throat.

She hurried back indoors further to make welcome the newcomers—Valancy, Karen, Davy, Jemmy. The women gathered Lala in with soft cries and shining eyes and she wept briefly upon them in response to their emotions, then leaped upon the fellows and nearly strangled them with her hugs.

Johannan briefed the four in what had happened and what was needed. They discussed the situation, glanced at the few salvaged pages on the desk and sent, eyes closed briefly, for someone else. His name was Remy and he had a special "Gift" for plans and diagrams. He arrived just before Mark got back, so the whole group of them confronted him when he flung the door open and stood there with his bundle of paper.

He blinked, glanced at Meris, then, shifting his burden to one arm, held out a welcoming hand. "I hadn't expected an invasion," he smiled. "To tell the truth, I didn't know what to expect." He thumped the package down on the table and grinned at Meris. "Chip's sure now that writers are psychos," he said. "Any normal person could wait till morning for paper or use flattened grocery bags!" He shrugged out of his jacket. "Now."

Jemmy said, "It's really quite simple. Since you wrote your book and have read it through several times, the thing exists as a whole in your memory, just as it was on paper. So all we have to do is put it on paper again." He gestured.

"That's *all*?" Mark's hands went back through his hair. "That's *all*? Man, that's all I had to do after my notes were organized, months ago! Maybe I should have settled for flattened grocery bags! Why, the sheer physical—" The light was draining out of his face.

"Wait—wait!" Jemmy's hand closed warmly over his sagging shoulder. "Let me finish."

"Davy, here, is our gadgeteer. He dreams up all kinds of knick-knacks and among other things, he has come forth with

36

a word scriber. Even better"—he glanced at Johannan—
"than the ones brought from the New Home. All you have to
do is think and the scriber writes down your thoughts. Here—
try it—" he said into Mark's very evident skepticism.

Davy put a piece of paper on the table in front of Mark
and, on it, a small gadget that looked vaguely like a small
sanding block in that it was curved across the top and flat on
the bottom. "Go on," urged Davy, "think something. You
don't even have to vocalize. I've keyed it to you. Karen
sorted your setting for me."

Mark looked around at the interested, watching faces, at
Meris's eyes, blurred with hesitant hope, and then down at
the scriber. The scriber stirred, then slid swiftly across the
paper, snapping back to the beginning of a line again, as
quick as thought. Davy picked up the paper and handed it to
Mark. Meris crowded to peer over his shoulder.

*Of all the dern-fool things! As if it were possible— Look
at the son-a-gun go!*

All neatly typed, neatly spaced, appropriately punctuated.
Hope flamed up in Mark's eyes. "Maybe so," he said, turning
to Jemmy. "What do I do, now?"

"Well," said Jemmy. "You have your whole book in your
mind, but a mass of other things, too. It'd be almost impossible for you to think through your book without any digres-
sions or side thoughts, so Karen will blanket your mind for
you except for your book—"

"Hypnotism—" Mark's withdrawal was visible.

"No," said Karen. "Just screening out interference. Think
how much time was taken up in your original draft by
distractions—"

Meris clenched her hands and gulped, remembering all the
hours Mark had had to—to *baby-sit* her while she was still
rocking her grief like a rag doll with all the stuffings pulled
out. She felt an arm across her shoulders and turned to
Valancy's comforting smile. "All over," said her eyes, kindly,
"all past."

"How about all the diagrams—" suggested Mark, "I can't
vocalize—"

"That's where Remy comes in," said Jemmy. "All you have
to do is visualize each one. He'll have his own scriber right
here and he'll take it from there."

The cot was pulled up near the table and Mark disposed
himself comfortably on it. The paper was unwrapped and
stacked all ready. Remy and Davy arranged themselves
strategically. Surrounded by briefly bowed heads, Jemmy

said, "We are met together in Thy name." Then Karen touched Mark gently on the forehead with one fingertip.

Mark suddenly lifted himself on one elbow. "Wait," he said, "things are going too fast. Why—why are you doing this for us, anyway? We're strangers. No concern of yours. Is it to pay us for taking care of Lala? In that case—"

Karen smiled. "Why *did* you take care of Lala? You could have turned her over to the authorities. A strange child, no relation, no concern of yours."

"That's a foolish question," said Mark. "She needed help. She was cold and wet and lost. Anyone—"

"You did it for the same reason we are doing this for you," said Karen. "Just because we had our roots on a different world doesn't make us of different flesh. There are no strangers in God's universe. You found an unhappy situation that you could do somehting about, so you did it. Without stopping to figure out the whys and wherefores. You did it just because that's what love does."

Mark lay back on the narrow pillow, "Thank you," he said. Then he turned his face to Meris. "Okay?"

"Okay." Her voice jerked a little past her emotion. "*Love* you, Mark!"

"*Love* you, Meris!"

Karen's fingertip went to Mark's forehead again. "I need contact," she said a little apologetically, "especially with an Outsider."

Meris fell asleep, propped up on the bunk, eyes lulled by the silent *sli-i-i-ide, flip! sli-i-i-ide, flip!* of the scriber, and the brisk flutter of finished pages from the tall pile of paper to the short one. She opened drowsy eyes to a murmur of voices and saw that the two piles of paper were almost balanced. She sat up to ease her neck where it had been bent against the cabin wall.

"But it's wrong, I tell you!" Remy was waving the paper. "Look, this line, here, where it goes—"

"Remy," said Jemmy, "are you sure it's wrong or is it just another earlier version of what we know now?"

"No!" said Remy. "This time it's not that. This is a real mistake. He couldn't possibly have meant it to be like that—"

"Okay," Jemmy nodded to Karen and she touched Mark's forehead. He opened his eyes and half sat up. The scriber flipped across the paper and Karen stilled it with a touch. "What is it?" he asked, "something go wrong?"

"No, it's this diagram." Remy brought it to him. "I think you have an error here. Look where this goes—"

The two bent over the paper. Meris looked around the cabin. Valancy was rocking a sleeping Lala in her arms. Davy was sound asleep in the upper bunk. At least his dangling leg looked very asleep. Johannan was absorbed in two books simultaneously. He seemed to be making a comparison of some sort. Meris lay back again, sliding down to a more comfortable position. For the first time in months and months the cabin was lapped from side to side with peace and relaxation. Even the animated discussion going on was no ruffling of the comfortable calmness. She heard, on the edge of her ebbing consciousness,

"Why no! That's not right at all!" Mark was astonished. "Hoo boy! If I'd sent that in with an error like that! Thanks, fella—" And sleep flowed over Meris.

She awoke later to the light chatter of Lala's voice and opened drowsy eyes to see her trailing back from the bathroom, her feet tucked up under her gown away from the chilly floor as she drifted back to Valancy's arms. The leg above Meris's head swung violently and withdrew, to be replaced by Davy's dangling head. He said something to Lala. She laughed and lifted herself up to his outstretched arms. There was a stirring around above Meris's head before sleeping silence returned.

Valancy stood and stretched widely. She moved over to the table and thumbed the stack of paper.

"Going well," she said softly.

"Yes," said Jemmy, "I feel a little like a midwife, snatching something new-born in the middle of the night."

"Dern shame to stop here, though," said Remy. "With such a good beginning—oh, barring a few excursions down dead ends—if we could only tack on a few more chapters."

"Uh-uh!" Jemmy stood and stretched, letting his arms fall around Valancy's shoulders. "You know better than that—"

"Not even one little hint?"

"Not even," Jemmy was firm.

Sleep flowed over Meris again until pushed back by Davy's sliding over the edge of the upper bunk.

"Right in the stomach!" he moaned as he dropped to the floor. "Such a kicking kid I never met. How'd *you* survive?" he asked Valancy.

"Nary a kick," she laughed. "Technique—that's what it takes."

39

"I was just wondering," said Davy, opening the stove and probing the coals before he put in another chunk of oak. "That kid Johannan was talking about—the one that's got interested in vintage cars. What about that place up on Bearcat Flat? You know, that little box canyon where we put all our old jalopies when we discarded them. Engines practically unused. Lifting's cheaper and faster. Of course the seats and the truck beds are kinda beat up, and the paint. Trees scratch the daylights out of paint. How many are there there? Let's see. The first one was about 19-ought-something —"

Johannan looked up from his books. "He said something about selling parts or cars to get money for college—"

"Or restoring them!" Davy cried. "Hey, that could be fun! If he's the kind that would—"

"He is," said Johannan and went back to his reading.

"It's almost daylight." Davy went to the window and parted the curtains. "Wonder how early a riser he is?"

Meris turned her back to the light and slid back under sleep again.

Noise and bustle filled the cabin.

Coffee was perking fragrantly, eggs cracking, bacon spitting itself to crispness. Remy was cheerfully mashing slices of bread down on the hot stove lid and prying up the resultant toast. Lala was flicking around the table, putting two forks at half the places and two knives at the others, then giggling her way back around with redistribution after Johannan pointed out her error.

Meris, reaching for a jar of peach marmalade on the top shelf of the cupboard, wondered how a day could feel so new and so wonderful. Mark sat at his desk opening and closing the box wherein lay the finished manuscript. He opened it again and fingered the top edge of the stack. He caught Jemmy's sympathetic grin and grinned back.

"Just making sure it's really there," he explained. "Magic put it in there. Magic might take it out again."

"Not this magic. I'll even ride shotgun for you into town and see that it gets sent off okay," said Jemmy.

"Magic or no," said Mark, sobering, "once more I can say Thank God! Thank God it's done!"

"Amen!" said a hovering Lala, and, laughing, Jemmy scooped her out of the air as they all found places at the table.

Tad was an early riser. He was standing under the hovering pickup, gaping upward in admiring astonishment.

"Oops!" said Davy, with a sidewise glance at Jemmy. Tad was swept up in a round of introductions during which the pickup lowered slowly to the ground.

Tad turned from the group back to the pickup. "Look at it!" he said. "It must be at least forty years old!" His voice pushed its genesis back beyond the pyramids.

"At least that," said Davy. "Wanta see the motor?"

"Do I!" He stood by impatiently as Davy wrestled with the hood. Then he blinked. "Hey! How did it get way up there? I mean, how'd it get down——"

"Look," said Davy hastily, "see this goes to the spark——"

The others, laughing, piled into Mark's car and drove away from the two absorbed autophiles-in-embryo.

The car pulled over onto a pine flat halfway back from town and the triumphal mailing of the manuscript. This was the parting place. Davy would follow later with the pickup.

"It's over," said Meris, her shoulders sagging a little as she put Lala's small bundle of belongings into Valancy's hands. "All over." Her voice was desolate.

"Only this little episode," comforted Valancy. "It's really only begun." She put Lala into Meris's arms. "Tell her good-by, Lala."

Lala hugged Meris stranglingly tight saying, "*Love* you, Meris!"

"*Love* you, Lala!" Meris's voice was shaken with laughter and sorrow.

"It's just that she filled up the empty places so wonderfully well," she explained to Valancy.

"Yes," said Valancy softly, her eyes tender and compassionate. "But, you know," she went on. "You *are* pregnant again!"

Before Meris could produce an intelligible thought, good-bys were finished and the whole group was losing itself in the tangle of creek-side vegetation. Lala's vigorous waving of Deeko was the last sign of them before the leaves closed behind them.

Meris and Mark stood there, Meris's head pressed to Mark's shoulder, both too drained for any emotion. Then Meris stirred and moved toward the car, her eyes suddenly shining. "I don't think I can wait," she said, "I don't think——"

"Wait for what?" asked Mark, following her.

"To tell Dr. Hilf—" She covered her mouth, dismayed. "Oh, Mark! We never did find out that doctor's name!"

"Not that Hilf is drooling to know," said Mark, starting the car, "but next time—"

"Oh, yes," Meris sat back, her mouth curving happily, "next time, next time!"

The next time wasn't so long by the calendar, but measured by the anticipation and the marking time, it seemed an endless eternity. Then one night Meris, looking down into the warm, moistly fragrant blanket-bundle in the crook of her elbow, felt time snap back into focus. It snapped back so completely and satisfyingly that the long, empty time of grief dwindled to a memory-ache tucked back in the fading past.

"And the next one," she said drowsily to Mark, "will be a brother for her."

The nurse laughed. "Most new mothers feel, at this point, that they are through with childbearing. But I guess they soon forget because we certainly get a lot of repeaters!"

The Saturday before the baby's christening, Meris felt a stir of pleasure as she waited for her guests to arrive. So much of magic was interwoven with her encounters with them, the magic of being freed from grief, of bringing forth a new life, and the magic of the final successful production of Mark's book. She was wondering, with a pleasurable apprehension, what means of transportation the guests would use, *treetop high, one wheel spinning lazily!* when a clanging clatter drew her to the front window.

There in all its glory, shining with love, new paint, and dignity, sailed the Overland that had been moldering behind Tad's barn. Flushed with excitement and pride, Tad, with an equally proud Johannan seated beside him, steered the vehicle ponderously over to the curb. There it hiccoughed, jumped, and expired with a shudder.

In the split second of silence after the noise cut off, there was a clinking rattle and a nut fell down from somewhere underneath and rolled out into the street.

There was a shout of relieved and amused laughter and the car erupted people apparently through and over every door. Meris shrank back a little, still tender in her social contact area. Then calling, "Mark, they're here," she opened the door to the babble of happy voices.

All the voices turned out to be female-type voices and she looked around and asked, "But where—?"

"The others?" Karen asked. "Behold!" And she gestured toward the old car where the only signs of life were three sets of feet protruding from under it, with a patient Jemmy leaning on a brightly black fender above them. "May I present, the feet, Tad, Davy, and Johannan?" Karen laughed. "Johannan is worse than either of the boys. You see, he'd never ever *seen* a car before he rode in yours!"

Finally everyone was met and greeted and all the faces swam up to familiarity again out of the remoteness of the time Before the Baby.

Lala—forever Lala in spite of translations!—peered at the bundle on Valancy's lap. "It's little," she said.

Meris was startled. Valancy smiled at her. "Did you expect her to un-English forever?" she teased. "Yes, Lala, it's a girl baby, very new and very little."

"I'm not little," said Lala, straightening from where she leaned against Meris and tightening to attention, her tummy rounding out in her effort to assume proportions. "I'm big!" She moved closer to Meris. "I had a birthday."

"Oh, how nice!" said Meris.

"We don't know what year to put on it, though," said Lala solemnly. "I want to put six, but they want to put five."

"Oh, six, of course!" exclaimed Meris.

Lala launched herself onto Meris and hugged her hair all askew. "*Love* you, Meris!" she cried. "Six, of course!"

"There has been a little discussion about the matter," said Valancy. "The time element differs between here and the New Home. And since she *is* precocious—"

"The *New* Home," said Meris thoughtfully. "The New Home. You know, I suspended all my disbelief right at the beginning of this Lala business, but now I feel questions bubbling and frothing—"

"I thought I saw question marks arising in both your eyes," laughed Valancy. "After church tomorrow, after this cherub receives her name before God and the congregation, we'll tackle a few of those questions. But now—" she hugged the wide-eyed, moist-mouthed child gently "—now this is the center of our interest."

The warm Sunday afternoon was slipping into evening. Davy, Tad, and Johannan were—again—three pairs of feet protruding from under the Overland. The three had managed to nurse it along all the way to the University City, but now it stubbornly sat in the driveway and merely rocked it, voiceless, no matter how long they cranked it.

The three of them had been having the time of their lives.

43

They had visited the Group's auto boneyard up-canyon and then, through avid reading of everything relevant that they could put their hands on, had slowly and bedazzledly come to a realization of what a wealth of material they had to work with.

Tad, after a few severe jolts from working with members of The People, such as seeing cars and parts thereof clattering massively unsupported through the air and watching Johannan weld a rip in a fender by tracing it with a fingertip, then concentrating on the task, had managed to compartmentalize the whole car business and shut it off securely from any need to make the methods of The People square with Outsiders' methods. And his college fund was building beautifully.

So there the three of them were under the Overland that was the current enthusiasm, ostensibly to diagnose the trouble, but also to delight in breathing deeply of sun-warmed metal and to taste the oily fragrance of cup grease and dust.

Mark and Jemmy were perched on the patio wall, immersed in some point from Mark's book. Lala was wrapped up in the wonder of Alicia's tiny, flailing fist, that if intercepted, would curl so tightly around a finger or thumb.

Meris smiled at Valancy and shifted the burden of 'Licia to her other arm. "I think I'd better park this bundle somewhere. She's gained ten pounds in the last five minutes so I think that a nap is indicated." With the help of Valancy, Karen, and Bethie, Meris gathered up various odds and ends of equipment and carried the already sleeping 'Licia into the house.

Later, in the patio, the women gathered again, Lala a warm weight in Valancy's lap.

"Now," said Meris, comfortably. "Now's the time to erase a few of my question marks. What is the Home? Where is the Home? Why is the *New* Home?"

"Not so fast—not so fast!" laughed Valancy. "This is Bethie's little red wagon. Let her drag it!"

"Oh, but—!" Bethie blushed and shook her head. "Why mine? I'd rather—"

"But you have been wanting to Assemble for Shadow, anyway, so that she'd have a verbalized memory of the Crossing. It's closer through your line." Her smile softened as she turned to Meris. "My parents were in the Crossing, but they were Called during the landing. Bethie's mother was *in* the Crossing and survived. Karen's grandparents did, too, but that's a step farther back. And, Bethie, haven't you already—"

"Yes," said Bethie softly, "from the Home to the beginning of the Crossing. Oh, how strange! How strange and wonderful! Oh, Valancy! To have lost the Home!"

"Now you're question-marking *my* eyes," laughed Valancy. "I've never gone by chapter and verse through that life myself. Jemmy—Mark—we're ready!"

"It'll be better, subvocal," said Bethie shyly. "Karen, you could touch Meris's hand so she can see, too. And Jemmy, you and Mark." The group settled comfortably.

"I went back through my mother's remembrances," Bethie's soft voice came through a comfortable dimming and fading of the patio. "Her grandmother before her verbalized a great deal. It was a big help. We can take it from her. We will begin on one happy morning—"

DELUGE

. . . and bare up the ark, and it was lift up above the earth.

GEN. 7:17

"The children are up already, Eva-lee?" asked David, lounging back in his chair after his first long, satisfying swallow from his morning cup.

"Foolish question, David, on Gathering Day," I laughed. "They've been up since before it was light. Have you forgotten how you used to feel?"

"Of course not." My son cradled his cup in his two hands to warm it and watched idly until steam plumed up fragrantly. "I just forgot—oh, momentarily, I assure you—that it was Gathering Day. So far it hasn't felt much like *failova* weather."

"No, it hasn't, I answered, puckering my forehead thoughtfully. "It has felt—odd—this year. The green isn't as— Oh, good morning, 'Chell," to my daughter-of-love, "I suppose the little imps waked you first thing?"

"At least half an hour before that," yawned 'Chell. "I suppose I used to do it myself. But just wait—they'll have their yawning time when they're parents."

"Mother! Mother! Father! Gramma!"

The door slapped open and the children avalanched in, all talking shrilly at once until David waved his cup at them and lifted one eyebrow. 'Chell laughed at the sudden silence.

"That's better," she said. "What's all the uproar?"

45

The children looked at one another and the five-year-old Eve was nudged to the fore, but, as usual, David started talking. "We were out gathering *panthus* leaves to make our Gathering baskets, and all at once—" He paused and nudged Eve again. "You tell, Eve. After all, it's you—"

"Oh, no!" cried 'Chell, "not my last baby! Not already!"

"Look," said Eve solemnly. "Look at me."

She stood tiptoe and wavered a little, her arms outstretched for balance, and then she lifted slowly and carefully up into her mother's arms.

We all laughed and applauded and even 'Chell, after blotting her surprised tears on Eve's dark curls, laughed with us.

"Bless-a-baby!" she said, hugging her tight. "Lifting all alone already—and on Gathering Day, too! It's not everyone who can have Gathering Day for her Happy Day!" Then she sobered and pressed the solemn ceremonial kiss on each cheek. "Lift in delight all your life, Eve!" she said.

Eve matched her parents' solemnity as her father softly completed the ritual. "By the Presence and the Name and the Power, lift to good and the Glory until your Calling." And we all joined in making the Sign.

"I speak for her next," I said, holding out my arms. "Think you can lift to Gramma, Eve?"

"Well ..." Eve considered the gap between her and me— the chair, the breakfast table—all the obstacles before my waiting arms. And then she smiled. "Look at me," she said. "Here I come, Gramma."

She lifted carefully above the table, overarching so high that the crisp girl-frill around the waist of her close-fitting briefs brushed the ceiling. Then she was safe in my arms.

"That's better than I did," called Simon through the laughter that followed. "I landed right in the *flahmen* jam!"

"So you did, son," laughed David, ruffling Simon's coppery-red hair. "A full dish of it."

"Now that that's taken care of, let's get organized. Are you all Gathering together?"

"No." Lytha, our teener, flushed faintly. "I—we—our party will be mostly—well—" She paused and checked her blush, shaking her dark hair back from her face. "Timmy and I are going with Beckie and Andy. We're going to the Mountain."

"Well!" David's brow lifted in mock consternation. "Mother, did you know our daughter was two-ing?"

"Not really, Father!" cried Lytha hastily, unable to resist

the bait though she knew he was teasing. "Four-ing, it is, really."

"*Adonday veeah!*" he sighed in gigantic relief. "Only half the worry it might be!" He smiled at her. "Enjoy," he said, "but it ages me so much so fast that a daughter of mine is two—oh, pardon, four-ing already."

"The rest of us are going together," said Davie. "We're going to the Tangle-meadows. The *failova* were thick there last year. Bet we three get more than Lytha and her two-ing foursome! They'll be looking mostly for *flahmen* anyway!" with the enormous scorn of the almost-teen for the activities of the teens.

"Could be," said David. "But after all, your sole purpose this Gathering Day is merely to Gather."

"I notice you don't turn up your nose at the *flahmen* after they're made into jam," said Lytha. "And you just wait, smarty, until the time comes—and it will," her cheeks pinked up a little, "when you find yourself wanting to share a *flahmen* with some gaggly giggle of a girl!"

"*Flahman!*" muttered Davie. "Girls!"

"They're both mighty sweet, Son," laughed David. "You wait and see."

Ten minutes later, 'Chell and David and I stood at the window watching the children leave. Lytha, after nervously putting on and taking off, arranging and rearranging her Gathering Day garlands at least a dozen times, was swept up by a giggling group that zoomed in a trio and went out a quartet and disappeared in long, low lifts across the pastureland toward the heavily wooded Mountain.

Davie tried to gather Eve up as in the past, but she stubbornly refused to be trailed, and kept insisting, "I can lift now! Let me do it. I'm big!"

Davie rolled exasperated eyes and then grinned and the three started off for Tangle-meadows in short hopping little lifts, with Eve always just beginning to lift as they landed or just landing as they lifted, her small Gathering basket bobbing along with her. Before they disappeared, however, she was trailing from Davie's free hand and the lifts were smoothing out long and longer. My thoughts went with them as I remembered the years I had Gathered the lovely luminous flowers that popped into existence in a single night, leafless, almost stemless, as though formed like dew, or falling like concentrated moonlight. No one knows now how the custom of loves sharing a *flahmen* came into being, but it's firmly entrenched in the traditions of the People. To share that luminous loveliness, petal by petal, one for me and one for you and all for us—

"How pleasant that Gathering Day brings back our loves," I sighed dreamily as I stood in the kitchen and snapped my fingers for the breakfast dishes to come to me. "People that might otherwise be completely forgotten come back so vividly every year—"

"Yes," said 'Chell, watching the tablecloth swish out the window, huddling the crumbs together to dump them in the feather-pen in back of the house. "And it's a good anniversary-marker. Most of us meet our loves at the Gathering Festival—or discover them there." She took the returning cloth and folded it away. "I never dreamed when I used to fuss with David over mud pies and playhouses that one Gathering Day he'd blossom into my love."

"*Me* blossom?" David peered around the doorjamb. "Have you forgotten how you looked, preblossom? Knobby knees, straggly hair, toothless grin—!"

"David, put me down!" 'Chell struggled as she felt herself being lifted to press against the ceiling. "We're too old for such nonsense!"

"Get yourself down, then, Old One," he said from the other room. "If I'm too old for nonsense, I'm too old to '*platt*' you."

"Never mind, funny fellow," she said, "I'll do it myself." Her down-reaching hand strained toward the window and she managed to gather a handful of the early morning sun. Quickly she platted herself to the floor and tiptoed off into the other room, eyes aglint with mischief, finger hushing to her lips.

I smiled as I heard David's outcry and 'Chell's delighted laugh, but I felt my smile slant down into sadness. I leaned my arms on the windowsill and looked lovingly at all the dear familiarity around me. Before Thann's Calling, we had known so many happy hours in the meadows and skies and waters of this loved part of the Home.

"And he is still here," I thought comfortably. "The grass still bends to his feet, the leaves still part to his passing, the waters still ripple to his touch, and my heart still cradles his name.

"Oh, Thann, Thann!" I wouldn't let tears form in my eyes. I smiled. "I wonder what kind of a grampa you'd have made!" I leaned my forehead on my folded arms briefly, then turned to busy myself with straightening the rooms for the day. I was somewhat diverted from routine by finding six mismated sandals stacked, for some unfathomable reason, above the middle of Simon's bed, the top one, inches above the rest, bobbing in the breeze from the open window.

The oddness we had felt about the day turned out to be more than a passing uneasiness and we adults were hardly surprised when the children came straggling back hours before they usually did.

We hailed them from afar, lifting out to them expecting to help with their burdens of brightness, but the children didn't answer our hails. They plodded on toward the house, dragging slow feet in the abundant grass.

"What do you suppose has happened?" breathed 'Chell. "Surely not Eve—"

"*Adonday veeah!*" murmured David, his eyes intent on the children. "Something's wrong, but I see Eve."

"Hi, young ones," he called cheerfully. "How's the crop this year?"

The children stopped, huddled together, almost fearfully.

"Look." Davie pushed his basket at them. Four misshapen *failova* glowed dully in the basket. No flickering, glittering brightness. No flushing and paling of petals. No crisp, edible sweetness of blossom. Only a dull glow, a sullen winking, an unappetizing crumbling.

"That's all," said Davie, his voice choking. "That's all we could find!" He was scared and outraged—outraged that his world dared to be different from what he had expected—had counted on.

Eve cried, "No, no! I have one. Look!" Her single flower was a hard-clenched *flahmen* bud with only a smudge of light at the tip.

"No *failova?*" 'Chell took Davie's proffered basket. "No *flahmen?* But they always bloom on Gathering Day. Maybe the buds—"

"No buds," said Simon, his face painfully white under the brightness of his hair. I glanced at him quickly. He seldom ever got upset over anything. What was there about this puzzling development that was stirring him?

"David!" 'Chell's face turned worriedly to him. "What's wrong? There have always been *failova!*"

"I know," said David, fingering Eve's bud and watching it crumble in his fingers. "Maybe it's only in the meadows. Maybe there's plenty in the hills."

"No," I said. "Look."

49

Far off toward the hills we could see the teeners coming, slowly, clustered together, *panthus* baskets trailing.

"No *failova*," said Lytha as they neared us. She turned her basket up, her face troubled. "No *failova* and no *flahmen*. Not a flicker on all the hills where they were so thick last year. Oh, Father, why not? It's as if the sun hadn't come up! Something's wrong."

"Nothing catastrophic, Lytha." David comforted her with a smile. "We'll bring up the matter at the next meeting of the Old Ones. Someone will have the answer. It is unusual, you know." (Unheard of, he should have said.) "We'll find out then." He boosted Eve to his shoulder. "Come on, young ones, the world hasn't ended. It's still Gathering Day! I'll race you to the house. First one there gets six *koomatka* to eat all by himself! One, two, three—"

Off shot the shrieking, shouting children, Eve's little heels pummeling David's chest in her excitement. The teeners followed for a short way and then slanted off on some project of their own, waving good-by to 'Chell and me. We women followed slowly to the house, neither speaking.

I wasn't surprised to find Simon waiting for me in my room. He sat huddled on my bed, his hands clasping and unclasping and trembling, a fine, quick trembling deeper than muscles and tendons. His face was so white it was almost luminous and the skiff of golden freckles across the bridge of his nose looked metallic.

"Simon?" I touched him briefly on his hair that was so like Thann's had been.

"Gramma." His breath caught in a half hiccough. He cleared his throat carefully as though any sudden movement would break something fragile. "Gramma," he whispered. "I can See!"

"See!" I sat down beside him because my knees suddenly evaporated. "Oh, Simon! You don't mean—"

"Yes, I do, Gramma." He rubbed his hands across his eyes. "We had just found the first *failova* and wondering what was wrong with it when everything kinda went away and I was—somewhere—Seeing!" He looked up, terrified. "It's my Gift!"

I gathered the suddenly wildly sobbing child into my arms and held him tightly until his terror spent itself and I felt his withdrawal. I let him go and watched his wet, flushed face dry and peal back to normal.

"Oh, Gramma," he said, "I don't want a Gift yet. I'm only ten. David hasn't found his Gift and he's twelve already. I don't *want* a Gift—especially this one—" He closed his eyes and shuddered. "Oh, Gramma, what I've seen already! Even the Happy scares me because it's still in the Presence!"

"It's not given to many," I said, at a loss how to comfort him. "Why, Simon, it would take a long journey back to our Befores to find one in our family who was permitted to See. It is an honor—to be able to put aside the curtain of time—"

"I don't *want* to!" Simon's eyes brimmed again. "I don't think it's a bit of fun. Do I have to?"

"Do you have to breathe?" I asked him. "You could stop if you wanted to, but your body would die. You can refuse your Gift, but part of you would die—the part of you the Power honors—your place in the Presence—your syllable of the Name." All this he knew from first consciousness, but I could feel him taking comfort from my words. "Do you realize the People have had no one to See for them since—since—why, clear back to the Peace! And now you are it! Oh, Simon, I am so proud of you!" I laughed at my own upsurge of emotion. "Oh, Simon! May I touch my thrice-honored grandson?"

With a wordless cry, he flung himself into my arms and we clung tightly, tightly, before his deep renouncing withdrawal. He looked at me then and slowly dropped his arms from around my neck, separation in every movement. I could see growing in the topaz tawniness of his eyes, his new set-apartness. It made me realize anew how close the Presence is to us always and how much nearer Simon was than any of us. Also, naked and trembling in my heart was the recollection that never did the People have one to See for them unless there lay ahead portentous things to See.

Both of us shuttered our eyes and looked away, Simon to veil the eyes that so nearly looked on the Presence, I, lest I be blinded by the Glory reflected in his face.

"Which reminds me," I said in a resolutely everyday voice, "I will now listen to explanations as to why those six sandals were left on, over, and among your bed this morning."

"Well," he said with a tremulous grin. "The red ones are too short—" He turned stricken, realizing eyes to me. "I won't ever be able to tell anyone anything any more unless the Power wills it!" he cried. Then he grinned again, "And the green ones need the latchets renewed—"

A week later the usual meeting was called and David and I—we were among the Old Ones of our Group—slid into our robes. I felt a pang as I smoothed the shimmering fabric over

51

my hips, pressing pleats in with my thumb and finger to adjust for lost weight. The last time I had worn it was the Festival the year Thann was Called. Since then I hadn't wanted to attend the routine Group meetings—not without Thann. I hadn't realized that I was losing weight.

'Chell clung to David. "I wish now that I were an Old One, too," she said. "I've got a nameless worry in the pit of my stomach heavy enough to anchor me for life. Hurry home, you two!"

I looked back as we lifted just before the turnoff. I smiled to see the warm lights begin to well up in the windows. Then my smile died. I felt, too, across my heart the shadow that made 'Chell feel it was Lighting Time before the stars had broken through the last of the day.

The blow—when it came—was almost physical, so much so that I pressed my hands to my chest, my breath coming hard, trying too late to brace against the shock. David's sustaining hand was on my arm but I felt the tremor in it, too. Around me I felt my incredulity and disbelief shared by the other Old Ones of the Group.

The Oldest spread his hands as he was deluged by a flood of half-formed questions. "It has been Seen. Already our Home has been altered so far that the *failova* and *flahmen* can't come to blossom. As we accepted the fact that there were no *failova* and *flahmen* this year, so we must accept the fact that there will be no more Home for us."

In the silence that quivered after his words, I could feel the further stricken sag of heartbeats around me and suddenly my own heart slowed until I wondered if the Power was stilling it now—now—in the midst of this confused fear and bewilderment.

"Then we are all Called?" I couldn't recognize the choked voice that put the question. "How long before the Power summons us?"

"*We* are not Called," said the Oldest. "Only the Home is Called. We—go."

"Go!" The thought careened from one to another.

"Yes," said the Oldest. "Away from the Home. Out."

Life apart from the Home? I slumped. It was too much to be taken in all at once. Then I remembered. Simon! Oh, poor Simon! If he were Seeing clearly already—but of course he was. He was the one who had told the Oldest! No wonder he was terrified! *Simon*, I said to the Oldest subvocally. *Yes*, answered the Oldest. *Do not communicate to the others. He*

52

scarcely can bear the burden now. To have it known would multiply it past his bearing. Keep his secret—completely.

I came back to the awkward whirlpool of thoughts around me.

"But," stammered someone, speaking what everyone was thinking, "can the People *live* away from the Home? Wouldn't we die like uprooted plants?"

"We can live," said the Oldest. "This we know, as we know that the Home can no longer be our biding place."

"What's wrong? What's happening?" It was Neil—Timmy's father.

"We don't know." The Oldest was shamed. "We have forgotten too much since the Peace to be able to state the mechanics of what is happening, but one of us Sees us go and the Home destroyed, so soon that we have no time to go back to the reasons."

Since we were all joined in our conference mind which is partially subvocal, all our protests and arguments and cries were quickly emitted and resolved, leaving us awkwardly trying to plan something of which we had no knowledge of our own.

"If we are to go," I said, feeling a small spurt of excitement inside my shock, "we'll have to make again. Make a tool. No, that's not the word. We have tools still. Man does with tools. No, it's a—a machine we'll have to make. Machines do to man. We haven't been possessed by machines—"

"For generations," said David. "Not since—" He paused to let our family's stream of history pour through his mind. "Since Eva-lee's thrice great-grandfather's time."

"Nevertheless," said the Oldest, "we must make ships." His tongue was hesitant on the long unused word. "I have been in communication with the other Oldest Ones around the Home. Our Group must make six of them."

"How can we?" asked Neil. "We have no plans. We don't know such things any more. We have forgotten almost all of it. But I do know that to break free from the Home would take a pushing something that all of us together couldn't supply."

"We will have the—the fuel," said the Oldest. "When the time comes. My Befores knew the fuel. We would not need it if only our motivers had developed their Gift fully, but as they did not—

"We must each of us search the Before stream of our lives and find the details that we require in this hour of need. By the Presence, the Name, and the Power, let us remember."

53

The evening sped away almost in silence as each mind opened and became receptive to the flow of racial memory that lay within. All of us partook in a general way of that stream that stemmed almost from the dawn of the Home. In particular, each family had some specialized area of the memory in greater degree than the others. From time to time came a sigh or a cry prefacing, "My Befores knew of the metals," or "Mine of the instruments"—the words were unfamiliar—"The instruments of pressure and temperature."

"Mine"—I discovered with a glow—and a sigh—"the final putting together of the shells of ships."

"Yes," nodded David, "and also, from my father's Befores, the settings of the—the—the settings that guide the ship."

"Navigation," said Neil's deep voice. "My Befores knew of the making of the navigation machine yours knew how to set."

"And all," I said, "all of this going back to nursery school would have been unnecessary if we hadn't rested so comfortably so long on the achievements of our Befores!" I felt the indignant withdrawal of some of those about me, but the acquiescence of most of them.

When the evening ended, each of us Old Ones carried not only the burden of the doom of the Home but a part of the past that, in the Quiet Place of each home, must, with the help of the Power, be probed and probed again, until—

"Until—" The Oldest stood suddenly, clutching the table as though he just realized the enormity of what he was saying. "Until we have the means of leaving the Home—before it becomes a band of dust between the stars—"

Simon and Lytha were waiting up with 'Chell when David and I returned. At the sight of our faces, Simon slipped into the bedroom and woke Davie and the two crept quietly back into the room. Simon's thought reached out ahead of him. *Did he tell?* And mine went out reassuringly. *No. And he won't.*

In spite of—or perhaps because of—the excitement that had been building up in me all evening, I felt suddenly drained and weak. I sat down, gropingly, in a chair and pressed my hands to my face. "You tell them, David," I said, fighting an odd vertigo.

David shivered and swallowed hard. "There were no *failova* because the Home is being broken up. By next Gathering Day there will be no Home. It is being destroyed. We can't even say why. We have forgotten too much and

54

there isn't time to seek out the information now, but long before next Gathering Day, we will be gone—out."

'Chell's breath caught audibly. "No Home!" she said, her eyes widening and darkening. "No Home? Oh, David, don't joke. Don't try to scare—"

"It's true." My voice had steadied now. "It has been Seen. We must build ships and seek asylum among the stars." My heart gave a perverse jump of excitement. "The Home will no longer exist. We will be homeless exiles."

"But the People away from the Home!" 'Chell's face puckered, close to tears. "How can we live anywhere else? We are a part of the Home as much as the Home is a part of us. We can't just amputate—"

"Father!" Lytha's voice was a little too loud. She said again, "Father, are all of us going together in the same ship?"

"No," said David. "Each Group by itself." Lytha relaxed visibly. "Our Group is to have six ships," he added.

Lytha's hands tightened. "Who is to go in which ship?"

"It hasn't been decided yet," said David, provoked. "How can you worry about a detail like that when the Home, *the Home* will soon be gone!"

"It's important," said Lytha, flushing. "Timmy and I—"

"Oh," said David. "I'm sorry, Lytha. I didn't know. The matter will have to be decided when the time comes."

It didn't take long for the resiliency of childhood to overcome the shock of the knowledge born on Gathering Day. Young laughter rang as brightly through the hills and meadows as always. But David and 'Chell clung closer to one another, sharing the heavy burden of leave-taking, as did all the adults of the Home. At times I, too, felt wildly, hopefully, that this was all a bad dream to be awakened from. But other times I had the feeling that this *was* an awakening. This was the dawn after a long twilight—a long twilight of slanting sun and relaxing shadows. Other times I felt so detached from the whole situation that wonder welled up in me to see the sudden tears, the sudden clutching of familiar things, that had become a sort of pattern among us as realization came and went. And then, there were frightening times when I felt weakness flowing into me like a river—a river that washed all the Home away on a voiceless wave. I was almost becoming more engrossed in the puzzle of me than in the puzzle of the dying Home—and I didn't like it.

David and I went often to Meeting, working with the rest

of the Group on the preliminary plans for the ships. One night he leaned across the table to the Oldest and asked, "How do we know how much food will be needed to sustain us until we find asylum?"

The Oldest looked steadily back at him. "We *don't* know," he said. "We don't know that we will ever find asylum."

"Don't know?" David's eyes were blank with astonishment.

"No," said the Oldest. "We found no other habitable worlds before the Peace. We have no idea how far we will have to go or if we shall any of us live to see another Home. Each Group is to be assigned to a different sector of the sky. On Crossing Day, we say good-by—possibly forever—to all the other Groups. It may be that only one ship will plant the seeds of the People upon a new world. It may be that we will all be Called before a new Home is found."

"Then," said David, "why don't we stay here and take our Calling with the Home?"

"Because the Power has said to go. We are given time to go back to the machines. The Power is swinging the gateway to the stars open to us. We must take the gift and do what we can with it. We have no right to deprive our children of any of the years they might have left to them."

After David relayed the message to 'Chell, she clenched both her fists tight up against her anguished heart and cried, "We can't! Oh, David! We can't! We can't leave the Home for—for—nowhere! Oh, David!" And she clung to him, wetting his shoulder with her tears.

"We can do what we must do," he said. "All of the People are sharing this sorrow so none of us must make the burden any heavier for the others. The children learn their courage from us, 'Chell. Be a good teacher." He rocked her close-pressed head, his hand patting her tumbled hair, his troubled eyes seeking mine.

"Mother—" David began—Eva-lee was for every day.

"Mother, it seems to me that the Presence is pushing us out of the Home deliberately and crumpling it like an empty eggshell so we can't creep back into it. We have sprouted too few feathers on our wings since the Peace. I think we're being pushed off the branch to make us fly. This egg has been too comfortable." He laughed a little as he held 'Chell away from him and dried her cheeks with the palms of his hands. "I'm afraid I've made quite an omelet of my egg analogy, but can you think of anything really new that we have learned about Creation in our time."

"Well," I said, searching my mind, pleased immeasurably

to hear my own thoughts on the lips of my son. "No, I can honestly say I can't think of one new thing."

"So if you were Called to the Presence right now and were asked, 'What do you know of My Creation?' all you could say would be 'I know all that my Befores knew—my immediate Befores, that is—I mean, my father—'" David opened his hands and poured out emptiness. "Oh, Mother! What we have forgotten! And how content we have been with so little!"

"But some other way." 'Chell cried. "This is so—so drastic and cruel!"

"All baby birds shiver," said David, clasping her cold hands. "Sprout a pin feather, 'Chell!"

And then the planning arrived at the point where work could begin. The sandal shops were empty. The doors were closed in the fabric centers and the ceramic workrooms. The sunlight crept unshadowed again and again across the other workshops and weeds began tentative invasions of the garden plots.

Far out in the surrounding hills, those of the People who knew how hovered in the sky, rolling back slowly the heavy green cover of the mountainsides, to lay bare the metal-rich underearth. Then the Old Ones, making solemn mass visits from Group to Group, quietly concentrated above the bared hills and drew forth from the very bones of the Home, the bright, bubbling streams of metal, drew them forth until they flowed liquidly down the slopes to the workplaces—the launching sites. And the rush and the clamor and the noise of the hurried multitudes broke the silence of the hills of the Home and sent tremors through all our windows—and through our shaken souls.

I often stood at the windows of our house, watching the sky-pointing monsters of metal slowly coming to form. From afar they had a severe sort of beauty that eased my heart of the hurt their having-to-be caused. But it was exciting! Oh, it was beautifully exciting! Sometimes I wondered what we thought about and what we did before we started all this surge out into space. On the days that I put in my helping hours on the lifting into place of the strange different parts that had been fashioned by other Old Ones from memories of the Befores, the upsurge of power and the feeling of being one part of such a gigantic undertaking, made me realize that we had forgotten without even being conscious of it, the warmth and strength of working together. Oh, the People are together even more than the leaves on a tree or the scales on a *dolfeo,* but *working* together? I knew this was my first experience with its pleasant strength. My lungs seemed to breathe deeper. My reach was longer, my grasp stronger. Odd, unfinished feelings welled up inside me and I wanted to *do.* Perhaps this was the itching of my new pin feathers. And then, sometimes when I reached an exultation that almost lifted me off my feet, would come the weakness, the sagging, the sudden desire for tears and withdrawal. I worried, a little, that there might come a time when I wouldn't be able to conceal it.

The Crossing had become a new, engrossing game for the children. At night, shivering in the unseasonable weather, cool, but not cold enough to shield, they would sit looking up at the glory-frosted sky and pick out the star they wanted for a new Home, though they knew that none they could see would actually be it. Eve always chose the brightest pulsating one in the heavens and claimed it as hers. Davie chose one that burned steadily but faintly straight up above them. But when Lytha was asked, she turned the question aside and I knew that any star with Timmy would be Home to Lytha.

Simon usually sat by himself, a little withdrawn from the rest, his eyes quiet on the brightness overhead.

"What star is yours, Simon?" I asked one evening, feeling intrusive but knowing the guard he had for any words he should not speak.

"None," he said, his voice heavy with maturity. "No star for me."

"You mean you'll wait and see?" I asked.

"No," said Simon. "There won't be one for me."

My heart sank. "Simon, you haven't been Called, have you?"

"No," said Simon. "Not yet. I will see a new Home, but I will be Called from its sky."

"Oh, Simon," I cried softly, trying to find a comfort for him. "How wonderful to be able to See a new Home!"

"Not much else left to See," said Simon. "Not that has words." And I saw a flare of Otherside touch his eyes. "But Gramma, you should see the Home when the last moment comes! That's one of the things I have no words for."

"But we will have a new Home, then," I said, going dizzily back to a subject I hoped I could comprehend. "You said—"

"I can't See beyond my Calling," said Simon. "I will see a new Home. I will be Called from its strange sky. I can't See what is for the People there. Maybe they'll all be Called with

58

me. For me there's flame and brightness and pain—then the Presence. That's all I know.

"But, Gramma"—his voice had returned to that of a normal ten-year-old—"Lytha's feeling awful bad. Help her."

The children were laughing and frolicking in the thin blanket of snow that whitened the hills and meadows, their clear, untroubled laughter echoing through the windows to me and 'Chell, who, with close-pressed lips, were opening the winter chests that had been closed so short a time ago. 'Chell fingered the bead stitching on the toes of one little ankle-high boot.

"What will we need in the new Home, Eva-lee?" she asked despairingly.

"We have no way of knowing," I said. "We have no idea of what kind of Home we'll find." *If any, if any, if any,* our unspoken thoughts throbbed together.

"I've been thinking about that," said 'Chell. "What will it be like? Will we be able to live as we do now or will we have to go back to machines and the kind of times that went with our machines? Will we still be one People or be separated mind and soul?" Her hands clenched on a bright sweater and a tear slid down her cheek. "Oh, Eva-lee, maybe we won't even be able to feel the Presence there!"

"You know better than that!" I chided. "The Presence is with us always, even if we have to go to the ends of the Universe. Since we can't know now what the new Home will be like, let's not waste our tears on it." I shook out a gaily patterned quilted skirt. "Who knows," I laughed, "maybe it will be a water world and we'll become fish. Or a fire world and we the flames!"

"We can't adjust quite that much!" protested 'Chell, smiling moistly as she dried her face on the sweater. "But it is a comfort to know we can change some to match our environment."

I reached for another skirt and paused, hand outstretched.

" 'Chell," I said, taken by a sudden idea, "what if the new Home is already inhabited? What if life is already there!"

"Why then, so much the better," said 'Chell. "Friends, help, places to live—"

"They might not accept us," I said.

"But refugees—homeless!" protested 'Chell. "If any in need came to the Home—"

"Even if they were different?"

"In the Presence, all are the same," said 'Chell.

59

"But remember," my knuckles whitened on the skirt. "Only remember far enough back and you will find the Days of Difference before the Peace."

And 'Chell remembered. She turned her stricken face to me. "You mean there might be no welcome for us if we do find a new Home?"

"If we could treat our own that way, how might others treat strangers?" I asked, shaking out the scarlet skirt. "But, please the Power, it will not be so. We can only pray."

It turned out that we had little need to worry about what kind of clothing or anything else to take with us. We would have to go practically possessionless—there was room for only the irreducible minimum of personal effects. There was considerable of an uproar and many loud lamentations when Eve found out that she could not take all of her play-People with her, and, when confronted by the necessity of making a choice—one, single one of her play-People, she threw them all in a tumbled heap in the corner of her room, shrieking that she would take none at all. A sharp smack of David's hand on her bare thighs for her tantrum, and a couple of enveloping hugs for her comfort, and she sniffed up her tears and straightened out her play-People into a staggering, tumbling row across the floor. It took her three days to make her final selection. She chose the one she had named the Listener.

"She's not a him and he's not a her," she had explained. "This play-People is to listen."

"To what?" teased Davie.

"To anything I have to tell and can't tell anyone," said Eve with great dignity. "You don't even have to verb'lize to Listener. All you have to do is to touch and Listener knows what you feel and it tells you why it doesn't feel good and the bad goes away."

"Well, ask the Listener how to make the bad grammar go away," laughed Davie. "You've got your sentences all mixed up."

"Listener knows what I mean and so do you!" retorted Eve.

So when Eve made her choice and stood hugging Listener and looking with big solemn eyes at the rest of her play-People, Davie suggested casually, "Why don't you go bury the rest of them? They're the same as Called now and we don't leave cast-asides around."

And from then until the last day, Eve was happy burying and digging up her play-People, always finding better, more

60

advantageous, or prettier places to make her miniature casting-place.

Lytha sought me out one evening as I leaned over the stone wall around the feather-pen, listening to the go-to-bed contented cluckings and cooings. She leaned with me on the rough gray stones and, snapping an iridescent feather to her hand, smoothed her fingers back and forth along it wordlessly. We both listened idly to Eve and Davie. We could hear them talking together somewhere in the depths of the *koomatka* bushes beyond the feather-pen.

"What's going to happen to the Home after we're gone?" asked Eve idly.

"Oh, it's going to shake and crack wide open and fire and lava will come out and everything will fall apart and burn up," said Davie, no more emotionally than Eve.

"Ooo!" said Eve, caught in the imagination. "Then what will happen to my play-People? Won't they be all right under here? No one can see them."

"Oh, they'll be set on fire and go up in a blaze of glory," said Davie.

"A blaze of glory!" Eve drew a long happy sigh. "In a blaze of glory! Inna blaza glory! Oh, Davie! I'd like to see it. Can I, Davie? Can I?"

"Silly *toola!*" said Davie. "If you were here to see it, *you'd* go up in a blaze of· glory, too!" And he lifted up from the *koomatka* bushes, the time for his chores with the animals hot on his heels.

"Inna blaza glory! Inna blaza glory!" sang Eve happily. "All the play-People inna blaza glory!" Her voice faded to a tuneless hum as she left, too.

"Gramma," said Lytha, "is it really true?"

"Is what really true?" I asked.

"That the Home won't be any more and that we will be gone."

"Why yes, Lytha, why do you doubt it?"

"Because—because—" She gestured with the feather at the wall. "Look, it's all so solid—the stones set each to the other so solidly—so—so *always-looking*. How can it all come apart?"

"You know from your first consciousness that nothing This-side is forever," I said. "Nothing at all except Love. And even that gets so tangled up in the things of This-side that when your love is Called—" The memory of Thann was a heavy burning inside me—"Oh, Lytha! To look into the face of your love and know that Something has come apart and that never again This-side will you find him whole!"

And then I knew I had said the wrong thing. I saw Lytha's too young eyes looking in dilated horror at the sight of her love—her not-quite-yet love, being pulled apart by this same whatever that was pulling the Home apart. I turned the subject.

"I want to go to the Lake for a good-by," I said. "Would you like to go with me?"

"No, thank you, Gramma." Hers was a docile, little girl voice—oh surely much too young to be troubled about loves as yet! "We teeners are going to watch the new metal-melting across the hills. It's fascinating. I'd like to be able to do things like that."

"You can—you could have—" I said, "—if we had trained our youth as we should have."

"Maybe I'll learn," said Lytha, her eyes intent on the feather. She sighed deeply and dissolved the feather into a faint puff of blue smoke. "Maybe I'll learn." And I knew her mind was not on metal-melting.

She turned away and then back again. "Gramma, The Love—" She stopped. I could feel her groping for words. "The Love is forever, isn't it?"

"Yes," I said.

"Love This-side is part of The Love, isn't it?"

"A candle lighted from the sun," I said.

"But the candle will go out!" she cried. "Oh, Gramma! The candle will go out in the winds of the Crossing!" She turned her face from me and whispered, "Especially if it never quite got lighted."

"There are other candles," I murmured, knowing how like a lie it must sound to her.

"But never the same!" She snatched herself away from my side. "It isn't fair! It isn't fair!" and she streaked away across the frost-scorched meadow.

And as she left, I caught a delightful, laughing picture of two youngsters racing across a little lake, reeling and spinning as the waves under their feet lifted and swirled, wrapping white lace around their slender brown ankles. Everything was blue and silver and laughter and fun. I was caught up in the wonder and pleasure until I suddenly realized that it wasn't my memory at all. Thann and I had another little lake we loved more. I had seen someone else's Happy Place that would dissolve like mine with the Home. Poor Lytha.

The crooked sun was melting the latest snow the day all of us Old Ones met beside the towering shells of the ships. Each Old One was wrapped against the chilly wind. No personal shields today. The need for power was greater for the task ahead than for comfort. Above us, the huge bright curved squares of metal, clasped each to each with the old joinings, composed the shining length of each ship. Almost I could have cried to see the scarred earth beneath them—the trampledness that would never green again, the scars that would never heal. I blinked up the brightness of the nearest ship, up to the milky sky, and blinked away from its strangeness.

"The time is short," said the Oldest. "A week."

"A week." The sigh went through the Group.

"Tonight the ship loads must be decided upon. Tomorrow the inside machines must be finished. The next day, the fuel." The Oldest shivered and wrapped himself in his scarlet mantle. "The fuel that we put so completely out of our minds after the Peace. Its potential for evil was more than its service to us. But it is there. It is still there." He shivered again and turned to me.

"Tell us again," he said. "We must complete the shells." And I told them again, without words, only with the shaping of thought to thought. Then the company of Old Ones lifted slowly above the first ship, clasping hands in a circle like a group of dancing children and, leaning forward into the circle, thought the thought I had shaped for them.

For a long time there was only the thin fluting of the cold wind past the point of the ship and then the whole shell of metal quivered and dulled and became fluid. For the span of three heartbeats it remained so and then it hardened again, complete, smooth, seamless, one cohesive whole from tip to base, broken only by the round ports at intervals along its length.

In succession the other five ships were made whole, but the intervals between the ships grew longer and grayer as the strength drained from us, and, before we were finished, the sun had gone behind a cloud and we were all shadows leaning above shadows, fluttering like shadows.

The weakness caught me as we finished the last one. David received me as I drifted down, helpless, and folded on myself. He laid me on the brittle grass and sat panting beside me, his head drooping. I lay as though I had become fluid and knew that something more than the fatigue of the task we had just finished had drained me. "But I *have* to be strong!" I said desperately, knowing weakness had no destiny

63

among the stars. I stared up at the gray sky while a tear drew a cold finger from the corner of my eye to my ear.

"We're just not used to using the Power," said David softly.

"I know, I know," I said, knowing that he did not know. I closed my eyes and felt the whisper of falling snow upon my face, each palm-sized flake melting into a tear.

Lytha stared from me to David, her eyes wide and incredulous. "But you *knew,* Father! I told you! I told you Gathering Night!"

"I'm sorry, Lytha," said David. "There was no other way to do it. Ships fell by lot and Timmy's family and ours will be in different ships."

"Then let me go to his ship or let him come to mine!" she cried, her cheeks flushing and paling.

"Families must remain together," I said, my heart breaking for her. "Each ship leaves the Home with the assumption that it is alone. If you went in the other ship, we might never all be together again."

"But Timmy and I—we might someday be a family! We might—" Lytha's voice broke. She pressed the backs of her hands against her cheeks and paused. Then she went on quietly. "I would go with Timmy, even so."

'Chell and David exchanged distressed glances. "There's not room for even one of you to change your place. The loads are computed, the arrangements finished," I said, feeling as though I were slapping Lytha.

"And besides," said 'Chell, taking Lytha's hands, "it isn't as though you and Timmy were loves. You have only started two-ing. Oh, Lytha, it was such a short time ago that you had your Happy Day. Don't rush so into growing up!"

"And if I told you Timmy is my love!" cried Lytha.

"Can you tell us so in truth, Lytha?" said 'Chell, "and say that Timmy feels that you are his love?"

Lytha's eyes dropped. "Not for sure," she whispered. "But in time—" She threw back her head impetuously, light swirling across her dark hair. "It isn't fair! We haven't had time!" she cried. "Why did all this have to happen now? Why not later? Or sooner?" she faltered, "before we started two-ing! If we have to part now, we might never know—or live our lives without a love because he is really—I am—" She turned and ran from the room, her face hidden.

I sighed and eased myself up from the chair. "I'm old,

David," I said. "I ache with age. Things like this weary me beyond any resting."

It was something after midnight the next night that I felt Neil call to me. The urgency of his call hurried me into my robe and out of the door, quietly, not to rouse the house.

"Eva-lee." His greeting hands on my shoulders were cold through my robe and the unfamiliar chilly wind whipped my hems around my bare ankles. "Is Lytha home?"

"Lytha?" The unexpectedness of the question snatched the last web of sleepiness out of my mind. "Of course. Why?"

"I don't think she is," said Neil. "Timmy's gone with all our camping gear and I think she's gone with him."

My mind flashed back into the house, Questing. Before my hurried feet could get there, I knew Lytha was gone. But I had to touch the undented pillow and lift the smooth spread before I could convince myself. Back in the garden that flickered black and gold as swollen clouds raced across the distorted full moon, Neil and I exchanged concerned looks.

"Where could they have gone?" he asked. "Poor kids. I've already Quested the whole neighborhood and I sent Rosh up to the hillplace to get something—he thought. He brought it back but said nothing about the kids."

I could see the tightening of the muscles in his jaws as he tilted his chin in the old familiar way, peering at me in the moonlight.

"Did Timmy say anything to you about—about anything?" I stumbled.

"Nothing—the only thing that could remotely—well, you know both of them were upset about being in different ships and Timmy—well, he got all worked up and said he didn't believe anything was going to happen to the Home, that it was only a late spring and he thought we were silly to go rushing off into Space—"

"Lytha's words Timmyized," I said. "We've got to find them."

"Carla's frantic." Neil shuffled his feet and put his hands into his pockets, hunching his shoulders as the wind freshened. "If only we had *some* idea. If we don't find them tonight we'll have to alert the Group tomorrow. Timmy'd never live down the humiliation—"

"I know—'Touch a teener—touch a tender spot.'" I quoted absently, my mind chewing on something long forgotten or hardly noticed. "Clearance," I murmured. And Neil closed his mouth on whatever he was going to say as I waited patiently for the vague drifting and isolated flashes in my mind to reproduce the thought I sought.

—Like white lace around their bare brown ankles—

"I have it," I said. "At least I have an idea. Go tell Carla I've gone for them. Tell her not to worry."

"Blessings," said Neil, his hands quick and heavy on my shoulders. "You and Thann have always been our cloak against the wind, our hand up the hill—" And he was gone toward Tangle-meadows and Carla.

You and Thann—you and Thann. I was lifting through the darkness, my personal shield activated against the acceleration of my going. Even Neil forgets sometimes that Thann is gone on ahead, I thought, my heart lifting to the memory of Thann's aliveness. And suddenly the night was full of Thann—of Thann and me—laughing in the skies, climbing the hills, dreaming in the moonlight. Four-ing with Carla and Neil. Two-ing after Gathering Day. The bittersweet memories came so fast that I almost crashed into the piny sighings of a hillside. I lifted above it barely in time. One treetop drew its uppermost twig across the curling of the bare sole of my foot.

Maybe Timmy's right! I thought suddenly. Maybe Simon and the Oldest are all wrong. How can I possibly leave the Home with Thann still here—waiting. Then I shook myself, quite literally, somersaulting briskly in mid-air. Foolish thoughts, trying to cram Thann back into the limitations of an existence he had outgrown!

I slanted down into the cup of the hills toward the tiny lake I had recognized from Lytha's thought. This troubled night it had no glitter or gleam. Its waves were much too turbulent for walking or dancing or even for daring. I landed on a pale strip of sand at its edge and shivered as a wave dissolved the sand under my feet into a shaken quiver and then withdrew to let it solidify again.

"Lytha!" I called softly, Questing ahead of my words. "Lytha!" There was no response in the wind-filled darkness. I lifted to the next pale crescent of sand, feeling like a driven cloud myself. "Lytha! Lytha!" Calling on the family band so it would be perceptible to her alone and Timmy wouldn't have to know until she told him. "Lytha!"

"Gramma!" Astonishment had squeezed out the answer. "Gramma!" The indignation was twice as heavy to make up for the first involuntary response.

"May I come to you?" I asked, taking refuge from my own emotion in ritual questions that would leave Lytha at least the shreds of her pride. There was no immediate reply. "May I come to you?" I repeated.

"You may come." Her thoughts were remote and cold as she guided me in to the curve of hillside and beach.

She and Timmy were snug and secure and very unhappily restless in the small camp cubicle. They had even found some Glowers somewhere. Most of them had died of the lack of summer, but this small cluster clung with their fragile-looking legs to the roof of the cubicle and shed a warm golden light over the small area. My heart contracted with pity and my eyes stung a little as I saw how like a child's playhouse they had set up the cubicle, complete with the two sleeping mats carefully the cubicle's small width apart with a curtain hiding them from each other.

They had risen ceremoniously as I entered, their faces carefully respectful to an Old One—no Gramma-look in the face of either. I folded up on the floor and they sat again, their hands clasping each other for comfort.

"There is scarcely time left for an outing," I said casually, holding up one finger to the Glowers. One loosed itself and glided down to clasp its wiry feet around my finger. Its glowing paled and flared and hid any of our betraying expressions. Under my idle talk I could feel the cry of the two youngsters—wanting some way in honor to get out of this impasse. Could I find the way or would they stubbornly have to—

"We have our lives before us." Timmy's voice was carefully expressionless.

"A brief span if it's to be on the Home," I said. "We must be out before the week ends."

"We do not choose to believe that." Lytha's voice trembled a little.

"I respect your belief," I said formally, "but fear you have insufficient evidence to support it."

"Even so," her voice was just short of a sob. "Even so, however short, we will have it together—"

"Yes, without your mothers or fathers or any of us," I said placidly. "And then finally, soon, without the Home. Still it has its points. It isn't given to everyone to be—in—at the death of a world. It's a shame that you'll have no one to tell it to. That's the best part of anything, you know, telling it—sharing it."

Lytha's face crumpled and she turned it away from me.

"And if the Home doesn't die," I went on, "that will truly be a joke on us. We won't even get to laugh about it because

67

we won't be able to come back, being so many days gone, not knowing. So you will have the whole Home to yourself. Just think! A whole Home! A new world to begin all over again—alone—" I saw the two kids' hands convulse together and Timmy's throat worked painfully. So did mine. I knew the aching of having to start a new world over—alone. After Thann was Called. "But such space! An emptiness from horizon to horizon—from pole to pole—for you two! Nobody else anywhere—anywhere. *If* the Home doesn't die—"

Lytha's slender shoulders were shaking now, and they both turned their so-young faces to me. I nearly staggered under the avalanche of their crying out—all without a word. They poured out all their longing and uncertainty and protest and rebellion. Only the young could build up such a burden and have the strength to bear it. Finally Timmy came to words.

"We only want a chance. Is that too much to ask? Why should this happen, now, to us?"

"Who are we," I asked sternly, "to presume to ask *why* of the Power? For all our lives we have been taking happiness and comfort and delight and never asking *why,* but now that sorrow and separation, pain and discomfort are coming to us from the same Power, we are crying *why.* We have taken unthinkingly all that has been given to us unasked, but now that we must take sorrow for a while, you want to refuse to take, like silly babies whose milk is cold!"

I caught a wave of desolation and lostness from the two and hurried on. "But don't think the Power has forgotten you. You are as completely enwrapped now as you ever were. Can't you trust your love—or your possible love to the Power that suggested love to you in the first place? I promise you, I *promise* you, that no matter where you go, together or apart if the Power leaves you life, you will find love. And even if it turns out that you do not find it together, you'll never forget these first magical steps you have taken together towards your own true loves."

I let laughter into my voice. "Things change! Remember, Lytha, it wasn't so long ago that Timmy was a—if you'll pardon the expression—'gangle-legged, clumsy *poodah* that I'd rather be caught dead than ganging with, let alone twoing.'"

"And he was, too!" Lytha's voice had a hiccough in it, but a half smile, too.

"You were no vision of delight, yourself," said Timmy. "I never saw such stringy hair—"

"I was *supposed* to look like that—"

Their wrangling was a breath of fresh air after the unnatural, uncomfortable emotional binge they had been on.

"It's quite possible that you two might change—" I stopped abruptly. "Wait!" I said. "Listen!"

"To what?" Lytha's face was puzzled. How could I tell her I heard Simon crying. "Gramma! Gramma!" Simon at home, in bed miles and miles—

"Out, quick!" I scrambled up from the floor. "Oh, hurry!" Panic was welling up inside me. The two snatched up their small personal bundles as I pushed them, bewildered and protesting ahead of me out into the inky blackness of the violent night. For a long terrified moment I stood peering up into the darkness, trying to interpret! Then I screamed, "Lift! Lift!" and, snatching at them both, I launched us upward, away from the edge of the lake. The clouds snatched back from the moon and its light poured down onto the convulsed lake. There was a crack like the loudest of thunder—a grinding, twisting sound—the roar and surge of mighty waters, and the lake bed below us broke cleanly from one hill to another, pulling itself apart and tilting to pour all its moon-bright waters down into the darkness of the gigantic split in the earth. And the moon was glittering only on the shining mud left behind in the lake bottom. With a frantic speed that seemed so slow I enveloped the children and shot with them as far up and away as I could before the ear-splitting roar of returning steam threw us even farther. We reeled drunkenly away, and away, until we stumbled across the top of a hill. We clung to each other in terror as the mighty plume of steam rose and rose and split the clouds and still rose, rolling white and awesome. Then, as casually as a shutting door, the lake bed tilted back and closed itself. In the silence that followed, I fancied I could hear the hot rain beginning to fall to fill the emptiness of the lake again—a pool of rain no larger than my hand in a lake bottom.

"Oh, poor Home," whispered Lytha, "poor hurting Home! It's dying!" And then, on the family band, Lytha whispered to me *Timmy's my love, for sure, Gramma, and I am his, but we're willing to let the Power hold our love for us, until your promise is kept.*

I gathered the two to me and I guess we all wept a little, but we had no words to exchange, no platitudes, only the promise, the acquiescence, the trust—and the sorrow.

We went home. Neil met us just beyond our feather-pen

and received Timmy with a quiet thankfulness and they went home together. Lytha and I went first into our household's Quiet Place and then to our patient beds.

I stood with the other Old Ones high on the cliff above the narrow valley, staring down with them at the raw heap of stones and earth that scarred the smooth valley floor. All eyes were intent on the excavation and every mind so much with the Oldest as he toiled out of sight, that our concentrations were almost visible flames above each head.

I heard myself gasp with the others as the Oldest slowly emerged, his clumsy heavy shielding hampering his lifting. The brisk mountain breeze whined as it whipped past suddenly activated personal shields as we reacted automatically to possible danger even though our shields were tissue paper to tornadoes against this unseen death should it be loosed. The Oldest stepped back from the hole until the sheer rock face stopped him. Slowly a stirring began in the shadowy depths and then the heavy square that shielded the thumb-sized block within lifted into the light. It trembled and turned and set itself into the heavy metal box prepared for it. The lid clicked shut. By the time six boxes were filled, I felt the old—or rather, the painfully new—weariness seize me and I clung to David's arm. He patted my hand, but his eyes were wide with dreaming and I forced myself upright. "I don't like me any more," I thought. "Why do I do things like this? Where has *my* enthusiasm and wonder gone? I am truly old and yet—" I wiped the cold beads of sweat from my upper lip and, lifting with the others, hovered over the canyon, preparatory to conveying the six boxes to the six shells of ships that they were to sting into life.

It was the last day. The sun was shining with a brilliance it hadn't known in weeks. The winds that wandered down from the hills were warm and sweet. The earth beneath us that had so recently learned to tremble and shift was quietly solid for a small while. Everything about the Home was suddenly so dear that it seemed a delirious dream that death was less than a week away for it. Maybe it was only some pre-adolescent, unpatterned behavior— But one look at Simon convinced me. His eyes were aching with things he had had to See. His face was hard under the soft contours of childhood and his hands trembled as he clasped them. I hugged him with my heart and he smiled a thank you and relaxed a little.

'Chell and I set the house to rights and filled the vases with fresh water and scarlet leaves because there were no flowers. David opened the corral gate and watched the beasts walk slowly out into the tarnished meadows. He threw wide the door of the feather-pen and watched the ruffle of feathers, the inquiring peering, the hesitant walk into freedom. He smiled as the master of the pen strutted vocally before the flock. Then Eve gathered up the four eggs that lay rosy and new in the nests and carried them into the house to put them in the green egg dish.

The family stood quietly together. "Go say good-by," said David. "Each of you say good-by to the Home."

And everyone went, each by himself, to his favorite spot. Even Eve burrowed herself out of sight in the *koomatka* bush where the leaves locked above her head and made a tiny Eve-sized green twilight. I could hear her soft croon, "Inna blaza glory, play-People! Inna blaza glory!"

I sighed to see Lytha's straight-as-an-arrow flight toward Timmy's home. Already Timmy was coming. I turned away with a pang. Supposing even after the lake they— No, I comforted myself. They trust the Power—

How could I go to any one place I wondered, standing by the windows of my room. All of the Home was too dear to leave. When I went I would truly be leaving Thann—all the paths he walked with me, the grass that bent to his step, the trees that shaded him in summer, the very ground that held his cast-aside. I slid to my knees and pressed my cheek against the side of the window frame. "Thann, Thann!" I whispered. "Be with me. Go with me since I must go. Be my strength!" And clasping my hands tight, I pressed my thumbs hard against my crying mouth.

We all gathered again, solemn and tear-stained. Lytha was still frowning and swallowing to hold back her sobs. Simon looked at her, his eyes big and golden, but he said nothing and turned away. 'Chell left the room quietly and, before she returned, the soft sound of music swelled from the walls. We all made the Sign and prayed the Parting prayers, for truly we were dying to this world. The whole house, the whole of the Home was a Quiet Place today and each of us without words laid the anguishing of this day of parting before the Presence and received comfort and strength.

Then each of us took up his share of personal belongings and was ready to go. We left the house, the music reaching after us as we went. I felt a part of me die when we could no longer hear the melody.

We joined the neighboring families on the path to the ships and there were murmurs and gestures and even an occasional excited laugh. No one seemed to want to lift. Our feet savored every step of this last walk on the Home. No one lifted, that is, except Eve, who was still intrigued by her new accomplishment. Her short little hops amused everyone and, by the time she had picked herself out of the dust three times and had been disentangled from the branches of overhanging trees twice and finally firmly set in place on David's shoulder, there were smiles and tender laughter and the road lightened even though clouds were banking again.

I stood at the foot of the long lift to the door of the ship and stared upward. People brushing past me were only whisperings and passing shadows.

"How can they?" I thought despairingly out of the surge of weakness that left me clinging to the wall. "How can they do it? Leaving the Home so casually!" Then a warm hand crept into mine and I looked down into Simon's eyes. "Come on, Gramma," he said. "It'll be all right."

"I—I—" I looked around me helplessly, then, kneeling swiftly, I took up a handful of dirt—a handful of the Home— and, holding it tightly, I lifted up the long slant with Simon.

Inside the ship we put our things away in their allotted spaces and Simon tugged me out into the corridor and into a room banked with dials and switches and all the vast array of incomprehensibles that we had all called into being for this terrible moment. No one was in the room except the two of us. Simon walked briskly to a chair in front of a panel and sat down.

"It's all set," he said, "for the sector of the sky they gave us, but it's wrong." Before I could stop him, his hands moved over the panels, shifting, adjusting, changing.

"Oh, Simon!" I whispered, "you mustn't!"

"I must," said Simon. "Now it's set for the sky I See."

"But they'll notice and change them all back," I trembled.

"No," said Simon. "It's such a small change that they won't notice it. And we will be where we have to be when we have to be."

It was as I stood there in the control room that I left the Home. I felt it fade away and become as faint as a dream. I said good-by to it so completely that it startled me to catch a glimpse of a mountaintop through one of the ports as we hurried back to our spaces. Suddenly my heart was light and lifting, so much so that my feet didn't even touch the floor. Oh, how wonderful! What adventures ahead! I felt as though

I were spiraling up into a bright Glory that outshone the sun—

Then, suddenly, came the weakness. My very bones dissolved in me and collapsed me down on my couch. Darkness rolled across me and breathing was a task that took all my weakness to keep going. I felt vaguely the tightening of the restraining straps around me and the clasp of Simon's hand around my clenched fist.

"Half an hour," the Oldest murmured.

"Half an hour," the People echoed, amplifying the murmur. I felt myself slipping into the corporate band of communication, feeling with the rest of the Group the incredible length and heartbreaking shortness of the time.

Then I lost the world again. I was encased in blackness. I was suspended, waiting, hardly even wondering.

And then it came—the Call.

How unmistakable! I was Called back into the Presence! My hours were totaled. It was all finished. This-side was a preoccupation that concerned me no longer. My face must have lighted as Thann's had. All the struggle, all the sorrow, all the separation—finished. Now would come the three or four days during which I must prepare, dispose of my possessions, say my good-bys— Good-bys? I struggled up against the restraining straps. But we were leaving! In less than half an hour I would have no quiet, cool bed to lay me down upon when I left my body, no fragrant grass to have pulled up over my cast-aside, no solemn sweet remembrance by my family in the next Festival for those Called during the year!

Simon I called subvocally. *You know!* I cried. *What shall I do?*

I See you staying. His answer came placidly.

Staying? Oh how quickly I caught the picture! How quickly my own words came back to me, coldly white against the darkness of my confusion. *Such space and emptiness from horizon to horizon, from pole to pole, from skytop to ground. And only me. Nobody else anywhere, anywhere!*

Stay here all alone? I asked Simon. But he wasn't Seeing me any more. Already I was alone. I felt the frightened tears start and then I heard Lytha's trusting voice—*until your promise is kept.* All my fear dissolved. All my panic and fright blazed up suddenly in a repeat of the Call.

"Listen!" I cried, my voice high and excited, my heart surging joyously, "Listen!"

"Oh, David! Oh, 'Chell! I've been Called! Don't you hear it? Don't you hear it!"

73

"Oh, Mother, no! No! You must be mistaken!" David loosed himself and bent over me.

"No," whispered 'Chell. "I feel it. She is Called."

"Now I can stay," I said, fumbling at the straps. "Help me, David, help me."

"But you're not summoned right now!" cried David. "Father knew four days before he was received into the Presence. We can't leave you alone in a doomed, empty world!"

"An empty world!" I stood up quickly, holding to David to steady myself. "Oh, David! A world full of all dearness and nearness and remembering! And doomed? It will be a week yet. I will be received before then. Let me out! Oh, let me out!"

"Stay with us, Mother!" cried David, taking both my hands in his. "We need you. We can't let you go. All the tumult and upheaval that's to start so soon for the Home——"

"How do we know what tumult and upheaval you will be going through in the Crossing?" I asked. "But beyond whatever comes there's a chance of a new life waiting for you. But for me— What of four days from now? What would you do with my cast-aside? What could you do but push it out into the black nothingness. Let it be with the Home. Let it at least become dust among familiar dust!" I felt as excited as a teener. "Oh, David! To be with Thann again!"

I turned to Lytha and quickly unfastened her belt. "There'll be room for one more in this ship," I said.

For a long moment, we looked into each other's eyes and then, almost swifter than thought, Lytha was up and running for the big door. My thoughts went ahead of her and before Lytha's feet lifted out into the open air, all the Old Ones in the ship knew what had happened and their thoughts went out. Before Lytha was halfway up the little hills that separated ship from ship, Timmy surged into sight and gathered her close as they swung around toward our ship.

Minutes ran out of the half hour like icy beads from a broken string, but finally I was slanting down from the ship, my cheeks wet with my own tears and those of my family. Clearly above the clang of the closing door I heard Simon's call. *Good-by, Gramma! I told you it'd be all right. See— you—soon!*

Hurry hurry hurry whispered my feet as I ran. *Hurry hurry hurry* whispered the wind as I lifted away from the towering ships. *Now now now* whispered my heart as I

74

turned back from a safe distance, my skirts whipped by the rising wind, my hair lashing across my face.

The six slender ships pointing at the sky were like silver needles against the rolling black clouds. Suddenly there were only five—then four—then three. Before I could blink the tears from my eyes, the rest were gone, and the ground where they had stood flowed back on itself and crackled with cooling.

The fingers of the music drew me back into the house. I breathed deeply of the dear familiar odors. I straightened a branch of the scarlet leaves that had slipped awry in the blue vase. I steadied myself against a sudden shifting under my feet and my shield activated as hail spattered briefly through the window. I looked out, filled with a great peace, to the swell of browning hills, to the upward reach of snow-whitened mountains, to the brilliant huddled clumps of trees sowing their leaves on the icy wind. "My Home!" I whispered, folding my heart around it all, knowing what my terror and lostness would have been had I stayed behind without the Call.

With a sigh, I went out to the kitchen and counted the four rosy eggs in the green dish. I fingered the stove into flame and, lifting one of the eggs, cracked it briskly against the pan.

That night there were no stars, but the heavy rolls of clouds were lighted with fitful lightnings and somewhere far over the horizon the molten heart of a mountain range was crimson and orange against the night. I lay on my bed letting the weakness wash over me, a tide that would soon bear me away. The soul is a lonely voyager at any time, but the knowledge that I was the last person in a dying world was like a weight crushing me. I was struggling against the feeling when I caught a clear, distinct call—

"Gramma!"

"Simon!" My lips moved to his name.

"We're all fine, Gramma, and I just Saw Eve with two children of her own, so they *will* make it to a new Home."

"Oh, Simon! I'm so glad you told me!" I clutched my bed as it rocked and twisted. I heard stones falling from the garden wall, then one wall of my room dissolved into dust that glowed redly before it settled.

"Things are a little untidy here," I said. "I must get out another blanket. It's a little drafty, too."

75

"You'll be all right, Gramma," Simon's thought came warmly. "Will you wait for me when you get Otherside?"

"If I can," I promised.

"Good night, Gramma," said Simon.

"Good night, Simon." I cradled my face on my dusty pillow. "Good night."

"Oh!" breathed Meris, out of her absorption. "All alone like that! The last, *last* anyone, anywhere—"

"But she had the Home longer than anyone else," said Valancy. "She had that dear familiarity to close her eyes upon before opening them in the Presence—"

"But how could Bethie possibly remember—" began Meris.

"It's something we can't quite explain," said Jemmy. "It's a Group consciousness that unites us across time and distance. I guess Simon's communicating with Eva-lee before he was Called brought her Assembling more directly to us. Eve, you know, was Bethie's mother."

"It's overwhelming," said Karen soberly. "We know, of course, about the Home and how it was lost, but until you're actually inside an emotion, you can't really comprehend it. Just imagine, to know that the solidness of earth beneath your feet is to become dust scattered across the sky so soon—so soon!"

The group was silent for a while, listening to memories and to a Past that was so Present.

The silence was suddenly shattered by a crashing roar that startled everyone into an awareness of Now.

"Good heavens!" cried Meris. "What's that!"

"*Adonday veeah!*" muttered Jemmy. "They've got that old clunker going again. Johannan must have done something drastic to it."

"Well, he started it just in time to stop it," said Valancy. "We've got a journey to go and we'd better eat and run. Karen, is it all ready?"

"Yes," said Karen, heading for the shadowy house. "Meris has a lovely kitchen. I move that we move in there to eat. It's chilling a little out here now. Jemmy, will you get the boys?"

"I'll set the table!" cried Lala, launching herself airborne toward the kitchen door.

"Lala." Valancy's voice was quiet, but Lala checked in mid-flight and tumbled down to her feet.

"Oh!" she said, her hands over her mouth. "I *did* forget, after I promised!"

"Yes, you did forget," said Valancy, her voice disappointed, "and after you promised."

"I guess I need some more discipline," said Lala solemnly. "A promise is not lightly broken."

"What would you suggest?" asked Karen from the kitchen door, as solemnly as Lala.

"Not set the table?" suggested Lala, with a visible reluctance. "Not tonight," she went on gauging carefully the adult reaction. "Not for a week?" She sighed and capitulated. "Not set the table for a whole month. And every meal remember a promise is not lightly broken. Control is necessary. Never be un-Earth away from the Group unless I'm told to." And she trudged, conscientiously heavy-footed, into the house with Karen.

"Isn't that a little harsh?" asked Meris. "She does so love to set the table."

"She chose the discipline," said Valancy. "She must learn not to act thoughtlessly. Maybe she has a little more to remember in the way of rules and regulations than the usual small child, but it must become an automatic part of her behavior."

"But at six—" protested Meris, then laughed "—or is it five?"

"Five or six, she understands," said Valancy. "An undisciplined child is an abomination under any circumstances. And doubly so when it's possible to show off as spectacularly as Lala could. Debbie had quite a problem concerning control when she returned from the New Home, and she was no child."

"Returned from the New Home?" said Meris, pausing in the door. "Someone else? Oh, Valancy, do you *have* to go home tonight? Couldn't you stay for a while and tell me some more? You want to Assemble anyway, don't you? Couldn't you now? You can't leave me hanging like this!"

"Well," Valancy smiled and followed Meris into the kitchen. "That's an idea. We'll take it up after supper."

Jemmy sipped his after-supper coffee and leaned back in his chair. "I've been thinking," he said. "This business of Assembling. We have already Assembled our history from when Valancy joined our Group up to the time Lala and the ship came. We did it while we were all trying to make up our minds whether to leave Earth or stay. Davy's recording

77

gadget has preserved it for us. I think it would be an excellent idea for us to get Eva-lee's story recorded, too, and whatever other ones are available to us or can be made available."

"Mother Assembled a lot because she was separated from the People when she was so young," said Bethie softly. "Assembling was almost her only comfort, especially before and after Father. She didn't know anything about the rest of her family—" Bethie whitened. "Oh, *must* we remember the bad times! The aching, hurting, cruel times?"

"There was kindness and love and sacrifice for us interwoven with the cruel times, too, you know," said Jemmy. "If we refuse to remember those times, we automatically refuse to remember the goodness that we found along with the evil."

"Yes," admitted Bethie. "Yes, of course."

"Well, if I can't persuade all of you to stay, why can't Bethie stay a while longer and Assemble?" asked Meris. "Then she'll have a lot of material ready for Davy's gadget when she gets home."

And so it was that Meris, Mark, and Bethie stood in the driveway and watched the rest of the party depart prosaically by car for the canyon—if you can call prosaic the shuddering, slam-bang departing of the Overland, now making up clamorously for its long afternoon of silence.

Assembling is not a matter of turning a faucet on and dodging the gushing of memories. For several days Bethie drifted, speechless and perhaps quite literally millions of miles away, through the house, around the patio, up and down the quiet street and back into the patio. She came to the table at mealtimes and sometimes ate. Other times her eyes were too intent on far away and long ago to notice food. At times tears streaked her face and once she woke Mark and Meris with a sharp cry in the night. Meris was worried by her pallor and the shadows on her face as the days passed.

Then finally came the day when Bethie's eyes were suddenly back in focus and, relaxing with a sigh onto the couch, she smiled at Meris.

"Hi!" she said shyly. "I'm back."

"And all in one piece again," said Meris. "And about time, too! 'Licia has a drake-tail in her hair now—all both of them. And she smiled once when it couldn't possibly have been a gas pain!"

So, after supper that night, Mark and Meris sat in the deepening dusk of the patio, each holding lightly one of Bethie's hands.

"This one," said Bethie, her smile fading, "is one I didn't enjoy. Not all of it. But, as Jemmy said, it had good things mixed in."

Hands tightened on hands, then relaxed as the two listened to Bethie Assembling, subvocally.

ANGELS UNAWARES

HEBREWS 13:2

I still have it, the odd, flower-shaped piece of metal, showing the flow marks on top and the pocking of sand and gravel on its bottom. It fits my palm comfortably with my fingers clasped around it, and has fitted it so often that the edges are smooth and burnished now, smooth against the fine white line of the scar where the sharp, shining, still-hot edge gashed me when I snatched it up, unbelievingly, from where it had dripped, molten, from the sloping wall to the sandy floor of the canyon beyond Margin. It is a Remembrance thing and, as I handled it just now, looking unseeingly out across the multiple roofs of Margin Today, it recalled to me vividly Margin Yesterday—and even before Margin.

We had been on the road only an hour when we came upon the scene. For fifteen minutes or so before, however, there had been an odd smell on the wind, one that crinkled my nose and made old Nig snort and toss his head, shaking the harness and disturbing Prince, who lifted his patient head, looked around briefly, then returned to the task.

We were the task, Nils and I and our wagonload of personal belongings, trailing behind us Molly, our young Jersey cow. We were on our way to Margin to establish a home. Nils was to start his shining new mining engineering career, beginning as superintendent of the mine that had given birth to Margin. This was to be a first step only, of course, leading to more accomplished, more rewarding positions culminating in all the vague, bright, but most wonderful of futures that could blossom from this rather unprepossessing present seed. We were as yet three days' journey from

Margin when we rounded the sharp twist of the trail, our iron tires grating in the sand of the wash, and discovered the flat.

Nils pulled the horses up to a stop. A little below us and near the protective bulge of the gray granite hillside were the ruins of a house and the crumpled remains of sheds at one end of a staggering corral. A plume of smoke lifted finger-straight in the early morning air. There was not a sign of life anywhere.

Nils flapped the reins and clucked to the horses. We crossed the flat, lurching a little when the left wheels dipped down into one of the cuts that, after scoring the flat, disappeared into the creek.

"Must have burned down last night," said Nils, securing the reins and jumping down. He lifted his arms to help me from the high seat and held me in a tight, brief hug as he always does. Then he released me and we walked over to the crumple of the corral.

"All the sheds went," he said, "and apparently the animals, too." He twisted his face at the smell that rose from the smoldering mass.

"They surely would have saved the animals," I said, frowning. "They wouldn't have left them locked in a burning shed."

"If they were here when the fire hit," said Nils.

I looked over at the house. "Not much of a house. It doesn't look lived in at all. Maybe this is an abandoned homestead. In that case, though, what about the animals?"

Nils said nothing. He had picked up a length of stick and was prodding in the ashes.

"I'm going to look at the house," I said, glad of an excuse to turn away from the heavy odor of charred flesh.

The house was falling in on itself. The door wouldn't open and the drunken windows spilled a few shards of splintered glass out onto the sagging front porch. I went around to the back. It had been built so close to the rock that there was only a narrow roofed-over passage between the rock and the house. The back door sagged on one hinge and I could see the splintered floor behind. It must have been quite a nice place at one time—glass in the windows—a board floor—when most of us in the Territory made do with a hard trampled dirt floor and butter muslin in the windows.

I edged through the door and cautiously picked my way across the creaking, groaning floor. I looked up to see if there was a loft of any kind and felt my whole body throb one huge throb of terror and surprise! Up against the sharp splintering of daylight through a shattered roof, was a face—looking down at me! It was a wild, smudged, dirty face, surrounded by a frizz of dark hair that tangled and wisped across the filthy cheeks. It stared down at me from up among the tatters of what had been a muslin ceiling, then the mouth opened soundlessly, and the eyes rolled and went shut. I lunged forward, almost instinctively, and caught the falling body full in my arms, crumpling under it to the floor. Beneath me the splintered planks gave way and sagged down into the shallow air space under the floor.

I screamed, "Nils!" and heard an answering, "Gail!" and the pounding of his running feet.

We carried the creature outside the ruined house and laid it on the scanty six-weeks grass that followed over the sand like a small green river the folds in the earth that held moisture the longest. We straightened the crumpled arms and legs and it was a creature no longer but a girl-child. I tried to pull down the tattered skirt to cover more seemly, but the bottom edge gave way without tearing and I had the soft smudge of burned fabric and soot between my fingers. I lifted the head to smooth the sand under it and stopped, my attention caught.

"Look, Nils, the hair. Half of it's burned away. This poor child must have been in the fire. She must have tried to free the animals—"

"It's not animals," said Nils, his voice tight and angered. "They're people."

"People!" I gasped. "Oh, no!"

"At least four," nodded Nils.

"Oh, how awful!" I said, smoothing the stub of hair away from the quiet face. "The fire must have struck in the night."

"They were tied," said Nils shortly. "Hand and foot."

"Tied? But, Nils—"

"Tied. Deliberately burned—"

"Indians!" I gasped, scrambling to my feet through the confusion of my skirts. "Oh, Nils!"

"There have been no Indian raids in the Territory for almost five years. And the last one was on the other side of the Territory. They told me at Margin that there had never been any raids around here. There are no Indians in this area."

"Then who—what—" I dropped down beside the still figure. "Oh, Nils," I whispered. "What kind of a country have we come to?"

81

"No matter what kind it is," said Nils, "we have a problem here. Is the child dead?"

"No." My hand on the thin chest felt the slight rise and fall of breathing. Quickly I flexed arms and legs and probed lightly. "I can't find any big hurt. But so dirty and ragged!"

We found the spring under a granite overhang halfway between the house and the corral. Nils rummaged among our things in the wagon and found me the hand basin, some rags, and soap. We lighted a small fire and heated water in a battered bucket Nils dredged out of the sand below the spring. While the water was heating, I stripped away the ragged clothing. The child had on some sort of a one-piece undergarment that fitted as closely as her skin and as flexible. It covered her from shoulder to upper thigh and the rounding of her body under it made me revise my estimate of her age upward a little. The garment was undamaged by the fire but I couldn't find any way to unfasten it to remove it so I finally left it and wrapped the still unconscious girl in a quilt. Then carefully I bathed her, except for her hair, wiping the undergarment, which came clean and bright without any effort at all. I put her into one of my nightgowns, which came close enough to fitting her since I am of no great size myself.

"What shall I do about her hair?" I asked Nils, looking at the snarled, singed tousle of it. "Half of it is burned off clear up to her ear."

"Cut the rest of it to match," said Nils. "Is she burned anywhere?"

"No," I replied, puzzled. "Not a sign of a burn, and yet her clothing was almost burned away and her hair—" I felt a shiver across my shoulders and looked around the flat apprehensively, though nothing could be more flatly commonplace than the scene. Except—except for the occasional sullen wisp of smoke from the shed ruins.

"Here are the scissors." Nils brought them from the wagon. Reluctantly, because of the heavy flow of the tresses across my wrist, I cut away the long dark hair until both sides of her head matched, more or less. Then, scooping out the sand to lower the basin beneath her head, I wet and lathered and rinsed until the water came clear, then carefully dried the hair, which, released from length and dirt, sprang into profuse curls all over her head.

"What a shame to have cut it," I said to Nils, holding the damp head in the curve of my elbow. "How lovely it must have been." Then I nearly dropped my burden. The eyes were

82

open and looking at me blankly. I managed a smile and said, "Hello! Nils, hand me a cup of water."

At first she looked at the water as though at a cup of poison, then, with a shuddering little sigh, drank it down in large hasty gulps.

"That's better now, isn't it?" I said, hugging her a little. There was no answering word or smile, but only a slow tightening of the muscles under my hands until, still in my arms, the girl had withdrawn from me completely. I ran my hand over her curls. "I'm sorry we had to cut it, but it was—" I bit back my words. I felt muscles lifting, so I helped the girl sit up. She looked around in a daze and then her eyes were caught by a sullen up-puff of smoke. Seeing what she was seeing, I swung my shoulder between her and the ashes of the shed. Her mouth opened, but no sound came out. Her fingers bit into my arm as she dragged herself to see past me.

"Let her look," Nils said. "She knows what happened. Let her see the end of it. Otherwise she'll wonder all her life." He took her from me and carried her over to the corral. I couldn't go. I busied myself with emptying the basin and burying the charred clothing. I spread the quilt out to receive the child when they returned.

Nils finally brought her back and put her down on the quilt. She lay, eyes shut, as still as if breath had left her, too. Then two tears worked themselves out of her closed lids, coursed down the sides of her cheeks, and lost themselves in the tumble of curls around her ears. Nils took the shovel and grimly tackled the task of burying the bodies.

I built up the fire again and began to fix dinner. The day was spending itself rapidly but, late or not, when Nils finished, we would leave. Eating a large meal now, we could piece for supper and travel, if necessary, into the hours of darkness until this place was left far behind.

Nils finally came back, pausing at the spring to snort and blow through double handful after double handful of water. I met him with a towel.

"Dinner's ready," I said. "We can leave as soon as we're finished."

"Look what I found." He handed me a smudged tatter of paper. "It was nailed to the door of the shed. The door didn't burn."

I held the paper gingerly and puzzled over it. The writing was almost illegible—Ex. 22:18.

"What is it?" I asked. "It doesn't say anything."

"Quotation," said Nils. "That's a quotation from the Bible."

"Oh," I said. "Yes. Let's see. Exodus, Chapter 22, verse 18. Do you know it?"

"I'm not sure, but I have an idea. Can you get at the Bible? I'll verify it."

"It's packed in one of my boxes at the bottom of the load. Shall we—"

"Not now," said Nils. "Tonight when we make camp."

"What do you think it is?" I asked.

"I'd rather wait," said Nils. "I hope I'm wrong."

We ate. I tried to rouse the girl, but she turned away from me. I put half a slice of bread in her hand and closed her fingers over it and tucked it close to her mouth. Halfway through our silent meal, a movement caught my eye. The girl had turned to hunch herself over her two hands that now clasped the bread, tremblingly. She was chewing cautiously. She swallowed with an effort and stuffed her mouth again with bread, tears streaking down her face. She ate as one starved, and, when she had finished the bread, I brought her a cup of milk. I lifted her shoulders and held her as she drank. I took the empty cup and lowered her head to the quilt. For a moment my hand was caught under her head and I felt a brief deliberate pressure of her cheek against my wrist. Then she turned away.

Before we left the flat, we prayed over the single mound Nils had raised over the multiple grave. We had brought the girl over with us and she lay quietly, watching us. When we turned from our prayers, she held out in a shaking hand a white flower, so white that it almost seemed to cast a light across her face. I took it from her and put it gently on the mound. Then Nils lifted her and carried her to the wagon. I stayed a moment, not wanting to leave the grave lonely so soon. I shifted the white flower. In the sunlight its petals seemed to glow with an inner light, the golden center almost fluid. I wondered what kind of flower it could be. I lifted it and saw that it was just a daisy-looking flower after all, withering already in the heat of the day. I put it down again, gave a last pat to the mound, a last tag of prayer, and went back to the wagon.

By the time we made camp that night we were too exhausted from the forced miles and the heat and the events of the day to do anything but care for the animals and fall onto our pallets spread on the ground near the wagon. We had not made the next water hole because of the delay, but

84

we carried enough water to tide us over. I was too tired to eat, but I roused enough to feed Nils on leftovers from dinner and to strain Molly's milk into the milk crock. I gave the girl a cup of the fresh, warm milk and some more bread. She downed them both with a contained eagerness as though still starved. Looking at her slender shaking wrists and the dark hollows of her face, I wondered how long she had been so hungry.

We all slept heavily under the star-clustered sky, but I was awakened somewhere in the shivery coolness of the night and reached to be sure the girl was covered. She was sitting up on the pallet, legs crossed tailor-fashion, looking up at the sky. I could see the turning of her head as she scanned the whole sky, back and forth, around and around, from zenith to horizon. Then she straightened slowly back down onto the quilt with an audible sigh.

I looked at the sky, too. It was spectacular with the stars of a moonless night here in the region of mountains and plains, but what had she been looking for? Perhaps she had just been enjoying being alive and able, still, to see the stars.

We started on again, very early, and made the next watering place while the shadows were still long with dawn.

"The wagons were here," said Nils, "night before last, I guess."

"What wagons?" I asked, pausing in my dipping of water.

"We've been in their tracks ever since the flat back there," said Nils. "Two light wagons and several riders."

"Probably old tracks—" I started. "Oh, but you said they were here night before last. Do you suppose they had anything to do with the fire back there?"

"No signs of them before we got to the flat," said Nils. "Two recent campfires here—as if they stayed the night here and made a special trip to the flat and back here again for the next night."

"A special trip." I shivered. "Surely you can't think that civilized people in this nineteenth century could be so violent—so—so—I mean people just don't—" My words died before the awful image in my mind.

"Don't tie up other people and burn them?" Nils started shifting the water keg back toward the wagon. "Gail, our next camp is supposed to be at Grafton's Vow. I think we'd better take time to dig out the Bible before we go on."

So we did. And we looked at each other over Nils's pointing finger and the flattened paper he had taken from the shed door.

85

"Oh, surely not!" I cried horrified. "It can't be! Not in this day and age!"

"It can be," said Nils. "In any age when people pervert goodness, love, and obedience and set up a god small enough to fit their shrunken souls." And his finger traced again the brief lines: *Thou shalt not suffer a witch to live.*

"Why did you want to check that quotation before we got to Grafton's Vow?" I asked.

"Because it's that kind of place," said Nils. "They warned me at the county seat. In fact, some thought it might be wise to take the other trail—a day longer—one dry camp—but avoid Grafton's Vow. There have been tales of stonings and—"

"What kind of place is it, anyway?" I asked.

"I'm not sure," said Nils. "I've heard some very odd stories about it though. It was founded about twenty years ago by Arnold Grafton. He brought his little flock of followers out here to establish the new Jerusalem. They're very strict and narrow. Don't argue with them and no levity or lewdness. No breaking of God's laws of which they say they have all. When they ran out of Biblical ones, they received a lot more from Grafton to fill in where God forgot."

"But," I was troubled, "aren't they Christians?"

"They say so." I helped Nils lift the keg. "Except they believe they have to conform to all the Old Testament laws, supplemented by all those that Grafton has dictated. Then, if they obey enough of them well enough after a lifetime of struggle, Christ welcomes them into a heaven of no laws. Every law they succeed in keeping on earth, they will be exempted from keeping for all of eternity. So the stricter observance here, the greater freedom there. Imagine what their heaven must be—teetotaler here—rigidly chaste here—never kill here—never steal here—just save up for the promised Grand Release!"

"And Mr. Grafton had enough followers of *that* doctrine to found a town?" I asked, a little stunned.

"A whole town," said Nils, "into which we will not be admitted. There is a campground outside the place where we will be tolerated for the night if they decide we won't contaminate the area."

At noon we stopped just after topping out at Millman's Pass. The horses, lathered and breathing heavily, and poor dragged-along Molly, drooped grateful heads in the shadows of the aspen and pines.

I busied myself with the chuck box and was startled to see

the girl sliding out of the wagon where we had bedded her down for the trip. She clung to the side of the wagon and winced as her feet landed on the gravelly hillside. She looked very young and slender and lost in the fullness of my nightgown, but her eyes weren't quite so sunken and her mouth was tinged with color.

I smiled at her. "That gown is sort of long for mountain climbing. Tonight I'll try to get to my other clothes and see if I can find something. I think my old blue skirt—" I stopped because she very obviously wasn't understanding a word I was saying. I took a fold of the gown she wore and said, "Gown."

She looked down at the crumpled white muslin and then at me but said nothing.

I put a piece of bread into her hands and said, "Bread." She put the bread down carefully on the plate where I had stacked the other slices for dinner and said nothing. Then she glanced around, looked at me and, turning, walked briskly into the thick underbrush, her elbows high to hold the extra length of gown up above her bare feet.

"Nils!" I called in sudden panic. "She's leaving!"

Nils laughed at me across the tarp he was spreading. "Even the best of us," he said, "have to duck into the bushes once in a while!"

"Oh, Nils!" I protested and felt my face redden as I carried the bread plate to the tarp. "Anyway, she shouldn't be running around in a nightgown like that. What would Mr. Grafton say! And have you noticed? She hasn't made a sound since we found her." I brought the eating things to the tarp. "Not one word. Not one sound."

"Hmm," said Nils, "you're right. Maybe she's a deaf-mute."

"She hears," I said, "I'm sure she hears."

"Maybe she doesn't speak English," he suggested. "Her hair is dark. Maybe she's Mexican. Or even Italian. We get all kinds out here on the frontier. No telling where she might be from."

"But you'd think she'd make some sound. Or try to say something," I insisted.

"Might be the shock," said Nils soberly. "That was an awful thing to live through."

"That's probably it, poor child." I looked over to where she had disappeared. "An awful thing. Let's call her Marnie, Nils," I suggested. "We need some sort of name to call her by."

87

Nils laughed. "Would having the name close to you reconcile you a little to being separated from your little sister?"

I smiled back. "It does sound homey—Marnie, Marnie."

As if I had called her, the girl, Marnie, came back from the bushes, the long gown not quite trailing the slope, completely covering her bare feet. Both her hands were occupied with the long stem of red bells she was examining closely. *How graceful she is,* I thought, *How smoothly*— Then my breath went out and I clutched the plate I held. That gown was a good foot too long for Marnie! She couldn't possibly be walking with it not quite trailing the ground without holding it up! And where was the pausing that came between steps? I hissed at Nils. "Look!" I whispered hoarsely, "she's— she's floating! She's not even touching the ground!"

Just at that moment Marnie looked up and saw us and read our faces. Her face crumpled into terror and she dropped down to the ground. Not only down to her feet, but on down into a huddle on the ground with the spray of flowers crushed under her.

I ran to her and tried to lift her, but she suddenly convulsed into a mad struggle to escape me. Nils came to help. We fought to hold the child who was so violent that I was afraid she'd hurt herself.

"She's—she's afraid!" I gasped. "Maybe she thinks—we'll— kill her!"

"Here!" Nils finally caught a last flailing arm and pinioned it. "*Talk* to her! Do something! I can't hold her much longer!"

"Marnie, Marnie!" I smoothed the tangled curls back from her blank, tense face, trying to catch her attention. "Marnie, don't be afraid!" I tried a smile. "Relax, honey, don't be scared." I wiped her sweat- and tear-streaked face with the corner of my apron. "There, there, it doesn't matter— we won't hurt you—" I murmured on and on, wondering if she was taking in any of it, but finally the tightness began to go out of her body and at last she drooped, exhausted, in Nils's arms. I gathered her to me and comforted her against my shoulder.

"Get her a cup of milk," I said to Nils, "and bring me one, too." My smile wavered. "This is hard work!"

In the struggle I had almost forgotten what had started it, but it came back to me as I led Marnie to the spring and demonstrated that she should wash her face and hands. She did so, following my example, and dried herself on the flour-sack towel I handed her. Then, when I started to turn away, she sat down on a rock by the flowing water, lifted the sadly bedraggled gown, and slipped her feet into the stream. When she lifted each to dry it, I saw the reddened, bruised soles and said, "No wonder you didn't want to walk. Wait a minute." I went back to the wagon and got my old slippers, and, as an afterthought, several pins. Marnie was still sitting by the stream, leaning over the water, letting it flow between her fingers. She put on the slippers—woefully large for her, and stood watching with interest as I turned up the bottom of the gown and pinned it at intervals.

"Now," I said, "now at least you can walk. But this gown will be ruined if we don't get you into some other clothes."

We ate dinner and Marnie ate some of everything we did, after a cautious tasting and a waiting to see how we handled it. She helped me gather up and put away the leftovers and clear the tarp. She even helped with the dishes—all with an absorbed interest as if learning a whole new set of skills.

As our wagon rolled on down the road, Nils and I talked quietly, not to disturb Marnie as she slept in the back of the wagon.

"She's an odd child," I said. "Nils, do you think she really was floating? How could she have? It's impossible."

"Well, it looked as if she was floating," he said. "And she acted as if she had done something wrong—something—" Nils's words stopped and he frowned intently as he flicked at a roadside branch with the whip "—something we would hurt her for. Gail, maybe that's why—I mean, we found that witch quotation. Maybe those other people were like Marnie. Maybe someone thought they were witches and burned them —"

"But witches are evil!" I cried. "What's evil about floating—"

"Anything is evil," said Nils. "It lies on the other side of the line you draw around what you will accept as good. Some people's lines are awfully narrow."

"But that's murder!" I said, "to kill—"

"Murder or execution—again, a matter of interpretation," said Nils. "*We* call it murder, but it could never be proved—"

"Marnie," I suggested. "She saw—"

"Can't talk—or won't," said Nils.

I hated the shallow valley of Grafton's Vow at first glance. For me it was shadowed from one side to the other in spite of the down-flooding sun that made us so grateful for the shade of the overhanging branches. The road was running between rail fences now as we approached the town. Even the horses seemed jumpy and uneasy as we rattled along.

"Look," I said, "there's a notice or something on that fence post."

Niles pulled up alongside the post and I leaned over to read: " 'Ex. 20:16.' That's all it says!"

"Another reference," said Nils. " 'Thou shalt not bear false witness.' This must be a habit with them, putting up memorials on the spot where a law is broken."

"I wonder what happened here." I shivered as we went on.

We were met at a gate by a man with a shotgun in his hands who said, "God have mercy," and directed us to the campgrounds safely separated from town by a palisade kind of log wall. There we were questioned severely by an anxious-faced man, also clutching a shotgun, who peered up at the sky at intervals as though expecting the wrath of heaven at any moment.

"Only one wagon?" he asked.

"Yes," said Nils. "My wife and I and—"

"You have your marriage lines?" came the sharp question.

"Yes," said Nils patiently, "they're packed in the trunk."

"And your Bible is probably packed away, too!" the man accused.

"No," said Nils, "here it is." He took it from under the seat. The man sniffed and shifted.

"Who's that?" He nodded at the back of Marnie's dark head where she lay silently, sleeping or not, I don't now.

"My niece," Nils said steadily, and I clamped my mouth shut. "She's sick."

"Sick!" The man backed away from the wagon. "What sin did she commit?"

"Nothing catching," said Nils, shortly.

"Which way you come?" asked the man.

"Through Millman's Pass," Nils answered, his eyes unwavering on the anxious questioning face. The man paled and clutched his gun tighter, the skin of his face seeming to stretch down tight and then flush loose and sweaty again.

"What—" he began, then he licked dry lips and tried again. "Did you—was there—"

"Was there what?" asked Nils shortly. "Did we what?"

"Nothing," stammered the man, backing away. "Nothing.

"Gotta see her," he said, coming reluctantly back to the wagon. "Too easy to bear false witness—" Roughly he grabbed the quilt and pulled it back, rolling Marnie's head toward him. I thought he was going to collapse. "That's—

that's the one!" he whimpered hoarsely. "How did she get—Where did you—" Then his lips clamped shut. "If you say it's your niece, it's your niece.

"You can stay the night," he said with an effort. "Spring just outside the wall. Otherwise keep to the compound. Remember your prayers. Comport yourself in the fear of God." Then he scuttled away.

"Niece!" I breathed. "Oh, Nils! Shall I write out an Ex. 20:16 for you to nail on the wagon?"

"She'll have to be someone," said Nils. "When we get to Margin, we'll have to explain her somehow. She's named for your sister, so she's our niece. Simple, isn't it?"

"Sounds so," I said. "But, Nils, *who* is she? How did that man know—? If those were her people that died back there, where are their wagons? Their belongings? People don't just drop out of the sky—"

"Maybe these Graftonites took the people there to execute them," he suggested, "and confiscated their goods."

"Be more characteristic if they burned the people in the town square," I said shivering. "And their wagons, too."

We made camp. Marnie followed me to the spring. I glance daround, embarrassed for her in the nightgown, but no one else was around and darkness was falling. We went through the wall by a little gate and were able for the first time to see the houses of the village. They were very ordinary looking except for the pale flutter of papers posted profusely on everything a nail could hold to. How could they think of anything *but* sinning, with all these ghosty reminders?

While we were dipping the water, a small girl, enveloped in gray calico from slender neck to thin wrists and down to clumsy shoes, came pattering down to the spring, eyeing us as though she expected us to leap upon her with a roar.

"Hello," I said and smiled.

"God have mercy," she answered in a breathless whisper. "Are you right with God?"

"I trust so," I answered, not knowing if the question required an answer.

"She's wearing white," said the child, nodding at Marnie. "Is she dying?"

"No," I said, "but she's been ill. That is her nightgown."

"Oh!" The child's eyes widened and her hand covered her mouth. "How wicked! To use such a bad word! To be in her—her—to be like that outside the house! In the daytime!" She plopped her heavy bucket into the spring and, dragging it

91

out, staggered away from us, slopping water as she went. She was met halfway up the slope by a grim-faced woman, who set the pail aside, switched the weeping child unmercifully with a heavy willow switch, took a paper from her pocket, impaled it on a nail on a tree, seized the child with one hand and the bucket with the other, and plodded back to town.

I looked at the paper. Ex. 20:12. "Well!" I let out an astonished breath. "And she had it already written!" Then I went back to Marnie. Her eyes were big and empty again, the planes of her face sharply sunken.

"Marnie," I said, touching her shoulder. There was no response, no consciousness of me as I led her back to the wagon.

Nils retrieved the bucket of water and we ate a slender, unhappy supper by the glow of our campfire. Marnie ate nothing and sat in a motionless daze until we put her to bed.

"Maybe she's subject to seizures," I suggested.

"It was more likely watching the child being beaten," said Nils. "What had she done?"

"Nothing except to talk to us and be shocked that Marnie should be in her nightgown in public."

"What was the paper the mother posted?" asked Nils.

"Exodus, 20:12," I said. "The child must have disobeyed her mother by carrying on a conversation with us."

After a fitful, restless night the first thin light of dawn looked wonderful and we broke camp almost before we had shadows separate from the night. Just before we rode away, Nils wrote large and blackly on a piece of paper and fastened it to the wall near our wagon with loud accusing hammer blows. As we drove away, I asked, "What does it say?"

"Exodus, Chapter 22, verses 21 through 24," he said. "If they want wrath, let it fall on them!"

I was too unhappy and worn out to pursue the matter. I only knew it must be another Shalt Not and was thankful that I had been led by my parents through the Rejoice and Love passages instead of into the darkness.

Half an hour later, we heard the clatter of hooves behind us and, looking back, saw someone riding toward us, waving an arm urgently. Nils pulled up and laid his hand on his rifle. We waited.

It was the anxious man who had directed us to the campsite. He had Nils's paper clutched in his hand. At first he couldn't get his words out, then he said, "Drive on! Don't stop! They might be coming after me!" He gulped and wiped his nervous forehead. Nils slapped the reins and we moved off down the road. "Y—you left this—" He jerked the paper toward us. " 'Thou shalt neither vex a stranger, nor oppress him—' " the words came in gasps. " 'Ye shalt not afflict any widow or fatherless child. If you afflict them in any wise, I will surely hear their cry and my wrath shall wax hot—' " He sagged in the saddle, struggling for breath. "This is exactly what I told them," he said finally. "I showed it to them—the very next verses—but they couldn't see past 22:18. They—they went anyway. That Archibold told them about the people. He said they did things only witches could do. I had to go along. Oh, God have mercy! And help them tie them and watch them set the shed afire!"

"Who were they?" asked Nils.

"I don't know." The man sucked air noisily. "Archibold said he saw them flying up in the trees and laughing. He said they floated rocks around and started to build a house with them. He said they—they walked on the water and didn't fall in. He said one of them held a piece of wood up in the air and it caught on fire and other wood came and made a pile on the ground and that piece went down and lighted the rest." The man wiped his face again. "They *must* have been witches! Or else how could they do such things! We caught them. They were sleeping. They fluttered up like birds. I caught that little girl you've got there, only her hair was long then. We tied them up. I didn't want to!" Tears jerked out of his eyes. "I didn't put any knots in my rope and after the roof caved in, the little girl flew out all on fire and hid in the dark! I didn't know the Graftonites were like that! I only came last year. They—they *tell* you exactly what to do to be saved. You don't have to think or worry or wonder—" He rubbed his coat sleeve across his face. "Now all my life I'll see the shed burning. What about the others?"

"We buried them," I said shortly. "The charred remains of them."

"God have mercy!" he whispered.

"Where did the people come from?" asked Nils. "Where are their wagons?"

"There weren't any," said the man. "Archibold says they came in a flash of lightning and a thunderclap out of a clear sky—not a cloud anywhere. He waited and watched them three days before he came and told us. Wouldn't *you* think they were witches?" He wiped his face again and glanced back down the road. "They might follow me. Don't tell them. Don't say I told." He gathered up the reins, his face drawn and anxious, and spurred his horse into a gallop, cutting away from the road, across the flat. But before the hurried hoofbeats were muffled by distance, he whirled around and galloped back.

"But!" he gasped, back by our wagon side. "She must be a witch! She should be dead. You are compromising with evil—"

"Shall I drag her out so you can finish burning her here and now?" snapped Nils. "So you can watch her sizzle in her sin!"

"Don't!" The man doubled across the saddle horn in an agony of indecision. " 'No man having put his hand to the plow and looking back is fit for the kingdom.' What if they're right? What if the Devil is tempting me? Lead me not into temptation! Maybe it's not too late! Maybe if I confess!" And he tore back down the road toward Grafton's Vow faster than he had come.

"Well!" I drew a deep breath. "What Scripture would you quote for that?"

"I'm wondering," said Nils. "This Archibold. I wonder if he was in his right mind—"

" 'They fluttered up like birds,' " I reminded him, "and Marnie was floating."

"But floating rocks and making fire and coming in a flash of lightning out of a clear sky!" Nils protested.

"Maybe it was some kind of a balloon," I suggested. "Maybe it exploded. Maybe Marnie *doesn't* speak English. If the balloon sailed a long way—"

"It couldn't sail too far," said Nils. "The gas cools and it would come down. But how else could they come through the air?"

I felt a movement behind me and turned. Marnie was sitting up on the pallet. But what a different Marnie! It was as though her ears had been unstopped or a window had opened into her mind. There was an eager listening look on her tilted face. There was light in her eyes and the possibility of smiles around her mouth. She looked at me. "Through the air!" she said.

"Nils!" I cried. "Did you hear that! How did you come through the air, Marnie?"

She smiled apologetically and fingered the collar of the garment she wore and said, "Gown."

"Yes, gown," I said, settling for a word when I wanted a volume. Then I thought, *Can I reach the bread box?* Marnie's bright eyes left my face and she rummaged among the boxes and bundles. With a pleased little sound, she came up

94

with a piece of bread. "Bread," she said, "bread!" And it floated through the air into my astonished hands.

"Well!" said Nils. "Communication has begun!" Then he sobered. "And we have a child, apparently. From what that man said, there is no one left to be responsible for her. She seems to be ours."

When we stopped at noon for dinner, we were tired. More from endless speculation than from the journey. There had been no signs of pursuit and Marnie had subsided onto the pallet again, eyes closed.

We camped by a small creek and I had Nils get my trunk out before he cared for the animals. I opened the trunk with Marnie close beside me, watching my every move. I had packed an old skirt and shirtwaist on the top till so they would be ready for house cleaning and settling-in when we arrived at Margin. I held the skirt up to Marnie. It was too big and too long, but it would do with the help of a few strategic pins and by fastening the skirt up almost under her arms. Immediately, to my surprise and discomfort, Marnie skinned the nightgown off over her head in one motion and stood arrow-slim and straight, dressed only in that undergarment of hers. I glanced around quickly to see where Nils was and urged the skirt and blouse on Marnie. She glanced around too, puzzled, and slipped the clothing on, holding the skirt up on both sides. I showed her the buttons and hooks and eyes and, between the two of us and four pins, we got her put together.

When Nils came to the dinner tarp, he was confronted by Marnie, all dressed, even to my clomping slippers.

"Well!" he said, "a fine young lady we have! It's too bad we had to cut her hair."

"We can pretend she's just recovering from typhoid," I said, smiling. But the light had gone out of Marnie's face as if she knew what we were saying. She ran her fingers through her short-cropped curls, her eyes on my heavy braids I let swing free, Indian-fashion, traveling as we were, alone and unobserved.

"Don't you mind," I said, hugging her in one arm. "It'll grow again."

She lifted one of my braids and looked at me. "Hair," I said.

"Hair," she said and stretched out a curl from her own head. "Curl."

What a wonderful feeling it was to top out on the flat

above Margin and to know we were almost home. Home! As I wound my braids around my head in a more seemly fashion, I looked back at the boxes and bundles in the wagon. With these and very little else we must make a home out here in the middle of nowhere. Well, with Nils, it would suffice.

The sound of our wheels down the grade into town brought out eager, curious people from the scattering of houses and scanty town buildings that made up Margin. Margin clung to the side of a hill—that is, it was in the rounded embrace of the hill on three sides. On the other side, hundreds and hundreds of miles of territory lost themselves finally in the remote blueness of distance. It was a place where you could breathe free and unhampered and yet still feel the protectiveness of the everlasting hills. We were escorted happily to our house at the other end of town by a growing crowd of people. Marnie had fallen silent and withdrawn again, her eyes wide and wondering, her hand clutching the edge of the seat with white-knuckled intensity as she tried to lose herself between Nils and me.

Well, the first few days in a new place are always uncomfortable and confused. All the settling-in and the worry about whether Marnie would go floating off like a balloon or send something floating through the air as she had the bread combined to wear me to a frazzle. Fortunately Marnie was very shy of anyone but us, so painfully so that as soon as the gown was washed and clean again and we borrowed a cot, I put Marnie into both of them, and she lay in a sort of doze all day long, gone to some far place I couldn't even guess at.

Of course we had to explain her. There had been no mention of her when we arranged to come, and she had no clothes and I didn't have enough to cover both of us decently. So I listened to myself spin the most outrageous stories to Mrs. Wardlow. Her husband was the schoolmaster-lay-preacher and every other function of a learned man in a frontier settlement. She was the unofficial news spreader and guardian of public morals.

"Marnie is our niece," I said. "She's my younger sister's girl. She is just recovering from typhoid and—and brain fever."

"Oh, my!" said Mrs. Wardlow. "Both at once?"

"No," I said, warming to my task. "She was weakened by the typhoid and went into a brain fever. She lost her hair from all the fever. We thought we were going to lose her, too." It didn't take play acting to shiver, as, unbidden into my mind, came the vision of the smoke pluming slowly up—

"My sister sent her with us, hoping that the climate out here will keep Marnie from developing a consumption. She hopes, too, that I can help the child learn to talk again."

"I've heard of people having to learn to walk again after typhoid, but not to talk—"

"The technical name for the affliction is aphasia," I said glibly. "Remember the brain fever. She had just begun to make some progress in talking, but the trip has set her back."

"She—she isn't—unbalanced, is she?" whispered Mrs. Wardlow piercingly.

"Of course not!" I said indignantly. "And, please! She can hear perfectly."

"Oh," said Mrs. Wardlow, reddening, "of course. I didn't mean to offend. When she is recovered enough, Mr. Wardlow would be pleased to set her lessons for her until she can come to school."

"Thank you," I said, "that would be very kind of him." Then I changed the subject by introducing tea.

After she left, I sat down by Marnie, whose eyes brightened for my solitary presence.

"Marnie," I said, "I don't know how much you understand of what I say, but you are my niece. You must call me Aunt Gail and Nils, Uncle Nils. You have been sick. You are having to learn to speak all over again." Her eyes had been watching me attentively, but not one flick of understanding answered me. I sighed heavily and turned away. Marnie's hand caught my arm. She held me, as she lay, eyes closed. Finally I made a movement as if to free myself, and she opened her eyes and smiled.

"Aunt Gail, I have been sick. My hair is gone. I want bread!" she recited carefully.

"Oh, Marnie!" I cried, hugging her to me in delight. "Bless you! You *are* learning to talk!" I hugged my face into the top of her curls, then I let her go. "As to bread, I mixed a batch this morning. It'll be in the oven as soon as it rises again. There's nothing like the smell of baking bread to make a place seem like home."

As soon as Marnie was strong enough, I began teaching her the necessary household skills and found it most disconcerting to see her holding a broom gingerly, not knowing, literally, which end to use, or what to do with it. Anybody knows what a needle and thread are for! But Marnie looked upon them as if they were baffling wonders from another world. She watched the needle swing back and forth sliding down the thread until it fell to the floor because she didn't know enough to put a knot in the end.

She learned to talk, but very slowly at first. She had to struggle and wait for words. I asked her about it one day. Her slow answer came. "I don't know your language," she said. "I have to change the words to my language to see what they say, then change them again to be in your language." She sighed. "It's so slow! But soon I will be able to take words from your mind and not have to change them."

I blinked, not quite sure I wanted anything taken from my mind by anyone!

The people of Margin had sort of adopted Marnie and were very pleased with her progress. Even the young ones learned to wait for her slow responses. She found it more comfortable to play with the younger children because they didn't require such a high performance in the matter of words, and because their play was with fundamental things of the house and the community, translated into the simplest forms and acted out in endless repetition.

I found out, to my discomfort, a little of how Marnie was able to get along so well with the small ones—the day Merwin Wardlow came roaring to me in seven-year-old indignation.

"Marnie and that old sister of mine won't let me play!" he tattled wrathfully.

"Oh, I'm sure they will, if you play nicely," I said, shifting my crochet hook as I hurried with the edging of Marnie's new petticoat.

"They won't neither!" And he prepared to bellow again. His bellow rivaled the six o'clock closing whistle at the mine, so I sighed, and laying my work down, took him out to the children's play place under the aspens.

Marnie was playing with five-year-old Tessie Wardlow. They were engrossed in building a playhouse. They had already outlined the various rooms with rocks and were now furnishing them with sticks and stones, shingles, old cans and bottles, and remnants of broken dishes. Marnie was arranging flowers in a broken vase she had propped between two rocks. Tessie was busily bringing her flowers and sprays of leaves. And not one single word was being exchanged! Tessie watched Marnie, then trotted off to get another flower. Before she could pick the one she intended, she stopped, her hand actually on the flower, glanced at Marnie's busy back, left that flower and, picking another, trotted happily back with it.

"Marnie," I called, and blinked to feel a wisp of something say *Yes?* inside my mind. "Marnie!" I called again. Marnie jumped and turned her face to me. "Yes, Aunt Gail," she said carefully.

"Merwin says you won't let him play."

"Oh, he's telling stories!" cried Tessie indignantly. "He won't do anything Marnie says and she's the boss today."

"She don't tell me nothing to do!" yelled Merwin, betraying in his indignation, his father's careful grammar.

"She does so!" Tessie stamped her foot. "She tells you just as much as she tells me! And you don't do it."

I was saved from having to arbitrate between the warring two by Mrs. Wardlow's calling them in to supper. Relieved, I sank down on the southwest corner of the parlor—a sizable moss-grown rock. Marnie sat down on the ground beside me.

"Marnie," I said. "How did Tessie know what flowers to bring you?"

"I told her," said Marnie, surprised. "They said I was boss today. Merwin just wouldn't play."

"Did you tell him things to do?" I asked.

"Oh, yes," said Marnie. "But he didn't do nothing."

"Did nothing," I corrected.

"Did nothing," she echoed.

"The last flower Tessie brought," I went on. "Did you ask for that special one?"

"Yes," said Marnie. "She started to pick the one with bad petals on one side."

"Marnie," I said patiently, "I was here and I didn't hear a word. Did you *talk* to Tessie?"

"Oh, yes," said Marnie.

"With words? Out loud?" I pursued.

"I think—" Marnie started, then she sighed and sagged against my knees, tracing a curve in the dirt with her forefinger. "I guess not. It is so much more easy ("Easier," I corrected.) easier to catch her thoughts before they are words. I can tell Tessie without words. But Merwin—I guess he needs words."

"Marnie," I said, taking reluctant steps into the wilderness of my ignorance of what to do with a child who found "no words more easy," "you must always use words. It might seem easier to you—the other way, but you *must* speak. You see, most people don't understand *not* using words. When people don't understand, they get frightened. When they are frightened, they get angry. And when they get angry, they—they have to hurt."

I sat quietly watching Marnie manipulate my words, frame a reply, and make it into words for her stricken, unhappy lips.

"Then it was because they didn't understand, that they killed us," she said. "They made the fire."

"Yes," I said, "exactly.

"Marnie," I went on, feeling that I was prying, but needing to know. "You have never cried for the people who died in the fire. You were sad, but—weren't they your own people?"

"Yes," said Marnie, after an interval. "My father, my mother, and my brother—" She firmed her lips and swallowed. "And a neighbor of ours. One brother was Called in the skies when our ship broke and my little sister's life-slip didn't come with ours."

And I saw them! Vividly, I saw them all as she named them. The father, I noticed before his living, smiling image faded from my mind, had thick dark curls like Marnie's. The neighbor was a plump little woman.

"But," I blinked, "don't you grieve for them? Aren't you sad because they are dead?"

"I am sad because they aren't with me," said Marnie slowly. "But I do not grieve that the Power Called them back to the Presence. Their bodies were so hurt and broken." She swallowed again. "My days are not finished yet, but no matter how long until I am Called, my people will come to meet me. They will laugh and run to me when I arrive and I—" She leaned against my skirt, averting her face. After a moment she lifted her chin and said, "I *am* sad to be here without them, but my biggest sorrow is not knowing where my little sister is, or whether Timmy has been Called. We were two-ing, Timmy and I." Her hand closed over the hem of my skirt. "But, praise the Presence, I have you and Uncle Nils, who do not hurt just because you don't understand."

"But where on Earth—" I began.

"Is this called Earth?" Marnie looked about her. "Is Earth the place we came to?"

"The whole world is Earth," I said. "Everything—as far as you can see—as far as you can go. You came to this Territory—"

"Earth—" Marnie was musing. "So this refuge in the sky is called Earth!" She scrambled to her feet. "I'm sorry I troubled you, Aunt Gail," she said. "Here, this is to promise not to be un-Earth—" She snatched up the last flower she had put in the playhouse vase and pushed it into my hands. "I will set the table for supper," she called back to me as she

100

hurried to the house. "This time forks at each place—not in a row down the middle."

I sighed and twirled the flower in my fingers. Then I laughed helplessly. The flower that had so prosaically grown on, and had been plucked from our hillside, was glowing with a deep radiance, its burning gold center flicking the shadows of the petals across my fingers, and all the petals tinkled softly from the dewdrop-clear bits of light that were finely pendant along the edges of them. Not un-Earth! But when I showed Nils the flower that evening as I retold our day, the flower was just a flower again, limp and withering.

"Either you or Marnie have a wonderful imagination," Nils said.

"Then it's Marnie," I replied. "I would never in a million years think up anything like the things she said. Only, Nils, how can we be sure it isn't true?"

"That what isn't true?" he asked. "What do you think she has told you?"

"Why—why—" I groped, "that she can read minds, Tessie's anyway. And that this is a strange world to her. And—and—"

"If this is the way she wants to make the loss of her family bearable, let her. It's better than hysterics or melancholia. Besides, it's more exciting, isn't it?" Nils laughed.

That reaction wasn't much help in soothing my imagination! But *he* didn't have to spend his days wrestling hand to hand with Marnie and her ways. He hadn't had to insist that Marnie learn to make the beds by hand instead of floating the covers into place—nor insist that young ladies wear shoes in preference to drifting a few inches above the sharp gravel and beds of stickers in the back yard. And he didn't have to persuade her that, no matter how dark the moonless night, one doesn't cut out paper flowers and set them to blooming like little candles around the corners of the rooms. Nils had been to the county seat *that* weekend. I don't know where she was from, but this *was* a New World to her and whatever one she was native to, I had no memory of reading about or of seeing on a globe.

When Marnie started taking classes in Mr. Wardlow's one-room school, she finally began to make friends with the few children her age in Margin. Guessing at her age, she seemed to be somewhere in her teens. Among her friends were Kenny, the son of the mine foreman, and Loolie, the daughter of the boardinghouse cook. The three of them ranged the hills together, and Marnie picked up a large vocabulary from them and became a little wiser in the ways of behaving unexceptionally. She startled them a time or two by doing impossible things, but they reacted with anger and withdrawal which she had to wait out more or less patiently before being accepted back into their companionship. One doesn't forget again very quickly under such circumstances.

During this time, her hair grew and she grew, too, so much so that she finally had to give up the undergarment she had worn when we found her. She sighed as she laid it aside, tucking it into the bottom dresser drawer. "At Home," she said, "there would be a ceremony and a pledging. All of us girls would know that our adult responsibilities were almost upon us—" Somehow, she seemed less different, less, well I suppose, alien, after that day.

It wasn't very long after this that Marnie began to stop suddenly in the middle of a sentence and listen intently, or clatter down the plates she was patterning on the supper table and hurry to the window. I watched her anxiously for a while, wondering if she was sickening for something, then, one night, after I blew out the lamp, I thought I heard something moving in the other room. I went in barefootedly quiet. Marnie was at the window.

"Marnie?" Her shadowy figure turned to me. "What's troubling you?" I stood close beside her and looked out at the moonlight-flooded emptiness of hills around the house.

"Something is out there," she said. "Something scared and bad—frightened and evil—" She took the more adult words from my mind. I was pleased that being conscious of her doing this didn't frighten me any more the way it did the first few times. "It goes around the house and around the house and is afraid to come."

"Perhaps an animal," I suggested.

"Perhaps," she conceded, turning away from the window. "I don't know your world. An animal who walks upright and sobs, 'God have mercy!' "

Which incident was startling in itself, but doubly so when Nils said casually next day as he helped himself to mashed potatoes at the dinner table, "Guess who I saw today. They say he's been around a week or so." He flooded his plate with brown meat gravy. "Our friend of the double mind."

"Double mind?" I blinked uncomprehendingly.

"Yes." Nils reached for a slice of bread. "To burn or not to burn, that is the question—"

"Oh!" I felt a quiver up my arms. "You mean the man at Grafton's Vow. What was his name anyway?"

"He never said, did he?" Nils's fork paused in mid-air as the thought caught him.

"Derwent," said Marnie shortly, her lips pressing to a narrow line. "Caleb Derwent, God have mercy."

"How do you know?" I asked. "Did he tell you?"

"No," she said, "I took it from him to remember him with gratitude." She pushed away from the table, her eyes widening. "That's it—that's the frightened evil that walks around the house at night! And passes by during the day! But he saved me from the fire! Why does he come now?"

"She's been feeling that something evil is lurking outside," I explained to Nils's questioning look.

"Hmm," he said, "the two minds. Marnie, if ever he—"

"May I go?" Marnie stood up. "I'm sorry. I can't eat when I think of someone repenting of good." And she was gone, the kitchen door clicking behind her.

"And she's right," said Nils, resuming his dinner. "He slithered around a stack of nail kegs at the store and muttered to me about still compromising with evil, harboring a known witch. I sort of pinned him in the corner until he told me he had finally—after all this time—confessed his sin of omission to his superiors at Grafton's Vow and they've excommunicated him until he redeems himself—" Nils stared at me, listening to his own words. "Gail! You don't suppose he has any mad idea about taking her back to Grafton's Vow, do you!"

"Or *killing* her!" I cried, clattering my chair back from the table. "Marnie!" Then I subsided with an attempt at a smile. "But she's witch enough to sense his being around," I said. "He won't be able to take her by surprise."

"Sensing or not," Nils said, eating hastily, "next time I get within reach of this Derwent person, I'm going to persuade him that he'll be healthier elsewhere."

In the days that followed, we got used to seeing half of Derwent's face peering around a building, or a pale slice of his face appearing through bushes or branches, but he seemed to take out his hostility in watching Marnie from a safe distance, and we decided to let things ride—watchfully.

Then one evening Marnie shot through the back door and, shutting it, leaned against it, panting.

"Marnie," I chided. "I didn't hear your steps on the porch. You *must* remember—"

"I—I'm sorry, Aunt Gail," she said, "but I had to hurry. Aunt Gail, I have a trouble!" She was actually shaking.

"What have you done now to upset Kenny and Loolie?" I asked, smiling.

"Not—not that," she said. "Oh, Aunt Gail! He's down in the shaft and I can't get him up. I know the inanimate lift, but he's not inanimate—"

"Marnie, sit down," I said, sobering. "Calm down and tell me what's wrong."

She sat, if that tense tentative conforming to a chair could be called sitting.

"I was out at East Shaft," she said. "My people are Identifiers, some of them are, anyway—my family is especially—I mean—" She gulped and let loose all over. I could almost see the tension drain out of her, but it came flooding back as soon as she started talking again. "Identifiers can locate metals and minerals. I felt a pretty piece of chrysocolla down in the shaft and I wanted to get it for you for your collection. I climbed through the fence—oh, I know I shouldn't have, but I did—and I was checking to see how far down in the shaft the mineral was when—when I looked up and he was there!" She clasped her hands. "He said, 'Evil must die. I can't go back because you're not dead. I let you out of a little fire in this life, so I'll burn forever. "He who endures to the end—" ' Then he pushed me into the shaft—"

"Into the—" I gasped.

"Of course, I didn't fall," she hastened. "I just lifted to the other side of the shaft out of reach, but—but he had pushed me so hard that he—he fell!"

"He fell!" I started up in horror. "He fell? Child, that's hundreds of feet down onto rocks and water—"

"I—I caught him before he fell all the way," said Marnie, apologetically. "But I had to do it our way. I stopped his falling—only—only he's just staying there! In the air! In the shaft! I know the inanimate lift, but he's alive. And I—don't —know—how—to—get—him—up!" She burst into tears. "And if I let him go, he will fall to death. And if I leave him there, he'll bob up and down and up and—I *can't* leave him there!" She flung herself against me, wailing. It was the first time she'd ever let go like that.

Nils had come in at the tail end of her explanation and I filled him in between my muttered comforting of the top of Marnie's head. He went to the shed and came back with a coil of rope.

"With a reasonable amount of luck, no one will see us," he said. "It's a good thing that we're out here by ourselves."

Evening was all around us as we climbed the slope behind

the house. The sky was high and a clear, transparent blue, shading to apricot, with a metallic orange backing the surrounding hills. One star was out, high above the evening-hazy immensity of distance beyond Margin. We panted up the hill to East Shaft. It was the one dangerous abandoned shaft among all the shallow prospect holes that dotted the hills around us. It had been fenced with barbwire and was forbidden territory to the children of Margin—including Marnie. Nils held down one strand of the barbwire with his foot and lifted the other above it. Marnie slithered through and I scrambled through, snatching the ruffle of my petticoat free from where it had caught on the lower barbs.

We lay down on the rocky ground and edged up to the brink of the shaft. It was darker than the inside of a hat.

"Derwent!" Nils's voice echoed eerily down past the tangle of vegetation clinging to the upper reaches of the shaft.

"Here I am, Lord." The voice rolled up flatly, drained of emotion. "Death caught me in the midst of my sin. Cast me into the fire—the everlasting fire I traded a piddlin' little shed fire for. Kids—dime a dozen! I sold my soul for a scared face. Here I am, Lord. Cast me into the fire."

Nils made a sound. If what I was feeling was any indication, a deep sickness was tightening his throat. "Derwent!" he called again, "I'm letting down a rope. Put the loop around your waist so we can pull you up!" He laid the rope out across a timber that slanted over the shaft. Down it went into the darkness—and hung swaying slightly.

"Derwent!" Nils shouted. "Caleb Derwent! Get hold of that rope!"

"Here I am, Lord," came the flat voice again, much closer this time. "Death caught me in the midst of my sin—"

"Marnie," Nils said over the mindless mechanical reiteration that was now receding below. "Can you do anything?"

"May I?" she asked. "May I, Uncle Nils?"

"Of course," said Nils. "There's no one here to be offended. Here, take hold of the rope and—and go down along it so we'll know where you are."

So Marnie stepped lightly into the nothingness of the shaft and, hand circling the rope, sank down into the darkness. Nils mopped the sweat from his forehead with his forearm. "No weight," he muttered, "not an ounce of weight on the rope!"

Then there was a shriek and a threshing below us. "No! No!" bellowed Derwent, "I repent! I repent! Don't shove me down into everlasting—!" His words broke off and the rope jerked.

"Marnie!" I cried. "What—what—"

"He's—his eyes turned up and his mouth went open and he doesn't talk," she called up fearfully from the blackness. "I can't find his thoughts—"

"Fainted!" said Nils. Then he called. "It's all right, Marnie. He's only unconscious from fright. Put the rope around him."

So we drew him up from the shaft. Once the rope snatched out of our hands for several inches, but he didn't fall! The rope slacked, but he didn't fall! Marnie's anxious face came into sight beside his bowed head. "I can hold him from falling," she said, "but you must do all the pulling. I can't lift him."

Then we had him out on the ground, lying flat, but in the brief interval that Nils used to straighten him out, he drifted up from the ground about four inches. Marnie pressed him back.

"He—he isn't fastened to the Earth with all the fastenings. I loosed some when I stopped his fall. The shaft helped hold him. But now I—I've got to fasten them all back again. I didn't learn that part very well at home. Everyone can do it for himself. I got so scared when he fell that I forgot all I knew. But I couldn't have done it with him still in the shaft anyway. He would have fallen." She looked around in the deepening dusk. "I need a source of light—"

Light? We looked around us. The only lights in sight were the one star and a pinprick or so in the shadows of the flat below us.

"A lantern?" asked Nils.

"No," said Marnie. "Moonlight or sunlight or enough starlight. It takes light to '*platt*'—" She shrugged with her open hands.

"The moon is just past full," said Nils. "It'll be up soon—"

So we crouched there on boulders, rocks, and pebbles, holding Derwent down, waiting for the moonrise to become an ingredient in fastening him to the Earth again. I felt an inappropriate bubble of laughter shaking my frightened shoulders. What a story to tell to my grandchildren! If I live through this ever to have any!

Finally the moon came, a sudden flood through the transparency of the evening air. Marnie took a deep breath, her face very white in the moonlight. "It's—it's frightening!" she said. " '*Platting*' with moonlight is an adult activity. Any child can 'platt' with sunlight, but," she shivered, "only the Old Ones dare use moonlight and sunlight together! I—I think I can handle the moonlight. I hope!"

She lifted her two cupped hands. They quickly filled with a double handful of moonlight. The light flowed and wound across her palms and between her fingers, flickering live and lovely. Then she was weaving the living light into an intricate design that moved and changed and grew until it hid her arms to the elbows and cast light up into her intent face. One curve of it touched me. It was like nothing I'd ever felt before, so I jerked away from it. But, fascinated, I reached for it again. A gasp from Marnie stopped my hand.

"It's too big," she gasped. "It's too powerful! I—I don't know enough to control—" Her fingers flicked and the intricate light enveloped Derwent from head to foot. Then there was a jarring and a shifting. The slopes around us suddenly became unstable and almost fluid. There was a grinding and a rumbling. Rocks clattered down the slopes beyond us and the lip of East Shaft crumpled. The ground dimpled in around where the shaft had been. A little puff of dust rose from the spot and drifted slowly away in the cooling night air. We sorted ourselves out from where we had tumbled, clutched in each other's arms. Marnie looked down at the completely relaxed Derwent. "It got too big, too fast," she apologized. "I'm afraid it spoiled the shaft."

Nils and I exchanged glances and we both smiled weakly. "It's all right, Marnie," I said, "it doesn't matter. Is he all right now?"

"Yes," said Marnie, "his thoughts are coming back."

"Everything's fine," muttered Nils to me. "But what do you suppose that little earth-shaking has done to the mine?"

My eyes widened and I felt my hands tighten. What, indeed, *had* it done to the mine?

Derwent's thoughts came back enough that he left us the next day, sagging in his saddle, moving only because his horse did, headed for nowhere—just away—away from Margin, from Grafton's Vow, from Marnie. We watched him go, Marnie's face troubled.

"He is so confused," she said. "If only I were a Sorter. I could help his mind—"

"He tried to *kill* you!" I burst out, impatient with her compassion.

"He thought he would never be able to come into the Presence because of me," she said quickly. "What might I have done if I had believed that of him?"

So Derwent was gone—and so was the mine, irretrievably. The shaft, laboriously drilled and blasted through solid rock, the radiating drifts, hardly needing timbering to support them because of the composition of the rock—all had splintered and collapsed. From the mine entrance, crushed to a cabin-sized cave, you could hear the murmur of waters that had broken through into, and drowned, the wreckage of the mine. The second day a trickle of water began a pool in the entrance. The third day the stream began to run down the slope toward town. It was soaked up almost immediately by the bone-dry ground, but the muddy wetness spread farther and farther and a small channel began to etch itself down the hill.

It doesn't take long for a town to die. The workmen milled around at the mine entrance for a day or two, murmuring earthquakes and other awesome dispensations from the hand of God, hardly believing that they weren't at work. It was like a death that had chopped off things abruptly instead of letting them grow or decrease gradually. Then the first of the families left, their good-bys brief and unemotional to hide the sorrow and worry in their eyes. Then others followed, either leaving their shacks behind them to fall into eventual ruin, or else their houses moved off down the road like shingled turtles, leaving behind them only the concrete foundation blocks.

We, of course, stayed to the last, Nils paying the men off, making arrangements about what was left of the mining equipment, taking care of all the details attendant on the last rites of his career that had started so hopefully here in Margin. But, finally, we would have been packing, too, except for one thing. Marnie was missing.

She had been horrified when she found what had happened to the mine. She was too crushed to cry when Loolie and Kenny and the Wardlows came to say good-by. We didn't know what to say to her or how to comfort her. Finally, late one evening, I found her sitting, hunched on her cot, her face wet with tears.

"It's all right, Marnie," I said, "we won't go hungry. Nils will always find a way to—"

"I am not crying for the mine," said Marnie and I felt an illogical stab of resentment that she wasn't. "It is a year," she went on. "Just a year."

"A year?" Then remembrance flooded in. A year since the sullen smoke plumed up from the burning shed, since I felt the damp curling of freshly cut hair under my fingers—since

Nils grimly dug the multiple grave. "But it should be a little easier now," I said.

"It's only that on the Home it would have been Festival time—time to bring our flowers and lift into the skies and sing to remember all who had been Called during the year. We kept Festival only three days before the angry ones came and killed us." She wiped her cheeks with the backs of her hands. "That was a difficult Festival because we were so separated by the Crossing. We didn't know how many of us were echoing our songs from Otherside."

"I'm not sure I understand," I said. "But go on—cry for your dead. It will ease you."

"I am not crying for those who have been Called," said Marnie. "They are in the Presence and need no tears. I am crying for the ones—if there are any—who are alive on this Earth we found. I am crying because— Oh, Aunt Gail!" She clung to me. "What if I'm the only one who was not Called? The only one!"

I patted her shaking shoulders, wishing I could comfort her.

"There was Timmy," she sniffed and accepted the handkerchief I gave her. "He—he was in our ship. Only at the last moment before Lift Off was there room for him to come with us. But when the ship melted and broke and we each had to get into our life-slips, we scattered like the baby quail Kenny showed me the other day. And only a few life-slips managed to stay together. Oh, I wish I knew!" She closed her wet eyes, her trembling chin lifting. "If only I knew whether or not Timmy is in the Presence!"

I did all that I could to comfort her. My all was just being there.

"I keep silent Festival tonight," she said finally, "trusting in the Power—"

"This is a solemn night for us, too," I said. "We will start packing tomorrow. Nils thinks he can find a job nearer the Valley—" I sighed. "This would have been such a nice place to watch grow up. All it lacked was a running stream, and now we're even getting that. Oh, well—such is life in the wild and woolly West!"

And the next morning, she was gone. On her pillow was a piece of paper that merely said, "Wait."

What could we do? Where could we look? Footprints were impossible on the rocky slopes. And for a Marnie, there could well be *no* footprints at all, even if the surroundings were pure sand. I looked helplessly at Nils.

"Three days," he said, tightly angry. "The traditional three days before a funeral. If she isn't back by then, we leave."

By the end of the second day of waiting in the echoless ghostiness of the dead town, I had tears enough dammed up in me to rival the new little stream that was cutting deeper and deeper into its channel. Nils was up at the mine entrance watching the waters gush out from where they had oozed at first. I was hunched over the stream where it made the corner by the empty foundation blocks of the mine office, when I heard—or felt—or perceived—a presence. My innards lurched and I turned cautiously. It was Marnie.

"Where have you been?" I asked flatly.

"Looking for another mine," she said matter-of-factly.

"Another mine?" My shaking hands pulled her down to me and we wordlessly hugged the breath out of each other. Then I let her go.

"I spoiled the other one," she went on as though uninterrupted. "I have found another, but I'm not sure you will want it."

"Another? Not want it?" My mind wasn't functioning on a very high level, so I stood up and screamed, "Nils!"

His figure popped out from behind a boulder and, after hesitating long enough to see there were two of us, he made it down the slope in massive leaps and stood panting, looking at Marnie. Then he was hugging the breath out of her and I was weeping over the two of them, finding my tears considerably fewer than I had thought. We finally all shared my apron to dry our faces and sat happily shaken on the edge of our front porch, our feet dangling.

"It's over on the other side of the flat," said Marnie. "In a little canyon there. It's close enough so Margin can grow again here in the same place, only now with a running stream."

"But a new mine! What do you know about mining?" asked Nils, hope, against his better judgment, lightening his face.

"Nothing," admitted Marnie. "But I can identify and I took these—" She held out her hands. "A penny for copper. Your little locket," she nodded at me apologetically, "for gold. A dollar—" she turned it on her palm, "for silver. By the identity of these I can find other metals like them. Copper—there is not as much as in the old mine, but there is *some* in the new one. There is quite a bit of gold. It feels like much more than in the old mine, and," she faltered, "I'm

110

sorry, but mostly there is only silver. Much, much more than copper. Maybe if I looked farther—"

"But, Marnie," I cried, "silver is better! Silver is better!"

"Are you serious?" asked Nils, the planes of his face stark and bony in the sunlight. "Do you really think you have found a possible mine?"

"I don't know about mines," repeated Marnie, "but I know these metals are there. I can feel them tangling all over in the mountainside and up and down as the ground goes. Much of it is mixed with other matter, but it's like the ore they used to send out of Margin in the wagons with the high wheels. Only some of it is penny and locket and dollar feeling. I didn't know it could come that way in the ground."

"Native silver," I murmured, "native copper and gold."

"I—I could try to open the hill for you so you could see," suggested Marnie timidly to Nils's still face.

"No," I said hastily. "No, Marnie. Nils, couldn't we at least take a look?"

So we went, squeezing our way through the underbrush and through a narrow entrance into a box canyon beyond the far side of the flat. Pausing to catch my breath, almost pinned between two towering slabs of tawny orange granite, I glanced up to the segment of blue sky overhead. A white cloud edged into sight and suddenly the movement wasn't in the cloud, but in the mountain of granite. It reeled and leaned and seemed to be toppling. I snatched my eyes away from the sky with a gasp and wiggled on through, following Marnie and followed by Nils.

Nils looked around the canyon wonderingly. "Didn't even know this was here," he said. "No one's filed on this area. It's ours—if it's worth filing on. Our own mine—"

Marnie knelt at the base of the cliff that formed one side of the canyon. "Here is the most," she said, rubbing her hand over the crumbling stone. "It is all through the mountain, but there is some silver very close here." She looked up at Nils and read his skepticism.

"Well," she sighed. "Well—" And she sank down with the pool of her skirts around her on the sandy ground. She clasped her hands and stared down at them. I could see her shoulders tighten and felt something move—or change—or begin. Then, about shoulder high on the face of the rock wall, there was a coloring and a crumbling. Then a thin, bright trickle came from the rock and ran molten down to the sand, spreading flowerlike into a palm-sized disk of pure silver!

111

"There," said Marnie, her shoulders relaxing. "That was close to the outside—"

"Nils!" I cried. "Look!" and snatching up the still-hot metallic blossom, I dropped it again, the bright blood flowing across the ball of my thumb from the gashing of the sharp silver edge.

It doesn't take long for a town to grow. Not if there's a productive mine and an ideal flat for straight, wide business streets. And hills and trees and a running stream for residential areas. The three of us watch with delighted wonder the miracle of Margin growing and expanding. Only occasionally does Marnie stand at the window in the dark and wonder if she is the only one—the last one—of her People left upon Earth. And only occasionally do I look at her and wonder where on Earth—or off it—did this casual miracle, this angel unawares, come from.

"This angel unawares." Bethie's whisper echoed the last phrase of the Assembly.

"Why I've *been* in Margin!" cried Meris. "I was there their last Founding Day and I didn't hear a word about Marnie!"

"What did you hear?' asked Bethie, interested.

"Well, about the first mine collapsing and starting the creek and about the new mine's being found—"

"I suppose that's enough," said Bethie. "How would you have included Marnie?"

"At least mention her name!" cried Meris. "Why even the burro a prospector hit with a piece of ore and found Tombstone or Charleston or wherever is remembered. And not word one about Marnie—"

"Maybe," suggested Bethie, "maybe because that wasn't her real name."

"It wasn't!" Meris's eyes widened.

"Do you think she was called Marnie on the Home?" teased Mark. "Look what we did to Lala's name. At least 'Marnie' couldn't be that bad a miss."

"Who was she then?" asked Meris. "What was her real name?"

"Why I thought you knew—" Bethie started.

"Marnie was Lytha. She used both names later on—Marnie Lytha."

"Lytha!" Meris sat down absently, almost off the chair, and scooted back slowly. "Lytha and Timmy. Oh! Of course! Then Eva-lee's promise to them must have come true—"

"She didn't promise them each other," reminded Mark. "Only love."

"Only love!" mocked Meris. "Oh, Mark! *Only* love?"

"I was just thinking," said Mark slowly. "If Marnie was Lytha, then all those people who died in the fire—"

"Oh, Mark!" Meris drew a breath of distress. "Oh, Mark! But Eve wasn't one of them. Bethie's mother escaped!"

"Others did, too," said Bethie. "The flow of Assembling about Marnie kept right on in the same general area and I didn't stop when Marnie's segment was finished. The next part—" She hesitated. "It's hard to tell what is bright and happy and what is dark and sad. I'll let you decide. The boy—well, he wasn't sure either—"

Bethie gathered up the two willing hands gently and began—

TROUBLING OF THE WATER

Sometimes it's like being a castaway, being a first settler in a big land. If I were a little younger, maybe I'd play at being Robinson Crusoe, only I'd die of surprise if I found a footprint, especially a bare one, this place being where it is.

But it's not only being a castaway in a place, but in a time. I feel as though the last years of the century were ruffling up to my knees in a tide that will sweep me into the next century. If I live seven more years, I'll not only be of age but I'll see the Turn of the Century! Imagine putting 19 in front of your years instead of 18! So, instead of playing Crusoe and scanning the horizon for sails, I used to stand on a rock and measure the world full circle, thinking—the Turn of the Century! The Turn of the Century! And seeking and seeking as though Time were a tide that would come racing through the land at midnight 1899 and that I could see the front edge of the tide beginning already!

But things have happened so fast recently that I'm not sure about Time or Place or Possible or Impossible any more. One thing I am sure of is the drought. It was real enough.

It's the responsibility of the men of the house to watch out for the welfare of the women of the house, so that day I went with Father up into the hills to find out where Sometime

Creek started. We climbed up and up along the winding creek bed until my lungs pulled at the hot air and felt crackly clear down to their bottoms. We stopped and leaned against a boulder to let me catch my breath and cool off a little in what shadow there was. We could see miles and miles across the country—so far that the mountains on the other side of Desolation Valley were swimmy pale against the sky. Below us, almost at our feet because of the steepness of the hill, was the thin green line of mesquites and river willows that bordered Chuckawalla River and, hidden in a clump of cottonwoods down to our left, was our cabin, where Mama, if she had finished mixing the bread, was probably standing in the doorway with Merry on her hip, looking up as I was looking down.

"What if there isn't a spring?" I asked, gulping dryly, wanting a drink. I thought Father wasn't going to answer. Sometimes he doesn't—maybe for a day or so. Then suddenly, when you aren't even thinking of the same thing, he'll answer and expect you to remember what you'd asked.

"Then we'll know why they call this Sometime Creek," he said. "If you've cooled down some, go get a drink."

"But we've always got the river," I said, as I bellied down to the edge of the plunging water. It flowed so fast that I couldn't suck it up. I had to bite at it to get a mouthful. It was cold and tasted of silt. It was shallow enough that I bumped my nose as I ducked my hot face into its coldness.

"Not always." Father waited until I finished before he cupped his hands in a small waterfall a step upstream and drank briefly. "It's dropped to less than half its flow of last week. Tanker told me yesterday when he stopped for melons that there's no snow left in the Coronas Altas, this early in the summer."

"But our orchard!" I felt dread crawl in my stomach. "All our fields!"

"Our orchard," said Father, no comfort or reassurance in his voice. "And all our fields."

We didn't find a spring. We stood at the bottom of a slope too steep to climb and watched the water sheet down it from the top we couldn't see. I watched Father as he stood there, one foot up on the steep rise, his knee bent as if he intended to climb up sheer rock, looking up at the silver falling water.

"If the river dries up," I offered, "the creek isn't enough to water everything."

Father said nothing but turned back down the hill.

We went down in half the time it took us to climb. Part

114

way down I stumbled and fell sideways into a catclaw bush. Father had to pull me out, the tiny thorns clinging to my clothes like claws and striping the backs of my hands and one of my cheeks with smarting scratches.

"People have to drink," said Father. "And the animals."

We were leveling out on the flat by the house when I finally figured out what Father meant. He had already given our young orchard back to the wilderness and turned his back on the vegetable crops that were our mainstay and on the withering alfalfa fields. He was measuring water to keep us alive and still clinging to Fool's Acres Ranch.

Mama and Merry met us as we came down the path. I took the burden of Merry and carried her on down to the house. I wasn't supposed to know that Mama was going to have a baby in a couple of months. Boys aren't supposed to notice such things—not even boys who are past fifteen and so almost men.

That night we sat around the table as usual and read to each other. I read first. I was reading *Robinson Crusoe* for the second time since we came to the ranch and I had just got to where he was counting his wheat seeds and figuring out the best way to plant them. I like this part better than the long, close pages where he talks philosophy about being alone and uses big, hard to pronounce words. But sometimes, looking out across the plains and knowing there is only Father and Mama and Merry and me as far as my eye can reach, I knew how he felt. Well, maybe the new baby would be a boy.

I read pretty well. Father didn't have to correct my pronunciation very often. Then Mama read from *Sense and Sensibility* and I listened even if it was dull and sleepy to me. You never know when Father is going to ask you what a word means and you'd better have some idea!

Then Father read from *Plutarch's Lives,* which is fun sometimes, and we ended the evening with our Bible verses and prayers.

I was half asleep before the lamp was blown out, but I came wide awake when I heard Mama's low carrying voice.

"Maybe mining would have been better. This is good mining country."

"Mining isn't for me," said Father. "I want to take living things from the earth. I can feel that I'm part of growing things, and nothing speaks to me of God more than seeing a field ripening ready for harvest. To have food where only a few months before was only a handful of seed—and faith."

115

"But if we finally have to give the ranch up anyway—" Mama began faintly.

"We won't give it up." Father's voice was firm.

Father and I rode in the supply wagon from Raster Creek Mine over the plank bridge across the dwindling thread of the river to our last gate. I opened the gate, wrestling with the wire loop holding the top of the post, while Father thanked Mr. Tanker again for the newspapers he had brought us. "I'm sorry there is so little for you this time," he said, glancing back at the limp gunny sacks and half-empty boxes. "And it's the last of it all."

Mr. Tanker gathered up the reins. "Reckon now you're finding out why this is called Fool's Acres Ranch. You're the third one that's tried farming here. This is mining country. Never be nothing else. No steady water. Shame you didn't try in Las Lomitas Valley across the Coronas. Artesian wells there. Every ranch got two-three wells and ponds with trees and fish. Devil of a long way to drive for fresh garden truck, though. Maybe if we ever get to be a state instead of a Territory—"

Father and I watched him drive away, the wagon hidden in dust before it fairly started. We walked back to the planks across the stream and stopped to look at the few pools tied together with a thread of water brought down by Sometime Creek that was still flowing thinly. Father finally said, "What does Las Lomitas mean in English?" And I wrestled with what little Spanish I had learned until that evening at the table. I grinned to myself as I said, "It means 'The Little Hills,'" and watched Father, for a change, sort through past conversations to understand what I was talking about.

Mama's time was nearing and we were all worried. Though as I said, politeness had it that I wasn't supposed to know what was going on. But I knew about the long gap between Merry and me—almost fourteen years. Mama had borne and buried five children in that time. I had been as healthy as a horse, but after me none of the babies seemed able to live. Oh, maybe a week or so, at first, but finally only a faint gasp or two and the perfectly formed babies died. And all this back East where there were doctors and midwives and comfort. I guess Mama gave up after the fifth baby died, because none came along until after we moved to Fool's Acres. When we knew Merry was on the way, I could feel the suspense building up. I couldn't really remember all those other babies because I had been so young. They had come each year regularly after me. But it had been ten years between the last one and Merry. So when Merry was born out in the wilderness with Father for midwife, none of us dared breathe heavily for fear she'd die. But she was like me—big lungs, big appetite, and no idea of the difference between day and night.

Mama couldn't believe it for a long time and used to turn suddenly from her work and go touch Merry, just to be sure.

And now another baby was almost due and dust and desolation had settled down on the ranch and the whole area except for our orchard. Father explained the upside-down running of the rivers in a desert area that was, so far, keeping our young trees alive.

Anyway, there came a day that I took the water bucket and went to find a new dipping place because our usual one where the creek flowed into the river was so shallow even a tin dipper scooped up half sand at each attempt.

I had started up Sometime Creek hoping to find a deeper pool and had just stopped to lean in the thin hot shade of a boulder when it came.

Roaring! Blazing! A locomotive across the sky! A swept-back fountain of fire! A huge blazing something that flaked off flames as it roared away across Desolation Valley!

Scared half to death, I crouched against my boulder, my eyes blinking against the violence and thundering speed, my front hair fairly frizzling into beads from the impression of heat. Some of the flames that flaked off the main blaze blackened as they zigzagged down out of the sky like bits of charred paper from a bonfire. But some flakes darted away like angry hornets and one—one flame that kept its shape as it blackened and plunged like an arrow down through the roaring skies—headed straight for me! I threw my arms up to shield my face and felt something hit below me with a swishing thud that shook the hill and me.

And stillness came back to the ranch.

Only a brief stillness. I heard the crackle of flames and saw the smoke plume up! I scrambled downhill to the flat, seeing, like lightning, the flames racing across our cinder-dry fields, over our house, through our young orchard, across the crisped grass of Desolation Valley, leaving nothing but a smudge on the sky and hundreds of miles of scorched earth. It had happened other places in dry years.

I skidded to a stop in the edge of the flames, and, for lack of anything else I could do, I started stamping the small licking tongues of flame and kicking dirt over them.

117

"Barney!" I heard Father's shout. "Here's a shovel!"

I knuckled the smoke tears out of my eyes and stumbled to meet him as he ran toward me. "Keep it from going up the hill!" And he sped for the weed-grown edge of the alfalfa field.

Minutes later I plopped sand over the last smoking clump of grass and whacked it down with the back of my shovel. We were lucky. The fire area was pretty well contained between the rise of the hill and the foot of the field. I felt soot smudge across my face as I backhanded the sweat from my forehead. Father was out of my sight around the hill. Hefting the shovel, I started around to see if he needed my help. There was another plume of smoke! Alerted, I dropped the point of my shovel. Then I let it clatter to the ground as I fell to my knees.

A blackened hand reached up out of a charred bundle! Fingers spread convulsively, then clenched! And the bundle rolled jerkily.

"Father!" I yelled. "Father!" And grabbed for the smoldering blackness. I stripped away handsful of the scorching stuff and, by the time Father got there, my hands were scorching, too.

"Careful! Careful!" Father cautioned. "Here, let me." I moved back, nursing my blistered fingers. Father fumbled with the bundle and suddenly it ripped from one end to the other and he pulled out, like an ear of corn from its shuck, the twisting body of a person!

"He's badly burned," said Father. "Face and hands. Help me lift him." I helped Father get the body into his arms. He staggered and straightened. "Go tell your mother to brew up all the tea we have in the house—strong!"

I raced for the house, calling to Mama as soon as I saw her anxious face, "Father's all right! I'm all right! But we found someone burned! Father says to brew up all our tea—strong!"

Mama disappeared into the cabin and I heard the clatter of stove lids. I hurried back to Father and hovered anxiously as he laid his burden down on the little front porch. Carefully we peeled off the burned clothes until finally we had the body stripped down and put into an old nightshirt of Father's. The fire hadn't got to his legs nor to his body, but his left shoulder was charred—and his face! And arms! A tight cap thing that crumpled to flakes in our hands had saved most of his hair.

Father's mouth tightened. "His eyes," he said. "His eyes."

"Is he dead?" I whispered. Then I had my answer as one blackened hand lifted and wavered. I took it carefully in mine, my blisters drawing as I closed my fingers. The blackened head rolled and the mouth opened soundlessly and closed again, the face twisting with pain.

We worked over the boy—maybe some older than I—all afternoon. I brought silty half bucket after half bucket of water from the dipping place and strained it through muslin to get the silt out. We washed the boy until we located all his burns and flooded the places with strong cold tea and put tea packs across the worst ones. Mama worked along with us until the burden of the baby made her breathless and she had to stop.

She had given Merry a piece of bread and put her out in the little porch-side pen when we brought the boy in. Merry was crying now, her face dabbled with dirt, her bread rubbed in the sand. Mama gathered her up with an effort and smiled wearily at me over her head. "I'd better let her cry a little more, than her face will be wet enough for me to wash it clean!"

I guess I got enough tea on my hands working with the boy that my own burns weren't too bad. Blisters had formed and broken, but I only needed my right thumb and forefinger bandaged with strips from an old petticoat of Mama's. We left Mama with the boy, now clean and quiet on my cot, his face hidden under the wet packs, and went slowly down the path I had run so many times through the afternoon. We took our buckets on past the dipping place where a palm-sized puddle was all that was left of the water and retraced our steps to where the fire had been.

"A meteor?" I asked, looking across the ashy ground. "I always thought they came only at night."

"You haven't thought the matter over or you'd realize that night and day has nothing to do with meteors," said Father. "Is meteor the correct term?"

"How funny that that fellow happened to be at the exact place at the exact time the piece of the meteor hit here," I said, putting Father's question away for future reference.

" 'Odd' is a better word," Father corrected. "Where did the boy come from?"

I let my eyes sweep the whole wide horizon before us. No one on foot and alone could ever have made it from *any* where! Where had he come from? Up out of the ground? Down out of the sky?

"I guess he rode in on the meteor," I said, and grinned at the idea. Father blinked at me, but didn't return my smile.

"There's what set the fire," he said. We plopped through feathery ashes toward a black lump of something.

"Maybe we could send it to a museum," I suggested as we neared it. "Most meteors burn up before they hit the ground."

Father pushed the chunk with his foot. Flame flared briefly from under it as it rocked, and a clump of grass charred, the tips of the blades twisting and curling as they shriveled.

"Still hot," said Father, hunkering down on his heels beside it. He thumped it with a piece of rock. It clanged. "Metal!" His eyebrows raised. "Hollow!"

Carefully we probed with sticks from the hillside and thumped with rocks to keep our hands from the heat. We sat back and looked at each other. I felt a stir of something like fear inside me.

"It's—it's been made!" I said. "It's a long metal pipe or something! And I'll bet he was inside it! But how could he have been? How could he get so high in the sky as to come down like that? And if this little thing has been made, what was the big thing it came from?"

"I'll go get water," said Father, getting up and lifting the buckets. "Don't burn yourself any more."

I prodded the blackened metal. "Out of the sky," I said aloud. "As high and as fast as a meteor to get that hot. What was he doing up there?" My stick rocked the metal hulk and it rolled again. The split ends spread as it turned and a small square metal thing fell out into the ashes. I scraped it to one side and cautiously lifted it. The soot on it blackened my bandages and my palms. It looked like a box and was of a size that my two hands could hold. I looked at it, then suddenly overwhelmed and scared by the thought of roaring meteors and empty space and billowing grass fires, I scratched a hasty hole against a rock, shoved the box in, and stamped the earth over it. Then I went to meet Father and take one of the dripping buckets from him. We didn't look back at the crumpled metal thing behind us.

Father could hardly believe his eyes when he checked the boy's burns next morning. "They're healing already!" he said to Mama. "Look!"

I crowded closer to see, too, almost spilling the olive oil we were using on him. I looked at the boy's left wrist where I remembered a big, raw oozing place just where the cuff of

120

his clothes had ended. The wrist was dry now and covered with the faint pink of new skin.

"But his face," said Mama. "His poor face and his eyes!" She turned away, blinking tears, and reached for a cup of water. "He must have lots of liquids," she said, matter-of-factly.

"But if he's unconscious—" I clutched at my few lessons in home care of the sick.

Father lifted the boy's head and shoulders carefully, but even his care wasn't gentle enough. The boy moaned and murmured something. Father held the cup to his blistered mouth and tipped the water to the dry lips. There was a moment's pause, then the water was gulped eagerly and the boy murmured something again.

"More?" asked Father clearly. "More?"

The face rolled to him, then away, and there was no answer.

"He'll need much care for a while," Father said to Mama as they anointed his burns and put on fresh bandages. "Do you think you can manage under the circumstances?"

Mama nodded. "With Barney to help with the lifting."

"Sure I'll help," I said. Then to Father, "Should I have said meteorite?"

He nodded gravely. Then he said, "There are other planets." And left me to digest that one!

Father was spending his days digging for water in the river bottom. He had located one fair-sized pool that so far was keeping our livestock watered. We could still find drinking water for us up Sometime Creek. But the blue shimmer of the sky got more and more like heated metal. Heat was like a hand, pressing everything under the sky down into the powdery dead ground.

The boy was soon sitting up and eating a little of the little we had. But still no word from him, not a sound, even when we changed the dressings on his deeply charred left shoulder, or when the scabs across his left cheek cracked across and bled.

Then, one day, when all of us had been out of the cabin, straining our eyes prayerfully at the faint shadow of a cloud I thought I had seen over the distant Coronas, we came back, disheartened, to find the boy sitting in Mama's rocker by the window. But we had to carry him back to the cot. His feet seemed to have forgotten how to make steps.

Father looked down at him lying quietly on the cot. "If he

121

can make it to the window, he can begin to take care of his own needs. Mother is overburdened as it is."

So I was supposed to explain to him that there would be no more basin for his use, but that the chamberpot under the cot was for him! How do you explain to someone who can't see and doesn't talk and that you're not at all sure even hears you? I told Father I felt like a mother cat training a kitten.

"Come on, fellow," I said to him, glad we had the cabin to ourselves. I tugged at his unscarred right arm and urged him until, his breath catching between clenched teeth, he sat up and swung his feet over the cot edge. His hand went out to me and touched my cheek. His bandaged face turned to me and his hand faltered. Then quickly he traced my features— my eyes, my nose, my ears, across my head, and down to my shoulders. Then he sighed a relieved sigh and both his hands went out to rest briefly on my two shoulders. His mouth distorted in a ghost of a smile, and he touched my wrist.

"What did you expect?" I laughed. "Horns?"

Then I sat back, astonished, as his fingertip probed my temple just where I had visualized a horn, curled twice and with a shiny black tip.

"Well!" I said. "Mind reader!"

Just then Mama and Father came back into the cabin. The boy lay down slowly on the cot. Oh, well, the explanations could wait until the need arose.

We ate supper and I helped Mama clear up afterward. I was bringing the evening books to the pool of light on the table around the lamp when a movement from the cot drew my eyes. The boy was sitting on the edge, groping to come to his feet. I hurried to him, wondering what to do with Mama in the room, then as I reached for the boy's arm, I flicked a glance at Father. My mouth opened to wonder how I had known what the boy wanted and how *he* knew about the Little House outside. But a hand closed on my arm and I moved toward the door, with the boy. The door closed behind us with a *chuck*. Through the starry darkness we moved down the path to the Little House. He went in. I waited by the door. He emerged and we went back up the path and into the house. He eased himself down on the cot, turned his face away from the light, and became quiet.

I wet my astonished lips and looked at Father. His lips quirked. "You're some mother cat!" he said.

But Mama wasn't smiling as I slid into my place at the table. Her eyes were wide and dark. "But he *didn't* touch the floor, James! And he didn't take one single step! He—he floated!"

Not one single step! I swiftly reviewed our walk and I couldn't remember the rhythm of any steps at all—except my own. My eyes questioned Father, but he only said, "If he's to mingle with us, he must have a name."

"Timothy," I said instantly.

"Why Timothy?" asked Father.

"Because that's his name," I said blankly. "Timothy."

So after awhile Timothy came to the table to eat, dressed in some of my clothes. He was wonderfully at ease with knife and fork and spoon though his eyes were still scabbed over and hidden behind bandages. Merry babbled to him happily, whacking at him with her spoon, her few words meaning as much to him as all our talking, which apparently was nothing. He labored at making his feet take steps again and Mama didn't have his steplessness to worry about any more. He sat with us during our evening readings with no more response than if we sat in silence. Except that after the first evening he joined us, his right hand always made some sort of sign in the air at the beginning and end of our prayer time. His left arm wasn't working yet because of the deep burns on his shoulder.

Though Mama's worries over Timothy's steplessness were over, I had all kinds of worries to take my mind off the baking, dust-blown fields outside and even off the slow, heartbreaking curling of the leaves on our small orchard trees. I was beginning to hear things. I began to know when Timothy was thirsty or when he wanted to go to the Little House. I began to know what food he wanted more of and what he didn't care for. And it scared me. I didn't want to know—not without words.

Then Mama's time came. When at last the pains were coming pretty close together, Father sent me with Timothy and Merry away from the house, away from the task the two had before them. I knew the worry they had plaguing them besides the ordinary worry of childbirth and I prayed soundlessly as I lifted Merry and herded Timothy before me out to our orchard. And when my prayers tripped over their own anxiety and dissolved into wordlessness, I talked.

I told Timothy all about the ranch and the orchard and how Father had found me the other night pouring one of my cups of drinking water on the ground by my favorite smallest tree and how he'd told me it wouldn't help because the roots were too deep for so little water to reach. And I talked about all the little dead babies and how healthy Merry was but how worried we were for the new baby. And—and—well, I babbled until I ran out of words and sat under my dying favorite, shivering in the heat and hugging Merry. I pushed my face against her tumbled hair so no one could see my face puckering for tears. After I managed to snuff them back, I looked up and blinked.

Timothy was gone. He was streaking for the house, with not even one step! His feet were skimming above the furrows in the orchard. His arms were out in front of him like a sleepwalker but he was threading between the trees as though he could see. I started after him, fumbling with Merry, who was sliding out of my arms, leaving her crumpled clothes behind, her bare legs threshing and her cries muffling in her skirts. I snatched her up more securely and, shucking her dress down around her as I ran, dropped her into her porch-pen. Timothy was fumbling at the door latch. I opened it and we went into the house.

Father was working over a small bundle on the scrubbed kitchen table. Timothy crouched by Mama's bed, his hands holding one of hers tightly. Mama's breath was quieting down in shuddering gulps. She turned her face and pressed her eyes against her free wrist. "It hasn't cried," she whispered hopelessly. "Why doesn't it cry?"

Father turned from the table, his whole body drooping. "It never even breathed, Rachel. It's perfectly formed, but it never breathed at all."

Mama stared up at the roof of the cabin. "The clothes are in the trunk," she said quietly, "and a pink blanket."

And Father sent me out to find a burying place.

The light went out of our house. We went the weary round of things that had to be done to keep living and even Merry stood quietly, her hands on the top board of her porch-pen, her wide eyes barely overtopping it, and stared out at the hillside for long stretches of time. And Father, who had always been an unmoved mainstay no matter what happened, was broken, silent and uncommunicating.

We seldom mentioned the baby. We had buried my hoped-for little brother up on the hill under a scrub oak. When Mama was well enough, we all went up there and read the service for the dead, but no one cried as we stood around the tiny, powdery-dry, naked little grave. Timothy held Mama's hand all the way up there and all the way back. And Mama half smiled at him when we got back to the house.

124

Father said quietly, as he laid down the prayer book, "Why must he hang onto you?" Mama and I were startled at his tone of voice.

"But, James," Mama protested. "He's blind!"

"How many things has he bumped into since he's been up and around?" asked Father. "How often has he spilled food or groped for a chair?" He turned a bitter face toward Timothy. "And hanging onto you, he doesn't have to see—" Father broke off and turned to the window.

"James," Mama went to him quickly, "don't make Timothy a whipping boy for your sorrow. God gave him into our keeping. 'The Lord giveth—' "

"I'm sorry, Rachel." Father gathered Mama closely with one arm. "This 'taking away' period is bad. Not only the baby—"

"I know," said Mama. "But when Timothy touches me, the sorrow is lessened and I can feel the joy—"

"Joy!" Father spun Mama away from his shoulder. I shook for the seldom seen anger in his face.

"James!" said Mama. " 'Weeping may endure for a night but joy cometh in the morning.' Let Timothy touch your hand—"

Father left the house without a glance at any of us. He gathered up Merry from the porch-pen and trudged away through the dying orchard.

That night, while Mama was reading, I got up to get Timothy a drink.

"You're interrupting your mother," said Father quietly.

"I'm sorry," I said, "Timothy is thirsty."

"Sit down," said Father ominously. I sat.

When our evening was finished, I asked, "May I get him a drink now?"

Father slowly sat down again at the table. "How do you know he wants a drink?" he asked.

"I—I just know," I stumbled, watching Timmy leave the table. "It comes into my mind."

"Comes into your mind." Father seemed to lay the words out on the table in front of him and look at them. After a silence he said, "How does it come into your mind? Does it say, Timothy is thirsty—he wants a drink?"

"No," I said, unhappily, looking at Father's lamplight-flooded face, wondering if he was, for the first time in my life, ridiculing me. "There aren't any words. Only a feeling—only a *knowing* that he's thirsty."

"And you." His face shadowed as he turned it to look at

Mama. "When he touches your hand, are there words—Joy, have joy?"

"No," said Mama. "Only the feeling that God is over all and that sorrow is a shadow and that—that the baby was called back into the Presence."

Father turned back to me. "If Timothy can make you know he is thirsty, he can tell you he is. You are not to give him a drink until he asks for it."

"But, Father! He can't talk!" I protested.

"He has a voice," said Father. "He hasn't talked since he became conscious after the fire, but he said some words before then. Not our words, but words. If he can be blind and still not stumble, if he can comfort a bereaved mother by the touch of the hand, if he can make you know he's thirsty, he can talk."

I didn't argue. You don't with Father. They started getting ready for bed. I went to Timothy and sat beside him on the cot. He didn't put out his hand for the cup of water he wanted. He knew I didn't have it.

"You have to ask for it," I told him. "You have to say you're thirsty." His blind face turned to me and two of his fingers touched my wrist. I suddenly realized that this was something he often did lately. Maybe being blind he could hear better by touching me. I felt the thought was foolish before I finished it. But I said again, "You have to ask for it. You must tell me, 'I'm thirsty. I want a drink, please.' You must talk."

Timothy turned from me and lay down on the cot. Mama sighed sharply. Father blew out the lamp, leaving me in the dark to spread my pallet on the floor and go to bed.

The next morning we were all up before sunrise. Father had all our good barrels loaded on the hayrack and was going to Tolliver's Wells for water. He and Mama counted out our small supply of cash with tight lips and few words. In times like these water was gold. And what would we do when we had no more money?

We prayed together before Father left, and the house felt shadowy and empty with him gone. We pushed our breakfasts around our plates and then put them away for lunch.

What is there to do on a ranch that is almost dead? I took *Pilgrim's Progress* to the corner of the front porch and sat with it on my lap and stared across the yard without seeing anything, sinking into my own Slough of Despond. I took a deep breath and roused a little as Timothy came out onto the porch. He had a cup in his hand.

126

"I'm thirsty," he said slowly but distinctly, "I want a drink, please."

I scrambled awkwardly to my feet and took the cup from him. Mama came to the door. "What did you say, Barney?"

"I didn't say anything," I said, my grin almost splitting my face. "Timmy did!" We went into the house and I dipped a cup of water for Timmy.

"Thank you," he said and drank it all. Then he put the cup down by the bucket and went back to the porch.

"He could have got the drink himself," Mama said wonderingly, "he can find his way around. And yet he waited, thirsty, until he could ask you for it."

"I guess he knows he has to mind Father, too!" I laughed shakily.

It was a two days' round trip to Tolliver's Wells and the first day stretched out endlessly. In the heat of noon, I slept, heavily and unrefreshingly. I woke, drenched with sweat, my tongue swollen and dry from sleeping with my mouth open. I sat up, my head swimming and my heart thumping audibly in my ears. Merry and Mama were still sleeping on the big bed, a mosquito bar over them to keep the flies off. I wallowed my dry tongue and swallowed. Then I staggered up from my pallet. Where was Timothy?

Maybe he had gone to the Little House by himself. I looked out the window. He wasn't in sight and the door swung half open. I waited a minute but he didn't come out. Where was Timothy!

I stumbled out onto the front porch and looked around. No Timothy. I started for the barn, rounding the corner of the house, and there he was! He was sitting on the ground, half in the sun, half in the shade of the house. He had the cup in one hand and the fingers of the other hand were splashing in the water. His blind face was intent.

"Timmy!" I cried, and he looked up with a start, water slopping. "Daggone! You had me scared stiff! What are you doing with that water?" I slid to a seat beside him. His two wet fingers touched my wrist without fumbling for it. "We don't have enough water to play with it!"

He turned his face down toward the cup, then, turning, he poured the water carefully at the bottom of the last geranium left alive of all Mama had taken such tender care of.

Then, with my help, he got to his feet and because I could tell what he wanted and because he said, "Walk!" we walked. In all that sun and dust we walked. He led me. I only went along for the exercise and to steer him clear of cactus and holes in the way. Back and forth we went, back and forth. To the hill in front of the house, back to the house. To the hill again, a little farther along. Back to the yard, missing the house about ten feet. Finally, halfway through the weary monotony of the afternoon, I realized that Timmy was covering a wide area of land in ten-foot swaths, back and forth, farther and farther from the house.

By evening we were both exhausted and only one of Timmy's feet was even trying to touch the ground. The other one didn't bother to try to step. Finally Timmy said, "I'm thirsty. I want a drink, please." And we went back to the house.

Next morning I woke to see Timmy paddling in another cup of water and all morning we covered the area on the other side of the house, back and forth, back and forth.

"What *are* you doing?" Mama had asked.

"I don't know," I said. "It's Timmy's idea." And Timmy said nothing.

When the shadows got short under the bushes we went back to the porch and sat down on the steps, Merry gurgling at us from her porch-pen.

"I'm thirsty. I want a drink, please," said Timmy again, and I brought him his drink. "Thank you," he said, touching my wrist. "It's sure hot!"

"It sure is!" I answered, startled by his new phrase. He drank slowly and poured the last drop into his palm. He put the tin cup down on the porch by him and worked the fingers and thumb of his other hand in the dampness of his palm, his face intent and listening-like under his bandaged eyes.

Then his fingers were quiet and his face turned toward Merry. He got up and took the two steps to the porch-pen. He reached for Merry, his face turned to me. I moved closer and he touched my wrist. I lifted Merry out of the pen and put her on the porch. I lifted the pen, which was just a hollow square of wooden rails fastened together, and set it up on the porch, too.

Timmy sat down slowly on the spot where the pen had been. He scraped the dirt into a heap, then set it to one side and scraped again. Seeing that he was absorbed for a while, I took Merry in to be cleaned up for dinner and came back later to see what Timmy was doing. He was still scraping and had quite a hole by now, but the dirt was stacked too close so that it kept sliding back into the hole. I scraped it all away from the edge, then took his right arm and said, "Time to eat, Timmy. Come on."

He ate and went back to the hole he had started. Seeing that he meant to go on digging, I gave him a big old spoon Merry sometimes played with and a knife with a broken blade, to save his hands.

All afternoon he dug with the tools and scooped the dirt out. And dug again. By evening he had enlarged the hole until he was sitting in it, shoulder deep.

Mama stood on the porch, sagging under the weight of Merry who was astride her hip and said, "He's ruining the front lawn." Then she laughed. "Front lawn! Ruining it!" And she laughed again, just this side of tears.

Later that evening, when what cooling-off ever came was coming over the ranch, we heard the jingle of harness and then the creak of the hayrack and the plop of horses' hooves in the dust.

Father was home! We ran to meet him at our gate, suddenly conscious of how out-of-step everything had been without him. I opened the gate and dragged the four strands wide to let the wagon through.

Father's face was dust-coated and the dust did not crease into smiles for us. His hugs were almost desperate. I looked into the back of the wagon, as he and Mama murmured together. Only half the barrels were filled.

"Didn't we have enough money?" I asked, wondering how people could insist on hard metal in exchange for life.

"They didn't have water enough," said Father. "Others were waiting, too. This is the last they can let us have."

We took care of the horses but left the water barrels on the wagon. That was as good a place as any and the shelter of the barn would keep it—well, not cool maybe, but below the boiling point.

It wasn't until we started back to the house that we thought of Timmy. We saw a head rising from the hole Timmy was digging and Father drew back his foot to keep it from being covered with a handful of dirt.

"What's going on?" he asked, letting his tiredness and discouragement sharpen his voice.

"Timmy's digging," I said, stating the obvious, which was all I could do.

"Can't he find a better place than that?" And Father stomped into the house. I called Timmy and helped him up out of the hole. He was dirt-covered from head to heels and Father was almost through with his supper before I got Timmy cleaned up enough to come inside.

We sat around the table, not even reading, and talked. Timmy sat close to me, his fingers on my wrist.

"Maybe the ponds will fill a little while we're using up this water," said Mama, hopelessly.

Father was silent and I stared at the table, seeing the buckets of water Prince and Nig had sucked up so quickly that evening.

"We'd better be deciding where to go," said Father. "When the water's all gone—" His face shut down, bleak and still, and he opened the Bible at random, missing our marker by half the book. He looked down and read, " 'For in the wilderness shall waters break out, and streams in the desert.' " He clapped the book shut and sat, his elbows on each side of the book, his face buried in his two hands, this last rubbing of salt in the wound almost too much to bear.

I touched Timmy and we crept to bed.

I woke in the night, hearing a noise. My hand went up to the cot and I struggled upright. Timmy was gone. I scrambled to the door and looked out. Timmy was in the hole, digging. At least I guess he was. There was a scraping sound for a while then a—a wad of dirt would sail slowly up out of the hole and fall far enough from the edge that it couldn't run down in again. I watched the dirt sail up twice more, then there was a clatter and three big rocks sailed up. They hovered a little above the mound of dirt then thumped down—one of them on my bare foot.

I was hopping around, nursing my foot in my hands, when I looked up and saw Father standing stern and tall on the porch.

"What's going on?" He repeated his earlier question. The sound of digging below stopped. So did my breath for a moment.

"Timmy's digging," I said, as I had before.

"At night? What for?" Father asked.

"He can't see, night or light," I said, "but I don't know why he's digging."

"Get him out of there," said Father. "This is no time for nonsense."

I went to the edge of the hole. Timmy's face was a pale blur below. "He's too far down," I said. "I'll need a ladder."

"He got down there," said Father unreasonably, "let him get out!"

"Timmy!" I called down to him. "Father says come up!"

There was a hesitating scuffle, then Timmy came up! Straight up! As though something were lifting him! He came straight up out of the hole and hovered as the rocks had, then he moved through the air and landed on the porch so close to Father that he stumbled back a couple of steps.

"Father!" My voice shook with terror.

Father turned and went into the house. He lighted the lamp, the upflare of the flame before he put the chimney on showed the deep furrows down his cheeks. I prodded Timmy and we sat on the bench across the table from Father.

"Why is he digging?" Father asked again. "Since he responds to you, ask him."

I reached out, half afraid, and touched Timmy's wrist. "Why are you digging?" I asked. "Father wants to know."

Timmy's mouth moved and he seemed to be trying different words with his lips. Then he smiled, the first truly smile I'd ever seen on his face. " 'Shall waters break out and streams in the desert,' " he said happily.

"That's no answer!" Father exclaimed, stung by having those unfitting words flung back at him. "No more digging. Tell him so."

I felt Timmy's wrist throb protestingly and his face turned to me, troubled.

"Why no digging? What harm's he doing?" My voice sounded strange in my own ears and the pit of my stomach was ice. For the first time in my life I was standing up to Father! That didn't shake me as much as the fact that for the first time in my life I was seriously questioning his judgment.

"No digging because I said no digging!" said Father, anger whitening his face, his fists clenching on the table.

"Father," I swallowed with difficulty, "I think Timmy's looking for water. He—he touched water before he started digging. He felt it. We—we went all over the place before he settled on where he's digging. Father, what if he's a—a dowser? What if he knows where water is? He's different—"

I was afraid to look at Father. I kept my eyes on my own hand where Timmy's fingers rested on my wrist.

"Maybe if we helped him dig—" I faltered and stopped, seeing the stones come up and hover and fall. "He has only Merry's spoon and an old knife."

"And he dug that deep!" thundered Father.

"Yes," I said. "All by himself."

"Nonsense!" Father's voice was flat. "There's no water anywhere around here. You saw me digging for water for the stock. We're not in Las Lomitas. There will be no more digging."

"Why not!" I was standing now, my own fists on the table

131

as I leaned forward. I could feel my eyes blaze as Father's do sometimes. "What harm is he doing? What's wrong with his keeping busy while we sit around waiting to dry up and blow away? What's wrong with hoping!"

Father and I glared at each other until his eyes dropped. Then mine filled with tears and I dropped back on the bench and buried my face in my arms. I cried as if I were no older than Merry. My chest was heavy with sorrow for this first real anger I had ever felt toward Father, with the shouting and the glaring, and especially for his eyes falling before mine.

Then I felt his hand heavy on my shoulder. He had circled the table to me. "Go to bed now," he said quietly. "Tomorrow is another day."

"Oh, Father!" I turned and clung to his waist, my face tight against him, his hand on my head. Then I got up and took Timmy back to the cot and we went to bed again.

Next morning, as though it was our usual task, Father got out the shovels and rigged up a bucket on a rope and he and I and Timmy worked in the well. We called it a well now, instead of a hole, maybe to bolster our hopes.

By evening we had it down a good twelve feet, still not finding much except hard, packed-down river silt and an occasional clump of round river rocks. Our ladder was barely long enough to help us scramble up out and the edges of the hole were crumbly and sifted off under the weight of our knees.

I climbed out. Father set the bucket aside and eased his palms against his hips. Timmy was still in the well, kneeling and feeling the bottom.

"Timmy!" I called. "Come on up. Time to quit!" His face turned up to me but still he knelt there and I found myself gingerly groping for the first rung of the ladder below the rim of the well.

"Timmy wants me to look at something," I said up to Father's questioning face. I climbed down and knelt by Timmy. My hands followed his tracing hands and I looked up and said, "Father!" with such desolation in my voice that he edged over the rim and came down, too.

We traced it again and again. There was solid rock, no matter which way we brushed the dirt, no matter how far we poked into the sides of the well. We were down to bedrock. We were stopped.

We climbed soberly up out of the well. Father boosted me up over the rim and I braced myself and gave him a hand

132

up. Timmy came up. There was no jarring of his feet on the ladder, but he came up. I didn't look at him.

The three of us stood there, ankle-deep in dust. Then Timmy put his hands out, one hand to Father's shoulder and one to mine. " '*Shall* waters break out and streams in the desert,' " he said carefully and emphatically.

"Parrot!" said Father bitterly, turning away.

"If the water is *under* the stone!" I cried. "Father, we blasted out the mesquite stumps in the far pasture. Can't we blast the stone—"

Father's steps were long and swinging as he hurried to the barn. "I haven't ever done this except with stumps," he said. He sent Mama and Merry out behind the barn. He made Timmy and me stay away as he worked in the bottom of the well, then he scrambled up the ladder and I ran out to help pull it up out of the well and we all retreated behind the barn, too.

Timmy clung to my wrist and when the blast came, he cried out something I couldn't understand and wouldn't come with us back to the well. He crouched behind the barn, his face to his knees, his hands clasped over the top of his head.

We looked at the well. It was a dimple in the front yard. The sides had caved in. There was nothing to show for all our labor but the stacked-up dirt beside the dimple, our ladder, and a bucket with a rope tied to the bale. We watched as clod broke loose at the top of the dimple and started a trickle of dirt as it rolled dustily down into the hole.

" 'And streams in the desert,' " said Father, turning away.

I picked up the bucket, dumped out a splinter of stone, and put the bucket carefully on the edge of the porch.

"Supper," said Mama quietly, sagging under Merry's weight.

I went and got Timmy. He came willingly enough. He paused by the dimple in the front yard, his hand on my wrist, then went with me into the shadowy cabin.

After supper I brought our evening books to the table, but Timmy put out seeking hands and gathered them to him. He put both hands, lapping over each other, across the top of the stack and leaned his chin on them, his face below the bandage thoughtful and still.

"I have words enough now," he said slowly. "I have been learning them as fast as I could. Maybe I will not have them always right, but I must talk now. You must not go away, because there *is* water."

133

Father closed his astonished mouth and said wearily, "So you have been making fools of us all this time!"

Timmy's fingers went to my wrist in the pause that followed Father's words. "I have not made fools of you," Timmy went on. "I could not speak to anyone but Barney without words, and I must touch him to tell and to understand. I had to wait to learn your words. It is a new language."

"Where are you from?" I asked eagerly, pulling the patient cork out of my curiosity. "How did you get out there in the pasture? What is in the—" Just in time I remembered that I was the only one who knew about the charred box.

"My *cahilla!*" cried Timmy—then he shook his head at me and addressed himself to Father. "I'm not sure how to tell you so you will believe. I don't know how far your knowledge—"

"Father's smarter than anyone in the whole Territory!" I cried.

"The Territory—" Timmy paused, measuring Territory. "I was thinking of your world—this world—"

"There are other planets—" I repeated Father's puzzling words.

"Then you *do* know other planets," said Timmy. "Do you—" he groped for a word. "Do you transport yourself and things in the sky?"

Father stirred. "Do we have flying machines?" he asked. "No, not yet. We have balloons—"

Timmy's fingers were on my wrist again. He sighed. "Then I must just tell and if you do not know, you must believe only because I tell. I tell only to make you know there *is* water and you must stay.

"My world is another planet. It *was* another planet. It is broken in space now, all to pieces, shaking and roaring and fire—and all gone." His blind face looked on desolation and his lips tightened. I felt hairs crisp along my neck. As long as he touched my wrist I could see! I couldn't tell you what all I saw because lots of it had no words I knew to put to it, but I saw!

"We had ships for going in Space," he said. I saw them, needlesharp and shining, pointing at the sky and the heavy red-lit clouds. "We went into space before our Home broke. Our Home! Our—Home." His voice broke and he leaned his cheek on the stack of books. Then he straightened again.

"We came to your world. We did not know of it before. We came far, far. At the last we came too fast. We are not Space travelers. The big ship that found your world got too hot. We had to leave it in our life-slips, each by himself. The life-slips got hot, too. I was burning! I lost control of my life-slip. I fell—" He put his hands to his bandages. "I think maybe I will never see this new world."

"Then there are others, like you, here on Earth," said Father slowly.

"Unless they all died in the landing," said Timmy. "There were many on the big ship."

"I saw little things shoot off the big thing!" I cried, excited. "I thought they were pieces breaking off only they—they *went* instead of falling!"

"Praise to the Presence, the Name, and the Power!" said Timmy, his right hand sketching his sign in the air, then dropping to my wrist again.

"Maybe some still live. Maybe my family. Maybe Lytha—"

I stared, fascinated, as I saw Lytha, dark hair swinging, smiling back over her shoulder, her arms full of flowers whose centers glowed like little lights. Daggone, I thought, Daggone! She sure isn't his Merry!

"Your story is most interesting," said Father, "and it opens vistas we haven't begun to explore yet, but what bearing has all this on our water problem?"

"We can do things you seem not able to do," said Timmy. "You must always touch the ground to go, and lift things with tools or hands, and know only because you touch and see. We can know without touching and seeing. We can find people and metals and water—we can find almost anything that we know, if it is near us. I have not been trained to be a finder, but I have studied the feel of water and the—the—what it is made of—"

"The composition," Father supplied the word.

"The composition of water," said Timmy. "And Barney and I explored much of the farm. I found the water here by the house."

"We dug," said Father. "How far down is the water?"

"I am not trained," said Timmy humbly. "I only know it is there. It is water that you think of when you say 'Las Lomitas.' It is not a dipping place or—or a pool. It is going. It is pushing hard. It is cold." He shivered a little.

"It is probably three hundred feet down," said Father. "There has never been an artesian well this side of the Coronas."

"It is close enough for me to find," said Timmy. "Will you wait?"

"Until our water is gone," said Father. "And until we have decided where to go.

"Now it's time for bed." Father took the Bible from the stack of books. He thumbed back from our place to Psalms and read the "When I consider the heavens" one. As I listened, all at once the tight little world I knew, overtopped by the tight little Heaven I wondered about, suddenly split right down the middle and stretched and grew and filled with such a glory that I was scared and grabbed the edge of the table. If Timmy had come from another planet so far away that it wasn't even one we had a name for—! I knew that never again would my mind think it could measure the world—or my imagination, the extent of God's creation!

I was just dropping off the edge of waking after tumbling and tossing for what seemed like hours, when I heard Timmy.

"Barney," he whispered, not being able to reach my wrist. "My *cahilla*— You found my *cahilla?*"

"Your what?" I asked, sitting up in bed and meeting his groping hands. "Oh! That box thing. Yeah, I'll get it for you in the morning."

"Not tonight?" asked Timmy, wistfully. "It is all I have left of the Home. The only personal things we had room for—"

"I can't find it tonight," I said. "I buried it by a rock. I couldn't find it in the dark. Besides, Father'd hear us go, if we tried to leave now. Go to sleep. It must be near morning."

"Oh yes," sighed Timmy, "oh, yes." And he lay back down. "Sleep well."

And I did, going out like a lamp blown out, and dreamed wild, exciting dreams about riding astride ships that went sailless across waterless oceans of nothingness and burned with white hot fury that woke me up to full morning light and Merry bouncing happily on my stomach.

After breakfast, Mama carefully oiled Timmy's scabs again. "I'm almost out of bandages," she said.

"If you don't mind having to see," said Timmy, "don't bandage me again. Maybe the light will come through."

We went out and looked at the dimple by the porch. It had subsided farther and was a bowl-shaped place now, maybe waist-deep to me.

"Think it'll do any good to dig it out again?" I asked Father.

136

"I doubt it," he answered heavily. "Apparently I don't know how to set a charge to break the bedrock. How do we know we could break it anyway? It could be a mile thick right here." It seemed to me that Father was talking to me more like to a man than to a boy. Maybe I wasn't a boy any more!

"The water is there," said Timmy. "If only I could *'platt'*—" His hand groped in the sun and it streamed through his fingers for a minute like sun through a knothole in a dusty room. I absently picked up the piece of stone I had dumped from the bucket last evening. I fingered it and said, "Ouch!" I had jabbed myself on its sharp point. Sharp point!

"Look," I said, holding it out to Father. "This is broken! All the other rocks we found were round river rocks. Our blasting broke *something!*"

"Yes." Father took the splinter from me. "But where's the water?"

Timmy and I left Father looking at the well and went out to the foot of the field where the fire had been. I located the rock where I had buried the box. It was only a couple of inches down—barely covered. I scratched it out for him. "Wait," I said, "it's all black. Let me wipe it off first." I rubbed it in a sand patch and the black all rubbed off except in the deep lines of the design that covered all sides of it. I put it in his eager hands.

He flipped it around until it fitted his two hands with his thumbs touching in front. Then I guess he must have thought at it because he didn't do anything else but all at once it opened, cleanly, from his thumbs up.

He sat there on a rock in the sun and felt the things that were in the box. I couldn't tell you what any of them were except what looked like a piece of ribbon, and a withered flower. He finally closed the box. He slid to his knees beside the rock and hid his face on his arms. He sat there a long time. When he finally lifted his face, it was dry, but his sleeves were wet. I've seen Mama's sleeves like that after she has looked at things in the little black trunk of hers.

"Will you put it back in the ground?" he asked. "There is no place for it in the house. It will be safe here."

So I buried the box again and we went back to the house.

Father had dug a little, but he said, "It's no use. The blast loosened the ground all around and it won't even hold the shape of a well any more."

We talked off and on all day about where to go from here, moneyless and perilously short of provisions. Mama wanted so much to go back to our old home that she couldn't talk about it, but Father wanted to go on, pushing West again. *I* wanted to stay where we were—with plenty of water. I wanted to see that tide of Time sweep one century away and start another across Desolation Valley! There would be a sight for you!

We began to pack that afternoon because the barrels were emptying fast and the pools were damp, curling cakes of mud in the hot sun. All we could take was what we could load on the hayrack. Father had traded the wagon we came West in for farm machinery and a set of washtubs. We'd have to leave the machinery either to rust there or for us to come back for.

Mama took Merry that evening and climbed the hill to the little grave under the scrub oak. She sat there a long time with her back to the sun, her wistful face in the shadow. She came back in silence, Merry heavily sleepy in her arms.

After we had gone to bed, Timmy groped for my wrist. "You do have a satellite to your earth, don't you?" he asked. His question was without words.

"A satellite?" Someone turned restlessly on the big bed when I hissed my question.

"Yes," he answered. "A smaller world that goes around and is bright at night."

"Oh," I breathed. "You mean the moon. Yes, we have a moon but it's not very bright now. There was only a sliver showing just after sunset." I felt Timmy sag. "Why?"

"We can do large things with sunlight and moonlight together," came his answer. "I hoped that at sunrise tomorrow—"

"At sunrise tomorrow, we'll be finishing our packing," I said. "Go to sleep."

"Then I must do without," he went on, not hearing me. "Barney, if I am Called, will you keep my *cahilla* until someone asks for it? If they ask, it is my People. Then they will know I am gone."

"Called?" I asked. "What do you mean?"

"As the baby was," he said softly. "Called back into the Presence from which we came. If I must lift with my own strength alone, I may not have enough, so will you keep my *cahilla?*"

"Yes," I promised, not knowing what he was talking about. "I'll keep it."

"Good. Sleep well," he said, and again waking went out of me like a lamp blown out.

138

All night long I dreamed of storms and earthquakes and floods and tornadoes all going past me—fast! Then I was lying half awake, afraid to open my eyes for fear some of my dreaming might be true. And suddenly, it was!

I clutched my pallet as the floor humped, snapping and groaning, and flopped flat again. I heard our breakfast pots and pans banging on the shelf and then falling with a clatter. Mama called, her voice heavy with sleep and fear, "James! James!"

I reached for Timmy, but the floor humped again and dust rolled in through the pale squares of the windows and I coughed as I came to my knees. There was a crash of something heavy falling on the roof and rolling off. And a sharp hissing sound. Timmy wasn't in bed. Father was trying to find his shoes. The hissing noise got louder and louder until it was a burbling roar. Then there was a rumble and something banged the front of the house so hard I heard the porch splinter. Then there was a lot of silence.

I crept on all fours across the floor. Where was Timmy? I could see the front door hanging at a crazy angle on one hinge. I crept toward it.

My hands splashed! I paused, confused, and started on again. I was crawling in water! "Father!" My voice was a croak from the dust and shock. "Father! It's water!"

And Father was suddenly there, lifting me to my feet. We stumbled together to the front door. There was a huge slab of rock poking a hole in the siding of the house, crushing the broken porch under its weight. We edged around it, ankle-deep in water, and saw in the gray light of early dawn our whole front yard awash from hill to porch. Where the well had been was a moving hump of water that worked away busily, becoming larger and larger as we watched.

"Water!" said Father. "The water has broken through!"

"Where's Timmy?" I said. *"Where's Timmy!"* I yelled and started to splash out into the yard.

"Watch out!" warned Father. "It's dangerous! All this rock came out of there!" We skirted the front yard searching the surface of the rising water, thinking every shadow might be Timmy.

We found him on the far side of the house, floating quietly, face up in a rising pool of water, his face a bleeding mass of mud and raw flesh.

I reached him first, floundering through the water to him. I lifted his shoulders and tried to see in the dawn light if he was still breathing. Father reached us and we lifted Timmy to dry land.

"He's alive!" said Father. "His face—it's just the scabs scraped off."

"Help me get him in the house," I said, beginning to lift him.

"Better be the barn," said Father. "The water's still rising." It had crept up to us already and seeped under Timmy again. We carried him to the barn and I stayed with him while Father went back for Merry and Mama.

It was lucky that most of our things had been packed on the hayrack the night before. After Mama, a shawl thrown over her nightgown and all our day clothes grabbed up in her arms, came wading out with Father, who was carrying Merry and our lamp, I gave Timmy into her care and went back with Father again and again to finish emptying the cabin of our possessions.

Already the huge rock had gone on down through the porch and disappeared into the growing pond of water in the front yard. The house was dipping to the weight of our steps as though it might float off the minute we left. Father got a rope from the wagon and tied it through the broken corner of the house and tethered it to the barn. "No use losing the lumber if we don't have to," he said.

By the time the sun was fully up, the house was floating off its foundation rocks. There was a pond filling all the house yard, back and front, extending along the hill, up to the dipping place, and turning into a narrow stream going the other way, following the hill for a while then dividing our dying orchard and flowing down toward the dry river bed. Father and I pulled the house slowly over toward the barn until it grated solid ground again.

Mama had cleaned Timmy up. He didn't seem to be hurt except for his face and shoulder being peeled raw. She put olive oil on him again and used one of Merry's petticoats to bandage his face. He lay deeply unconscious all of that day while we watched the miracle of water growing in a dry land. The pond finally didn't grow any wider, but the stream widened and deepened, taking three of our dead trees down to the river. The water was clearing now and was deep enough over the spring that it didn't bubble any more that we could see. There was only a shivering of the surface so that circles ran out to the edge of the pond, one after another.

Father went down with a bucket and brought it back

brimming over. We drank the cold, cold water and Mama made a pack to put on Timmy's head.

Timmy stirred but he didn't waken. It wasn't until evening when we were settling down to a scratch-meal in the barn that we began to realize what had happened.

"We have water!" Father cried suddenly. "Streams in the desert!"

"It's an artesian well, isn't it!" I asked. "Like at Las Lomitas? It'll go on flowing from here on out, won't it?"

"That remains to be seen," Father said. "But it looks like a good one. Tomorrow I must ride to Tolliver's Wells and tell them we have water. They must be almost out by now!"

"Then we don't have to move?" I asked.

"Not as long as we have water," said Father. "I wonder if we have growing time enough to put in a kitchen garden—"

I turned quickly. Timmy was moving. His hands were on the bandage, exploring it cautiously.

"Timmy," I reached for his wrist. "It's all right, Timmy. You just got peeled raw. We had to bandage you again."

"The—the water—" His voice was barely audible.

"It's all over the place!" I said. "It's floated the house off the foundations and you should see the pond! And the stream! And it's cold!"

"I'm thirsty," he said. "I want a drink, please."

He drained the cup of cold water and his lips turned upward in a ghost of a smile. "Shall waters break out!"

"Plenty of water," I laughed. Then I sobered. "What were you doing out in it, anyway?"

Mama and Father were sitting on the floor beside us now.

"I had to lift the dirt out," he said, touching my wrist. "All night I lifted. It was hard to hold back the loose dirt so it wouldn't slide back into the hole. I sat on the porch and lifted the dirt until the rock was there." He sighed and was silent for a minute. "I was not sure I had strength enough. The rock was cracked and I could feel the water pushing, hard, hard, under. I had to break the rock enough to let the water start through. It wouldn't break! I called on the Power again and tried and tried. Finally a piece came loose and flew up. The force of the water—it was like—like—blasting. I had no strength left. I went unconscious."

"You dug all that out alone!" Father took one of Timmy's hands and looked at the smooth palm.

"We do not always have to touch to lift and break," said

141

Timmy. "But to do it for long and heavy takes much strength." His head rolled weakly.

"Thank you, Timothy," said Father. "Thank you for the well."

So that's why we didn't move. That's why Promise Pond is here to keep the ranch green. That's why this isn't Fool's Acres any more but Full Acres. That's why *Cahilla* Creek puzzles people who try to make it Spanish. Even Father doesn't know why Timmy and I named the stream *Cahilla*. The pond had almost swallowed up the little box before we remembered it.

That's why the main road across Desolation Valley goes through our ranch now for the sweetest, coldest water in the Territory. That's why our big new house is built among the young black walnut and weeping willow trees that surround the pond. That's why it has geraniums windowsill high along one wall. That's why our orchard has begun to bear enough to start being a cash crop.

And that's why, too, that one day a wagon coming from the far side of Desolation Valley made camp on the camping grounds below the pond.

We went down to see the people after supper to exchange news. Timmy's eyes were open now, but only light came into them, not enough to see by.

The lady of the wagon tried not to look at the deep scars on the side of Timmy's face as her man and we men talked together. She listened a little too openly to Timmy's part of the conversation and said softly to Mama, her whisper spraying juicily, "He your boy?"

"Yes, our boy," said Mama, "but not born to us."

"Oh," said the woman. "I thought be talked kinda foreign." Her voice was critical. "Seems like we're gettin' overrun with foreigners. Like that sassy girl in Margin."

"Oh?" Mama fished Merry out from under the wagon by her dress tail.

"Yes," said the woman. "She talks foreign too, though they say not as much as she used to. Oh, them foreigners are smart enough! Her aunt says she was sick and had to learn to talk all over again, that's why she sounds like that." The woman leaned confidingly toward Mama, lowering her voice. "But I heard in a roundabout way that there's something queer about that girl. I don't think she's really their niece. I

142

think she came from somewhere else. I think she's really a foreigner!"

"Oh?" said Mama, quite unimpressed and a little bored.

"They say she does funny things and Heaven knows her name's funny enough. I *ask* you! Doesn't the way these foreigners push themselves in—"

"Where did your folks come from?" asked Mama, vexed by the voice the lady used for "foreigner."

The lady reddened. "*I'm* native born!" she said, tossing her head. "Just because my parents— It isn't as though England was—" She pinched her lips together. "Abigail Johnson for a name is a far cry from Marnie Lytha Something-or-other!"

"Lytha!" I heard Timmy's cry without words. *Lytha?* He stumbled toward the woman, for once his feet unsure. She put out a hasty hand to fend him off and her face drew up with distaste.

"Watch out!" she cried sharply. "Watch where you're going!"

"He's blind," Mama said softly.

"Oh," the woman reddened again. "Oh, well—"

"Did you say you knew a girl named Lytha?" asked Timmy faintly.

"Well, I never did have much to do with her," said the woman, unsure of herself. "I saw her a time or two—"

Timmy's fingers went out to touch her wrist and she jerked back as though burned. "I'm sorry," said Timmy. "Where are you coming from?"

"Margin," said the woman. "We been there a couple of months shoeing the horses and blacksmithing some."

"Margin," said Timmy, his hands shaking a little as he turned away. "Thanks."

"Well, you're welcome, I guess," snapped the woman. She turned back to Mama, who was looking after us, puzzled. "Now all the new dresses have—"

"I couldn't see," whispered Timmy to me as we moved off through the green grass and willows to the orchard. "She wouldn't let me touch her. How far is Margin?"

"Two days across Desolation Valley," I said, bubbling with excitement. "It's a mining town in the hills over there. Their main road comes from the other side."

"Two days!" Timmy stopped and clung to a small tree. "Only two days away all this time!"

"It might not be your Lytha," I warned. "It could be one

143

of us. I've heard some of the wildest names! Pioneering seems to addle people's naming sense."

"I'll call," said Timmy, his face rapt. "I'll call and when she answers—!"

"If she hears you," I said, knowing his calling wouldn't be aloud and would take little notice of the distance to Margin. "Maybe she thinks everyone is dead like you did. Maybe she won't think of listening."

"She will think often of the Home," said Timmy firmly, "and when she does, she will hear me. I will start now." And he threaded his way expertly through the walnuts and willows by the pond.

I looked after him and sighed. I wanted him happy and if it was his Lytha, I wanted them together again. But, if he called and called again and got no answer—

I slid to a seat on a rock by the pond, thinking again of the little lake we were planning where we would have fish and maybe a boat— I dabbled my hand in the cold water and thought, this was dust before Timmy came. He was stubborn enough to make the stream break through.

"If Timmy calls," I told a little bird balancing suddenly on a twig, bobbing over the water, "*someone* will answer!"

Meris leaned back with a sigh. "Well!" she said, "thank goodness! I never would have rested easy again if I hadn't found out! But after Timmy found The People, surely his eyes—"

"Never satisfied," said Mark. "The more you hear the more you want to hear—"

"I've never Assembled much beyond that," said Bethie. Then she held up a cautioning hand. "Wait—

"Oh," she said, listening. "Oh dear! Of course." She stood up, her face a pale blur in the darkness of the patio. "That was Debbie. She's on her way here. She says Dr. Curtis needs me back at the Group. Valancy sent her because she's the one who came back from the New Home and 'Peopled all over the place,' as she says. I have to leave immediately. There isn't time for a car. Luckily it's dark enough now. Debbie has her part all Assembled already so she can—"

"I wish you didn't have to leave so soon," said Meris, following her inside and helping her scramble her few belongings into her small case.

"There is so much— There's always so much— You'll enjoy Debbie's story." Bethie was drifting steplessly out the door. "And there are others—" She was a quickening shadow

144

rising above the patio and her whispered "Good-by," came softly down through the overarching tree branches.

"Hi!" The laughing voice startled them around from their abstraction. "Unless I've lost my interpretive ability, that's an awfully wet, hungry cry coming from in there!"

"Oh, 'Licia, honey!" Meris fled indoors, crooning abject apologies as she went.

"Well, hi, to you, then." The woman stepped out of the shadows and offered a hand to Mark. "I'm Debbie. Sorry to snatch Bethie away, but Dr. Curtis had to have her stat. She's our best Sensitive and he has a puzzlesome emergency to diagnose. She's his court of last resort!"

"Dr. Curtis?" Mark returned her warm firm clasp. "That must be the doctor Johannan was trying to find to lead him to the Group."

"Is so," said Debbie. "Our Inside-Outsider. He's a fixture with us now. Not that he stays with the Group, but he functions as One of Us."

"Come on in," said Mark, holding the kitchen door open. "Come in and have some coffee."

"Thank you kindly," laughed Debbie. "It's right sightly of you to ask a stranger to 'light and set a spell.' No," she smiled at Mark's questioning eyes. "That's not the way they talk on the New Home. It's only a slight lingual hangover from the first days of my Return. That's the Assembly Valancy sent me to tell you."

She sat at the kitchen table and Mark gathered up his battered, discolored coffee mug and Meris's handleless one and a brightly company-neat cup for Debbie. There wasn't much left of the coffee but by squeezing hard enough, he achieved three rather scanty portions.

After the flurry of building more coffee and Meris's return with a solemnly blinking 'Licia to be exclaimed over and inspected and loved and fed and adored and bedded again, they decided to postpone Debbie's installment until after their own supper.

"This Assembling business is getting to be as much an addiction as watching TV," said Mark, mending the fire in the fireplace.

"Well, there's addiction and addiction," said Meris as Mark returned to the couch to sit on the other side of Debbie. "I prefer this one. This is for real—hard as it is to believe."

"For real," mused Debbie, clasping their hands. "I could hardly believe it was for real then, either. Here is how I felt—"

RETURN

I was afraid. When the swelling bulk of the Earth blotted our ports, I was afraid for the first time. Fear was a sudden throb in my throat and, almost as an echo, a sudden throb from Child Within reminded me why it was that Earth *was* swelling in our ports after such a final good-by. Drawn by my mood, Thann joined me as the slow turning of our craft slid the Earth out of sight.

"Apprehensive?" he asked, his arm firm across my shoulders.

"A little." I leaned against him. "This business of trying to go back again is a little disquieting. You can't just slip back into the old mold. Either it's changed or you've changed—or both. I realize that."

"Well, the best we can do is give it the old college try," he said. "And all for Child Within. I hope he appreciates it."

"Or she." I glanced down at my unfamiliar proportions. "As the case may be. But you do understand, don't you?" Need for reassurance lifted my voice a little. "Thann, we just had to come back. I just couldn't bear the thought of Child Within being born in that strange—tidy—" My voice trailed off and I leaned more heavily, sniffing.

"Listen, Debbie-my-dear!" Thann shook me gently and hugged me roughly. "I know, I know! While I don't share your aching necessity for Earth, I agreed, didn't I? Didn't I sweat blood in that dern Motiver school, learning to manipulate this craft? Aren't we almost there?"

"Almost there! Oh, Thann! Oh, Thann!" Our craft had completed another of its small revolutions, and Earth marched determinedly across the port again. I pressed myself against the pane, wanting to reach—to gather in the featureless mists, the blurred beauties of the world, and hold them so close—so close that even Child Within would move to their wonder.

I'm a poor hand at telling time. I couldn't tell you even to within a year how long ago it was that Shua lifted the Ship from the flat at Cougar Canyon and started the trip from Earth to The Home. I remembered how excited I was. Even my

146

ponytail had trembled as the great adventure began. Thann swears he was standing so close to me at Takeoff that the ponytail tickled his nose. But I don't remember him. I don't even remember seeing him at all during the long trip when the excitement of being evacuated from Earth dulled to the routine of travel and later became resurrected as anxiety about what The Home would be like.

I don't remember him at all until that desolate day on The Home when I stood at the end of the so-precise little lane that wound so consciously lovely from the efficient highway. I was counting, through the blur of my tears, the precisely twenty-six trees interspersed at suitable intervals by seven clumps of underbrush. He just happened to be passing at the moment and I looked up at him and choked, "Not even a weed! Not one!"

Astonished, he folded his legs and hovered a little above eye level.

"What good's a weed?"

"At least it shows individuality!" I shut my eyes, not caring that by so doing the poised tears consolidated and fell. "I'm so sick of perfection!"

"Perfection?" He lifted a little higher above me, his eyes on some far sight. "I certainly wouldn't call The Home perfect yet. From here I can see the North Reach. We've only begun to nibble at that. The preliminary soil crew is just starting analysis." He dropped down beside me. "We can't waste time and space on weeds. It'll take long enough to make the whole of The Home habitable without using energy on nonessentials."

"They'll find out!" I stubbornly proclaimed. "Someday they'll find out that weeds *are* essentials. Man wasn't made for such—such *neatness*. He has to have unimportant clutter to relax in!"

"Why haven't you presented these fundamental doctrines to the Old Ones?" He laughed at me.

"Have I not!" I retorted. "Well, maybe not to the Old Ones, but I've already expressed myself, and further more, Mr.—Oh, I'm sorry, I'm Debbie—"

"I'm Thannel," he grinned.

"—Thannel, I'll have you know other wiser heads than mine have come to the same conclusion. Maybe not in my words, but they mean the same thing. This artificiality—this—this— The People aren't *meant* to live divorced from the—the—" I spread my hands. "Soil, I guess you could say. They lose something when everything gets—gets paved."

"Oh, I think we'll manage," he smiled. "Memory can sustain."

"Memory? Oh, Thann, remember the tangle of blackberry vines in back of Kroginold's house? How we used to burrow under the scratchy, cool, green twilight in under these vines and hunt for berries—cool ones from the shadows, and warm ones from the sun, and always at least one thorn in the thumb as payment for trespassing. Mmmm—" Eyes closed, I lost myself in the memory.

Then my eyes flipped open. "Or are you from the other Home? Maybe you've never even seen Earth."

"Yes, I have," he said, suddenly sober. "I'm from Bendo. I haven't many happy memories of Earth. Until your Group found us, we had a pretty thin time of it."

"Oh, I'm sorry," I said. "Bendo was our God Bless for a long time when I was little."

"Thank you." He straightened briskly and grinned. "How about a race to the twenty-third despiséd tree, just to work off a little steam!"

And the two of us lifted and streaked away, a yard above the careful gravel of the lane, but I got the giggles so badly that I blundered into the top of the twenty-first tree and had to be extricated gingerly from its limbs. Together we guiltily buried at its foot the precious tiny branch I had broken off in my blundering, and then, with muffled laughter and guilty back-glances, we went our separate ways.

That night I lay and waited for the pale blue moon of The Home to vault into the sky, and thought about Earth and the Other Home.

The other Home was first, of course—the beautiful prototype of this Home. But it had weeds! And all the tangled splendor of wooded hillsides and all soaring upreach naked peaks and the sweet uncaring, uncountable profusion of life, the same as Earth. But The Home died—blasted out of the heavens by a cosmic Something that shattered it and scattered the People like birds from a falling tree. Part of them found this Home—or the bare bones of it—and started to remake it into The Home. Others found refuge on Earth. We had it rough for a long time because we were separated from each other. Besides, we were Different, with a capital D, and some of us didn't survive the adjustment period. Slowly though, we were Gathered In until there were two main Groups—Cougar Canyon and Bendo. Bendo lived in a hell of concealment and fear long after Cougar Canyon had managed to adjust to an Outsider's world.

Then that day—even now my breath caught at the wonder of that day when the huge ship from the New Home drifted down out of the skies and came to rest on the flat beyond the schoolhouse!

And everyone had to choose. Stay or go. My family chose to go. More stayed. But the Oldest, Cougar Canyon's leader, blind, crippled, dying from what the Crossing had done to him, he went. But you should see him now! You should see him *see!* And Obla came too. Sometimes I went to her house just to touch her hands. She had none, you know, on Earth. Nor legs nor eyes, and hardly a face. An explosion had stripped her of all of them. But now, because of transgraph and regeneration, she is becoming whole again—except perhaps her heart—but that's another story.

Once the wonder of the trip and the excitement of living without concealment, without having to watch every movement so's not to shock Outsiders, had died a little, I got homesicker and homesicker. At first I fought it as a silly thing, a product of letdown, or idleness. But a dozen new interests, frenzied activities that consumed every waking moment, did nothing to assuage the aching need in me. I always thought homesickness was a childish, transitory thing. Well, most of it, but occasionally there is a person who actually sickens of it and does not recover, short of Return. And I guess I was one of those. It was as though I were breathing with one lung or trying to see with one eye. Sometimes the growing pain became an anguish so physical that I'd crouch in misery, hugging my hurt to me, trying to contain it between my knees and my chest—trying to ease it. Sometimes I could manage a tear or two that relieved a little—such as that day in the lane with Thann.

"Thann!" I turned from the port. "Isn't it about time—"

"One up on you, Debbie-my-dear," Thann called from the Motive room. "I'm just settling into the old groove. Got to get us slowed down before we scorch our little bottoms and maybe even singe Child Within."

"Don't joke about it!" I said. "Remember, the first time the atmosphere gave us too warm a welcome to Earth. Ask the Oldest."

"The Power be with us," came Thann's quick answering thought.

"And the Name and the Presence," I echoed, bowing my head as my fingers moved to the Sign and then clasped above

Child Within. I moved over to the couch and lay down, feeling the almost imperceptible slowing of our little craft.

Thann and I started two-ing not long after we met and, at *flahmen* Gathering time, we Bespoke one another and, just before Festival time, we were married.

Perhaps all this time I was hoping that starting a home of my own would erase my longing for Earth and perhaps Thann hoped the same thing. The Home offered him almost all he wanted and he had a job he loved. He felt the pioneering thrill of making a new world and was contented. But my need didn't evaporate. Instead, it intensified. I talked it over with the Sorter for our Group (a Sorter cares for our emotional and mental problems) because I was beginning to hate—oh, not hate! That's such a poisonous thing to have festering in your mind. But my perspective was getting so twisted that I was making both myself and Thann unhappy. She Sorted me deftly and thoroughly—and I went home to Thann and he started training to develop his latent Motive ability. We both knew we could well lose our lives trying to return to Earth, but we had to try. Anyway, I had to try, especially after I found out about Child Within. I told Thann and his face lighted up as I knew it would, but—

"This ought to make a bond between you and The Home," he said. "Now you'll find unsuspected virtues in this land you've been spurning."

I felt my heart grow cold. "Oh, no, Thann!" I said. "Now more than ever we must go. Our child *can't* be born here. He must be of Earth. And I want to be able to enjoy this Child Within—"

"This is quite a Child Without," said Thann, tempering the annoyance in his voice by touching my cheek softly, "crying for a lollipop, Earth flavored. Ah, well!" He gathered me into his arms. "Hippity-hop to the candy shop!"

A high thin whistle signaled the first brush of Earth's atmosphere against our craft—as though Earth were reaching up to scrape tenuous incandescent fingers against our underside. I cleared my mind and concentrated on the effort ahead. I'm no Motiver, but Thann might need my strength before we landed.

Before we landed! Setting down on the flat again, under Old Baldy! And seeing them all again! Valancy and Karen and the Francher Kid. Oh, the song the Kid would be singing would be nothing to the song my heart would be singing! *Home! Child Within! Home again!* I pressed my hands against

150

the swell of Child Within. *Pay attention* I admonished. *Be ready for your first consciousness of Earth.* "I won't look," I told myself. "Until we touch down on the flat. I'll keep my eyes shut!" And I did.

So when the first splashing crash came, I couldn't believe it. My eyes opened to the sudden inrush of water and I was gasping and groping in complete bewilderment trying to find air. "Thann! Thann!" I was paddling awkwardly, trying to keep my head above water. What had happened? How could we have so missed the Canyon—even as inexperienced a Motiver as Thann was? Water? Water to *drown* in, anywhere near the Canyon?

There was a gulp and the last bubble of air belched out of our turning craft. I was belched out through a jagged hole along with the air.

Thann! Thann! I abandoned vocal calling and spread my cry clear across the band of subspeech. No reply—no reply! I bobbed on the surface of the water, gasping. *Oh Child, stay Within. Be Careful. Be Careful! It isn't time yet. It isn't time!*

I shook my dripping hair out of my eyes and felt a nudge against my knees. Down I went into darkness, groping, groping—and found him! Inert, unresponsive, a dead weight in my arms. The breathless agony of struggle ended in the slippery mud of a rocky shore. I dragged him up far enough that his head was out of the water, listened breathlessly for a heartbeat, then, mouth to mouth, I breathed life back into him and lay gasping beside him in the mud, one hand feeling the struggle as his lungs labored to get back into rhythm. The other hand was soothing Child Within. *Not now, not now! Wait*—wait!

When my own breathing steadied, I tore strips off my tattered travel suit and bound up his head, staunching the blood that persistently threaded down from the gash above his left ear. Endlessly, endlessly, I lay there listening to his heart—to my heart—too weak to move him, too weak to move myself. Then the rhythm of his breathing changed and I felt his uncertain thoughts, questioning, asking. My thoughts answered his until he knew all I knew about what had happened. He laughed a ghost of a laugh.

"Is this untidy enough for you?" And I broke down and cried.

We lay there in mud and misery, gathering our strength. I started once to a slithering splash across the water from us and felt a lapping of water over my feet. I pulled myself up on one elbow and peered across at the barren hillside. A huge chunk of it had broken off and slithered down into the water. The scar was raw and ragged in the late evening sunshine.

"Where did it come from?" I asked, wonderingly. "All this water! And there *is* Baldy, with his feet all awash. What happened?"

"The rain is raining," said Thann, his voice choked with laughter, his head rolling on the sharp shale of the bank. "The rain is raining—and don't go near the water!" His nonsense ended with a small moan that tore my heart.

"Thann Thann! Let's get out of this mess. Come on. Can you lift? Help me—"

He lifted his head and let it fall back with a *thunk* against the rocks. His utter stillness panicked me. I sobbed as I reached into my memory for the inanimate lift. It seemed a lifetime before I finally got him up out of the mud and hovered him hand high above the bank. Cautiously I pushed him along, carefully guiding him between the bushes and trees until I found a flat place that crunched with fallen oak leaves. I *"platted"* him softly to the ground and for a long time I lay there by him, my hand on his sleeve, not even able to think coherently about what had happened.

The sun was gone when I shivered and roused myself. I was cold and Thann was shaken at intervals by an icy shuddering. I scrambled around in the fading light and gathered wood together and laid a fire. I knelt by the neat stack and gathered myself together for the necessary concentration. Finally, after sweat had gathered on my forehead and trickled into my eyes, I managed to produce a tiny spark that sputtered and hesitated and then took a shining bite out of a dry leaf. I rubbed my hands above the tiny flame and waited for it to grow. Then I lifted Thann's head to my lap and started the warmth circulating about us.

When our shivering stopped, I suddenly caught my breath and grimaced wryly. How quickly we forget! I was getting as bad as an Outsider! And I clicked my personal shield on, extending it to include Thann. In the ensuing warmth, I looked down at Thann, touching his mud-stained cheek softly, letting my love flow to him like a river of strength. I heard his breathing change and he stirred under my hands.

"Are we Home?" he asked.

"We're on Earth," I said.

"We left Earth years ago," he chided. "Why do I hurt so much?"

"We came back." I kept my voice steady with an effort. "Because of me—and Child Within."

"Child Within—" His voice strengthened. "Hippity-hop to the candy shop," he remembered. "What happened?"

"The Canyon isn't here any more," I said, raising his shoulders carefully into my arms. "We crashed into water. Everything's gone. We lost everything." My heart squeezed for the tiny gowns Child Within would never wear.

"Where are our People?" he asked.

"I don't know," I said. "I don't know."

"When you find them, you'll be all right," he said drowsily.

"*We'll* be all right," I said sharply, my arms tightening around him. "In the morning, we'll find them and Bethie will find out what's wrong with you and we'll mend you."

He sat up slowly, haggard and dirty in the upflare of firelight, his hand going to his bandaged head. "I'm broken," he said. "A lot of places. Bones have gone where bones should never go. I will be Called."

"Don't say it!" I gathered him desperately into my arms. "Don't say it, Thann! We'll find the People!" He crumpled down against me, his cheek pressed to the curve of Child Within.

I screamed then, partly because my heart was being torn shred by shred into an aching mass—partly because my neglected little fire was happily crackling away from me, munching the dry leaves, sampling the brush, roaring softly into the lower branches of the scrub oak. I had set the hillside afire! And the old terror was upon me, the remembered terror of a manzanita slope blazing on Baldy those many forgotten years ago.

I cradled Thann to me. So far the fire was moving away from us, but soon, soon—

"No! No!" I cried. "Let's go home. Thann! I'm sorry! I'm sorry! Let's go home! I didn't mean to bring you to death! I hate this world! I hate it! Thann, Thann!"

I've tried to forget it. It comes back sometimes. Sometimes again I'm so shaken that I can't even protect myself any more and I'm gulping smoke and screaming over Thann. Other times I hear again the rough, disgusted words, "Goldinged tenderfoots! Setting fire to the whole gol-dinged mountain. There's a law!"

Those were the first words I ever heard from Seth. My first sight of him was of a looming giant, twisted by flaring flames and drifting smoke and my own blurring tears.

It was another day before I thought again. I woke to find

153

myself on a camp cot, a rough khaki blanket itching my chin. My bare arms were clean but scratched. Child Within was rounding the blanket smoothly. I closed my eyes and lay lapped in peace for a moment. Then my eyes flew open and I called, "Thann! Thann!" and struggled with the blanket.

"Take it easy! Take it easy!" Strong hands pushed me back against the thin musty pillow. "You're stark, jay-nekkid under that blanket. You can't go tearing around that way." And those were the first words I heard from Glory.

She brought me a faded, crumpled cotton robe and helped me into it. "Them outlandish duds you had on'll take a fair-sized swatch of fixing 'fore they're fit t' wear." Her hands were clumsy but careful. She chuckled. "Not sure there's room for both of yens in this here wrapper."

I knelt by the cot in the other room. There were only three rooms in the house. Thann lay, thin and unmoving as paper, under the lumpy comforter.

"He wants awful bad to go home." Glory's voice tried to moderate to a sick room tone. "He won't make it," she said bluntly.

"Yes, he will. Yes, he will! All we have to do is find The People—"

"Which people?" asked Glory.

"*The* People!" I cried. "The People who live in the Canyon."

"The Canyon? You mean Cougar Canyon? Been no people there for three-four years. Ever since the dam got finished and the lake started rising."

"Where—where did they go?" I whimpered, my hands tightening on the edge of the cot.

"Dunno." Glory snapped a match head with her thumbnail and lighted a makin's cigarette.

"But if we don't find them, Thann will die!"

"He will anyway less'n them folks is magic," said Glory.

"They are!" I cried. "They're magic!"

"Oh?" said Glory, squinting her eyes against the eddy of smoke. "Oh?"

Thann's head moved and his eyes opened. I bent my head to catch any whisper from him, but his voice came loud and clear.

"All we have to do is fix the craft and we can go back Home."

"Yes, Thann." I hid my eyes against my crossed wrists on the cot. "We'll leave right away. Child Within will wait 'til we

154

get Home." I felt Child Within move to the sound of my words.

"He shouldn't oughta talk," said Glory. "He's all smashed inside. He'll be bleeding again in a minute."

"Shut up!" I spun on my knees and flared at her. "You don't know anything about it! You're nothing but a stupid Outsider. He won't die! He won't!"

Glory dragged on her cigarette. "I hollered some, too, when my son Davy got caught in a cave-in. He was smashed. He died." She flicked ashes onto the bare plank floor. "God calls them. They go—"

"I'm Called!" Thann caught the familiar word. "I'm Called! What will you do, Debbie-my-dear? What about Child—" A sudden bright froth touched the corner of his mouth and he clutched my wrist. "Home is so far away," he sighed. "Why did we have to leave? Why did we leave?"

"Thann, Thann!" I buried my face against his quiet side. The pain in my chest got worse and worse and I wished someone would stop that awful babbling and screaming. How could I say good-by to my whole life with that ghastly noise going on? Then my fingers were pried open and I lost the touch of Thann. The black noisy chaos took me completely.

"He's dead." I slumped in the creaky rocker. Where was I? How long had I been here? My words came so easily, so accustomedly, they must be a repetition of a repetition. "He's dead and I hate you. I hate Seth. I hate Earth. You're all Outsiders. I hate Child Within. I hate myself."

"There," said Glory as she snipped a thread with her teeth and stuck the needle in the front of her plaid shirt. My words had no impact on her, though they almost shocked me as I listened to them. Why didn't she notice what I said? Too familiar? "There's at least one nightgown for Child Within." She grinned. "When I was your age, folks woulda died of shock to think of calling a baby unborn a name like that. I thought maybe these sugar sacks might come in handy sometime. Didn't know it'd be for baby clothes."

"I hate you," I said, hurdling past any lingering shock. "No lady wears Levis and plaid shirts with buttons that don't match. Nor cuts her hair like a man and lets her face go all wrinkledy. Oh, well, what does it matter? You're only a stupid Outsider. You're not of The People, that's for sure. You're not on our level."

"For that, thanks be to the Lord." Glory smoothed the clumsy little gown across her knee. "I was taught people are people, no matter their clothes or hair. I don't know nothing about your folks or what level they're on, but I'm glad my arthritis won't let me stoop as low as—" She shrugged and laid the gown aside. She reached over to the battered dresser and retrieved something she held out to me. "Speaking of looks, take a squint at what Child Inside's got to put up with."

I slapped the mirror out of her hands—and the mad glimpse of rumpled hair, swollen eyes, raddled face, and a particularly horrible half sneer on lax lips—slapped it out of her hands, stopped its flight in mid-air, spun it up to the sagging plasterboard ceiling, swooped it out with a crash through one of the few remaining whole windowpanes, and let it smash against a pine tree outside the house.

"Do *that!*" I cried triumphantly. "Even child's play like that, you can't do. You're stupid!"

"Could be." Glory picked up a piece of the shattered window glass. "But today I fed my man and the stranger within my gates. I made a gown for a naked baby. What have you done that's been so smart? You've busted, you've ruined, you've whined and hated. If that's being smart, I'll stay stupid." She pitched the glass out of the broken window. "And I'll slap you silly, like I would any spoiled brat, if you break anything else."

"Oh, Glory, oh Glory!" I squeezed my eyes shut. "I killed him! I killed him! I made him come. If we'd stayed Home. If I hadn't insisted. If—"

"If," said Glory heavily, lifting the baby gown. "If Davy hadn'ta died, this'd be for my grandkid, most likely. If-ing is the quickest way I know to get the blue mullygrubs."

She folded the gown and put it away in the dresser drawer. "You haven't told me yet when Child Within is s'posed to come Without." She reached for the makin's and started to build a cigarette.

"I don't know," I said, staring down at my tight hands. "I don't care." What was Child Within compared to the pain within?

"You'll care plenty," snapped Glory around the smooth curve of the cigarette paper, "if'n you have a hard time and no doctor. You can go ahead and die if you want to, but I'm thinking of Child Within."

"It'd be better if he died, too," I cried. "Better than having to grow up in this stupid, benighted world, among savages—"

"What'd you want to come back so bad for then?" asked Glory. "You admit it was you wanted to come."

"Yes," I moaned, twisting my hands. "I killed him. If we'd only stayed Home. If I hadn't—"

I lay in the dusk, my head pillowed on Thann's grave. Thann's grave— The words had a horrible bitterness on my tongue. "How can I bear it, Thann?" I whimpered. "I'm lost. I can't go Home. The People are gone. What'll I do with Child Within? How can we ever bear it, living with Outsiders? Oh, Call me too, Call me too!" I let the rough gravel of the grave scratch against my cheek as I cried.

And yet I couldn't feel that Thann was there. Thann was a part of another life—a life that didn't end in the mud and misery of a lakeside. He was part of a happy adventure, a glad welcome back to the Earth we had thought was a thing of the past, a tumultuous reunion with all the dear friends we had left behind—the endless hours of vocal and subvocal news exchange—Thann was a part of that. Not a part of this haggard me, this squalid shack teetering on the edge of a dry creek, this bulging, unlovely, ungainly creature muddying her face in the coarse gravel of a barren hillside.

I roused to the sound of footsteps in the dark, and voices. "—nuttier than a fruitcake," said Glory. "It takes some girls like that, just getting pregnant, and then this here other shock—"

"What's she off on now?" It was Seth's heavy voice.

"Oh, more of the same. Being magic. Making things fly. She broke that lookin' glass Davy gave me the Christmas before the cave-in." She cleared her throat. "I picked up the pieces. They're in the drawer."

"She oughta have a good hiding!" Anger was thick in Seth's voice.

"She'll get one if'n she does anything like that again! Oh, and some more about the Home and flying through space and wanting them people again."

"You know," said Seth thoughtfully, "I heard stuff about some folks used to live around here. Funny stuff."

"All people are funny." Glory's voice was nearer. "Better get her back into the house before she catches her death of live-forevers."

I stared up at the ceiling in the dark. Time was again a word without validity. I had no idea how long I had huddled myself in my sodden misery. How long had I been here with Glory and Seth? Faintly in my consciousness, I felt a slight stirring of wonder about Seth and Glory. What did they live

157

on? What were they doing out here in the unfruitful hills. This shack was some forgotten remnant of an old ghost town—no electricity, no water, four crazy walls held together by, and holding up, a shattered roof. For food—beans, cornbread, potatoes, prunes, coffee.

I clasped my throbbing temples with both hands, my head rolling from side to side. But what did it matter? What did anything matter any more? Wild grief surged up in my throat and I cried out, "Mother! Mother!" and felt myself drowning in the icy immensity of the lonely space I had drifted across—

Then there were warm arms around me and a shoulder under my cheek, the soft scratch of hair against my face, a rough hand gently pressing my head to warmth and aliveness.

"There, there!" Glory's voice rumbled gruffly soft through her chest to my ear. "It'll pass. Time and mercy of God will make it bearable. There, there!" She held me and let me blot my tears against her. I didn't know when she left me and I slept dreamlessly.

Next morning at breakfast—before which I had washed my face and combed most of the tangles out of my hair—I paused over my oatmeal and canned milk, spoon poised. "What do you do for a living, Seth?" I asked.

"Living?" Seth stirred another spoonful of sugar into the mush. "We scratch our beans and bacon outa the Skagmore. It's a played-out mine, but there's a few two-bittin' seams left. We work it hard enough, we get by—but it takes both of us. Glory's as good as a man—better'n some."

"How come you aren't working at the Golden Turkey or the Iron Duke?" I wondered where I had got those names even as I asked.

"Can't," said Glory. "He's got silicosis and arthritis. Can't work steady. Times are you'd think he was coughing up his lungs. Hasn't had a bad time though since you came."

"If I were a Healer," I said, "I could cure your lungs and joints. But I'm not. I'm really not much of anything." I blinked down at my dish. *I'm nothing. I'm nothing without Thann.* I gulped. "I'm sorry I broke your window and your mirror, Glory. I shouldn't have. You can't help being an Outsider."

"Apology accepted," Glory grinned dourly. "But it's still kinda drafty."

"There's a whole window in that shack down-creek a ways," said Seth. "When I get the time, I'll go get it. Begins to look like the Skagmore might last right up into winter, though."

158

"Wish we could get some of that good siding—what's left of it—and fill in a few of our holes," said Glory, tipping up the scarred blue and white coffee pot for the last drop of coffee.

"I'll get the stuff soon's this seam pinches out," promised Seth.

I walked down-creek after breakfast, feeling for the first time the sun on my face, seeing for the first time the untidy tangle and thoughtless profusion of life around me, the dream that had drawn me back to this tragedy. I sat down against a boulder, clasping my knees. My feet had known the path to this rock. My back was familiar with its sun-warmed firmness, but I had no memory of it. I had no idea how long I had been eased of my homesickness.

Now that that particular need was filled and that ache soothed, it was hard to remember how vital and how urgent the whole thing had been. It was like the memory of pain—a purely intellectual thing. But once it had been acute—so acute that Thann had come to his death for it.

I looked down at myself and for the first time I noticed I was wearing jeans and a plaid shirt—Glory's, indubitably. The jeans were precariously held together, bulging under the plaid shirt, by a huge blanket pin. I smiled a little. Outsider makeshift—well, let it stay. They don't know any better.

Soon I aroused and went on down-creek until I found the shack Seth had mentioned. It had two good windows left. I stood in front of the first one, reaching into my memory for my informal training. Then I settled to the job at hand.

Slowly, steadily, nails began to withdraw from around the windows. With toil and sweat and a few frustrated tears, I got the two windows out intact, though the walls around them would never be the same again. I had had no idea how windows were put into a house. After the windows, it was fairly simple to detach the few good lengths of siding left. I stacked them neatly, one by one, drifting them into place. I jumped convulsively at a sudden crunching crash, then laughed shakily to see that the poor old shack had disintegrated completely, having been deprived of its few solid members. Lifting the whole stack of my salvage to carrying height, I started back up-creek, panting and sweating, stumbling and pushing the load ahead of me until I got smart and, lifting, perched on the pile of planks, I directed my airborne caravan up-creek.

Glory and Seth were up at the mine. I set the things down

159

by the house and then, suddenly conscious of weariness, made my way to Thann's grave. I patted the gravelly soil softly and whispered, "They'll like it won't they, Thann? They're so like children. Now Glory will forget about the mirror. Poor little Outsider!"

Glory and Seth were stupefied when they saw my loot leaning against the corner of the shack. I told them where I'd got the stuff and how I had brought it back.

Seth spat reflectively and looked sideways at Glory. "Who's nuts now?" he asked.

"Okay, okay," said Glory. "You go tell that Jick Bennett how this stuff got here. Maybe he'll believe you."

"Did I do something wrong?" I asked. "Did this belong to Mr. Bennett?"

"No, no," said Glory. "Not to him nor nobody. He's just a friend of ours. Him and Seth're always shooting the breeze together. No, it's just—just—" She gestured hopelessly then turned on Seth. "Well? Get the hammer. You want her to do the hammering too?"

We three labored until the sun was gone and a lopsided moon had pushed itself up over the shoulder of Baldy. The light glittered on the smug wholeness of the two windows of the shack and Glory sighed with tired satisfaction. Balling up the rag she had taken from the other broken window, she got it ready to throw away. "First time my windows've been wind-tight since we got here. Come winter that's nothing to sneeze at!"

"Sneeze at!" Seth shook with silent gargantuan laughter. "Nothing to sneeze at!"

"Glory!" I cried. "What have you there? Don't throw it away!"

"What?" Glory retrieved the wad from the woodpile. "It's only the rags we peeled off'n both of yens before we put you in bed. And another hunk we picked up to beat out the fire. Ripped to tatters. Heavy old canvassy stuff, anyway."

"Give it to me, Glory," I said. And took the bundle from her wondering hands. "It's *tekla*," I said. "It's never useless. Look." I spread out several of the rags on a flat stone near the creek. In the unreal blend of sunset and moonrise, I smoothed a fingernail along two overlapping edges. They merged perfectly into a complete whole. Quickly I sealed the other rips and snags and, lifting the sheet of *tekla* shook off the dirt and wrinkles. "See, it's as good as new. Bring the rest in the house. We can have some decent clothes again." I smiled at Glory's pained withdrawal. "After all, Glory, you

160

must admit this pin isn't going to hold Child Within much longer!"

Seth lighted the oil lamp above the table and I spread *tekla* all over it, mending a few rips I'd missed.

"Here's some more," said Glory. "I stuck it in that other stovepipe hole. It's the hunk we used to beat the fire out with. It's pretty holey."

"It doesn't matter," I said, pinching out the charred spots. "What's left is still good." And she and Seth hung fascinated around the table, watching me. I couldn't let myself think of Thann, flushed with excitement, trying to be so casual as he tried on his travel suit to show me, so long—so long ago—so yesterday, really.

"Here's a little bitty piece you dropped," said Seth, retrieving it.

"It's too little for any good use," said Glory.

"Oh, no!" I said, a little intoxicated by their wonder and by a sudden upsurge of consciousness that I was able to work so many—to them—miracles. "Nothing's too small. See. That's one reason we had it made so thick. To spread it thin when we used it." I took the tiny swatch of *tekla* and began to stretch and shape it, smoother and farther. Farther and farther until it flowed over the edges of the table and the worn design on the oilcloth began to be visible through it.

"What color do you like, Glory?" I asked.

"Blue," breathed Glory, wonderingly. "Blue."

I stroked blue into the *tekla*, quickly evened the edges and, lifting the fragile, floating chiffony material, draped it over Glory's head. For a half moment I saw my own mother looking with shining eyes at me through the lovely melt of color. Then I was hugging Glory and saying, "That's for the borrow of your jeans and shirt!" And she was fingering unbelievingly the delicate fabric. *There,* I thought, *I even hugged her. It really doesn't matter to me that she's just an Outsider.*

"Magic!" said Glory. "Don't touch it!" she cried, as Seth reached a curious hand toward it.

"He can't hurt it," I laughed. "It's strong enough to use for a parachute—or a trampoline!"

"How did you do it?" asked Seth, lifting another small patch of *tekla,* his fingers tugging at it.

"Well, first you have to—" I groped for an explanation. "You see, first— Well, then, after that— Oh, I don't know!" I cried. "I just know you do it." I took the piece from him and snatched it into scarf length, stroking it red and woolly, and wound it around his neck and bewildered face.

I slept that night in a gown of *tekla,* but Glory stuck to her high-necked crinkle-crepe gown and Seth scorned nightclothes. But after Glory blew out the light and before she disappeared behind the denim curtain that gave me part of the front room for a bedroom of my own, she leaned over, laughing in the moonlight, to whisper, "He's got that red thing under his pillow. I seen it sticking out from under!"

Next morning I busied myself with the precious *tekla,* thinning it, brushing up a soft nap, fashioning the tiny things Child Within would be needing some day. Glory stayed home from the mine and tried to help. After the first gown was finished, I sat looking at it, dreaming child-dreams any mother does with a first gown. I was roused by the sound of a drawer softly closing and saw Glory disappear into the kitchen. I went over and opened the drawer. The awkward little sugar-sack gown was gone. I smiled pityingly. *She realized,* I said to myself. *She realized how inappropriate a gown like that would be for child of The People.*

That night Seth dropped the lamp chimney and it smashed to smithereens.

"Well, early to bed," sighed Glory. "But I did want to get on with this shirt for Seth." She smoothed the soft, woolly *tekla* across her lap. We had figured it down pretty close, but it came out a dress for each of us and a shirt for Seth as well as a few necessities for Child Within. I blessed again the generousness of our travel clothes and the one small part of a blanket that had survived.

"If you've got a dime," I said, returning to the problem of light, "I haven't a cent—but if you've got a dime, I can make a light—"

Seth chuckled. "If we've got a dime, I'd like to see it. We're 'bout due for a trip into town to sell our ore. Got any change, Glory?"

Glory dumped her battered purse out on the bed and stirred the contents vigorously. "One dollar bill," she said. "Coffee and sugar for next week. A nickel and three pennies. No dime—"

"Maybe a nickel will work," I said dubiously. "We always used dimes or disks of *argen.* I never tried a nickel." I picked up the coin and fingered it. Boy! Would this ever widen their eyes! If I could remember Dita's instructions. I spun the coin and concentrated. I spun the coin and frowningly concentrat-

162

ed. I spun the coin. I blushed. I sweated. "It'll work," I reassured the skeptical side glances of Seth and Glory. I closed my eyes and whispered silently, "We need it. Bless me. Bless me."

I spun the coin.

I saw the flare behind my eyelids and opened them to the soft, slightly blue handful of light the nickel had become. Seth and Glory said nothing, but their eyes blinked and were big and wondering enough to please anyone, as they looked into my cupped hand.

"A dime is brighter," I said, "but this is enough for here, I guess. Only thing is, you can't blow it out."

The two exchanged glances and Seth smiled weakly. "Nutty as a fruitcake," he said. "But don't it shine pretty!"

The whole room was flooded with the gentle light. I put it down in the middle of the table, but it was too direct for our eyes, so Seth balanced it on the top of a windowsill and Glory picked up the half-finished shirt from the floor where it had fallen and asked in a voice that only slightly trembled, "Could you do this seam right here, Debbie? That'll finish this sleeve."

That night we had to put the light in a baking powder can with the lid on tight when we went to bed. The cupboard had leaked too much light and so had the dresser. I was afraid to damp the glow for fear I might not be able to do it again the next night. A Lady Bountiful has to be careful of her reputation.

I sat on the bank above the imperceptibly growing lake and watched another chunk of the base of Baldy slide down into the water. Around me was the scorched hillside and the little flat where I had started the fire. Somewhere under all that placid brown water was our craft and everything we had of The Home. I felt my face harden and tighten with sorrow. I got up awkwardly and made my way down the steep slant of the bank. I leaned against a boulder and stirred the muddy water with one sneaker-clad toe. That block of *tekla*, the seed box, the pictures, the letters. I let the tears wash downward unchecked. All the dreams and plans. The pain caught me so that I nearly doubled up. My lips stretched thinly. How physical mental pain can be! If only it could be amputated like— Pain caught me again. I gasped and clutched the boulder behind me. *This is pain,* I cried to myself. *Not Child Inside! Not out here in the wilds all alone!* I made my way back to the shack in irregular, staggering stages and put myself to bed. When Glory and Seth got back, I propped up wearily on one elbow and looked at them groggily, the pain having perversely quitted me just before they arrived.

"Do you suppose it *is* almost time? I have no way of knowing. Time is—is different here. I can't put the two times together and come out with anything. I'm afraid, Glory! I'm afraid!"

"We shoulda taken you into Kerry to the doctor a long time ago. He'd be able to tell you, less'n—" she hesitated "—less'n you are different, so'st he'd notice—"

I smiled weakly. "Don't tiptoe so, Glory. I won't be insulted. No, he'd notice nothing different except when birth begins. We can bypass the awfullest of the hurting time—" I gulped and pressed my hands to the sudden emptiness that almost caved me in. "That's what I was supposed to learn from our People here!" I wailed. "I only know about it. Our first child is our learning child. You can't learn it ahead."

"Don't worry," said Glory dryly. "Child Within will manage to get outside whether you hurt or not. If you're a woman, you can bear the burden women have since Eve."

So we planned to go into town the next day and just tell the doctor I hadn't been to a doctor yet—lots of people don't, even today. But it started to rain in the night. I roused first to the soft sound of rain on the old tin roof of the kitchen—the soft sound that increased and increased until it became a drumming roar. Even that sound was music. And the vision of rain falling everywhere, everywhere, patting the dusty ground, dimpling the lake, flipping the edges of curled leaves, soothed me into sleep. I was wakened later by the sound of Seth's coughing. *That* wasn't a soothing sound. And it got worse and worse. It began to sound as though he actually were coughing up his lungs as Glory had said. He could hardly draw a breath between coughing spasms. I lay there awake in the dark, hearing Glory's murmurs and the shuff-shuff of her feet as she padded out to the kitchen and back to the bedroom. But the coughing went on and on and I began to get a little impatient. I tossed in bed, suddenly angrily restless. I had Child Within to think of. They knew I needed my rest. They weren't making any effort to be quiet— Finally I couldn't stand it any longer. I padded in my turn to their bedroom and peered in. Seth was leaning back against the head of the iron bedstead, gasping for breath. Glory was sitting beside him, tearing up an old pillowcase to make handkerchiefs for him. She looked up at me in the half light of the uncovered baking powder can, her face drawn and worn.

"It's bad, this time," she said. "Makin' up for lost time, I guess."

"Can't you do something to stop his coughing?" I asked. I really hadn't meant it to sound so abrupt and flat. But it did, and Glory let her hands fall slowly to her lap as her eyes fixed on me.

"Oh," she said. "Oh." Then her eyes fairly blazed and she said, "Can't *you?*"

"I'm not a Healer," I said, feeling almost on the defensive. "If I were, I could give—"

"You wouldn't give anybody anything," said Glory, her face closed and cold. "Less'n you wanted to show off or make yourself comfortable. Go back to bed."

I went, my cheeks burning in the dark. How dare she talk to me like this! An Outsider to one of The People! She had no right— My anger broke into tears and I cried and cried on my narrow Outsider bed in that falling down Outsider house, but under all my anger and outrage, so closely hidden that I'd hardly admit it to myself even, was a kernel of sorrow. I'd thought Glory liked me.

Morning was gray and clammy. The rain fell steadily and the bluish light from the baking powder can was cold and uncheerful. The day dragged itself to a watery end, nothing except a slight waning and waxing of the light outdoors to distinguish one hour from the next. Seth's coughing eased a little and by the second rain-loud morning it had finally stopped.

Seth prowled around the cramped rooms, his shoulders hunched forward, his chest caved in as though he had truly coughed out his lungs. His coughing had left him, but his breath still caught in ragged chunks.

"Set," said Glory, tugging at his sleeve. "You'll wear yourself and me out too, to-ing and fro-ing like that."

"Don't ease me none to set," said Seth hoarsely. "Leave me be. Let me move while I can. Got a hunch there won't be much moving for me after the next spell."

"Now, Seth." Glory's voice was calm and a little reprimanding, but I caught her terror and grief. With a jolt I realized how exactly her feelings were mine when I had crouched beside Thann, watching him die. *But they're old and ugly and through with life!* I protested. *But they love* came the answer, *and love can never be old nor ugly nor through with life.*

" 'Sides, I'm worried," said Seth, wiping the haze of his breath off the newly installed window. "Rain like this'll fill
165

every creek around here. Then watch the dam fill up. They told us we'd be living on an island before spring. When the lake's full, we'll be six foot under. All this rain—" He swiped at the window again, and turning away, resumed his restless pacing. "That slope between here and the highway's getting mighty touchy. Wash it out a little at the bottom and it'll all come down like a ton of bricks. Dam it up there, we'd get the full flow right across us and I ain't feeling much like a swim!" He grinned weakly and leaned against the table.

"Glory." His breathing was heavy and ragged. "Glory, I'm tired."

Glory put him to bed. I could hear the murmur of her voice punctuated at intervals by a heavy monosyllable from him.

I shivered and went to the little bandy-legged cast-iron stove. Lifting one of its four lids, I peered at the smoldering pine knot inside. The heaviness outside pushed a thin acrid cloud of smoke out at me and I clattered the lid back, feeling an up-gush of exasperation at the inefficiency of Outsiders. I heated the stove up until the top glowed dull red, and reveled in the warmth.

Glory came back into the kitchen and hunched near the stove, rubbing her hands together.

"How'd you get the wood to burn?" she finally asked. "It was wet. 'S'all there is left."

"I didn't," I said. "I heated the stove."

"Thanks," said Glory shortly (not even being surprised that I could do a thing like that!).

We both listened to the murmur of the rain on the roof and the pop and creak of the expanding metal of the stovepipe as the warmth reached upward.

"I'm sorry," said Glory. "I shouldn'ta spoken so short the other night, but I was worried."

"It's all right," I said magnanimously. "And when my People come—"

"Look, Debbie." Glory turned her back to the stove and clasped her hands behind her. "I'm not saying you don't have folks and that they won't come some day and set everything right, but they aren't here *now*. They can't help *now*, and we got troubles—plenty of troubles. Seth's worrying about that bank coming down and shifting the water. Well, he don't know, but it came down in the night last night and we're already almost an island. Look out the window."

I did, cold apprehension clutching at my insides. The creek had water in it. Not a trickle, but a wide, stainless-steel

166

roadbed of water that was heavy with red silt where it escaped the color of the down-pressing clouds. I ran to the other window. A narrow hogback led through the interlacing of a thousand converging streams, off into the soggy grayness of the mountain beyond us. It was the trail—the hilltop trail Glory and Seth took to Skagmore.

"I hate to ask it of you," said Glory. "Especially after telling you off like I did, but we gotta get outa here. We gotta save what we can and hole up at the mine. You better start praying now that it'll be a few days more before the water gets that high. Meanwhile, grab your bedroll and git goin'."

I gaped at her and then at the water outside and, running to my cot, grabbed up the limp worn bedding and started for the door.

"Hold it! Hold it!" she called. "Fold the stuff so you can manage it. Put on this old hat of Seth's. It'll keep the rain outa your eyes for a while, maybe. Wait'll I get my load made up. I'll take the lead."

Oh no! Oh no! I cried to myself as panic trembled my hands and hampered my folding the bedclothes. *Why is this happening to me? Wasn't it enough to take Thann away? Why should I have to suffer any more?*..

"Ready?" Glory's intent eyes peered across her load. "Hope you've been praying. If you haven't, you better get started. We gotta make it there and back. Seth's gotta rest some before he tackles it."

"But I can lift!" I cried. "I don't have to walk! I have my shield. I don't have to get wet! I can go—"

"Go then," said Glory, her voice hard and unfriendly. "Git goin'!"

I caught at my panic and bit my lips—I needed Glory. "I only mean I could take your load and mine, too," I said, which wasn't what I had originally meant at all. "Then you could take something else. I can transport all this stuff and keep it dry."

I lifted my own burden and hovered it while I took hers from her reluctant arms. I lifted the two together and maneuvered the load out the door, extending my personal shield to cover it all. "How—how do I get there?" My voice was little and scared.

"Follow the hogback," said Glory, her voice still unwarmed, as though she had been able to catch my hidden emotion, as the People do. "You'll see the entrance up the hill a ways soon as you top out on the ridge. Don't go too far inside. The shoring's rotted out in lots of places."

"Okay," I said. "I'll come back."

"Stay there," said Glory. "Git goin'. I gotta get Seth up." My eyes followed hers and recoiled from the little brown snake of water that had welled up in one corner of the room. I got going.

Even inside my shield, I winched away from the sudden increased roar of descending rain. I couldn't see a yard ahead and had to navigate from boulder to boulder along the hogback. It was a horrible eternity before I saw the dark gap of the mine entrance and managed to get myself and my burden inside. For several feet around the low irregular arch of the entrance, the powdery ground was soggy mud, but farther back it was dry and the roof vaulted up until it was fairly spacious.

I put the bedding down and looked around me. Two narrow strips of rail disappeared back into the mine and an ore car tilted drunkenly off one side, two wheels off and half covered with dirt on the floor beside it. I unearthed one wheel and tugging it upright, rolled it, wobbling and uncooperative, over to the stack of bedding. I started heating the wheel, making slow work of so large a task because I had done so little with the basic Signs and Persuasions—the practices of my People.

Suddenly it seemed to me a long time since I'd left the shack. I ran to the entrance and peered out. No Glory or Seth! Where could they be! I couldn't be all alone here with no one around to help me! I swished out into the storm so fast my face was splattered with rain before my shielding was complete. Time and again I almost lost the hogback. It was an irregular chain of rocky little islands back toward the shack. I groped through the downpour, panting to Child Within, *Oh wait! Oh wait! You can't come now!* And tried to ignore a vague, growing discomfort.

Then the miracle happened! High above me I heard the egg-beater whirr of a helicopter! Rescue! Now all this mad rush and terror and discomfort would be over. All I had to do was signal the craft and make them take me aboard and take me somewhere away—I turned to locate it and signal it to me when I suddenly realized that I couldn't lift to it—I *couldn't* lift around Outsiders who would matter. This basic rule of The People was too deeply engrained in me. Hastily I dipped down until I perched precariously on one of the still-exposed boulders of the trail. I waved wildly up at the slow swinging 'copter. They had to see me! "Here I am! Here I am!" I cried, my voice too choked even to carry a yard. "Help me! Help me!" And, in despair as the 'copter slanted away into the gray falling rain, I slid past vocal calling into subvocal and spread my call over the whole band, praying that a receptor somewhere would pick up my message. "There's need!" I sobbed out the old childish distress cry of the Group. "There's need!"

And an answer came!

"One of us?" The thought came startled. "Who are you? Where are you?"

"I'm down here in the rain!" I sobbed, aloud as well as silently. "I'm Debbie! I used to live in the Canyon! We went to the Home. Come and get me! Oh, come and get me!"

"I'm coming," came the answer. "What on Earth are you doing on Earth, Debbie? No one was supposed to return so lightly—"

"So lightly!" Shattered laughter jabbed at my throat. All the time I'd spent on Earth already had erased itself, and I was caught up by the poignancy of this moment of meeting with Thann not here—this watery welcome to Earth with no welcome for Thann. "Who are you?" I asked. I had forgotten individual thought patterns so soon.

"I'm Jemmy," came the reply. "I'm with an Outsider Disaster Unit. We've got our hands full fishing people out of this dammed lake!" He chuckled. "Serves them right for damming Cougar Creek and spoiling the Canyon. But tell me, what's the deal? You shouldn't be here. You went back to the Home, didn't you?"

"The Home—" I burst into tears and all the rest of the time that the 'copter circled back and found a settling-down space on a flat already awash with two inches of water, Jemmy and I talked. Mostly I did the talking. We shifted out of verbalization and our thoughts speeded up until I had told Jemmy everything that had happened to me since that awful crashing day. It was telling of someone else—some other far, sad story of tragedy and graceless destitution—Outsider makeshifts. I had just finished when the 'copter door swung open and Jemmy stepped out to hover above the water that was sucking my sneakers off the slant of the boulder I was crouched on.

"Oh, thanks be to The Power," I cried, grabbing for Jemmy's hands, but stubbing my own on my personal shield. "Oh take me out of this, Jemmy! Take me back to The People! I'm so sick of living like an Outsider! And Child

169

Within doesn't want to be born on a dirt floor in a mine! Oh, Jemmy! How horrible to be an Outsider! You came just in time!" Tears of thankfulness wet my face as I tried to smile at him.

"Debbie!"

Surely that couldn't be my name! That cold, hard, accusing world! That epithet—that—

"Jemmy!" I collapsed my shield and reached for him. Unbelievably, he would not receive me. "Jemmy!" I cried, the rain wetting my lips. "What's the matter? What's wrong?"

He floated back so I couldn't reach him. "Where are Glory and Seth?" he asked sternly.

"Glory and Seth?" I had to think before I could remember them. They were another life ago. "Why back at the cabin, I guess." I was bewildered. "Why?"

"You have no concern of them?" he asked. "You ask for rescue and forget them? What did The Home do to you? You're apparently not one of Us any more. If you've been infected with some sort of virus, we want no spreading of it."

"You don't want me?" I was dazed. "You're going to leave me here! But—but you can't! You've got to take me!"

"You're not drowning," he said coldly. "Go back to the cave. I have a couple of blankets in the 'copter I can spare. Be comfortable. I have other people who need rescue worse."

"But, Jemmy! I don't understand. What's wrong? What have I done?" My heart was shattering and cutting me to pieces with its razor-sharp edges.

He looked at me coldly and speculatively. "If you have to ask, it'd take too long to explain," he said. He turned away and took the blankets from the 'copter. He aimed them at the mine entrance and, hovering them, gave them a shove to carry them through into the mine.

"There," he said, "curl up in your comfort. Don't get your feet wet."

"Oh, Jemmy, don't leave me! Help me!" I was in a state of almost complete collapse, darkness roaring over me.

"While you're curled up, all nice and safe," Jemmy's voice came back to me from the 'copter, "you might try thinking a little on 'Just who on Earth do you think you are!' And if you think you have the answer to that, try, 'I was hungry—' "

I didn't hear him go. I sat hunched in my sodden misery, too far gone even to try to puzzle it all out. All my hopes had been built on when my People would find me. They'd set everything right. I would be freed from all my worry and hardships—and now—and now—

A wave of discomfort that had been building up slowly for some time suddenly surged over me and my fingers whitened as I clutched the rock. How could I have mistaken that other pain for this? "Glory!" I whimpered. "It's Child Within!" *Now* I could remember Glory and Seth. I was back in the miserable half-life of waiting for my People. I scrambled to my feet and closed my shield, setting it to warmth to counteract the chill that stuck to my bones. "I can't face it alone! Anything, anything is better than being alone!"

I streaked back along the hogback that had almost disappeared under the creeping muddy tide. The cabin was in a lake. The back door was ajar. The whole thing tilted slightly off true as though it were thinking of taking off into the roar of the incredible river that swept the creek bed from bank to bank. I staggered against the door as another hard surge of pain tightened my hands and wrung an involuntary cry from me.

When it subsided, I wiped the sweat from my upper lip and pushed the door further open. I stepped into the magnified roaring of the rain on the roof. Blue light was flooding serenely from the baking powder can on the table in the empty kitchen. I snatched it up and ran to the bedroom.

Seth lay white and unmoving on his bed, his eyes sunken, his chest still. I pressed the back of my clenched hand hard against my mouth, feeling the bruise of my teeth. "Oh, no!" I whispered, and gasped with relief as a quick shallow breath lifted the one thin quilt Glory had left him from the bundle of bedding.

"You came back."

My eyes flew to Glory. She sat on the other side of the bed, a shoe box in her lap, one hand clutching a corner of the battered old quilt.

"You didn't come," I whispered. "I waited."

"No need to whisper." Her voice was quite as usual except for a betraying catch on the last word. "He can't hear you."

"But you must come!" I cried. "The house will go in a minute. The creek's already—"

"Why should I come," she asked without emphasis. "He can't come."

We both watched another of the shaken breaths come and go.

"But you'll be washed away—"

171

"So'll you if you don't git goin'." She turned her face away from me.

"But Glory—" Her name came, but twisted—a muffled cry of pain. I clenched both hands on the doorjamb and clung until the pain subsided.

"Child Within," said Glory—her eyes intent on me.

"Yes," I gasped. "I guess so."

Glory stood up and laid the shoe box on the corner of the sagging dresser. She leaned over and smoothed the covers under Seth's chin. "I'll be back," she told him. She waded through the ruffle of water that covered the floor ankle-deep and rounded the bed.

"We better go," she said. "You'll have to point me the way. The trail's gone—"

"You mean you'd leave him here alone!" I was stunned. "Your own husband!"

She looked back at Seth and her lips tightened. "We all die alone, anyway," she said, "He'd tell me to go, if'n he could."

Then I was still as I caught the passionate outpouring of her grief and love—her last, unspoken farewell to Seth. With an effort she turned her eyes back to me. "Our duty's to the living," she said. "And Child Within won't wait."

"Oh, Glory!" Anguish of sorrow filled my chest till I could only gasp again. "Oh, Glory! We can't, we can't!" My throat ached and I blinked against tears of quite a different sort than those I'd been shedding since Thann died.

I snatched the glowing nickel out of the baking powder can and shoved it into my pocket. "Tuck him in good," I said, nodding at Seth. "Bring whatever you need."

Glory looked at me briefly, hope flaring in her eyes, then, with hasty shaken hands, she tucked the covers tight around Seth and, grabbing up her shoe box, she pushed it under the covers next to him. There was a grating grind and the whole shack swung a quarter circle around.

"Can we get the bed through the doors?" I asked shrilly.

"Not unless we take it apart," said Glory, the quietness of her voice steadying me, "and there isn't time."

"Then—then—"

"The mattress will bend," she said. "If both of us—"

With all my faith and power I withdrew into the Quiet within me. *Help me now*, I prayed. *I can do nothing of myself. Strengthen me, guide me, help me—*

The last words came audibly as I clutched the foot of the bed, waiting until the wave subsided. Then, slowly, deliberately, quietly and unhurried, I lifted the mattress Seth lay on

172

and bent its edges enough to get it out of the bedroom. I hovered it in the kitchen. Glory and I both staggered as the house swayed underfoot—swayed and steadied.

"Have you something to put over him to keep the rain off?" I asked, "I can't extend my shield that far and lift that much at the same time."

"Our slickers," said Glory, her eyes intent on me with that different look in them. "They'll help a little."

"Get them then," I said, "and you'll have to get on the mattress, too, to keep him covered."

"But can you—" Glory began.

"I will," I said, holding my Quietness carefully in my mind. "Hurry—the house is going."

Hastily, Glory snatched the two yellow slickers from the nails behind the front door. She scrambled into one and spread the other over Seth. "His head, too," I said, "or he'll nearly drown. You'd better cover your head, too. It'll be easier to take. Hurry! Hurry!"

Glory gave one look at the hovering mattress and, setting her lips grimly, crawled on and lay beside Seth, one arm protectively across his chest. She'd hardly closed her eyes before I started the mattress out the door. The house began spinning at the same time. By the time we got outside, it had turned completely around and, as we left it, it toppled slowly into the creek and was lost in the tumult of the waters.

It's no more than the windows and siding, I whispered to myself. *In fact, it's less because there's no glass to break.* But all my frantic reassurances didn't help much. There were still two olives hanging on my ability to do the inanimate lift and transport them. Doggedly I pushed on, hardly able to see beyond the cascade of rain that arched down my shield. Below me the waters were quieting because they were getting so deep that they no longer quarreled with the boulders and ridges. They smothered them to silence. Ahead and a little below me, rain ran from Glory and Seth's slickers, and the bed, other than where they lay, was a sodden mess.

Finally I could see the entrance of the mine, a darker blot in the pervading grayness. "There it is, Glory!" I cried. "We're almost there. Just a little—" And the pain seized me. Gasping, I felt myself begin to fall. All my power was draining out thinly—my mind had only room for the all-enveloping anguish. I felt the soggy end of the mattress under one arm, and then two strong hands grabbed me and began to tug me onto the bed.

173

"Try—" Glory's voice was almost too far away. "Help yourself! Onto the bed! Help yourself!"

Deliberately I pushed all thought of pain aside. As though in slow motion I felt myself lift slightly and slide onto the end of the bed. I lay half on half off and tried to catch my breath.

"Debbie," Glory's voice came calmly and deliberately. "We're almost in the water. Can you lift us up a little?"

Oh no, I thought. *It's too much to ask! Let me rest.*

Then for no reason at all I heard Jemmy's voice again. "Where's Glory and Seth?" as though in some way I were responsible. *I am!* I cried to myself. *I am responsible for them. I took their lives in my hands when we left the bedroom. Even before that! I made myself responsible for them when they took me in—*

With infinite effort I pushed myself into the background and reached out again to lay hold on The Power and, slowly, the bed rose from the lapping of the waters and, slowly, it started again toward the mine entrance and I held Glory's hand in such a bruising grasp you would have thought I was birthing something or someone out there in the pelting rain.

The events of the next few minutes ran hurriedly and clear, but as far removed from me as though I were watching everything through the wrong end of binoculars. I settled the mattress near the glowing wheel. Glory was off in unflurried haste. She spread my bedclothes and got me undressed by the light of the nickel she had propped up on a ledge on the wall. I cried out when I felt the warmth of my *tekla* nightgown gliding over my head. I'd forgotten the clothes for Child Within! The muddy waters were tumbling all their softness and smallness now.

Another pain came and when it subsided, Glory had brought a coffee pot from somewhere—one of those huge enameled camp pots—and had filled it from somewhere and put it on the wheel-stove to heat. The cases were gone from our pillows and they lay beside my bed torn into neat squares in a little heap, topped by a battered old jackknife with one sharp blade open. One of the thin blankets had been ripped in four.

Glory's face appeared over me, rugged, comforting. "We're doin' fine," she said. "Me and Seth had a few things stashed here in the mine. You got nothing to worry about now 'ceptin' Child Within. Nothing to worry about there neither 'ceptin' what you'll name him now that he won't be within any more."

"Oh, Glory!" I whispered and turned my cheek to press against her hand.

From there on, I was three people—one who cried out and gasped and struggled with the pain and against the pain and was bound up in the blindness of complete concentration on the task at hand, and an accusing one—one sitting in judgment. And the third me was standing before the bar of that judgment, defenseless and guilty.

The indictment was read from the big Book.

"I was hungry," came the accusation, "and they fed me."

"I ate their food," I admitted. "Unearned—"

"I was naked and they clothed me—"

" 'Now we can have decent clothes,' " I heard myself saying again.

"I was a stranger and they took me in—"

"I condescended to let them care for me," I admitted.

"I was in the prison of my grief and they visited me."

"And I accepted their concern and care of me as an unquestioned right. I took and took and took and gave nothing—" Remorse was sharper than the pain that made the other cry out and struggle on the thin bedclothes.

Think no more highly of yourself than you should. The voice had stopped. Now the words ran in ribbons of flames, wavering before my closed eyes, searing the tears dry.

To whom much is given, much is expected. Who would be first must be last. Who would be greatest must be the servant of all.

Whatsoever you do unto the least of these—

Then suddenly the separation was over and the three of me coalesced in a quick blind rush and I listened blissfully to the lusty, outraged cry of My Child.

"Oh, Thann!" I whispered as I slid into a cloud of comfort and relaxation. "Oh, Thann, he's here. Our child—our Thann-too."

"You're mighty sure, aren't you?" Glory's voice was amused. "But you're right. He's a boy."

I pushed sleep away from me a little to fret, "Let me see my poor naked baby. All his little clothes—"

"Not so naked," said Glory. "Here, hold him while I get things squared around." She laid the blanket-wrapped bundle beside me and I lifted up on one elbow to look down into the miracle of the face of my child. I brushed my forefinger across the dark featherdown of his damp hair and lost myself in the realization that here was Child Within. This was what had been Becoming, serenely untouched, within me during all

175

the tumultuous things that had happened. I protested from my half sleep when Glory came back for my child.

"Just going to dress him," said Glory. "You can have him back."

"Dress him?" I asked fuzzily.

"Yes," said Glory, unwrapping the blanket. "I had that sugar-sack gown in my shoe box and them old pillowcases make pretty soft diapers. Not very wetproof though, I'm afraid."

"A boy?" It was Seth's voice, shaken but clear—his first words since the cabin.

"A boy!" Glory's voice was a hymn of thankfulness. "Want to see him?"

"Sure. Us men gotta stick together!"

I lay and smiled to keep from crying as I heard their murmuring over my child.

"Dark like Davy," Glory finally said softly. "Well, better give him back, I guess." She laid him beside me.

"Glory," I said, "the gown could have been for Davy's child. So you and Seth must be grandparents for my Thann-too."

"I—" Glory bit her lips and smoothed his blanket with a trembling hand. "We—" She swallowed hard. "Sure. It's a pleasure."

"Hey, Grandma," called Seth, hardly above a whisper. "I could do with some coffee!"

"Okay, Grampa, keep your shirt on," said Glory. "One coffee coming up!"

That night after Glory had got us all settled and the nickel light was tucked under a rusty tin can and sleep was flowing warmly around us all, I roused a little and leaned up on one elbow, instinctively curving myself around the precious bundle of my child. The wheel-stove glowed on, taking a little of the raw chill off the rocky room. Glory and Seth were sleeping on the other side of the wheel, their bedding augmented by one of the blankets Jemmy had left. When I told Glory where they were, but not where they came from, she got them and, looking at me over the folded bulk of them, opened her mouth, closed it again, and silently spread one blanket for me and one for them. Now they were both asleep and I was awake listening to the "voice of many waters, praising—" and added my praise to theirs. Outside, the sky was clearing, but the murmuring lap of the waters reminded that the numberless creeks in the hills had not yet emptied themselves and the tide was rising higher.

I turned over in my mind the odd duality of events of the night. I heard and saw again all the accusations, all the admonitions. They must have all been waiting for just such a chance when the Distorted Me wasn't watching, to break through and confront me with myself. I had known all the words before. Their pertinent wisdom had been familiar to The People before they ever arrived on Earth and it was one of the endearing things of Earth that we had there found such beautifully rhythmic paraphrases of them.

As I had laid down the burden of Child Within only to assume the greater burden of Thann-too, so also must I lay down the burden of my spoiled-brat self and take up the greater burden of my responsibility as one of The People toward Glory and Seth and whatever the Power sent into my life. Jemmy had been right. I *wasn't* of The People. I had made myself more of an Outsider than an Outsider, even. Well, remorse is useless except insofar as it changes your way of doing things. And change I would—the Power being my helper.

Then I closed my eyes and felt them begin to dampen a little, as I wondered wistfully how long it would be before Jemmy would come again. Thann-too stirred in the curve of my arm. I looked down into the shadow that held him. "But I do think Jemmy was unnecessarily hard on Child Within!" I whispered as I gathered the warm little life closer.

"I do, too," came a voice—subvocally.

Startled, I glanced up. There were two of them standing in the cave entrance.

"And I told him so, too." The figures moved in, quiet inches above the crunch of the mine floor. "Remember me, Debbie? It's Valancy. Maybe you've forgotten—"

"Forgotten? Oh, Valancy!" And we were hugging each other tightly. There was a lovely, warm intermingling of thoughts among the three of us, and all sorts of explanations— Jemmy had had no idea Child Within was so nearly ready to be born—and apologies—"If I'd had *any* idea, but when you—" and acceptances and reasons why and such things as Necessary Patterns— "Since you had the situation in hand I went to see if someone else—" until finally, chastened and relaxed, I watched Valancy cuddling my child.

How could I ever have forgotten Jemmy and Valancy— the glamorous Grown-ups—the Old Ones of the Group of my People in Cougar Canyon, when the Canyon was still habitable. We had all waved them good-by when our ship left for the Home so long ago.

"You can look," said Valancy to Jemmy. "But don't touch." Then she contradicted herself by putting the sleeping bundle into his arms. She snapped her fingers and a small bundle floated in from the mine entrance.

"I brought some clothes," she said. "Though it looks as if Glory has things well in hand. But here are some of Our Child's clothes. She grew so fast that she hardly got to use some of them. If we don't tell him, Thann-too will never know he had to wear girl-type clothes." She unfolded the torn blanket square from around the baby. "And there's the gown," she said, smiling, fingering the hem of it, now regrettably damp.

"There's the gown," I said. "Oh, Valancy, wasn't I the luckiest person in the whole world to have Glory with me? I didn't deserve it a bit! What a mess I was!"

"The Glorys of this world have to put up with a lot of messes," said Valancy, deftly changing my child from the skin out, and returning him, still blissfully sleeping, to my arms. She folded the wet clothes and bundled them up.

"We're taking you and the child back with us," said Jemmy. "We'd better wake Glory and tell her."

"Glory!" I called softly and audibly.

Instantly she was awake and out of bed, blinking in the dimness. "Glory, my People have come," I said. "They want to take me and Thann-too back with them. But I'll be back, just as soon as I can."

Valancy surrendered the baby into Glory's waiting arms. She held him close. "I reckon you do have to go," she said, her voice muffled against his blanket. "He's going to be needing diapers by the dozen pretty darn soon. It'd keep us hopping, washing out what we have."

"We brought some supplies for you," said Jemmy. "They're from the disaster unit. We're working all around this area helping people who got flooded out."

"Is Jicker all right?" Seth's voice came huskily.

"Jicker?" Jemmy did some fast scanning— "Oh, yes," chuckled Jemmy. "I remember him. We fished him off the roof of his cabin. Never heard such cussing in all my life. Ten minutes solid without repeating himself once!"

"That's Jicker," grinned Seth and settled back down. "I'm glad the old cuss is okay."

Jemmy was looking around the shadowy room. "This is the

178

Skagmore, isn't it?" he said. "I thought she was played out a long time ago."

"She was—a couple of times," said Seth. "But we managed to find a few more pockets. Enough to keep us going for a while, but I reckon she's about done for now, with all this water and stuff."

"We had a mine on the other side of Baldy," said Jemmy. "When we moved on up into the hills we didn't think there was enough left to make it worthwhile to leave a crew behind. I think there's pretty good pickin's there for a couple of willing workers. A sort of shack's there, too, where the fellows bunked when it was their shift. I think we piped the spring into the kitchen the last summer. It's not bad. As soon as we get Debbie settled at home, we'll come back and take you there. You can look the setup over and see if you'd like to take a whack at it."

"Thanks," said Glory huskily. "We'll give her a look. We're kinda wiped out here. This is it." She gestured at the few possessions huddled around the glowing wheel.

"And only the clothes they stand in," I added. "And Glory's treasure box." I lifted the shoe box from the edge of Seth's bed and floated it to Glory's hands. "Glory," I said on sudden impulse, "do you have your mirror in there?"

"The pieces." Glory's face reddened slightly. "Silly, keeping useless things."

"Show it to them," I asked. "They know I broke it."

Slowly Glory took the lid off the box and carefully lifted out the mirror. She had fitted all the broken pieces together and they caught and cut into pieces what little light there was in the cave. I took the mirror from her and looked into it at my shattered, shamed face. "Jemmy," I said, holding it out to him. "I broke it. I ruined something I can't make right. Can you help me?"

Jemmy took the mirror and stared down into it, his face tight with concentration. After long seconds, there was a sudden liquid flow of light and the broken pieces of glass melted into one another and glazed across. He gave the mirror back to me and I saw myself mended and whole again.

"Here, Glory," I said, putting it into her hands. "It's only a part of all the apologies and makings-up for what I owe you."

She ran her finger across the mended glass, her face tender with memories.

"Thanks," she said. "I appreciate it."

Jemmy was bringing in a carrycase for me so I wouldn't

179

have to exert myself at all on the return trip. Glory held Thann-too while Valancy and Jemmy got me settled. She fingered the soft warmth of the baby blanket and burrowed in to uncover one of the tiny pink hands. She tucked it back gently, folding the cuff of the gown around it first.

"Where's the other stuff?" she asked. "No sense taking makeshifts back with you."

"No," I said. "You can't have the gown back, even if you *do* want to keep it. That's Thann-too's very first gown, and might have been his only gown if things hadn't worked out as they did. It's staying in our family, every thoughtful stitch of it, and Thann-too's first child will wear it—" I broke off, overwhelmed by a sudden thought. "Oh, Valancy! I'm a *mother!* And when Thann-too grows up, I'll be a *grandmother!"*

They all laughed at my shocked astonishment. And the emotional temperature of our parting eased.

When Jemmy and Valancy were ready to transport me out into a sky aglow with moonlight and puffy leftover clouds, Glory knelt to surrender my baby into my arms. I reached up and hugged her fiercely to me. "You're Thann-too's grandma, and don't you forget it," I whispered. "I'll be back. We'll both be back, and make everything as right as we can after such a horrible beginning. Honestly, all the People aren't as bad as I make them seem. Don't judge them by me."

"Your folks seem to be mighty nice." Glory was ignoring the tears that stood in her eyes. "I—I never minded you too much. Kids will be kids and then there was Child Within—" Her finger touched his sleeping cheek and she stood up abruptly. "Lordee! Here I am in my nightclothes in front of ever'body!" And she retreated into the shadows to find her slicker to use for a robe.

I waved good-by once as we launched out over the waters. Glory's arm went up in brief salute and she turned back into the darkness without waiting to see us gone.

"You certainly lucked out there, didn't you?" said Jemmy from behind me.

"Didn't I?" I murmured drowsily. "I didn't expect an angel in jeans and plaid shirt. That's not an excuse. It's an explanation."

Jemmy chuckled and in silence we streaked across the sky. I closed my eyes against the brightness of the moon. Swallowing sorrow and hugging my child close against me, I whispered, "Oh, Thann—oh, Thann—oh, Thann!"

And felt him very near.

"Chee!" Meris's breath came out in a long sigh.

"Hmm," said Mark, unfolding his long legs to attend again to the fire. "Not exactly—" He broke off, absorbed in poking the coals.

Debbie laughed. "Not exactly the behavior you would expect from one of the People?" she said.

"Well, I guess that's it." He reached for another length of wood.

"Don't think it wasn't a big blow to me, too, when I finally stepped back for a good look." Debbie sobered, the flaring fire lighting her face. "Of course the People are far from perfect, but it was terribly humbling to me to realize that I was a big, fat part of the clay on the feet thereof and an excellent object lesson to the rising generation. Believe me, I've learned to check myself often against a standard more reliable than my own egocentric two-foot yardstick."

"Thann-too," mused Meris. "Eva-lee's husband was named Thann."

"Yes," said Debbie. "He was one of my Thann's Befores. Thann is a fairly common name among us."

"Speaking of names," said Meris casually, "do you know a Timmy and—"

"And a Lytha?" Debbie laughed. "I passed Bethie on my way in! She said you were wondering— Maybe someday you can hear their story from them in person. I don't have it well enough to pass it on."

"Well, I just thought," Meris smiled.

"Bed." Mark stood and stretched. "Bed for our guest along with our many thanks. How long can you stay?"

"Only tonight and tomorrow night," said Debbie. "I have involvements back with the Group, but Bethie wants me to stay long enough to tell you about Shadow."

"Shadow?" Meris laughed.

Mark laughed. "Look at her ears prick up!"

"Yes, Shadow," said Debbie. "She's a Too, too. In fact she is Bethie-too. She and—you know her brother—Remy had quite an experience not so long ago. In the light of recent developments, Bethie thought you might like to hear of it. Also, it all started pretty close to your summer cabin. You see, from where you live, you go northeast about—" She broke off. "Bed," she said firmly. "Bed, right now. Talking is almost as addictive as listening."

The next evening—school keeps, guest or no guest, and Mark had daily duties—Debbie settling down on the couch between Mark and Meris said, "I suppose that Bethie was relieved to be called away before she could tell you this segment of our story. It concerns mostly her own family and she's so shy about talking of herself or those close to her." Debbie laughed. "It is to smile a little ruefully for me to realize how parallel my actions and thinking were with Remy's, only he's really a Teener and I was supposed to be a responsible married woman.

"Well, anyway, give me your hands and listen to Shadow—"

SHADOW ON THE MOON

"No, we can't even consider it." Father smoothed his hand along the board he was planing. It was to be a small table for Mother's birthday. I curled one of the good smelling shavings around my finger as I listened.

"But, Father—" I could see Remy's hands clenching themselves as he tried to control his voice and keep it low and reasonable—a real job for the volatile person he was. "If you'd only—"

Father put the plane down and looked at Remy. I mean really looked at him, giving him his full attention. "Has anything changed materially since last we discussed the matter?" he asked.

"Apparently not." Remy laughed shortly. "I hoped *you* might have— If you'd only consider it—"

"You know I'm not the only one that thinks this way," said Father. "Though I concur heartily with the thinking of the rest of the Old Ones. No good would be served. Can't you see that, Remy?"

"I can't see any flat statement like that!" cried Remy, his control of his impatience beginning to slip. "Every step of progress anyone makes is some good. Why don't you let us—"

"Look, Remy." Father sat on one hip on the edge of the workbench. "Shall we A B C it again. A—we couldn't possibly let anyone else know we had gone to the moon in a spacecraft. B—to the best of our knowledge, there is no immediate need for anything to be found on the moon. C"—he smiled—" 'We bin there already.' At least on our

182

way in. And that was enough for most of us. It looked as good to us as the Statue of Liberty did to the flood of immigrants that used to come over from Europe, but we're most of us content to stay where we are now—looking at it from this side, not that." He grinned at Remy. "Unless you have any information that would materially alter any of these three checkpoints, I'm afraid the discussion is closed—"

"Why *couldn't* we tell?" cried Remy desperately, feeling the whole situation going down the drain. "Why do we have to keep it a secret? Isn't everyone risking their lives and spending fortunes trying to get into Space? Why can't we help?" He broke off because his throat got so tight with anger and frustrated tears that he couldn't talk any more.

Father sighed patiently. "So we go to the moon and back and announce it. So they all swarm around. Can't you hear them screaming?— What propellant? What engine? Escape velocity—air pressure—radiation—landing—return launching —reentry! What would you tell them? Go on, boy-type, answer the nice people. Show them the engines. What? No engines! Show them the fuel tank. ¿Que? No fuel tank! Show them our protection against radiation. Quoi? No protection?

"No, Remy. I wish, because you want it so much, that we could make this expedition for you. Your grandfather's memories of Space can hardly be much comfort to you at your age. But it's out of the question. We cannot deliver ourselves over to the Outsiders for the whim of just one of us. If only you'd reconcile yourself to it—"

"What's the use then?" Remy flung at Father. "What's the use of being able to if we don't?"

"Being able to is not always the standard to go by," said Father. He flicked his fingers at the ceiling and we three watched the snowflakes drift down starrily to cover the workbench. "Your mother loves to watch the snow," he said, "but she doesn't go around snowing all the time." He stopped the snow with a snap of his fingers and it dampened the wood shavings with its melting. "No, just being able to is not a valid reason. And reason there must be before action."

Remy kicked a block of wood out of the workshop and all the way up the slope to our walnut tree on the hill above the twisted, glittering string that was Cayuse Creek. I followed along. I always follow along—Remy's shadow, they call me— and he usually pays about that much attention to me. What can I expect else, being a girl and his sister besides. But I like it because Remy does things—lots of things—and he can

183

usually use a listening ear. I am the willing ear. I'm Bethie-too, because Mother is Bethie.

"Then we'll do it by ourselves!" he muttered as he dug a rock out of the ground where it was poking his shoulder when he tried to relax against the hillside. "We'll build our own craft and we'll go by ourselves!" He was so used to me that he automatically said "we"—though it usually meant *he* had decided *he'd* do something—a sort of royal "we." He lay back under the tree, his hands under his head, his eyes rebelliously on the leaves above. I sat by him, trying to snow like Father had, but all I got was cold fingertips and one big drop of rain that I flicked at Remy. He wiped it off and glared up at the canopy of leaves. "Derned old birds!"

I laughed.

"Go on! Laugh!" he said, jerking upright. "Fine deal when my own sister laughs!"

"Remy." I looked at him, smiling. "You're acting about ten years below yourself and a seven-year-old isn't very attractive in a frame the size of yours!"

He sank back and grinned. "Well, I bet I could. A craft wouldn't be so hard to build. I could use scrap metal— though why does it have to be metal? And we could check in the newspaper for when Canaveral says is the best time—"

"Remy"—the light in his eyes quenched at the tone of my voice—"how far is it to the moon?"

"Well, us—I'm not for sure. I think it's about 250,000 miles, give or take a couple of blocks."

"How far have you ever lifted a vehicle?" I asked.

"Well, at least five miles—with your help! With your help!" he hastened as I looked at him.

"And how far out of the atmosphere?" I asked.

"Why none at all, of course! Father won't let me—"

"And in free fall? And landing in no air? And coming back?"

"All right! All right! Don't rub it in," he said sulkily. "But you wait!" he promised. "I'll get into Space yet!"

That evening, Father quirked an eyebrow when Remy said he wanted to start training to become a Motiver. Oh, he could learn it—most any of The People could—but it's a mighty uphill job of it if you aren't especially gifted for it. A gifted Motiver hardly needs any training except in how to concentrate on a given project for the time necessary. But Remy would have to start from scratch, which is only a notch or two above Outsider performance—which is mostly nil. Father and Remy both knew Remy was just being stubborn because he so wanted to go out into Space, but Father let him go to Ron for study and I got pretty lonely in the hours he spent away from camp. After all, what is there for a shadow to do when there's no one to follow around?

For a day or two I ranged above the near slopes and hills, astonishing the circling buzzards by peering over their thin, wide wings, or catching a tingly downward slide on the last slants of the evening sun through the Chimneys. The Chimneys are spare, angular fingers of granite that thrust themselves nakedly up among the wooded hills along one bank of the Cayuse. But exploring on your own stops being fun after a while and I was pretty lonesome the evening I brought Mother a little cottontail rabbit I'd taken away from a coyote on the edge of night.

"I can tell he's hurt," I said, holding the soft, furry thing gently in my hands and securely in my Concern. It lay unwinking on my palms, its quick nose its only movement. "But I can't decide whether it's a break or a strain. Tell me again how to tell the difference."

Mother laid her hand softly on the creature after reassuring it with her Concern. "It's a strain," she said softly. "Don't you sense——" And the rest of it was thinking that has no separate words for it so I can't write it down. And I did finally Sense the strain in the rabbit's muscles and the difference between it and how a break in a bone would feel.

"Oh, yes," I said. "I won't forget again. Shall I let him go, then?"

"Better put him in the patient-pen," said Mother. "At least for the night. Nothing will fright him there and we can let him go tomorrow."

So we slipped him into the pen and Mother and I leaned over to watch him hide himself in the green tangle of growing things at the far end. Then I carefully did as Mother did. We reached inside ourselves to channel away the pain we had Sensed. That's one of the most important things to be learned if you're a Sensitive—which we both are. When Mother was a girl, she lived among Outsiders and she was almost destroyed before she found our Group and was taught how to Channel.

Still full of the warm, prayerlike feeling that follows the Channeling, we walked back toward the house in the half dark.

"You've been missing Remy," said Mother.

"Yes," I sighed. "It wouldn't be so bad if we were back

with the Group, but being up here till Father's shift is over makes it kinda lonesome. Even with Remy coming back here to sleep, it's not the same. There's nothing to do—"

Mother laughed. "I'd like a dime for every time a child has said that to a parent! Why not use this so empty time to develop a new Gift or Persuasion?"

"Like what?" I wasn't very enthusiastic.

"Well." Mother considered. "Why not something that would go along with being a Sensitive? You're Gifted with that already. Choose something that has to do with Sensing things. Take metal or water or some Awareness like that. It might come in handy sometime, and you could map the springs or ore deposits for the Group. Your father has the forestry maps for this area, but the People haven't mapped it yet."

Well, the idea was better than nothing, so that evening Mother helped me review the Awareness of water and metal and I set my mind to Group Memory that night so by morning I had a pretty good idea of the Basics of the job. It'd take years really to be an expert, but I could play around with it for the rest of the summer.

Water wasn't scarce enough in Cayuse Canyon to make looking for it much fun, though I loved the little blind stream I found in a cave above the creek, so I tried the metal Awareness and got pretty adept by the evening of the first day. Adept, that is, at finding campers' dumps and beef cans—which isn't much to brag about. It's like finding a telephone pole when you're really looking for a toothpick.

By the end of the week, I had fined down my Sensing. Hovering a hundred feet or so over the surface, I had found an old, two-tined fork buried under two and a half feet of silt at the base of one of the Chimneys, and an ox shoe caught in a cleft of rock six feet above the creek on another of the Chimneys. Don't ask me how it got there.

"Big deal!" Remy shoved the shoe with his finger when I showed the family my spoils after supper that night. "Both of them iron—both manufactured. Big deal!"

I flushed and talked right back at him as I practically never do. "How far did you move the world today, wise guy? Was that the house I heard roaring past me this afternoon or a matchbox you managed to tilt off the table?"

Which was hardly fair of me because he was having a lot of trouble with his Motiving and had got his reactions so messed up that he could hardly lift anything now. Sort of a centipede trying to watch his feet when he walks. The trouble would clear up, of course, with further training, but Remy's not the patient type.

"Who's a wise guy?" Before I knew it, I was pressed against the ceiling, the light fixture too hot near the back of my neck.

"Remy!" Mother cried out. "Not at the table!"

"Put her down." Father didn't raise his voice, but I was tumbled back so fast that the hem of my skirt caught the flower bowl and nearly pulled it off the table.

"I'm sorry." Remy glared at his clenched hands on the table and shut us all out so completely that we all blinked, and he kept us out all the rest of the evening.

He hardly said good-by when he left next morning, kicking petulantly at the top of the pinyon tree by the gate as he went by. Mother and Father looked at each other and shook their heads like parents and Father folded his mouth like a father and I was sorry I had started the whole thing—though I'm not sure I did.

I had fun all day. I was so absorbed in sorting out the different junk I Sensed that I lost track of time and missed lunch completely. When I checked the shadows for the time, it was long past the hour and I was too far to bother with going home. I wanted to finish this part of the Chimneys before going home anyway. So I sighed and filled my empty stomach with fresh cold spring water and took off again, enjoying the sweep of wind that brushed my hair back from my neck and dried the perspiration.

Well, concentration paid off! Around about four o'clock I sensed a metal deep inside the last of the towering Chimneys. Or the first one, depending on which mountain you started counting from. Anyway, I sensed a metal near the base of the last one—and not iron and not manufactured! Excitedly I landed on the flank of the mountain and searched out the exact spot. I tore my shirt and scratched my cheek and broke two fingernails before I found the spot in the middle of a brush pile. I traced with my finger the short, narrow course. Wire gold. Six feet inside the solid rock beneath me. Almost four inches of it, as thick as a light bulb filament! I laughed at my own matchbox I'd tilted off the table, but I was pleased anyway. It was small, for sure, but I'd found it, hadn't I? From over a hundred feet up?

It was getting late and I was two-meal hungry, so I lifted up to the top of the last Chimney and teetered on its crumbling granite capstone to check my directions. I could short-cut home in a fraction of the time I'd taken to get here. The panorama laid out at my feet was so breathtakingly lovely that I could hardly leave it, but I finally launched myself in the direction of home. I cut diagonally away from the Chimneys, headed for the notch in the hills just beyond the old Selkirk mine. Half unconsciously I checked off metal as I passed above it. It was all ABC easily detected stuff like *barbwire fence, tin can, roofing, barrel hoop*—all with the grating feeling that meant rust.

Then suddenly there it was in my Awareness—slender and shiny and smooth and complicated! I checked in mid-air and circled. *Beer can, wire fence, horseshoe—slender and shiny and smooth and not iron!* I slid to a landing on the side of the mountain. What could it be? A water tank? Some mining equipment? But it was unrusted, sleek and shiny and slender. But how tall? If only I knew a little about sizes and contents. I could tell sizes of things I was familiar with, but not of this thing. I lifted and circled till I caught it again and narrowed my circle smaller and smaller until I was hovering. Over the old Selkirk mine. I grimaced, disappointed, and Sensed, a little annoyed, the tangly feeling of all the odds and ends of silver left in the fifty-years-abandoned old mine, and the traces of a lot of other metals I didn't know yet. Then I sighed. Must have misinterpreted, but big and shiny, smooth and complicated—that's what it still felt like to me. Nasty break! Back to the Differentiations again, girl!

My hunger hurried my lifting for home so much that I had to activate my personal shield to cut the wind.

Before I even got in sight of the ranger station where we were spending our summer in our yearly required shift for the Group, I felt Remy calling for me. Well, maybe not me by name, but he was needing comfort in large quantities and who better than his shadow to give it to him. So I zeroed in on our walnut tree and stumbled to a stop just behind him as he sat hunched morosely over himself.

"I'm grounded," he said. "Ron says not to come back until I'm Purged. Father says I can start clearing brush out of the campsites tomorrow."

"Oh, Remy!" I cried, dismayed for his unhappiness. "Why?"

He grinned unhappily. "Ron says I can't learn as long as I'm trying to learn for the wrong reason."

"Wrong reason?" I asked.

"Yeah. He said I don't want to be a Motiver just to be a Motiver. I want to learn to be one so I can show people up, like Father and you and the Old Ones. He says I don't want to get into Space because of any real interest in Space, but because I'm mad at The People for not telling the world they can do it right now if they want to. He says—" Remy pulled a double handful of grass with sharp, unhappy yanks "—he says he has no intention of teaching me anything as long as I only want to learn it for such childish reasons. What does he think I'm going to do, drop another Hiroshima bomb?"

I checked firmly the surge of remembered sorrow at his words. "One of us *was* there in that plane," I said. "Remember?"

"But he didn't use any of the Designs or Persuasions in the dropping of the Bomb—"

"No. If he had, we probably never would have been able to help him out of the Darkness afterward. Maybe Ron's afraid you might do something as bad as that if you learn to be a Motiver and then get mad."

"That's silly!" cried Remy. "I wasn't even born when the Bomb fell! And as if I'd ever do a thing like that anyway!"

"Maybe you wouldn't, but if you don't know how to be a Motiver, you can't. Remember, every person who ever did anything bad was seventeen once, and anger starts awfully early. Some kids start to crook their trigger fingers in their cradles—"

"I still think it's a lot of foolish fuss over nothing—"

"If it's nothing," I said, "give it up."

"Why should I?" he flared. "I want—"

"What's the matter with you this summer, Remy?" I asked. "Why are you so prickly?"

"I'm not—!" he began. Then he flushed and lay back against the hillside, covering his eyes with his arm. "Sorry, Shadow," he said gently after a while. "I don't know what it is. I just feel restless and irritable. Growing pains, I guess. And I guess it bothers me that I don't have any special outstanding Gift like you do. I gues I'm groping to find out what I'm supposed to do. Do you think it's because we're part Outsider? Remember, Mother's a Blend."

"I know," I said, "but Mother managed to work out all her difficulties. You will too. You wait and see. Besides, a lot of kids that aren't Blends don't develop their Gifts until later. Just be patient." Then I sighed without sound, thinking that to tell Remy to be patient was like telling the Cayuse to flow uphill.

It wasn't until we were at the supper table that I remembered my find of the day. "I found gold today!" I said, feeling a flush of pleasure warming my face. "Real unmanufactured gold!"

"Well!" Father's fork paused in mid-air. "That's pretty good for a second week. When do we start carting it away? Will a bucket do, or shall I get a wheelbarrow?"

"Oh, Father, don't tease," I said. "You know this isn't gold-like-that country! It was just a short wire of it, six feet inside a granite slope. But now I know what gold feels like—and silver and—and something slender and shiny—"

I broke off, suddenly not wanting to detail all my findings. Fortunately my last words were swallowed up in activity as Remy cleared the table so Mother could bring in the dessert. It was his table week and my dishes week.

Remy put in the next morning hacking and grubbing to clear the underbrush out of some of the campsites along Cayuse Creek. Very few people ever come this far into the wilderness, but the Forestry Service has set up several camp places for them just in case, and Father had this area this summer. Any other year he'd be spending his time in his physics lab back with The Group, trying to find gadgets to help Outsiders do what The People do without gadgets.

Anyway, Father released Remy after lunch and I talked him into going metal Sensing with me.

"Shall I bring Father's bucket?" he teased. "It might be diamonds this time!"

"Diamonds!" I wrinkled my nose at him. "I'm *metal* Sensing, goon-child. Even you know diamonds aren't metal!"

I didn't do much Sensing on the way out, what with his chasing me over the ridge for my impertinence to my elders— he's a year older—and my chasing him up-creek for chasing me across the ridge. We were both laughing and panting by the time we got to the Chimneys.

The Chimneys? "Wait—" I held out my hand and we stopped in mid-flight. "I just remembered. Remy, what's slender and shiny and not iron and complicated?"

"What do you mean, slender? How slender? How complicated?" Remy sat cross-legged in the air beside me. "Is it a riddle?"

"It's a riddle, all right, but I don't know the answer." And I told him all about it.

"Well, let's go over and see," he said, his eyes shining, his ears fairly quivering with interest. "If it's something at the Selkirk, at least we know *where* it is." We started off again.

"Can't you remember anything that'd give you any idea of its size?"

"No-o-o," I said thoughtfully. "It could be most any size from a needle up to—up to—" I was measuring myself alongside my memory. "Gee, Remy! It could be higher than my head!"

"And shiny?" he asked. "Not rusted?"

"Shiny and not rusted."

We were soon hovering over the old Selkirk mine, looking down on the tailings dump, the scant clutter of falling-apart shacks at the mine opening.

"Somewhere there—" I started, when suddenly Remy caught me by the arm and we plummeted down like falling stars. I barely had time to straighten myself for landing before we were both staggering into the shelter of the aspens at the foot of the dump.

"What on earth!" I began.

"Hush!" Remy gestured violently. "Someone came out of the shack up there. An Outsider! You know we can't let Outsiders see us lifting! And we were right overhead!"

"I didn't even know there was anyone in the area," I said. "No one has checked in since we got here this spring. Can you see them from here?"

Remy threaded his way through the clump of aspen and was peering out dramatically, twining himself around the trunk of a tree that wasn't nearly big enough to hide him. "No," he said. "The hill hides him. Or them. I wonder how many there are."

"Well, let's stop lurking like criminals and go up and see," I said. "It's only neighborly—"

The trail up to the Selkirk was steep, rocky, and overgrown with brush and we were both panting when we got to the top.

"Hi!" yelled Remy, "anybody home?" There was no answer except the squawk of a startled jay. "Hey!" he yelled again, "anyone here?"

"Are you sure you saw someone?" I asked, "or is this another—"

"Sure I saw someone!" Remy was headed for the sagging shack that drooped against the slope of the hill.

It was too quick for me even to say a word to Remy. It would have been forever too late to try to reach him, so I just lifted his feet out from under him and sent him sprawling to the ground under the crazy paneless window of the shack. His yell of surprise and anger was wiped out by an explosive roar. The muzzle of a shotgun stabbed through the window, where smoke was eddying.

"Git!" came a tight, cold voice. "Git going back down that trail. There's plenty more buckshot where that came from."

"Hey, wait a minute." Remy hugged the wall under the window. "We just came to see—"

"That's what I thought." The gun barrel moved farther out. "Sneaking around. Prying—"

"No," I said. "You don't yell 'hi' when you're sneaking. We just wondered who our neighbors were. We don't want to pry. If you'd rather, we'll go away. But we'd like to visit with you—" I could feel the tension lessening and saw the gun waver.

"Doesn't seem like they'd send kids," the voice muttered, and a pale, old face wavered just inside the window. "You from the FBI?" the old man asked.

"FBI?" Remy knelt under the window, his eyes topping the sill. "Heck, no. What would the FBI be wanting up here?"

"Allen says the government—" He stopped and blinked. I caught a stab of sorrow from him that made me catch my breath. "Allen's my son," he said, struggling with some emotion or combination of emotions I hadn't learned to read yet. "Allen says nobody can come around, especially G-men—" He ran one hand through his heavy white hair. "You don't look like G-men."

"We're not," I laughed. "You just ask your son."

"My son?" The gun disappeared and I could hear the thump of the butt on the splintered old floor of the shack. "My son—" It was a carefully controlled phrase, but I could hear behind it a great soaring wail. "My son's busy," he said briskly. "And don't ask what's he doing. I won't tell you. Go on away and play. We got no time for kids."

"We just wanted to say 'hi,'" I hastened before Remy could cloud up at being told to go play. "And to see if you need anything—"

"Why should we need anything?" The voice was cold again and the muzzle of the gun came back up on the sill, not four inches from Remy's startled eyes. "I have the plans. Practically everything was ready—" Again the hurting stab of sorrow came from him and another wave of that mixture of emotions, so heavy a wave that it almost blinded me and the next thing I knew, Remy was helping me back down the trail. As soon as we were out of sight of the shack, we lifted back to the aspen thicket. There I lay down on the wiry grass

192

and, closing my eyes, I Channeled whatever the discomfort was, while Remy sat by sympathetically silent.

"I wonder what he's so tender of up there," he finally said after I had sighed and sat up.

"I don't know, but he's suffering from something. His thoughts don't pattern as they should. It's as though they were circling around and around a hard something he can't accept nor deny."

"Something slender and shiny and complicated?" said Remy idly.

"Well, yes," I said, casting back into my mind. "Maybe it does have something to do with that, but there's something really bad that's bothering him."

"Well, then, let's figure out what that slender, shiny thing is, then maybe we can help him figure out that much— By the way, thanks for getting me out of range. I could have got perforated, but good—"

"Oh, I don't know," I said. "I don't think he was really aiming at you."

"Aiming or not, I sure felt drafty there when I saw what he was holding."

I smiled and went on with the original topic. "If only we could get up closer," I said. "I'm not an expert at this Sensing stuff yet."

"Well, try it anyway," said Remy. "Read it to me and I'll draw it and then we'll see what it is." He cleared a little space, shoving the aspen litter aside, and taking up a twig, held it poised.

"I've studied hardly a thing about shapes yet," I said, lying back against the curve of the slope, "but I'll try." So I cleared my mind of everything and began to coax back the awareness of whatever the metal was at the Selkirk. I read it to Remy—all that metal so closely surrounded by the granite of the mountain and yet no intermingling! If you took away the metal there'd be nothing left but a tall, slender hole—

My eyes flipped open. "The mine shaft!" I cried. "Whatever it is, it's filling the mine shaft—the one that goes straight down. All the drifts take off from there!"

"So now we have a hole," said Remy. "Fill it up. And I'll bet it's just the old workings—the hoist—the cage—"

"No, it isn't." I closed my eyes and concentrated again, Sensing diagonally up through the hill and into the Selkirk. Carefully I detailed it to Remy contour by contour.

"Hey!" I sat up, startled at Remy's cry. "Look what we've

193

made!" I leaned over his sketch, puzzling over the lines in the crumbly soil.

"It looks a little like a shell," I said. "A rifle shell. Oh, my gosh! Do you suppose that's what it is? That we've spent all of this time over a rifle shell?"

"If only we had some idea of relative size." Remy deepened one of the lines.

"Well, it fills the hole it's in," I said. "The hole felt like a mine shaft and that thing fills it."

"A rifle shell that big?" Remy flicked a leaf away with his twig. "Why that'd be big enough to climb into—"

Remy stiffened as though he had been jabbed. Rising to his knees, he grabbed my arm, his mouth opening wordlessly. He jabbed his twig repeatedly at the tailings dump, yanking my arm at the same time.

"Remy!" I cried, alarmed at his antics. "What on earth's the matter?"

"It's—" he gasped. "It's a rocket! A rocket! A spaceship! That guy's building a spaceship and he's got it down in the shaft of the Selkirk!"

Remy babbled in my ear all the way home, telling again and again why it *had* to be a spaceship and, by the time we got home, I began to believe him. The sight of the house acted as an effective silencer for Remy.

"This is a secret," he hissed as we paused on the porch before going into the house. "Don't you dare say a word to anyone!"

I promised and kept my promise but I was afraid for Remy all evening. He's as transparent as a baby when he gets excited and I was afraid he'd give it away any minute. Both Mother and Father watched him and exchanged worried looks—he acted feverish. But somehow we made it through the evening.

His arguments weren't nearly so logical by the cold light of early morning and his own conviction and enthusiasms were thinned by the hard work he had to put in before noon at the campsites.

Armed with half a cake and a half-dozen oranges, we cautiously approached the Selkirk that afternoon. My shoulders felt rigid as we approached the old shack and I Sensed apprehensively around for the shotgun barrel—I knew *that* shape! But nothing happened. No one was home.

"Well, dern!" Remy sat down by me on a boulder near the door. "Where d'you suppose he went?"

"Fishing, maybe," I suggested. "Or to town."

"We would have seen him if he were fishing on the Cayuse. And he's an Outsider—he'd have to use the road to go to town, and that goes by our place."

"He could have hiked across the hills instead,"

"That'd be silly. He'd just parallel the road that way."

"Well, since he isn't here—" I paused, lifting an inquiring eyebrow.

"Yeah! Let's do. Let's go take a look in the shaft!" Remy's eyes were bright with excitement. "Put this stuff somewhere where the ants won't get into the cake. We'll eat it later, if he doesn't turn up."

We scrambled across the jumble of broken rock that was the top of the dump, but when we arrived where the mouth of the shaft should be, there was nothing but more broken rock. We stumbled and slipped back and forth a couple of times before I perched up on a boulder and, closing my eyes, Sensed for metal.

It was like being in a shiny, smooth flood. No matter on which side of me I turned, the metal was there and, with that odd illusion that happens visually sometimes, the metal under me suddenly seemed to cup upward and contain me instead of my perching over it. It was frightening and I opened my eyes.

"Well?" asked Remy, impatiently.

"It's there," I said. "It's covered over, but it's there. We're too close, now, though. I can't get any idea of shape at all. It could be a barn door or a sheet of foil or a solid cube. All I know is that it's metal, it's under us, and there's lots of it."

"That's not much help." Remy sagged with disappointment.

"No, it's not," I said.

"Let's lift," said Remy. "You did better from the air."

"Lift? With him around?"

"He's not around now," said Remy.

"He might be and we just don't Sense him."

"How could we keep from it?" asked Remy. "We can always Sense Outsiders. He has no way to shield—"

"But if that thing is a rocket and he's in it, that means he'd be shielded—and that means there's some way to get in it—"

We looked at each other and then scrambled down the dump. It was pretty steep and rugged and we lifted part of the way. Otherwise we might have ended up at the bottom of a good-sized rockslide—us under. We searched the base of the hill, trying to find an entrance. We searched all afternoon, stopping only a few minutes to shake the ants off of and out of the cake and eat it and the oranges, burying the peels carefully before we went back to work. We finally gave up, just before sunset, and sprawled in the aspen thicket at the base of the dump, catching our breath before heading home.

I raised up on one elbow, peering upward to the heights I couldn't see. "He's there now," I said, exasperated. "He's back. How'd he get past us?"

"I'm too tired to care," said Remy, rubbing the elbow he'd banged against a rock—and that's pretty tired for Remy.

"He's crying," I said softly. "He's crying like a child."

"Is he hurt?" Remy asked, straightening.

"No-o-o, I don't think so," I said, trying to reach him more fully. "It's sorrow and loneliness—that's why he's crying."

We went back the next day. This time I took a deep-dish apple pie along. Most men have a sweet tooth and miss desserts the most when they're camping. It was a juicy pie and, after I had dribbled juice down the front of me and down onto Remy where he lifted below, I put it into a nice, level inanimate lift and let it trail behind me.

I don't know exactly what we expected, but it was rather an anticlimax to be welcomed casually at the Selkirk—no surprise, no shotgun, no questions, but plenty of thanks for the pie. Between gulps and through muffling mouthfuls, we learned that the old man's name was Thomas.

"Should have been Doubting Thomas," he told us unhappily. "Didn't believe a word my son said. And when he used up all our money buying—" He swallowed hard and blinked and changed the subject.

We never did find out much about him and, of course, ignored completely whatever it was in the shaft of the Selkirk. At least we did that trip and for many more that followed. Remy was learning patience the hard way, but I must admit he was doing wonderfully well for Remy. One thing we didn't find out was the whereabouts of his son. Most of the time for Thomas his son had no other name except My Son. Sometimes he taked as though his son were just over the hill. Other times he was so long gone that he was half forgotten.

Not long after we got on visiting terms with Tom, I felt I'd better alert Remy. "He's not completely sane," I told him. "Sometimes he's as clear as can be. Other times his thoughts are as tangled as baling wire."

"Old age," suggested Remy. "He's almost eighty."

"It might be," I said. "But he's carrying a burden of some

kind. If I were a Sorter, I could Go-In to him and tell what it is, but every time he thinks of whatever is troubling him, his thoughts hurt him and get all tangled up."

"Harmless, though," said Remy.

"Yes?" I brought back to his mind the shotgun blast we had been greeted with. Remy moved uneasily. "We startled him then," he said.

"No telling what will startle him. Remember, he's not always tracking logically. We'd better tread lightly for a while."

One day about a week later, a most impatient week for Remy, we were visiting with Tom again—or rather watching him devour half a lemon pie at one sitting—when we got off onto mines and mining towns.

"Father said the Selkirk was quite a mine when it was new. They took over a million dollars' worth of silver out of her. Are you working her any?" Remy held his breath as he waited Tom's response to this obvious fishing.

"No," said Tom. "I'm not a miner. Don't know anything about mines and ores and stuff. I was a sheet metal man before I retired." He frowned and stirred uneasily. "I can't remember much of what I used to do. My memory isn't so good any more. Not since my son filled me up with this idea of getting to the moon." I felt Remy freeze beside me. "He's talked it so much and worked at it so hard and sunk everything we ever owned into it that I can't think of anything else any more either. It's like a horn blaring in my ears all the time. Gets so bad sometimes—" He pressed his hands to his ears and shook his head.

"How soon will you be blasting off?" Remy asked carefully casually.

"My son says there's only a little left to do. I ought to be able to figure it out from the plans."

"Where is your son?" asked Remy softly.

"My son's—" Tom stopped and frowned, "My son's—" His eyes clouded over and his face set woodenly. "My son said no one was to come around. My son said everyone had to stay away." His voice was rising and he came to his feet. "My son said they'd come and try to stop us!" The voice went up another notch. "He said they'd come snooping and take the ship away!" He was yelling now. "He said to keep them away! Keep them away until he—until he—" His voice broke and he grabbed for the nearest chunk of rock. I reached out quickly with my mind and opened his hand so it dropped the rock and, while he was groping for another,

197

Remy and I took off down the hill, wordless and shaken. We clutched each other at the foot of the slope.

"It *is* a rocket!" stuttered Remy, shaken with delight. "I told you so! A real rocket! A moon rocket!"

"He kept saying 'my son said,'" I shivered. "Something's wrong about that son of his."

"Why worry about that?" exulted Remy. "He's got a spacecraft of some kind and it's supposed to go to the moon."

"I worry about that," I said, "because every time he says 'my son' his mind tangles more. That's what triggered this madness."

Well, when we got back home, almost bursting with the news we couldn't share, Mother was brisking around gathering up some essential things. "It's an emergency," she said. "Word came from the Group. Dr. Curtis is bringing a patient out to us and he needs me. Shadow, you're to come with me. This will be a good chance for you to begin on real diagnosis. You're old enough now. Remy, you be good and take care of your father. You'd better be the cook and no more than two meals a day of fried eggs!"

"But, Mother—" Remy looked at me and frowned. "Shadow—"

"Yes?" Mother turned from the case she was packing.

"Oh, nothing," he said, his bottom lip pushing forward in his disappointment.

"Well, this'll have to be your exclusive little red wagon, now," I murmured as he reached down a case for me from the top shelf of the closet. "But drag it mighty carefully. If in doubt—lift!"

"I'll wave to you as we go by, headed for the moon!" he teased.

"Remy," I paused with a handful of nightgown poised above the case. "It might still be all a mad dream of Tom's. We've never seen the rocket. We've never seen the son. I could be misreading the metal completely. It'll be fun if you can find out for sure, but don't get your heart set on it too much. And be careful!"

Mother and I decided to take the pickup truck because Father had the forestry jeep and we might need transportation if we went among Outsiders. So we loaded in our cases. Mother got in touch with Father and told him good-by. As the pickup lifted out of the yard and drifted upward and away over the treetops, I leaned out and waved at Remy, who was standing forlornly on the front porch.

It was a wonderful two weeks—in a solemn sort of way. We have a very small hospital. The People are pretty healthy, but Dr. Curtis, who is an Outsider friend of ours, brings patients out every so often for Mother to help him diagnose. That's her Gift—to put her hands on the suffering and read what the trouble is. So when he's completely puzzled with a case, he brings it out to Mother. She's too shy to go Outside. Besides, the People function more efficiently when they are among their own.

It wasn't an easy two weeks because a Sensitive must experience whatever the patient is experiencing. Even if it is vicarious, it's still very real and very uncomfortable, especially for a beginner such as I am. One evening I thought I was going to die when I got so caught up in the smothering agony of a seizure that I forgot to Channel and lost my way in the suffering. Mother had to rescue me and give me back my breath.

When we finally finished at the hospital, we headed home again. I felt as though I were ten years older—as though I had left home as a child and returned as an adult. I had forgotten completely about Tom and the rocket and had to grope for memory when Remy hissed to me, "It's real!" Then memory went off like a veritable rocket of its own and I nearly burst with excitement.

There was no opportunity that night to find out any details, but it made pleasant speculation before I fell asleep. Next morning we left right after breakfast, lifting into the shivery morning chill, above the small mists that curled up from the *cienega* where antelope grazed, ankle-deep in the pooling water or belly-deep in dew-heavy wild flowers.

"No campsites?" I asked, as we left the flats behind us.

"I finished them last week," said Remy. "Father said I could have some time off. Which is a real deal because Tom needs so much help now." Remy frowned down at me as he lifted above me. "I'm worried, Shadow. He's sick. I mean more than a wandery mind. I'm afraid he'll be Called before—"

"Before the ship is done?" I asked with a squeeze in my heart that he should be still so preoccupied with his own dream.

"Exactly!" flashed Remy. "But I'm not thinking of myself alone. Sure I want the ship finished, and I want in it and out into Space. But I know Tom now and I know he's only living

199

for this flight and it's bigger to him than his hope of Heaven or fear of Hell. You see, I've met his son—"

"You have!" I reached for his arm. "Oh, Remy! Really! Is he as—uh—eccentric as Tom? Do you like him? Is he—" I stopped. Remy was close to me. I should have been able to read his "yes" or "no" from the plainest outer edges of his thinking, but he was closed to me.

"What's wrong, Remy?" I asked in a subdued voice. "Is he worse than Tom? Won't he let you—"

"Wait and ask Tom," said Remy. "He tells me every day. He's like a child and he's decided he can trust me so he talks and talks and talks and always the same thing." Remy swallowed visibly. "It takes some getting used to—at least for me. Maybe for you—"

"Remy!" I interrupted. "We're almost there and we're still airborne. We'd better—"

"Not necessary," he said. "Tom's seen me lift lots of times and use lots of our Signs and Persuasions." Remy laughed at my astonishment. "Don't worry. It's no betrayal. He just thinks I've gone to a newfangled school. He marvels at what they teach nowadays and is quite sure I can't spell for sour apples or tell which is the longest river in South America. I told you he's like a child. He'll accept anything except the fact—" We were slanting down to the Selkirk.

"The fact—" I prompted. Then instinctively looked for a hiding place. Tom was waiting for us.

"Hi!" His husky, unsurprised voice greeted us as we landed. "So the sister got back? She's almost as good in the air as you are, isn't she? You two must have got an early start this morning. I haven't had breakfast yet."

I was shocked by his haggard face and the slow weakness of his movements. I could read illness in his eyes, but I winced away from the idea of touching his fragile shoulders or cramped chest to read the illness that was filling him to exhaustion. We sat quietly on the doorstep and smelled the coffee he brewed for breakfast and waited while he worried down a crumbly slice of bread. And that was his breakfast.

"I told my sister about the ship," Remy said gently.

"The ship—" His eyes brightened. "Don't trust many people to show them the ship, but if she's your sister, I trust her. But first—" His eyes closed under the weight of sorrow that flowed almost visibly down over his face. "First I want her to meet my son. Come on in." He stepped back and Remy followed him into the shack. I bundled up my astonishment and followed them.

"Remember how we looked for an entrance?" grinned Remy. "Tom's not so stupid!"

I don't know what all Tom did with things that clanked and pulleys that whined and boards that parted in half, but the end result was a big black square in the middle of the floor of the shack. It led down into a dark nothingness.

"He goes down a ladder," whispered Remy as Tom's tousled head disappeared. "But I've been having to help him hold on. He's getting awfully weak."

So, as we dropped down through the trapdoor, I lent my help along with Remy's and held the trembling old hands around the ladder rungs and steadied the feeble old knees as Tom descended. At the bottom of the ladder, Tom threw a switch and the subdued glow of a string of lights lead off along a drift.

"My son rigged up the lights," Tom said, "The generator's over by the ship." There was a series of thuds and clanks and a shower of dust sprinkled us liberally as the door above swung shut again.

We walked without talking along the drift behind Tom as he scurried along the floor that had been worn smooth in spots by countless comings and goings.

The drift angled off to one side and when I rounded the corner I cried out softly. The roof had collapsed and the jaggedy tumble of fallen rock almost blocked the drift. There was just about edging-through space between the wall and the heaped-up debris.

"You'd better Channel," whispered Remy.

"You mean when we have to scrape past—" I began.

"Not that kind of Channeling," said Remy.

The rest of his words were blotted out in the sudden wave of agony and sorrow that swept from Tom and engulfed me—not physical agony, but mental agony. I gasped and Channeled as fast as I could, but the wet beads from that agony formed across my forehead before I could get myself guarded against it.

Tom was kneeling by the heaped-up stones, his eyes intent upon the floor beside them. I moved closer. There was a small heap of soil beside a huge jagged boulder. There was a tiny American flag standing in the soil, and, above it on the boulder, was painted a white cross, inexpertly, so that the excess point wept down like tears.

"This," mourned Tom almost inaudibly, "is my son—"

"Your son!" I gasped. "Your son!"

"I can't take it again," whispered Remy. "I'm going on to

the ship and get busy. He'll tell it whether anyone's listening or not. But each time it gets a little shorter. It took all morning the first time." And Remy went on down the drift, a refugee from a sorrow he couldn't ease.

"—so I said I'd come out and help him." Tom's voice became audible and I sank down on the floor beside him.

"His friends had died—Jug, of pneumonia, Buck, from speeding in his car to tell my son he'd figured out some angle that had them stopped. And there my son was—no one to help him finish—no one to go out to Space with, so I said I'd come out and help him. We could live on my pension. We had to, because all our money was spent on the ship. All our money and a lot more has gone into the ship. I don't know how they got started or who got the idea or who drew the plans or which one of them figured out how to make it go, but they were in the service together and I think they must have pirated a lot of the stuff. That's maybe why they were so afraid the government would find them. I don't hold with dishonesty and mostly my son don't either, but he was in on it along with the other two and I think he wanted to go more than any of them. It was like a fever in his blood. He used to say, 'If I can't make it alive, I want to make it dead. What a burial! Blackness of Outer Space for my shroud—a hundred million stars for my candles and the music of the spheres for my requiem!' And here he lies—all in the dark—" Tom's whole body dropped and he nearly collapsed beside me.

"I heard the crack and crumble," he whispered urgently. "I heard the roof give away. I heard him yell, 'No! Not down here!' and I saw him race for the ship and I saw the rocks come down and I saw the dust billow out—" His voice was hardly audible, his face buried in his hands. "The lights didn't go. They're strung along the other wall. After the dust settled, I saw—I saw my son. Only his hand—only his hand reaching—reaching for Space and a hundred million stars. Reaching—asking—wanting." He turned to me, his face awash with tears. "I couldn't move the rock. I couldn't push life back into him. I couldn't save my son, but I swore that I'd take his ship into Space—that I'd take something of his to say he made it, too. So I gave him the flag to hold. The one he meant to put where the other moon-shot landed. 'Litter-bugs!' he called them for messing up the moon. He was going to put this flag there instead—so small it wouldn't clutter up the landscape. So he's been holding it—all this time—and as soon as Remy and I get the ship to going, we'll take the flag and—and—"

202

His eyes brightened and I helped him—shielding strongly from him—to his feet. "You can come, too, if you bring one of those lemon pies!" He had paid his admission ticket of sorrow and was edging past the heap of fallen rock.

"We'll save that to celebrate with when we get back," I said.

"Get back?" He smiled over his shoulder. "We're only going. We have a capsule to send back with all the information, and a radio to keep in touch as long as we can, but we never said anything about coming back. Why should we ever come back?"

Stunned, I watched him edge out of sight off down the drift, his sorrow for the moment behind him. I leaned against the wall, waiting for my Channeling to be complete. I looked down at the small mound of earth and the quietly drooping flag and cried in a sudden panic—"We can't handle this alone! Not a one-way trip."

I clasped my hands over my mouth, but Tom was gone. I hurried after him, the echo of my feet slipping on the jagged rocks canceling out the frightened echo of my voice.

As I followed Tom down the drift I was trying frantically to find some way out of this horrible situation. Finally I smiled, relieved. "We just won't go," I said aloud. "We just won't go—"

And then I saw the ship, curving gently up into the darkness of the covered shaft. It was almost with a feeling of recognition that I saw and sensed the quiet, efficient beauty of her, small, compact, lovely, and I saw inside where everything flowed naturally into everything else, where one installation merged so logically and beautifully into another. I stood and felt the wonderful wholeness of the ship. It wasn't something thrown together of tags and leftovers. It had grown, taking into itself each component part and assimilating it. It was a beautiful, functional whole, except for—

I followed the unfinished feeling and found Tom and Remy where they were working together. Tom's working consisted of holding a corner of a long sheet of diagrams while he dozed the facile doze of age and weariness. Remy had wound himself around behind some sort of panel and was making mysterious noises.

"Finally get here?" His voice came hollowly. "Take a look at the plans, will you? Tom left his reading specs in the shack. See where—" and his speech went off into visualization of something that was lovely to look at but completely incomprehensible to me. I gently took the sheet from Tom.

He snorted and his eyes opened. He half grinned and closed his eyes again. I looked at the sheet. Lines went all over it. There were wiggly lines bisecting other lines and symbols all over it, but I couldn't find anywhere the thing Remy had showed me.

"He must have the wrong paper," I said. "There's nothing here like you want. There's only—" and I visualized back at him.

"Why, it's right there!" And he showed me a wiggly sign and equated it to the picture he had given me.

"Well, how am I to tell what's what when it's put down in such a mysterious way!" I was annoyed. Remy's feet wiggled and he emerged backward.

"Ha!" he said, taking the sheet from me. "Anybody knows what a schematic diagram is. Anybody can see that this"—he waved it at me—"is *this*." And he showed me mentally a panel full of complications that I never could have conceived of.

"Well, maybe anyone can, but I can't," I said. "When did you learn to read this? In school?"

" 'Course not in school," said Remy. "Tom showed me all the plans of the stuff that was left to do. He couldn't figure them out, so I'm doing it. No sweat."

"Remy," I said, pointing to a cluster of symbols on the page. "What's that?"

"Why, this, of course." And he visualized back the things that were symbolized.

"Had you ever seen any of those parts before?" I asked seriously.

"No." Remy put down his tools and his own seriousness matched mine. "What use would they be around The People? They're things Tom's son brought."

"But you looked at all this—this—" I waved the page at him. "And you knew what went where?"

"Why, of course," said Remy. "How could I help it when there the thing is before me, big as life and twice as natural. Anybody—"

"Stop saying 'of course' and 'anybody,' " I said. "Remy, don't you realize that to most people these marks are nonsense until they put in hours and even years of study? Don't you realize that most people can't see three dimensionally from something two dimensioned? Don't you know even with study it takes a special knack to *see* the thing complete when you're working with blueprints and diagrams? A special knack—" My voice slowed. "A special Gift? Oh, Remy!"

"Special Gift?" Remy took the plan from my hand and looked at it. "You mean you can't see this solid enough that you could almost pick it up off the paper?"

"No," I said. "It's just lines and odd marks."

"And when we looked at the plans for the addition to the cabin the other night, couldn't you see that funny little room sitting on the paper?"

"No," I said, smiling at the memory. "Is that why you pinched at the paper?"

"Yes," Remy grinned. "I was trying to pick it up, to show Father that it wasn't quite right along the back wall, but he found the mistake in the plans and changed it. That straightened the back wall out okay."

"Remy," I caught his eyes with mine. "Maybe you *do* have a special Gift. Maybe this is what you've been looking for! Oh, Remy!"

"Special Gift—" Remy's eyes were clouded with speculation. "Special Gift?"

I looked around the compartment where we were. "You changed some things, didn't you?"

"Not much," he said absently, still busy with his thoughts. "A few minor shapings that didn't look right—didn't fit exactly."

"That's why it all goes together so wonderfully, now. Oh, Remy, I'll bet you've found your Gift!"

Remy looked down at the paper. "My Gift!" His eyes glowed. "And it's to take me into Space!"

"But not back!" Tom's shaken voice startled us. "Strictly a one-way trip. We've got a capsule—"

"Yeah, Tom, yeah," said Remy, rolling his eyes at me. "Strictly a one-way trip."

I felt an awful cave-in inside me and my lips were stiff with fear. "Remy, you can't mean that! To go into Space and never come back!"

"It'd be worth it, wouldn't it?" he asked, beginning to crawl back behind the panel again. "Tom, will you go get my yellow-handled screwdriver? I left it in the drift by the tool chest."

"Sure, sure!" Tom scrambled to his feet and shuffled away.

"For Pete's sake" hissed Remy, his eyes glaring around the end of the panel. "Go along with the gag! Don't get into an argument with Tom. I tried it once and he nearly died of it—and so did I. He got his shotgun again. He's going out to Space, like making a trip to the cemetery. He knows he'll never make it back and he wouldn't want it any other way.

205

All he wants is that little flag on the moon and his body somewhere out there. But he wants it so much we've *got* to give it to him. I'm not fool enough to want to leave my bones out there. Give me credit for a little brains!"

"Then it's okay? There is a way to bring the ship back?"

"It's okay! It's okay!" Remy's voice came muffled from behind the panel. "Hand me back the screwdriver when Tom gets here with it."

So the days went, much too fast for us. We were working against the deadline of summer's ending and the fatal moment when Father and Mother would finally question our so-long absence from the cabin. So far we'd skipped the explanations. So it was that I felt a great release of tension on the day when Remy put down a tool, wiped his hands slowly on his jeans, and said quietly, "It's finished."

Tom's face went waxen and I was afraid he'd faint. I felt my face go scarlet and I was afraid I'd explode.

"Finished," whispered Tom. "Now my son can go into Space. I'll go tell him." And he shuffled off.

"How are we ever going to talk Mother and Father into letting us go?" I asked. "I doubt that even with the ship all ready—"

"We can't tell them," said Remy. "They don't have to know."

"Not tell them?" I was aghast. "Go on an expedition like this and not tell them? We can't!"

"We must." Remy had put on a measure of maturity he had never showed before. "I know very well they'd never let us go if they knew. So you've got to keep the secret—even after we're gone."

"Keep the secret! You're not going without me. Where did you get such a fool idea! If you think for one minute—" I was shrieking now. Remy took hold of my arm.

"Be quiet!" he said, shaking me lightly. "I couldn't possibly let you go along under the circumstances. You've got to stay—"

"Under the circumstances," I repeated, my eyes intent on his face. "Remy, *is* there a way to bring the ship back?"

"I said there was, didn't I?" Remy returned my look steadily.

"To bring the ship back under its own power?"

Remy's hand dropped from my arm. "It'll get back all right. Stop worrying."

"Remy." It was my turn to take his arm. "Have you the instructions for a return flight? Tom said—"

"No," said Remy. His voice was hard and impersonal. "There are no instructions for a return flight—nor for the flight out. But I'll make it—there and back. If not with the ship, then by myself."

"Remy! You can't!" My protest crowded out of the horrified tumult of my thoughts. "Even the Old Ones wouldn't try it without a ship and they have *all* the Signs and Persuasions among them. You can't Motive the whole craft by yourself. You're not strong enough. You can't break it out of orbit— Oh, Remy!" I was almost sobbing. "You don't even know all the things—inertia—trajectory—gravitational pull— it's too complicated. No one could do it by himself! Not even the two of us together!"

Remy moved away from my hand. "There's no question of your going," he said. "You told me—this is my own little red wagon and I'll find some way of dragging it, even if a wheel comes off along the way." He smiled a little and then sobered.

"Look, Shadow, it's for Tom. He's so wrapped up in this whole project that there's literally nothing for him in this life but the ship and the trip. He'd have died long ago if this hope hadn't kept him alive. You haven't touched him unshielded or you'd know in a second that he was Called months ago and is stubbornly refusing to go. I doubt if he'll live through blast-off, even with all the shielding I can give him. But I've *got* to take him, Shadow. I've just got to. It—it—I can't explain it so it makes sense, but it's as necessary for me to do this for Tom as it is for Tom to do it. Why he's even forgotten God except as a spy who might catch us in the act and stop us. I think even the actual blast-off or one look at the Earth from Space will Purge him and he will submit to being Called and go to where his son is waiting, just the Otherside.

"I've got to give him his dream." Remy's voice faltered. "Young people have time to dream and change their dreams, but old people like Tom have time for only one dream, and if that fails them—"

"But, Remy," I whispered forlornly. "You might never make it back."

"It is in the hands of The Power," he said soberly. "If I'm to be Called, I'm to be Called."

"I don't think you're right," I said thickly, finding it difficult after all these years to contradict Remy in anything of importance. "You're trying to catch the sun in a sieve—and

207

you'll die of it!" Tears were wet on my face. "I can't let you—I can't—"

"It isn't for you to say 'no' or 'go,' " said Remy, flatly. "If you won't help, don't hinder—"

Tom was back, holding out his hands, bloodstained across the palms.

"Come help me," he panted. "I can't get the rocks off my son—"

Remy and I exchanged astonished glances.

"But, Tom—" I took one of his hands in mine to examine the cut flesh—and was immediately caught up in Death! Death rolled over me like a smothery cloud. Death shrieked at me from every corner of my mind. Death! Death! Rebellious, struggling Death! Nothing of the solemn Calling. Nothing of preparation for returning to the Presence. I forced my stiff fingers to open and dropped his hand. Remy had my other hand, pulling me away from Tom, his eyes anxiously on me.

"But, Tom," he said into the silence my dry mouth couldn't fill, "we're going to take the little flag. Remember? That's to be the memorial for your son—"

"I promised my son I'd go into Space with him," said Tom serenely. "It cuts both ways. He's going into Space with me. Only there are so many rocks. Come help me, you kids. We don't want to be late." He wiped his palms on the seat of his pants and started back down the drift.

"Wait," called Remy. "You help us first. We can't go anywhere until we fuel up. You've got to show me the fuel dump. You promised you would when the ship was finished. Well, it's finished now—all but pumping the fuel in."

Tom stopped. "That's right," nodded his head. "That's right." He laughed. The sound of it crinkled my spine. "I'm nobody's fool. Always keep an ace in the hole."

We followed him down another drift. "Wonder what fuel they have," said Remy. "Tom either wouldn't say, or didn't know. Never could get a word out of him about it except it would be there when we were ready for it. The fuel compartment was finished before we ever found him. He wouldn't let me go in there. He has the key to it."

"It's awfully far from the ship," I worried. "How're we going to get it back there?"

"Don't know," Remy frowned. "They must have had something figured out. But if it's liquid—"

Tom had stopped at the padlocked door. He fumbled for a key and, after several abortive attempts, found the right one and opened the lock. He flung the door wide. There was a solid wall of metal blocking the door, a spigot protruding from it was the only thing that broke its blank expanse.

"Liquid, then," whispered Remy. "Now, how on earth—"

Tom giggled at our expressions. "Used to keep water in here. 'S'all gone now. Nothing but the fuel—" He pushed a section of the metal. It swung inward. It had been cut into a rude door.

"There 'tis," cried Tom. "There 'tis."

At first we could see nothing because our crowding into the door shut out all the light that came from behind us; then Tom shuffled forward and the shaft of light followed him. He stopped and fumbled, then turned to us, lifting his burden triumphantly. "Here 'tis," he repeated. "You gotta put it in the ship. Here's the key to the compartment. I'll go get my son."

Remy grasped and almost dropped the thing Tom had given him. It was a box or something like a box. A little more rectangular than square, but completely featureless except for a carrying handle on each end and a smooth, almost mirrorlike surface on the top.

"What is it?" I asked. "How does it work?"

"I don't know." Remy was hunkered down by it on the floor, prodding at it with curious fingers.

"Maybe it's a solid fuel of some kind. It must be. Tom says it's the fuel."

"But why such a big fuel compartment if this is all that goes in it?" I had sensed the big empty chamber several times—padlock and all.

"Well, the only answer I have to that is let's go put it where it belongs and maybe we'll see."

We carried the object between us, back to the ship and into the fuel compartment—at least what was so labeled on the plans. We put it down on the spot indicated for it and fastened it down with the metal clamps that were situated in just the right places to hold the object. Then we stepped back and looked the situation over. The object sat there in the middle of the floor—plenty of room all around it and above it. The almost mirror surface reflected cloudily the ceiling above. There were no leads, no wires, no connections, nothing but the hold-clamps and they went no farther into the structure of the floor than was necessary to hold them secure.

"Remy?" I looked at his mystified face. "How does it work? Do the plans say?"

"There aren't any plans about this room," he said blankly, searching back in his memory of the plans that were available. "Only a label that says 'fuel room.' There's one notation. I couldn't figure it out before. It says, 'After clamps are secure, coordinate and lift off!!!!' With four exclamation points. That's all. You see, Tom had only the plans for finishing the ship. Nothing for the actual trip."

"And you thought you could—" I was horrified.

"Oh, relax, Shadow," said Remy. "Of course I could see how everything fitted into everything and what the dial readings meant *after* we got started, but—" His voice stopped and his thoughts concentrated on the plans again. "Nowhere a starter button or lever—" He bit his lip and frowned down at the object. In the silence we heard a clatter of rock and Tom's voice echoing eerily. "Come on out, Son. It's time to go! Rise and shine!"

Both of us listened to Tom's happy chant and we just looked at each other.

"What'll we do, Shadow?" asked Remy helplessly. "What'll we do?"

"Maybe Tom knows more about this," I suggested. "Maybe we can get him to talk." I shuddered away from the memory of his hand in mine.

So we went to Tom where he was clawing at the broken rock, trying to free his son, the tiny flag still standing upright in the little mound of earth. Tom was prying at a rock that, if he freed it, would bring half the slide roaring down upon him.

"Tom!" Remy called. "Tom!" And finally got his attention. "Come down here. I need help."

Tom scrambled awkwardly down the slope, half falling the last little way. And I let him stumble because I couldn't bear to touch him again.

"Tom, how does that fuel work?" Remy asked.

"Work? Why just like you'd think a fuel would work," said Tom wonderingly. "You just install it and take off."

"What connects it to the engines?" asked Remy. "You didn't give me that part of the plans."

"What engines?" grinned Tom.

"Whatever makes the ship go!" Remy's patience was running out rapidly.

"My son makes the ship go," said Tom, chuckling.

"Tom!" Remy took him by his frail shoulders and held him until the wander-eyes focused on his face. "Tom, the ship's

210

all ready to go, but I don't know how to start it. Unless you can tell me, *we—can't—go!*"

"Can't go?" Tom's eyes blinked with shock. "Can't go? We have to go! We have to! I promised!" The contours of his face softened and sagged to a blur under the force of his emotion. "We gotta go!" He took Remy's hands roughly off his shoulders and pushed him staggering away. "Stupid brat! 'Course you can't make it go! My son's the only one that knows how!" He turned back to the heap of stone. "Son!" His voice was that of a stern parent. "Get outa there. There's work to be done and you lie there lazing!" He began tearing again at the jagged boulders.

We moved away from him—away from the whirlwind of his emotions and the sobbing, half vocal panting of his breath. We retreated to the ladder that lead up to the cabin, and, leaning against it, looked at each other.

"His son's been under there for months—maybe a year," Remy said dully. "If he uncovers him now—" He gulped miserably. "And I can't make the ship go. After all your fussing about making the trip, and here I am stuck. But there *are* engines—at least there are mechanisms that work from one another after the flight begins. I don't think that little box is all the fuel. I'll bet there was liquid fuel somewhere and it's all evaporated or run off or something." He gulped again and leaned against the foot of the ladder.

"Oh, Shadow," he mourned. "At first this was going to be my big deal. I was going to help Tom find his dream—and all on my own. It was my declaration of independence to show Father and Ron that I could do something besides show off—and I guess that was showing off, too. But, Shadow, I gave that all up—I mean showing them. All I wanted was for Tom—" His voice broke and he blinked fast. "And his son—" He turned away from me and my throat ached with his unshed tears.

"We're not finished yet," I said. "Come on back."

There was a silence in the drift that sounded sudden. Nowhere could we hear Tom. Not a stone grated against another stone. Not a cry nor a mumbled word. Remy and I exchanged troubled looks as we neared the jagged heap of broken rock.

"Do you suppose he had a heart attack?" Remy hurried ahead of me, edging past the rockfall.

"Remy!" I gasped. "Oh, Remy, come back!" I had Sensed ahead of him and gulped danger like a massive swallow of fire. "Remy!" But it was too late. I heard him cry out and the sudden triumphant roar of Tom's voice. "Gotcha!"

I pressed myself against the far side of the drift away from the narrow passageway and listened.

"Hey, Tom!" Remy's voice was carefully unworried. "What you got that cannon for? Looks big enough from this end for me to crawl in."

" 'Tain't a cannon," said Tom. "It's a shotgun my son gave me to guard the ship so'st you couldn't kill him and keep the ship from taking off. Now you've killed him anyway, but that's not going to stop us."

"I didn't kill—"

"Don't lie to me!" The snarling fury in Tom's voice scared me limp-legged. "He's dead. I uncovered his hand—my son's dead! And you did it! You pushed all that stuff down on him to try to hide your crime, but murder will out. You killed my son!"

"Tom, Tom," Remy's voice was coaxing. "I'm Remy, remember? You showed me where your son lay. Remember the little flag—"

"The little flag—" Tom's voice was triumphant. "Sure, the little flag. He was going to put it on the moon. So you killed him. But now *you're* going to put it on the moon—or die in the attempt." He laughed. It sounded like two stones being rapped together. "Or die in the attempt! Get going!"

"But, Tom—there's no fuel!" protested Remy.

"You got what was in the tank room, didn't you?" demanded Tom. "Well, then, get to flying. My son said it would go. It'll go!"

And I heard their footsteps die off down the drift and Remy's distress came back to me like a scarlet banner. "Shadow! Shadow!"

I don't remember racing back to the ladder or opening the trapdoor or leaving the shack. My first consciousness of where I was came as I streaked over the ridge, headed for home. The stars—when had night come?—the treetops, the curves of the hills all lengthened themselves into flat ribbons of speed behind me. I didn't remember to activate my shield until my eyes were blinded with tears.

I hit the front porch so fast that I stumbled and fell and was brought up sharp with a rolling crash against the front door. Before I could get myself untangled, Mother and Father were there and Mother was checking me to see if I was hurt.

"I'm all right," I gasped. "But Remy—Remy!"

"Shadow, Shadow—" Father gathered me up, big as I am, and carried me into the house and put me down on the couch. "Shadow, clear yourself before you try to begin. It'll save time." And I forced myself to lie back quietly, though my tears ran hotly down into both my ears—and let all the wild urgency and fear and distress drain out of my mind. Then, as we held each others' hands, our three minds met in the wordless communication of The People.

Thoughts are so much faster than words and I poured out all the details in a wild rush—now and then feeling the guidance of my father leading me back to amplify or make clear some point I'd skidded by too fast.

"And now he's there with a madman pointing a shotgun at him and he can't do a thing—or maybe he's already dead—"

"Can we handle him?" Father had turned to Mother.

"Yes," she whispered whitely. "If we can get there in time."

Again the meteoric streaking across the dark hills. And Mother's reaching out ahead, trying to find Tom—reaching, reaching. After an eternity, we swung around the shoulder of a hill and there was the Selkirk—but different! Oh, different!

A shiny, needle-sharp nose was towering above the shack, the broken rock and shale had been shed off on all sides like silt around an ant hole. And the ship! The ship was straining toward the stars! Even as we watched, the nose wavered and circled a wobbly little circle and settled back again, out of sight in the shadows.

"Remy's trying to lift it!" I cried. "A thing that size! He'll never make it— And then Tom—"

We watched the feeble struggle as the nose of the ship emerged again from the shaft—not so far this time—much more briefly. It settled back with an audible crash and Mother caught her breath. "There!" she breathed, clasping her hands. "There!" Slowly she drifted down toward the shack, holding firmly whatever it was that she had caught. Father and I streaked to the shack and down the ladder. We rushed along the drift, past the huddle of rocks, and into the shaft. It took Father a fumbling eternity to find how to get into the ship. And there we found them both—Tom sprawled across his gun, his closed eyes sunken, his face a death mask of itself. And Remy—Remy was struggling to a sitting position, his hand pushing against the useless box from the tank room. He smiled a wavery smile and said in a dazed voice, "I have a little Shadow—That goes in and out with me—And what can be the use of her—I see, I see, I see—"

Then he was held tight in Father's arms and I turned my tears away only to be gathered into Mother's arms. And Tom slept peacefully the quiet sleep Mother had given him as we had a family-type wallow in tears and sobs and murmurs and exasperated shakings and all sorts of excited explanations and regrets.

It was a much more solemn conclave back at the house later on. Tom was still sleeping, but in our back bedroom now. I think Mother was afraid to waken him for fear the shock of opening his eyes on Earth might kill him. She had experienced his gigantic, not-to-be-denied, surge toward Space before she had Slept him, and knew it for the unquenchable fire it was.

Of course by the time we finally reduced to vocal words, most of the explanations had been made—the incredulity expressed, the reprimands given, and the repentance completed—but the problem of Tom was still unanswered.

"The simplest way, of course," said Remy, "is just to write 'finis' to the whole thing, wake Tom up, and then hold his funeral."

"Yes," said Father. "That would be the simplest."

"Of course, Mother and Shadow will have to be ready to Channel instantly to bypass that agonized moment when Tom realizes he has been betrayed." Remy was inspecting his jagged thumbnail and didn't meet Father's eyes.

"Bethie, what do you think?" Father turned to Mother.

She blushed pinkly—that's where I get my too-ready coloring up—and murmured, "I think we ought to look at the ship at least," she said. "Maybe that would help us decide, especially if we have Ron look it over, too."

"Okay, tomorrow." Father parted the curtain at the big window. "Today." He amended as he blinked at the steely gray light of dawn. "Today we'll get in touch with him and take a look. After all, the ship *is* finished." And he turned away with a sigh, only a faint quirk at the corner of his mouth to betray the fact that he knew Remy and I were having a hard time containing our jubilation.

After lunch—even our frantic impatience couldn't pry Mother and Father away from what seemed such minor matters—Ron finally arrived and we all went out to look the ship over. Remy and I streaked on ahead of the others and I laughed as I caught myself visualizing me dusting the ship frantically from end to end so it'd look its best for our visitors.

There it was! The shaft at least, with the concealing shale and rock shed away on all sides. When we arrived above it, we could see the gleam of the nose of the ship. In all the excitement the night before, we had forgotten to conceal it. But it didn't matter now. Soon that bright nose would be lifting! Remy and I turned joyous somersaults as we shot down to the old shack.

The men—I include Remy in that—were like a bunch of kids with a new toy. They toured the ship, their eyes eager and seeking, their manner carefully casual, their hands touching and drinking in the wonder of it. A spacecraft! Remy's replies to their questions were clipped and practically monosyllabic. His containment surprised me and I wondered if this was a foretaste of what he'd be like as an adult. Of course, Ron's being there—the head Motiver of the Group— may have awed him a little, but it wasn't awe in his eyes, it was assurance. He *knew* the ship.

Mother took advantage of the preoccupation of the men to get in touch with Valancy and, through her, with Dr. Curtis, who hadn't gone back Outside yet. I suppose they discussed Tom's condition and what—if anything—could be done for him. Mother was sitting near a wall of the fuel room, to all appearances, daydreaming.

So again I was a Shadow. Not a part of the inspection team—not meshed with Mother. I sighed and wandered over to the fuel box where it sat lonesomely in the middle of the floor. I lay down on my stomach beside it and looked at the shining upper surface. It reflected softly the light in the room, but the reflection seemed to come from deeper into the box than just the upper surface. It had depth to it. It was like looking at the moon. I have never quite believed that the light of the moon is just a reflection of the sun, especially a full moon when the light seems to have such depth, such dimension. And now—and now—if the ship were found spaceworthy, we'd be able to see firsthand if the moon had any glowing of its own.

I caught my own eyes shadowed in the surface and thought, *We'll be going up and up and more up than anyone has ever been before—lifting, soaring, rising—*

Mother cried out. Everything shook and moved and there was a grinding, grating sound. I heard the men shout from somewhere in the ship. Frightened, I rolled away from the fuel box and cried, "Mother!"

215

There was another scraping sound that shook the ship, and then a crunching thud. For a half second there was silence and then a clatter of feet as the men rushed into the fuel room, and Father, seeing us unhurt, was demanding, "Who lifted the ship!"

"Lifted the ship?" Remy's jaw was ajar. Father's eyes stabbed him. "Did you, Remy?"

"I was with you!" Remy protested.

"Bethie?"

Mother colored deeply and her eyes drifted shyly away from the sternness of Father's face. "No," she said, "I'm not a Motiver. I was talking with Valancy."

I scrambled to my feet, my eyes wide, my color rising as Mother's had. "Father, I'll bet I did it!"

"You *bet* you did it?" Father was annoyed. "Don't you know?"

"I'm—I'm not sure," I said. "You know I'm not even as much a Motiver as Mother is. I still have to struggle to lift the pickup, but—but I was looking at the fuel box and thinking. Father, I'll try it again. You and Ron had better stand by, just in case."

I lay down beside the box again, my eyes intent on the surface, and consciously lifted with all my might.

There was no grinding, grating this time. There was a shriek of metal on stone, a gasp from Mother as her knees buckled under the sudden upthrust, and Father's voice came clear and commanding, "Let go, Shadow. I've got it."

Light was streaming into the ship from windows we'd hardly noticed before. We all exchanged astonished looks then rushed to look out. We were hovering above the Selkirk—hundreds of feet above the gaping shaft visible off to one side. The scraping on its walls had thrown us sideways.

Father turned to Ron and said, "Take over and maintain, will you?" Then he knelt beside the little box, prodding it with his fingers, smoothing it with his palm. Then he said, "Release to me," and, kneeling there, he brought the nose of the ship down so we lay horizontal to the ground. We all started sliding down as the floor slanted, but we lifted and waited until a wall became a floor, then Father moved the ship to an open flat below the Selkirk and brought it down gently on its side.

We all gathered around him as he stood looking at the box that was now head-high on the wall. We all looked at it and then Father's voice came slow and wonderingly, "It's an

216

amplifier! Why, with that, it wouldn't even take a Motiver to make it to the moon. Three or four people lifting, coordinating in this, this amplifier, could do it, if they didn't tire."

"'Coordinate and lift off!'" cried Remy. "*Four* exclamation points!"

Father had laid the ship on its side so we could find what damage had been done by Remy and me when we churned the poor thing up and down in the shaft. Mother and I went back home to check on Tom and to ready things for the voyage. No one needed to say we'd go. We all knew we'd go. The men were busy repairing the beat-up undercarriage or whatever you'd call that part of the ship, and we brought a picnic supper out to them a little while before sunset.

We all sat around on the flat. I sat on an anthill first and moved in a hurry. We ate and feasted our eyes on the ship. Remy had come out the other side of ecstasy and was serenely happy. Father and Ron were more visibly excited than he. But then they hadn't lived with the ship and the idea as long as Remy had.

Finally a silence fell and we just sat and watched the night come in from the east, fold by fold of deepening darkness. In the half light came Ron's astonished voice.

"Why, that's what it is! That's what it is!"

"That's what what is?" came Father's voice, dreamily from where he lay looking up at the darkening sky.

"The ship," said Ron. "I've been trying all afternoon to remember what it reminds me of. Now I know. It's almost the same pattern as our life-slips."

"Our life-slips?" Father sat up slowly. "You mean the ones the People escaped in when their ships were disabled entering Earth's atmosphere?"

"Exactly!" Ron's voice quickened. "It's bigger and it's cluttered with a lot of gadgets we didn't have, but basically, it's almost identical! Where did those fellows get the design of our life-slips? We didn't keep any. We don't need to with our Group memory—"

"And it's motive power." Father's voice was thoughtful. "It's the power the People use. And Tom's son was supposed to know how to make it go. Did you suppose Tom—"

"No." Mother's voice came softly in the darkness. "I Sorted him after we took him to the house. He's not one of Us."

"His wife then, maybe," I said. "So many of us were scattered after the Crossing. And their son could have inherited—" My voice trailed off as I remembered what his son

217

had inherited—the darkness, the heap of stones, and no chance ever for the stars, not even a reflection of them.

"We could rouse Tom and ask?" offered Remy questioningly.

"Tom is past remembering," said Mother. "He's long since been Called and as soon as we waken him, he will be gone."

"Well," Ron sighed, "we don't *need* to know."

"No," I admitted. "But it would be fun to know if Our Own built the ship."

"Whoever did," said Father, "is Our Own whether he ever knew the Home or not."

So we went, the next day.

But first, Ron and Father spent a quiet hour or so in the drift and emerged bearing between them a slender pine box with a small flag fluttering atop it. By now the ship was upright again and Remy, Mother, and I had provisioned it. When we were ready to go, we all went back to the house and got Tom, still and lifeless except for the flutter of a pulse faintly in his throat and a breathing that seemed to stop forever after each outflowing sigh. We brought him, cot and all, and put him in the ship.

And then, our Voyage Prayer and the lift-off—not blast-off. No noise pushed us on our way nor stayed behind to shout of our going.

Slowly, at first, the Earth dropped behind us, alternately convex and concave, changing sometimes from one to the other at a blink of the eyes. I won't tell you in detail how it all looked. I'll let you find it all new when you make your first trip. But I will say my breath caught in a sob and I almost wept when first the whole of Earth outlined itself against the star-blazing blackness of space. At that point, Ron and Father put the ship on maintain while they came and looked. We had very little to say. There are no word patterns yet for such an experience. We just stood and worshiped. I could feel unsaid words crowding up against my wonder-filled heart.

But even a wonder like that can't hold the restlessness of a boy for long, and Remy soon was drifting to all parts of the ship, clucking along with the different machines that were now clucking back at him as they activated to keep the ship habitable for us. He was loving every bolt and rivet, every revolution and flutter of dial, because they were his, at least by right of operation.

Mother and I lasted longer at the windows than Remy. We

were still there when Ron and Father finally could leave the ship on maintain and rejoin us.

I'm the wrong one to be telling this story if you want technical data. I'm an illiterate for anything like that. I can't even give you the time it took. Time is the turning of the Earth and we were free of that tyranny for the first time in our lives.

I know that finally Father and Ron took the ship off maintain and swung it around to the growing lunar wonder in our windows and I watched again that odd curve and collapse sequence as we plunged downward.

Then we were there, poised above the stripped unmovingness of the lunar landscape. We landed with barely a thud and Father was out, testing his personal shield to see if that would be sufficient protection for the time needed to do what we had to do. It was. We all activated our shields and stepped out, closing the door carefully behind us to safeguard the spaced gasping of Tom.

We stood there looking up at the full Earth, losing ourselves in its flooding light, and I found myself wondering if perhaps it wasn't only the reflection of the sun, if Earth had its own luminousness.

After a while we went back in and warmed ourselves a little and then the men brought out the slender pine box and laid it on the pumicey crunch of the ground. I stirred the little flag with my fingers so that it might flutter its last flutter.

Then inside the ship they lifted Tom to a window. Mother Went-in to him before she woke him completely and told him where we were and where his son was. Then she awakened him gently. For a moment his eyes were clouded. His lips trembled and he blinked slowly—or closed his eyes, waiting for strength. He opened them again and looked for a long moment at the bright curve of the plain and the spangled darkness of the sky.

"The moon," he murmured, his thin hand clenching on the rim of the window. "We made it, Son, we made it! Let me out. Let me touch it."

Father's eyebrows questioned Mother and her eyes answered him. We lifted him from the cot and, enveloping him in our own shields, moved him out the door. We sustained him for the few staggering steps he took. He half fell across the box, one hand trailing on the ground. He took up a handful of the rough gravel and let it funnel from his hand to the top of the box.

"Son," he said, his voice surprisingly strong. "Son, dust thou art, go back to dust. Look out of wherever you are up there and see where your body is. We're close enough that you ought to be able to see real good." He slid to his knees, his face resting against the undressed pine. "I told you I'd do it for you, Son."

We straightened him and covered him with Mother's double wedding ring patchwork quilt, tucking him gently in against the long, long night. And I know at least four spots on the moon where water has fallen in historical time—four salty, wet drops, my own tears. Then we said the Parting Prayers and returned to the ship.

We went looking for the littering that had annoyed Tom's son so much. I found it, Sensing its metal from miles farther than I could have among the distractions of earth. Remy wanted to lift it right back out into Space, but Father wouldn't let him. "It wouldn't change things," he said. "It did get here first. Let it stay."

"Okay, then," said Remy, "but with this on it." He pulled a flag out of his pocket and unfolded it. He spread it carefully as far as it would go over the metal and laid a chunk of stone on each corner. "To keep the wind from blowing it away," he grinned, stepping back to look it over. "There, that takes the cuss off it!"

So we took off again. We made a swoop around behind the moon, just to see what it was like, and we were well on our way home before it dawned on me that I hadn't even got one pebble for a souvenir.

"Don't mind," said Mother, smiling as she remembered other rock-collecting trips of mine. "You know they never look as pretty when you get them home."

Now we're back. The ship is stashed away in the shaft. We may never use it again. The fire of Remy's enthusiasm has turned to plans and blueprints and all things pertaining to his Gift, his own personal Gift, apparently the first evidence of a new Gift developing among us. He's gone in so much for signs and symbols and schematic diagrams that he'd talk in them if he could. Personally I think he went a trifle too far when he drew a schematic diagram of me and called it a portrait. After all! Mother and Father laughed at the resultant horror, but Remy thinks if he keyed colors in he might have a new art form. Talk about things changing!

But what will never, never change is the wonder, the

indescribable wonder to me of seeing Earth lying in space as in the hollow of God's hand. Every time I return to it, I return to the words of the Psalmist—the words that welled up in me unspoken out there half way to the moon.

When I consider thy heavens, the work of thy fingers, the moon and the stars which thou hast ordained; What is man that thou art mindful of him—

AVON ◆ MEANS THE BEST IN FANTASY AND SCIENCE FICTION

URSULA K. LE GUIN

The Lathe of Heaven	25338	1.25
The Dispossessed	24885	1.75

ISAAC ASIMOV

Foundation	29579	1.50
Foundation and Empire	30627	1.50
Second Foundation	29280	1.50
The Foundation Trilogy (Large Format)	26930	4.95

ROGER ZELAZNY

Doorways in the Sand	32086	1.50
Creatures of Light and Darkness	35956	1.50
Lord of Light	33985	1.75
The Doors of His Face, The Lamps of His Mouth	18846	1.25
The Guns of Avalon	31112	1.50
Nine Princes in Amber	− 36756	1.50
Sign of the Unicorn	30973	1.50
The Hand of Oberon	33324	1.50

Include 25¢ per copy for postage and handling, allow 4-6 weeks for delivery.

Avon Books, Mail Order Dept.
250 W. 55th St., N.Y., N.Y. 10019

SF 10-77

SUPERIOR
FANTASY AND SCIENCE FICTION
FROM AVON BOOKS

Available at better bookstores everywhere, or order direct from the publisher.

AVON BOOKS, Mail Order Dept., 250 West 55th St., New York, N.Y. 10019

Please send me the books checked above. I enclose $_____ (please include 25¢ per copy for postage and handling). Please use check or money order—sorry, no cash or COD's. Allow 4-6 weeks for delivery.

Mr/Mrs/Miss_____

Address_____

City_____State/Zip_____

SSF 11-77